REMEMBRANCE DAY

Leah Fleming was born in Lancashire of Scottish parents, and is married with four grown-up children and six grand-children. She lives in the Yorkshire Dales and is currently working on her next novel, *Winter's Children*, to be published in 2010.

Find out more about Leah at www.leahfleming.co.uk and visit www.BookArmy.co.uk for exclusive updates.

LEAH FLEMING

Remembrance Day

AVON

This novel is entirely a work of fiction.
The names, characters and incidents portrayed in it are
the work of the author's imagination. Any resemblance to
actual persons, living or dead, events or localities is
entirely coincidental.

AVON

A division of HarperCollins*Publishers*
77–85 Fulham Palace Road,
London W6 8JB

www.harpercollins.co.uk

A Paperback Original 2009
1

Copyright © Leah Fleming 2009

Leah Fleming asserts the moral right to
be identified as the author of this work

A catalogue record for this book is
available from the British Library

ISBN-13: 978-1-84756-103-9

Set in Minion by Palimpsest Book Production Limited,
Grangemouth, Stirlingshire

Printed and bound in Great Britain by
Clays Ltd, St Ives plc

All rights reserved. No part of this publication may be reproduced, stored in a
retrieval system, or transmitted, in any form or by any means, electronic,
mechanical, photocopying, recording or otherwise,
without the prior permission of the publishers.

Mixed Sources

Product group from well-managed
forests and other controlled sources
www.fsc.org Cert no. SW-COC-1806
© 1996 Forest Stewardship Council

FSC is a non-profit international organisation established
to promote the responsible management of the world's forests.
Products carrying the FSC label are independently certified
to assure consumers that they come from forests that are managed
to meet the social, economic and ecological needs
of present and future generations.

Find out more about HarperCollins and the environment at
www.harpercollins.co.uk/green

Not forgetting the fifteen men
of Langcliffe who never made it home.

Who made the law that men should die in meadows?
Who spake the word that blood should splash in lanes?
Who gave it forth that gardens should be bone-yards?
Who spread the hills with flesh, and blood, and brains?

'Who Made the Law?' Leslie Coulson

11 November 2000

The ceremony is about to begin, the shuffling feet and coughing settle as the dignitaries line up in uniforms, cassocks and mayoral chains. A silence descends over the crowds on this most solemn of mornings.

We stand before the new war memorial in Elm Tree Square while a scuffle of film crews jockey for position. There is a chill Martinmas wind from the north but I am well wrapped with quilt and cushions in my wheelchair.

At last after all these years justice has been done, the dead are honoured; all of them by name. These cobble-stones, once heavy with old sorrows, damp with tears and bloodshed, now sparkle with hope and pride. I never thought to see this day.

No more arguing about things that can't be altered, no more dissention in the village about planning permissions. The names of the dead say it all, etched here on marble tablets.

That I have made the effort to witness this moment is miracle enough at my great age. My eyes are dimming, my hands tremble and my limbs disobey commands. Old age comes not alone, they say, and my heart leaps to see such a crowd of supporters. I hope our menfolk would be proud that we've settled things at last.

We wait in patience in the chill air, all the West Sharland faithful and their far-flung relatives, all the families represented where possible, prosperous in thick overcoats and stylish black hats with grandchildren, tall as saplings, and great-grandchildren on their knees, bemused by the pageantry unfolding.

There are faces I don't recognise but in their features are echoes of village folk long buried. There is new life and fresh growth here, and that is good.

The clouds part as a ray of weak sun beams down for a second, haloing all the hand-held wreaths and circlets. Blood-red poppies flash on lapels like medals. The golden light glides across the green fells and stone walls above us, across the slate rooftops of familiar old buildings, and my eye turns to the forge in Prospect Row, but it is long gone.

They have put me in the front as one of the honoured guests, alongside the great and the good of the district; just another old matriarch, an 'ancient of days' waiting to pay her respects. There are plans to interview me later but I have other ideas.

In my fancy I see sepia faces hidden in the shadows, a crowd of ghosts watching, waiting with us, faces of the long dead from the war who knew only suffering, sacrifice and shame. What would they make of all this now?

My daughter stands upright, breasted like a plump capon. I am so proud of the spirit she has shown in fighting our corner. By her side her grandson, the spit of his great-grandfather, built like a tree trunk, the wind and sun etched on his bronzed brow.

There is no one left to recognise me, though a few may

4

guess a little of my history. I am just one of the many visitors and want no fuss. I have been absent so many years but this place is at the heart of my being.

Nothing has changed but everything is changed. The familiar Yorkshire air is sweet after the dryness of the Arizona desert, the rooks caw in the churchyard ash trees even into my failing ears. I had forgotten how raucous and noisy they are.

The cars parked right through the village, the houses expanded into barns and outbuildings, speak of a prosperity and comfort we could only dream of as children.

My mind is flooding with memories. I have completed a circle in coming back to West Sharland, fulfilling a promise, honouring those closest to me, but it is hard to contain the ache still in my heart for their undeserved sufferings. What has driven me back here one last time is a strange yearning, a sense of the wanderer returning to this now sacred space for peace before my long sleep. My days are leaching away, but no matter.

To live long is not enough, and it is a wise soul who knows his beginning and his end and makes some answer for the life given him. Over the years I have thought it fitting to set my own story on paper, to turn over the pages in my mind and wonder where I would be if what was done long ago could be undone. This task has been a close companion in my widowhood. They would not let me fly back so, in my cabin suite on the Atlantic crossing I reread the chapters, relived those parts of my life that brought me from the West Riding to the New World and back.

This journal will be left among the archives of West Sharland when I'm gone, but not before. Perhaps someone will turn its pages with interest and profit from what I write. For, make no mistake, there are secrets within that belong to this village alone, secrets that explain the real reason why no war memorial was ever erected in our village until now.

But enough. The age-old ceremony begins. The silver band is marching down the hill, gathering a crowd just as it did all those years ago in the late summer of 1914. How trusting, how ignorant, how innocent we were back then. Little did any of us know what heartache lay ahead . . .

1

GOLDEN SUMMERS
Yorkshire, 1913–14

Pack up your troubles in your old kitbag
And smile, smile, smile . . .

George Asaf, 1915

1

It was just another Yorkshire afternoon in high summer with nothing to mark it out as a day that would change their lives for ever. The young Bartley brood had done their Saturday chores in the morning heat, watered the horses waiting to be shod under the shade of a clump of elderberry trees in the paddock behind the forge. Newton and Frankland, their broad shoulders tanned like leather, were pumping water from the well into the slate tank at the back of the yard for Father's wash in the zinc tub. It was time for his Bible class preparation. Asa Bartley never liked to touch the Holy Book with blacksmith's rusty fingers.

Selma, his young daughter, made her usual rounds of the village shops with her mother's wicker basket: off-cuts for stew from Stan, the butcher, soda crystals for Monday's wash tub from Mrs Marshbank at the Co-op, stopping to chat with neighbours taking advantage of the end of their shift at the cotton mill, and picking up a second-hand copy of the local *Gazette*. It was one of the hottest afternoons in the whole summer. Doors were wide open onto the street with strips of beaded rope pinned over the lintels, waving in the breeze to discourage the flies, windows propped up with bedding hanging out to bleach in the sunshine, stools set outside in the shade to catch passers-by for crumbs of gossip. Dogs panted in the shade and the forge cat, Jezebel, was curled up under a hedge.

The rooks were silent for once, high up in the ash trees of St Wilfred's, West Sharland as Selma scuttled through the ginnel short cut between Main Street and the forge, her striped cotton shirt clinging to her liberty bodice, her long skirt and petticoats sticking to her thin legs. She was boiling hot and dying for a swim.

'I'm going down to the Foss,' she announced when she brought in the paper and the change. Essie was laying down the best rug for the Sabbath, tidying away the bread, cheese and pickle dinner. It was too hot for a full meal. There was a pot jug of lemonade on the dresser, covered with a beaded cloth ready to be put back on the slate shelf under the stairs; the coolest place in the cottage.

'Not on your own, you're not,' Essie replied. 'You'll wait while Frank and Newt do their chores. You know I don't like you going down there alone. It's private land. I don't want her ladyship on my doorstep again and her with such a down on chapelgoers.'

The Cantrells owned everything in Sharland. They didn't mix in the village; they were more gentry folk than farmers. The colonel was serving in the army and his boys were away at school. They were churchers not chapellers, and lived at Waterloo House with their sons, servants and a carriage. Lady Hester was queen of the district: Father said she was above herself. Selma had never seen her sons except far down the field in the annual cricket match between the school and the village.

'Mam, I'm boiling in all these clothes and they'll be ages yet!' Selma protested. If only she could strip off like her brothers, who jumped in the water in their undershorts or, better still, with no clothes at all. As the youngest and the only girl she had to tag along with them to school, to chapel. Her best friends, Sybil and Annie, lived on scattered farms and it was over a two-mile walk uphill to play with them.

The path from the village to the Foss was well trodden by village children. It was a secret cavern, a hideaway, where the beck cascaded over silver stone shelves, falling head-long into a deep pool overhung with trees and bracken, a hiding place for salmon and trout, and the slabs were cool to bare feet. There was always lots of splashing and fooling about, but the water was cold and shallow in parts and fathoms deep in others. You had to know where to jump in. It was supposed to be haunted by a highwayman who fell to his death when chased by the squire's men in the good old days.

Half an hour later, Selma was trudging behind her brothers. They could hear squeals of laughter ahead echoing across the rocks. There would be the usual gang of village lads all vying for a good jumping-off point, with silly girls giggling, eyeing them up. Selma shivered by the cool shade of the trees. She thought all that romancing was embarrassing. She never knew where to look when the boys took off their shorts.

Now there were strangers in their pool, picnicking across the bank, boys she'd never seen before, dressed in proper one-piece swimming costumes, with a basket of food on a rug. They stared across at the intruders, nodded but said nothing.

'It must be them twinnies of Cantrells', alike as two peas,' whispered Newt with a respectful nod in their direction.

Selma eyed them up with interest. They were tall and gangly, about fifteen or so, fair-haired and slender as willows, not rugged and leathered like her brothers. She'd never seen a proper bathing suit before on a lad.

Newt and Frank stripped off their workday shirts and breeches to splash in the water. None of the Bartleys was a strong swimmer but they were good at diving under-water, turning circles and coming up somewhere far away from where they'd gone in. Selma dipped her toes in the water and screamed.

Not to be outdone, the two boys on the far bank started shouting. 'Fancy a diving match?' one of them turned and yelled. 'Come on, let's show these bumpkins how to dive!'

The other brother hung back, watching as first Newt and then Frank, intent on their own fun, ignored the jibe by jumping off the ledge midway. Selma edged herself into the water, embarrassed to take her clothes off now there was an audience. Better to paddle and not show off Monday's washing to strangers.

One of the boys swam across the beck and climbed up onto the slate ledge jutting out above where Newt had jumped in. Selma gawped up as the boy postured on the edge and made a perfect dive into the pool. He rose to the surface grinning, and that was the first time she clapped eyes on Guy Cantrell. The other twin was already clambering up even higher to the topmost shelf that none of them had dared use before.

Frank shook his head. 'I wouldn't go that high, chum. It's not safe.'

'I'm not your chum,' the boy pouted.

'Don't be a fool, Angus. Do what the young man says,' yelled his brother.

'Come on, Newt, can't let them toffs show us up!' Frank shouted in defiance.

'I never took you for a coward, Guy!' yelled his brother from his rocky perch.

It was then that Selma knew that something awful was about to happen and she couldn't stop it. 'Don't jump, please, Frank, on our mam's life. Showing off's not worth it!' Selma screamed. Frank hovered, shocked at her outburst, and backed off just as Angus Cantrell took a flying leap from the highest ledge, plunging down into the dark abyss, down and down and not bobbing up again.

Everyone was in the water, sensing something was wrong. Guy was splashing about, unsure of his bearings now. Selma pulled off her skirts and dived deep, opening her eyes to get her bearings. Newt was already down there, coming up for air, gasping before diving down again. It was Frank who spotted the boy curled up on the rock floor. Selma and Newt dived in to grab him but he was wedged.

'Over here!' she screamed to Guy, who dived with them to rescue his brother, pulling and tugging to set the boy free.

They dragged him to the surface. There was a gash on the side of his head. He was not breathing. Guy took over, turning him on his stomach, lifting his arms to raise his chest. 'Come on, Angus! Someone go and get help! Give me a hand,' he ordered Selma, while Frank ran off as bid. It felt like hours before the boy coughed and spluttered but then promptly fell back into unconsciousness.

'He's alive!' said the boy with the ink-blue eyes glinting

with fear and relief as he looked up at the Bartleys with gratitude.

Selma swam across the beck and waded back with the picnic rug over her head to cover Angus's cold body.

'What a daft thing to do!' Newt said.

Selma wanted to kick him. 'Shut yer gob! Let's get some warmth into his limbs. He's so cold. Pile all our clothes on him.' She felt so helpless. They must keep him warm and dry while they waited. That was what you did with a sick horse.

It was an age before the servants from the House arrived with a flurry of blankets and Angus was passed from arm to arm until he could be placed on a dog cart. Still he made no movement.

'Hell's bells! Mother will kill us for this,' sighed Guy, who looked close to tears.

Selma resisted the urge to reach her arm out to him. 'Praise God, he's alive and that's all that matters,' she whispered.

'Thanks to you and your brothers. My mother will be so grateful. What a frightful thing to happen – and I don't even know your names,' he said, reaching out to shake their hands. His fingers were like ice, his lips trembling with shock and chill.

'We're Bartleys from the forge, my two brothers, Newton and Frankland, and I'm Selima but everyone calls me Selma for short. Sorry we were trespassing on your land.'

'Thank God you were. From now on feel free to enjoy this cursed place. I don't think I'll ever dare come here again. We'll be gated by Mother when she hears about this. What unusual names you have . . . I'm Guy Cantrell, by the way, and you must call me Guy. How can we ever thank you?'

'It was nothing,' Frank blushed.

'Make sure your dad has his horses shoed at our place,' quipped Newt, the elder, apprenticed as a farrier, heir to Asa Bartley's smiddy and always one for the last word. Selma turned pink, embarrassed, and nudged him hard.

'Of course . . . Better go now. Mother will be back soon and Father will be furious. She will want to thank you in person, I'm sure,' Guy repeated, pausing to smile at Selma.

She stared back as if a magnet were pulling them together until they both dropped their eyes. One look into those deep blue pools and thirteen-year-old Selma felt to have grown three years in three hours. She had come to play at the Foss as a child; why did she now feel she was leaving here closer to a woman? Suddenly she felt naked, her chestnut hair dripping wet, hanging in rat-tails, shivering in her darned underwear, shabby, uncouth, ashamed to be just a blacksmith's daughter. One look from Master Cantrell and she didn't know who she was any more.

Hester Cantrell saw the doctor's new motor car parked in the drive, blocking her carriage from the front portico. Annoyance quickly changed to panic. What was he doing here? Not waiting for the step to be let down from the carriage, she stumbled out, rushing up the steps of Waterloo House with an energy that belied her fifty-three years. 'What the blazes is going on, Arkie?' she said, storming past the parlour maid, and looking to Mrs Arkholme, the house-keeper, standing at the foot of the stairs, wringing her hands.

'I'm sorry, Lady Hester, but it's Master Angus. He's had an accident in the Foss . . . I took the liberty of calling Dr Mac. He's with him now.'

'Why wasn't I summoned? You knew where I was . . .

Those Board of Guardians meetings at the workhouse are such a waste of time.'

'Beg pardon, ma'am, but there wasn't time.'

Hester raced up the stairs, tripping over her long silk skirt, her heart thumping and the wretched sweats making her cheeks flush like rouge. This was no time for her usual decorum.

Angus was lying on his bed, his face swollen and bruised and his eyes shut. There were stitches on his left temple.

Hester turned to her other son. 'What happened this time?'

Guy muttered the whole story about Angus going too high, the village boys warning him and his mistimed dive. 'If the Bartleys hadn't been there, and their sister, I dread to think . . . It was awful, Mother, and I was useless.'

Angus opened his eyes sheepishly, sighed and went back to sleep.

'Now don't get your mother in a state, young man,' ordered the doctor. 'It's no' as bad as it looks. He's a wee bit concussed and shaken, but lots of rest and sleep will sort him out in no time.'

'He ought to be in hospital,' said Hester, examining her son closely. Mackenzie was a fool, in her eyes, driving around in his car like a lord, living above his means with his silly wife called Amaryllis, for goodness' sake, and far too friendly with the natives. She would get a second opinion.

'Hospital would be fine if it weren't twenty miles away. Movement and sudden jerks would be unwise. Rest, but no sleeping draughts, mind, just in case.'

'In case of what?' she demanded.

'If he's sick and drowsy after tomorrow I want to know, but give the laddie a chance to settle himself. Nature

16

knows best. He's had a lucky escape. Yon Foss has seen a fair few into the next world. Ah, but boys will be boys . . . the wee devils!'

'Thank you, Doctor. You will call later,' she ordered.

'Of course, Lady Hester. Do you want a nurse?'

'That won't be necessary. I shall see to my son myself.'

'The colonel is abroad, I hear,' said the doctor, packing up his Gladstone bag.

'That is correct. I shall inform him immediately.' She was not going to endure his presence a moment longer, but he turned to Guy, who stood pale-faced by the window.

'You look like you need a brandy, young man. How old are you now? How time flies, and you so tall already . . . Don't worry, Angus'll live to plague the life out of you for a while longer. He's done far worse falling off his horse.'

How dare he be so familiar with her son? 'Arkie, show Dr Mackenzie to the door. I'm sure you've got plenty of patients waiting.'

'Funnily enough, I'm quiet. It's too braw a day to be sick and I've sewn up all the cut fingers at haytiming, but if it stays this hot, the old folk'll peg out if they're daft enough to go walking midday.'

'Yes, quite,' Hester sighed. Would the fool ever go? 'Goodbye, Doctor.' She waved him away, then pulled down the window blinds to stop the sunlight shining on Angus's face. 'Ask Shorrocks to organise a bath, Guy – it'll ease out any stiffness – and I'll get Cook to send you up a coddled egg and soldiers.'

'Mother, don't fuss, I'm fine . . . Angus was just showing off as usual. He can be such a chump.'

'I turn my back for five minutes and you get up to mischief again.'

17

'We're not babies. It was so hot and we just fancied a swim.'

'What were those village brats doing on my land?'

'You know everyone plays in the Foss when it's warm. It's tradition.'

'Not while we're in residence for the summer, they don't. I shall speak to the Parish Council.'

'Oh, Mother, the Bartleys saved Gus's life. You ought to be singing their praises, not punishing them. I told them you would be grateful,' Guy argued. He always stood his ground, just like his father. What a fine soldier he would make one day, she thought, but she must be firm.

'Sometimes, Guy, you overstep the mark . . . Over-familiarity with the lower orders breeds contempt and disobedience. Playing cricket against the village is one thing, but cavorting in front of locals is another. It is your duty to set an example, not make promises on my behalf. Ask Arkie to have tea sent up here. I'll sit and watch over Angus, just in case . . . He really ought to be in hospital.'

'I wish Father was here. He promised to be home for the hols.'

'The army needs him. There's talk of war with Germany. The situation demands all the staff officers to be making contingency plans. We mustn't worry him now about such folly. Run along. Have a warm bath, you're shivering in that indecent bathing suit.'

Hester needed to be alone. Angus looked so fragile and battered, poor darling. Nothing must harm either of her precious sons, her golden eggs. They were so late coming into her life. At nearly forty she had feared she was barren and then they came together one terrible night when all her dignity was abandoned in the struggle to bring them into the world. Guy Arthur Charles came first, all of a rush, and then the shock when another baby emerged, Garth Angus Charles, taking his time. Two for the pain of one, her beautiful boys, alike in every way. In one night her world was changed for ever and she loved them both with a devotion that knew no bounds.

Looking round at the mess in Angus's bedroom – cricket bats and fishing rods, horse crops, rugby shoes, clothes scattered on the floor – she sighed. He was such an energetic boy, full of pranks and madcap ideas. He was a skilled horseman, winning rosettes to prove his competitive spirit. On the wall were stag antlers, model ships and biplanes, and a map tracing Colonel Charles's campaigns in South Africa. The twins were as bad as each other when they were home. At school it was another matter. They were put in different houses, beaten for any misdemeanours but excelled on the sports field and in the Officers' Training Corps.

It was always so quiet when they were away. That was why she'd begged Charles to let her buy Waterloo House, so she could be close for their exeats and any public concerts at Sharland School, the great stone fortress that stood on the edge of the moor.

To think that life could have ended for one of them this beautiful afternoon didn't bear thinking about. Horse treks and camping out over the Dales would be out of bounds for the rest of the holidays after this escapade. Now she must be gracious and receive their rescuers, but of all the children to save Angus why did it have to be the blacksmith's brood of non-conformists?

Only last week she was in her carriage doing a round of charitable visiting when she chanced to see the blacksmith striding along the cobbled narrow street in his leather apron, shirtsleeves rolled up, showing muscled arms the colour of walnut oil. His black curly hair was far too long under his cap, more like a gypsy's locks. She looked down at him from her carriage, expecting him to doff his cap in deference but he swaggered on as if she was nobody of consequence.

'Stop the carriage!' she ordered Beaven. 'Go and ask that man why he has been so rude.'

'Yes, ma'am,' said her coachman, pulling up until Bartley was alongside them. 'Hey, you, why didn't you pay the usual respect to her ladyship?'

'Oh, aye,' said Asa Bartley, looking straight at her with those coal-black eyes. 'You tell your mistress I bows to no man but my Maker, and that's a fact!'

Hester flushed at such insolence and demanded that Beaven drive on. The blacksmith might own his business but he rented his cottage from the Waterloo estate. How dare he be so rude?

Men like him didn't know their place. These chapel ranters were behind all the stirrings of unrest in England: the Labour Movement and trade unions, socialist ideas of all being equal, women wanting to register for the Vote and such like. The Women's Suffrage Society had the cheek to send wagons round the villages canvassing for support from Sharland's millworkers, encouraging them to strike for better wages. She blamed all the unrest on the preachers in the pulpits of these stone chapels, giving workmen ideas above their station.

'God bless the squire and his relations, And keep us in our proper stations,' went the verse of a hymn. That was how society worked. How could any army survive without discipline and rank? Rank first and foremost. Orders must be given and obeyed, that was the key to social cohesion. Charles's generals and his staff knew how to plan battles, and their foot soldiers, under officers, must carry out the orders without question. It was always thus.

Bartley had insulted her rank and class by his insolence and now she must forbear this insult to show Christian fortitude to stomach making conversation with his children. But one thing was certain. No child of his would ever be employed on the estate. Dissenters' children had too much spirit to be knocked back, asked too many questions. They were difficult foals to break in. Their kind were best ignored and kept a bay: a different tribe, and long may that continue.

Angus seemed comfortable enough so she gathered up some of the mess on the floor. What must the doctor have thought of the clutter – that she was slack with her servants? The eye of the mistress was worth two of her hands, she mused. Arkie must make sure the room was more presentable for his next visit. She didn't want any tittle-tattling to his silly wife.

Hester caught a glimpse of herself in the dressing mirror. She'd never been an oil painting: tall, on the gaunt side of slender, but well corseted to give a robust shape and bolstered bosom like her heroine, the new Queen Mary. Her thin cream dress was a little frivolous for a Board of Workhouse Guardians meeting but the weather was so hot. That was the trouble with country living, you had to be so careful to set a suitable standard.

A military wife knew how to dress appropriately, to impress junior officers' wives as to what they must aspire. There were formal school visits to endure, dressing discreetly with nothing to cause the boys embarrassment, especially being such an older parent: no fancy jewellery or lavish trimmings on her picture hats. The risk of under- or over-dressing in such a backwater was a balancing act she found quite within her grasp. If she stuck to muted colours: mauve, taupe, eau-de-Nil, stone and her beloved silver grey for her palette, her spirits rose. Afternoon and tea gowns, skirts blended with tweed and dull plaids, furs and country tweeds were what she ordered from her dressmaker in London. Silk and wool, cotton lawns and simple lace trim distinguished her as top drawer at a glance.

Yorkshire might have smoke and soot but the best woollen cloth in the world was just over the hills in Leeds and Bradford. She felt dignified in such quiet shades. Colour was for the young fry and dress uniforms. She was a colonel's lady, daughter of an earl, albeit the youngest of many sisters, well enough placed to receive calling cards from the Birkwiths of Wellerby Hall and Lady Sommerton, the aunt of the headmaster of Sharland School. His wife, Maud, was the cousin of Lord Bankwell.

It was important to know where one was placed on this ladder. There were those who tried a little too hard to climb up a rung, like the vicar's poor wife, Violet Hunt.

Then there was Dr Mac, with his ambitious wife and their two pretty daughters, one of whom was old enough now to be brought to her sons' attention. All to no avail, of course; her boys were far too young for such entangle-ments. They were destined for the army and glittering careers.

Hester sat down on the window seat, suddenly exhausted, staring out across the walled garden, through the orchard that went down to the river, across to the great moors rising above. A patchwork of bronzed squares and golden greens caught her eye where the grass had been mown off for hay. Such was the heat haze that the stone walls dividing up the fell side shimmered like silver ribbons.

This part of the West Riding of Yorkshire was remote but not unpleasantly so. There were plenty of regular trains into Leeds and a direct line to London through the Midland Railway. The Dales' rough-hewn beauty, a grandeur of limestone scars and moor, was growing on her. She liked the fresh damp air, for they were removed from the worst of mill chimney smoke.

Most of the locals were pleasant plain folk who made few demands on her services. Once the boys were out of school and established she would think again about where to settle. Charles preferred the southern uplands, the Sussex Downs, to this rugged terrain. Soon he would finish off his career at a desk in London, if all went to plan. But she didn't like these rumours of war. He was far too old for battle service now. Her boys were nearly sixteen. Hester shivered. Surely they would be far too young to be mobilised, should any threat occur?

2

'You're not going up to Waterloo House looking like a pig in muck, Newton!' ordered Essie at the sight of her elder son strolling out of the forge, covered in soot. 'Go and scrub yoursel' down in the sink. There's hot water in the kettle.'

'Do I have to go?' he moaned, pumping the well handle and dunking his head in cold water.

'Yes, you do, and, our Frank, get into your Sunday best. It's all laid out upstairs. Sharp on! I'm not having her lady-ship peering down her nose at my family for want of a bowl of hot water. It's half-past already, get a move on.'

She'd laid out clean shirts and their serge chapel suits. Selma was already dressed in her white cotton best with the pintucked bodice and lace frill. They'd put rags in her hair last night to coil into ringlets. She had white canvas shoes and white socks which she was under pain of death not to get dirty. Everything was a little tight and short for her but it'd have to do until next year when a parcel of hand-me-downs from Essie's married sister, Ruth, in Bradford, would augment Selma's meagre wardrobe. There was no money for frills.

This presentation at Waterloo was a belated thank you to the Bartley family for the rescue of Angus. He was making excellent progress and now back at school, according to Bert Smedley, who worked in the grounds. Asa was all for refusing to send them, seeing that a whole month had passed since the accident. He stood by the forge door looking like thunder, his black brows clenched, but even he recognised that as the Cantrells were their landlords, things must be done proper.

When they were all tidied up and respectable, Frank's hair plastered down with water, Essie lined her children up against the wall. Where had her babies gone? These three were all she had to show for six labours of love; three of her babes already buried in St Wilfred's churchyard – nothing unusual in this village but still, precious lives lost before they were two years old – and there were the other two who never made it into the world. Such was life. Two fine sons and a clever daughter made up for all those other losses. And now a public thank you for her brave children. Her heart was bursting with pride at bringing three bright stars into the world.

How handsome they all were. Newt tall, broad-shouldered like his father; Frank softer round the edges and as fair as Selma was dark; Selma herself sprouting fast, sharp as a brass tack at her schooling. They all needed kicking with a different foot but they knew how to toe the line when it came to family matters.

Everyone was proud of their part in the rescue. They had saved a life and deserved a treat. Why shouldn't her ladyship receive them with gratitude? Working folk or not, they knew what was right and proper.

'Don't forget your manners and bob a curtsy when you're spoken to. Hold your head up and don't mumble. Remember, in the eyes of the Lord, we're all equal so no slouching.' Essie wished she could go with them and have a peep inside Waterloo House. Everyone knew it was very grandly furnished, with a beautiful walled garden, hidden from village eyes, but the invitation was addressed only to the children.

'Three o'clock sharp, and come by the side entrance through the door in the wall and not up the front drive to the grand entrance,' said Beaven, the coachman. What an experience to be received as guests. Selma would be full of it when she returned, Essie thought. Wick as weasel, the girl missed nothing.

The Bartleys were an old Sharland family, not offcomers like many of the cotton millworkers who kept the machines at High Mill on the go. There was a pecking order in any village: parish councillors, church wardens, school master, shopkeepers, tradesmen and farmers. Everyone came to them sooner or later for horseshoes, repairs of tools and harnesses, chains, pots and pans and iron bars. The Bartleys had been blacksmiths for three generations and Asa was a reliable fettler of anything reusable. He didn't waste his brass at the Hart's Head of a night that put so many families short of food and clothes. He liked to support the chapel reading room and took a men's Bible class.

Selma was the clever-clogs of her brood. Mr Pierce, the headmaster, was suggesting she become a pupil teacher when she was fourteen. Essie was so proud that her daughter might get the chance she never had. Not for her the grind of the mill or going into service but a proper training on the job

Selma was first to the side door of Waterloo, her brothers dawdling along as if they had all day. It was still warm for

26

September and they were red-faced in their Sunday best, playing football with fallen conkers, scuffing their polished boots.

'Hurry up, or we'll be late,' she yelled.

'So what? Let 'em wait. I've not heard the church clock chime the hour.'

'But I want to see inside . . . oh, do shift yourself,' Selma cried. Why did her brothers spoil everything? She was so excited to see where Guy lived.

Only last week he'd called in person at the forge with a horse, admiring the other beasts waiting in the paddock behind the cottage. Newt had shown him round and she'd hung on the gate, hoping for a chance to show off her own riding skills. He'd waved and then Mother had called her in and when she'd run back, he'd gone. She hoped against hope he'd be waiting behind the high stone wall with the copper beech hedge that divided the Cantrells from the village. This was her chance of a glimpse into another world and she promised Mam to notice every little detail so she could enjoy it too.

The side door was unlocked, a dog barked at their entrance and they crossed the cobbles of the yard, hearing horses neighing in the stable. The back door was opened by a stern woman in a black dress, whom Selma knew as Mrs Arkholme. She looked after the house while the Cantrells were away from Yorkshire.

'Wipe your boots on the mat,' she ordered, looking them up and down. 'Follow me and don't touch anything.' Her long black skirt swished in front of them, swaying from a gathering of material over her ample bottom.

Selma swallowed, awestruck, her eyes adjusting to the dark passageway. Would Guy and Angus be at the other

27

side of the door? She hoped so. How she wanted Guy to see her looking her very best.

On and on they marched until they came through a green door into a wide hall and staircase that spiralled up into the sunlight, which beamed down through rays of coloured glass like a kaleidoscope.

'Take your caps off, boys,' said the housekeeper. 'Wait here until you're called. I'll tell her ladyship you've arrived.'

Even Newt and Frank were silenced by the echoes of their boots on the marble floor, the grandeur of the carved furniture, the foot of a real elephant full of walking sticks, vases the size of great copper boilers, and the face of the tiger sprawling at their feet. There was a smell of rose petals and polish. It felt a bit like the inside of the parish church, Selma thought. They seemed to wait for hours until the double doors to another vast room opened and a maid in a stiff white apron ushered them inside.

A lady sat before them, her back as straight as a chapel pew. She wore a lavender dress with ruffles round her bosom, a choke of milk-white pearls, her face was pale and her white hair coiled high above her head like a helmet. She didn't rise but gestured like a queen receiving courtiers in one of Selma's old picture books.

'So here you are . . . the Bartley brood.' She examined each of them in turn. 'Sturdy workhorses, by the look of you . . . Your names?'

Selma bobbed a curtsy, suddenly struck dumb by the grandeur of the room, the marble fire surround, fine brass irons and a fire shield. Her dad would like the metalwork on display. There were silken rugs and cushions, silver candelabra and ornaments, draped curtains of heavy rust velvet, framed photographs gathered in a cluster. There was the scent of wood smoke and tobacco, and on the sideboard crystal bottles full of Satan's brew. Such luxuries she'd never seen before.

'Speak, girl,' said Lady Hester impatiently.

'This is Newton, the oldest, and my brother Frankland and I am Selima Bartley,' she offered, seeing her brothers standing tongue-tied.

'What peculiar names for Christian children,' the lady replied. 'You look more like Tom, Dick and Nellie to me. You will be pleased to know that Master Angus has made a full recovery, and is back at school with his brother. They wish me to thank you all for your part in the unfortunate accident. They wish you to know that they appreciate all the effort you made on their behalf. The Colonel and I of course endorse such sentiments. We agree therefore that you should all be given a token of our gratitude. Arkholme, fetch the tray.'

Selma thought they were in for a bun feast but a silver tray with curlicue edges was placed on the table with a lace cloth. There were three gold coins, three half sovereigns, glinting in the sunlight.

'Please take one each,' said Lady Hester. 'Tell your parents we are pleased that our tenants have brought up their children to be of such service to the community.'

Selma grabbed the first coin and bobbed her curtsy, not knowing what to do next. Frank and Newt did the same and bowed. There was a silence and then Lady Hester rang a bell and the parlour maid ushered them to the door.

'Just this once, let them go out the front entrance and down the steps. I expect they will want to admire the view to the river. Thank you and good day.'

The audience was over. No handshake, no cup of tea and

29

cake, no conversation. But most of all, no Guy or Angus in attendance.

Disappointment rose like bile in Selma's throat. All that dressing up for five minutes in a beautiful drawing room.

How pokey, cold, plain and homespun their front room, with its rag rug and chenille tablecloth, would appear when she got home. How ordinary everything was. A splinter of discontent pierced her heart and she felt shame and pain.

This was another world, a world of luxury and comfort the likes of which the Bartleys would never know. 'We are all equal in the eyes of the Lord.' Mam's words rang in her head like a tolling bell. Why at this moment were they sounding so hollow?

It was quite evident that they were not equal, or why did her ladyship not even stand or shake their hands? The gold coins meant nothing to the Cantrells. She had paid them for their services. Selma wanted to throw hers away in disgust. How dare they think so ill of them?

What would Dad make of it all? Half a guinea to spend or save? The boys weren't bothered either way, glad to be out in the fresh air, wanting to tear off their Sunday clothes.

Selma felt a strange sadness when she opened the back door to their cottage.

'Well? How did it go? That didn't take long.' Mam was anxious to hear every detail of the visit, stirring soup on the range.

'It were all right . . . She give us one of these each.' Selma plonked the coin on the table as if it was burning her fingers.

'That'll come in handy for your schooling,' Essie smiled, and then she saw her face. 'What's up?'

'Nothing. It were all so quick, in and out in five minutes as if we were the delivery boys.'

'You didn't get a look round, then?' Essie registered surprise. 'I thought the young masters would want to show you the horses.'

'They're back at school. It was a right thunder of nothing. I felt like a fool,' Newt added. 'She's a right proud madam, is that one. Had us through the door in a flash in case we might steal owt, I reckon.'

'Surely not.' Essie sighed and shook her head. 'I suppose we must expect that they do things different. Gentry folk don't mix, never have except when they want the rent. She's a bit stiff but I hear she's very fond of her boys. They say she never had a nursemaid to them. Anyhow, I'm sure she was grateful.'

'She didn't look it. She looked at us as if we were the scrapings off her boot,' muttered Frank.

'Happen she's just reserved with lower orders,' Essie consoled.

'You said we were all equal,' Selma jumped in.

'Aye, we are but that lot up there don't know it yet. One day perhaps . . . Things'll be better. You'll see.'

'I'm getting out of this clobber.' Newt made for the stairs.

'I'll put the kettle on the hob. I gather she didn't give you any tea then? I had hoped . . . never mind. Nowt as queer as folk.'

'You can say that again,' snapped Selma. 'I'm never going back there.' It wasn't right to be made to feel small or ashamed of their fancy names as if they didn't deserve them. Selima was her dad's choice. It was foreign different. How dare Lady Hester belittle his choosing?

The drill sergeant had them marching up and down the quadrangle of Sharland School. 'Forward . . . at the double.'

31

He wanted them drill perfect for the next inspection day. The officer cadets were soldiers-in-waiting, pride of the school parades, but today Guy was out of step and not his usual efficient self. He couldn't concentrate. Something was wrong and he didn't know what. It kept making him lose his rhythm. He kept looking over to where his twin brother was marching, head up, eyes forward, a glint of steel in his eye. He was a born drill merchant, far better than he.

Angus had made a remarkable recovery, only the gash on his left temple bearing evidence of his accident, and this was now hidden under a tuft of blond hair that fell like a forelock when it wasn't plastered down. In their uniforms they were identical, but now all those pranks and swapping identities would not be so easy to go undetected. Angus was the one with the scar.

Guy felt uneasy. Poor chap had no recollection of the accident or indeed the afternoon picnic or the jump when the Bartleys rescued him. It was as if the whole slate was wiped clean, had never happened until he looked in the mirror at his brow with disgust. Mother kept reminding him to be careful. She'd not wanted him back at school so soon. Angus had shrugged off her worries as fussing and brushed aside Guy's enquiries about how he was feeling.

Having a twin brother was both a blessing and a curse. There was always your own face looking back at you. It was always the two of them, dressed alike, objects of curiosity. Sometimes he felt as if they were one whole person split into two halves – or he did until the accident. Now he sensed Angus was changing and he was sure he was getting headaches because they throbbed in his own head. It was curious how when one of them was ill the other felt groggy too. Sometimes he sensed they could think each other's thoughts before they spoke them, knew instinctively what the other was going to say.

He'd noticed that Angus didn't concentrate on his studies for very long now, that he jumped up and paced round their study room, much more restless than last term. His tri-weekly test scores were much lower than his own and the competitive edge between them had vanished. All Angus wanted to do was run cross-country, chase up and down the rugger pitch and drill. They may still look like two peas in a pod but something had shifted. Guy had tried to speak to Mother and warn her something was up, but she put it all down to going back to school too early.

At least she'd had the Bartleys to tea one afternoon and given them a present each but he was horrified when she'd told them she'd given them a coin as a token. It wasn't his place to criticise her decision, though. He tried but failed to imagine her putting little Selma and her brothers at ease.

Father would've been more gracious, but he was never around these days. Colonel 'Give 'em hell' Cantrell was now an important member of Lord Kitchener's advisory staff. If war did come, as everyone was saying it would, they'd hardly see him.

'Eyes right!' shouted the drill sergeant.

Damn! Guy nearly tripped into the back of Forbes Senior.

'At ease, gentlemen. We will be stepping up training this term and for the foreseeable future. We want all Sharlanders to be prepared for every eventuality, to answer the call to arms, should the situation arise . . .'

Suddenly there was a commotion in the rear and a chorus of 'Sir!' Guy spun round, suddenly sensing that it would be Angus on the ground. 'It's Cantrell Junior, sir! He's fitting.'

Angus was lying on the ground, spasms of jerking limbs,

frothing at the mouth and a pool of wetness on his trousers. It was a frightful scene. Guy broke ranks to be at his side. 'For God's sake, give him some air!' he heard himself shouting.

'Take him to the san,' someone yelled, but the master shoved them all aside.

'Wait till he comes round.' He turned to Guy. 'How long has he had fits, Cantrell? Better put something on his tongue.'

Someone with a satchel brought out a ruler. Everyone stood around. Guy felt sick and shaky. Then the twitching tremors stopped and Angus woke up dazed, surprised to find himself the object of attention.

'What's up? Guy? Did I fall?'

'You'll be fine, old chum. You had a bit of a turn, that's all.' Guy wanted to cover his wet trousers with his army jacket to mask his brother's shame. The cadets were dismissed. Angus was carried to the san and the doctor summoned from the village.

'What's happened to him?' Guy asked Matron, suddenly scared at such a public exhibition.

'He had a seizure . . . nothing to worry about. It probably won't happen again. Too much drilling, I expect,' she fobbed him off. 'Run along now . . . we'll see what Dr Mackenzie has to say. Your parents will be informed in due course. It may be nothing but overtiredness.'

'Can I stay?' Guy pleaded, knowing Angus would be feeling strange on his own.

'No, the boy needs rest and privacy . . . And he's never done this before, you say?'

Guy shook his head. Fits were terrifying to witness. He'd felt so helpless.

'Ah well, growing pains and fits go hand in hand in my book,' Matron smiled. 'Doctor will know what's best for him.'

Guy ambled through the leafy grounds of Sharland School, puzzled, scared and confused. What if they made Angus leave? What if it happened again on the rugby pitch in a match, or riding across the moor, or with a gun in his hand? He was an outdoorsy chap, and Sharland was a school that fostered team spirit, personal challenges, fresh air and exercise. He'd never cope.

Mother would have him home-tutored in a flash if she thought there was any danger.

Guy stared up at the turrets of the stone building. He loved his Alma Mater, with its warren of study rooms, corridors, fine chapel and acres of playing fields.

Angus wasn't academic. He'd loathe being deskbound or cosseted. He needed open spaces, hunting over the fields to release all his spare energy. He bounded everywhere like an over excited Labrador puppy.

Guy found a hidey-hole under a huge black poplar and whipped out his forbidden pipe. Had Angus's jump from the Foss left permanent damage. Had it ruined his chance of an army career? Would he be an invalid? Guy couldn't bear to see him unhappy and frustrated.

Take a hold of yourself, he thought. Don't get so windy! One fit doesn't mean life in a basket chair. It was just a warning sign, that was all. If his brother calmed down and took enough rest and some pills, he'd be his old self again. Guy said a silent prayer to the Almighty to put everything back to normal.

Reluctantly he lifted himself out of his funk hole and made for the school. He'd face a barrage of questions from his house chums on his return. It was none of their business but news would have already gone round the school like wild fire. Cantrell Junior had had a fit. The question was, would he have another?

3

Selma stared into the window of Bow's Emporium on Market Square in Sowerthwaite. The window was lit up like a magic lantern with fairy figures in silhouette against a glowing sky. She couldn't wait for Christmas to come and the first carollers to sing at the door for a slice of spiced loaf and hot elderberry cordial. It was cold and her breath was steaming up the window. Mam was doing her secret shopping on market day but it was already darkening fast and the sky was full of snow feathers. Selma's feet were freezing on the stone pavement.

She wandered past the toy shop, glad she was grown up enough now not to be disappointed by the lack of the Christmas dolls and games her other friends bragged about. This year there might be a new knitted cardigan with matching beret and scarf, a parcel of clothes from Aunty Ruth when she called in on Boxing Day, some of which might fit her, if she was lucky.

Selma'd grown inches since the summer, and filled out. Her breasts were like two rubber balls sticking out of her thick vest, and with them came the curse one morning and all that messy business that Mam explained was a step on the way to being a proper young lady. But fourteen was not quite old enough to roll her hair over in pads like Marigold Plimmer did, the other pupil teacher and the bane of Selma's life.

Marigold was older by a year, pretty enough, clever too, but had a way of setting Selma's teeth on edge. The Plimmers ran the Hart's Head Inn on Elm Tree Square at the other end of Prospect Row, but not far enough from the teetotal Bartley forge for comfort on a noisy Saturday night. The pub had once been a house, with two fine bow windows and a large stable for horses at the back with benches for draymen to idle away their lunch times.

Marigold and her mother, Betty, were also on the horse-drawn bus to Sowerthwaite alongside the Bartleys, boasting about how big a turkey they were going to carve and how Marie was getting a new tartan dress with a crocheted collar for the Sunday school Christmas concert.

It was Marie who had pointed out that Selma and her brothers were heathens, since none of them had been baptised, and they would all go to Hell. Selma knew the Chapel didn't do infant christenings but preferred them to make a profession of faith when they were teenagers, but it had still worried her for days afterwards.

'What happens to my baby brothers and sisters who died before baptism?' she had cried to Mam in distress one night. 'Will they be saved?'

'Of course. The Lord only lent them to us for a season. They are angels now in Glory, too lovely to live long in this wicked world. Take no notice of Marie Plimmer's popish superstitions,' Essie had reassured her, but Marie had a way of insinuating that chapelgoers were the poor relations in this village.

The mill owner, Mr Best, was a big worker and Sunday

school teacher, as was their organist and schoolmaster, Mr Firth. They had a great concert party and outings to the seaside at Morecambe, fun and games at Christmas like everyone else.

Dad said that Christmas was the Lord's birthday, not theirs, and the heart of Christmas was in giving to others, not wanting for yourself. But on this chill December afternoon, the forthcoming Christmas festivities glowed like a beacon on a dark night with all the special baking, the scent of spices, roasting meat and the promise of fun and games.

Farmer Dinsdale up the dale had promised them a joint of pork as a thank you for Dad's good services to his Clydesdale horses over the year.

Selma knew all about pig sticking and slaughter at this time of year. The poor beasts were cornered and hung upside down with their throats cut to bleed into a bucket for black puddings. But she did love a roast with crunchy crackling and Mam's special herb stuffing. Her mouth was watering at the very thought, making her forget the chill of the wild north-easterly as it tore through her thin coat and scarf: a lazy wind, they called this, one as went through you not round you. It was time to make for the bus home.

Then she caught sight of a tall young man striding across the square, parcels under his arm and another identical figure chasing after him. They looked so smart in thick tweed suits with Sharland School scarves flapping behind them, those distinctive purple and gold stripes that marked the public school boys out from other town scholars. Who could miss the Cantrell twins doing their own Christmas shopping?

Selma tried not to stare and pulled her muffler over her

face to spare her blushes but not before she caught the eye of the first twin.

'Hello there, Miss Bartley . . . Busy with your Christmas shopping too,' he said. 'And you'll have a lot of folk to buy for.'

His brother marched on, hardly giving her a glance. 'Hang on, Angus! Let me introduce you to the young lady who helped save your life!'

Angus stared at her, his eyes blank and dull as if he had never seen her before. He nodded but said nothing. 'He doesn't remember a thing, sadly,' Guy explained. 'How are you? Looking forward to Christmas?'

Selma smiled back, not knowing what to say.

'It's jolly cold. There's snow on the way but I hope it holds off for the Boxing Day meet.'

Selma nodded, knowing her father had been hard at the forge shoeing fine hunters for the annual foxhunting gathering that started outside the Hart's Head.

'Spare a thought for us on our Christmas morning parade,' she offered. 'I don't fancy singing through a blizzard.'

'Parade?' Angus looked puzzled, fidgeting with the string on his parcel and looking at her sideways through drooping eyelids.

'The Christmas waits. We sing carols under the tree in the early hours and then we have a band . . .'

'Oh, the chapel thingy.' Angus shrugged. 'Spoiling everyone's lie in, Mama says.'

'Angus!' It was Guy's turn to be embarrassed. 'Oh, look, there's Beaven with his new toy. Father has bought a motor car. We'd offer you a lift only we're off to the station to meet the London Express. Father is home for the hols too.'

'I'm waiting for my mother. We're catching the bus, thank

40

you. I hope you both have a pleasant Christmas,' she offered, bobbing a short curtsy.

'And the same to you and yours. You know we are awfully grateful to you and your brothers, aren't we, Angus?' He turned to his brother, but Angus had already strolled off towards the big saloon. 'Forgive his rudeness. He's not been quite himself lately. I'd better be off. And you must go too. You look frozen.'

To Selma, Angus looked just as haughty as he had on that fateful afternoon when he was showing off. 'I hope he recovers soon,' she replied, more out of politeness than conviction.

Guy paused. 'Will you be watching the meet?'

'I might if the weather holds but we're expecting company from Bradford: my aunty Ruth and her husband.'

'And so are we, loads every day, Mother's friends mostly. It'll be charades, singsongs and cards, long walks and cross-country hacks; exhausting!'

'We have singsongs too but no card playing . . . we don't hold with gambling,' she answered, not telling him that they never imbibed alcohol either. 'Have fun then.'

'Merry Christmas, Selima,' Guy replied, raising his cap as he marched off.

She felt a glow of pride that he'd remembered her proper name. Guy was as warm as his brother was cool, sick or not. It was as if he saw her as a friend, an equal. Confusion and excitement fluttered in her chest as if butterflies were let loose from a cage.

Their families lived in separate worlds even within a small village, sectioned off by a high stone wall and beech hedge, but Christmas was a special time, she smiled, a time of goodwill to all men, rich or poor, high or low. Was it possible

41

that their two worlds might meet again? One thing was certain: she wanted to see Guy on horseback in his hunting dress.

Suddenly her reverie was halted by a sharp dig in the back from a passer-by.

'What were you hobnobbing with those two toffs about?'

Selma spun round to see the pinched face of Marigold Plimmer pursing her lips into a sneer. 'Never you mind!' Selma whispered back.

'Be like that but don't think you'll get any favours from *that* quarter. My mum says one of them's gone daft in the head. Had a fit in the school yard, or so Tilly Foster said. She works in the canteen and saw it all – well, one of her mates did. Just shows money can't buy you everything. It's only fair they should have some bad luck as well as us, isn't it?'

'That's sad,' murmured Selma. No wonder Angus looked so blank. 'His mother must be so worried.'

'Who, that stuck-up cow? Lady Muck of Waterloo? Serves her right. You should see her in church. Comes in through a side door just before the service, all dolled up with a thick veil like curtains round her head so she don't have to look at us. Then leaves the same way as soon as the organ strikes up at the end. I pity them boys. She'll not let them far off the leash. My mum got it off her that works in the kitchen that she—'

'Oh, there's Mam. I've got to go. See you on the bus!'

Selma couldn't wait to get away from Marie's gossiping. She didn't care for all that backbiting. Poor Guy and his brother – no wonder he looked tired and glassy-eyed. Her little brother, Dawson, had fitted badly when his temperature went sky high and never came down, all those years

42

ago. They'd tried to soak him with ice water from the slate tank in the yard and then piled on blankets to sweat it out of him but his heart was too weak, the doctor had said. Why did Marigold have to remind her of such sad memories?

Selma stood looking up to the grey-white hills rising above the town, sparkling with ice, and the trees dusted with air frost. How beautiful it looked at dusk. In two days it would be Christmas morning and they would be singing 'Joy to the World' around the village green. So no more sad thoughts when there was so much to look forward to. Mam was waving at her now to get in the queue. Time to go home.

On Christmas morning the wind would carry the sound of bells into every household, thought Essie, waking at dawn with excitement long before the peals filled the air with promise. This was the day for singing and feasting. However humble they were, each family managed some cheer at their fireside and kept good company together.

Essie had packed each stocking with love: a shilling, an orange, a bar of chocolate and some walnuts to crack, knitted socks for the boys, and a new scarf and beret for Selma, with some sweet-smelling lavender sachets for her pocket. How she wished she could do more than just these little tokens, but they were going to have a fine feast with all the trimmings later; plum pudding and a traditional dish of frumenty, fresh creamed wheat in a bowl and mince pies to share with visitors.

Tomorrow Ruth would bring treats from Bradford. She had been in service and married a wool sorter's apprentice who had done well in the trade and set them up comfortably. Sadly there were no little ones so Essie's own children were at the receiving end of much kindness. Not that they were short of anything this year.

Only two days ago she had laid out old Mrs Marshall, who had died in her sleep, well prepared with her best nightdress and pennies ready in the top drawer.

There was an art to laying out the dead with dignity and pride, plugging places that might leak, washing and dressing the body, tying the chin with a bandage, combing hair and changing all their linen for the first viewings.

Mrs Marshall was a good sort, plain spoken but kindly, and would be missed at the weekly Women's Bright Hour. Her son and widower were pleased and had left Essie two florins on the dresser for her willing services, a thank you that had come in useful in buying little extras for the coming days.

It was not that Asa made a poor living, but with the rent and their everyday expenses, the budget was always tight. Growing boys needed good boots and strong breeches and shirts. She was trying to save for Selma to have some fresh skirts and blouses for her new post as a pupil teacher assistant, and it was time she wore a good corset to hold her firm. They were blessed with work and not want.

As she crept down the dark stairs with a lamp she smiled at all the little trimmings Selma had dotted about the cottage, evergreen branches, winter berries, a kissing bough of holly hung from the kitchen. They didn't go in for decorated trees because Asa said they were pagan and killing perfectly good shelter for winter birds wasn't on, but he did light one candle at the window on Christmas Eve as a symbol of guidance to those who lived in dark ignorance.

Asa was a good husband and one who didn't put his

44

religion away with his Sunday suit like so many she could mention. He was strict and fair and honest to the point of being a stickler. Only last week he had refused thirty shillings for a piece of wrought iron work that had taken him hours of reshaping and finishing. 'Give me twenty-nine shillings, Alf,' he'd said. 'Never let it be said that I sold this for thirty pieces of silver. The Lord was betrayed for just that sum.' How could you not love such a man?

Now the front parlour smelled of elbow grease and beeswax polish, the pine needles added a rich tincture and the fire was laid and ready. They had roasted the joint overnight slowly, wrapped in greaseproof and cloth so it would fall apart and go further cold for Ruth's visit.

Every surface was cleaned and tidied, the best rag rug down and white linen cloth ready to receive the feast. Their boots were lined up for the Christmas procession they called the waits. Even she was not too old to feel a thrill on such a joyful morning.

Soon the children were stumbling bleary-eyed into the dawn light.

'Rise and shine! We shall stir the hearts of West Sharland with our songs of praise this merry morning.' Asa was wide awake, chivvying up his sons to wash and shave while Essie shoved hot porridge from the stove into bowls for them all. No one was going out on an empty stomach in this chill.

'Do we have to?' moaned Newt, who liked his lie abed.

'Faith before feasting, son! How can we honour the day without honouring Him first?' There was no arguing with Asa when it came to what was right and proper.

By the time they picked their way across the cobbled square there was a small crowd huffing and puffing, stamping their clogs; the faithful brigade of chapel stalwarts wrapped against the cold with caps, shawls and bonnets on their heads. Men in hobnail boots and hats holding baskets of hymn sheets, children, muffled with hoods, skating on icy flags.

The last to arrive was Mr Best from the mill, in his carriage with his son and daughter and a line of servants walking behind, looking pinched underneath their best cloaks. Harold Fothergill flourished his trumpet and the sober remnants of the village silver band gathered in a huddle. The drummer strapped on his instrument ready to lead the proceedings. They were ready for the off but not before a prayer.

'All present and correct,' shouted the pastor, raising his hat. Only the old and infirm were exempt from this morning's witness.

'Hurry up, I'm freezing!' yelled Frank, laughing. 'What's the first hymn?'

'As it always is,' Newt replied. '"Christians, awake" followed by "Hail, smiling morn".'

'That'll wake the dead then,' quipped Selma.

'If we're awake and doing, I don't see why those still in their beds should slumber on,' said the choirmaster. 'I want full throttle.'

There was a drum roll, a tuning up of the large euphonium and the procession stood to attention as the bass drum banged out the start of their parade. Everyone tried to stay in tune and on time but they kept parting company and stopping so stragglers could catch up as they stormed round the village green, past the church and through the side streets before back to the square.

'Christians, awake, salute the happy morn . . .' rang out

in the frosty air loud enough to wake the dead in the church-yard; 'O come, all ye faithful' and 'Once in royal David's city'. A few curtains twitched and then a head appeared from behind the shutters of the Hart's Head. An irate Charlie Plimmer was yelling his protest as he chucked the contents of his chamber pot out the window in their direction.

'Shut that bloody racket! Can't a man get a decent night's sleep without you caterwauling?'

'And a Merry Christmas to you and yours, Mr Plimmer . . .' The minister raised his hat and everyone cheered.

Essie smiled as they carried on singing until they were hoarse, standing under the elm tree that shaded both teetotallers and hard drinkers alike of a sunny evening. 'Who needs John Barleycorn to lift spirits on such a day?' whispered Asa, slipping his arm into hers. Essie smiled and patted his hand, her dark eyes flashing mischief.

'That was a good sing-along. We got in first before the church bells,' said the minister. 'Time for a slice of Christmas pie in the chapel room.'

Essie stood admiring the grey stone building, proud to see her family name, Ackroyd, carved into one of the foundation stones. We're built to last, she thought, looking at her bonny children growing into fine specimens. One day they would be leading the faithful in this age-old tradition.

The pastor handed small books to the children, full of terrible tales of poor little Eva who waited in the snow for her father to come out of the public house, dying with fever and bringing him to sign the pledge of her dying wish, alongside decorated biscuits. They sipped cups of tea with relish; glad of the warmth on their fingers.

Essie smiled, thinking she had brewed up her Christmas cordial from hedge berries; blackberries and elderberries, rosehips all steeped in sugar for weeks on end; all the good-ness of God's earth in a stone jar. Asa, Ruth and her husband, Sam, would wolf it down and complain of a puzzling funny headache in the morning. Essie was sure it must be the extra sweetness of the juice, but what if the fermentation was too strong? Perhaps it was better not to know. She was sure the Lord, who turned water into wine at the wedding in Cana, would not begrudge a little laxity on His birthday.

'You don't really believe there'll be war, do you, Charles?' Hester asked her husband, pressing her damask linen napkin to her lips, her grey eyes full of concern.

'Of course there will,' Colonel Cantrell snapped. 'Why do you think I'm setting up a Rifle Association in our bottom field for the local men to sharpen up their musketry and drills? Got to get 'em up to scratch, and the Territorials too. It's been coming for years. The Kaiser and his henchmen do nothing but boast about their navy. One of these days he'll want to pit it against us British, Lord Kitchener was reminding us only the other day,' he replied, wiping his waxed moustache.

'But what about the twins?' she countered. Her sons were now past their sixteenth birthday.

'Just the sort of trustworthy leaders of men the army will want. Officer cadet training is first class for stiffening the backbone.'

'But you heard what those doctors said about Angus. He's had two fits in the past few months. That blessed jump from the Foss is to blame, I'm sure.'

'He looks A1 to me; nothing a bit of drilling won't cure. Guy keeps an eye on him. They'll both make excellent officers.'

'But they're hardly out of short trousers.'

'Don't fuss, woman. Boys grow up fast these days, and when the time comes they'll want to do their duty for King and Country.'

'Not at sixteen, they won't . . . You mustn't let them do anything stupid, Charles,' she pleaded, stabbing the air with her cake fork.

'Huh! If every woman took your attitude, why bother with an army? We could just invite Kaiser Bill over the Channel to occupy us. Pass the cheeseboard and stop wittering. You'll make a baby of Angus with all those hospital appointments and rest cures.'

'Now who's being unrealistic? Who'll have rest cures if there's a war on? I think he should be tutored privately for the meantime, away from all that activity they go in for at Sharland School.'

'And I think you should go back to your tapestry and get things in proportion. I don't want my son raised as a spineless sissy. He's been bred to be tough and a skilled marksman.' Charles rose, grabbing the port decanter and heading for his library without a backward glance. Hester sighed and rang the bell for Shorrocks to clear away the debris of their supper.

There was no talking to Charles when he was in one of his belligerent moods, his eyes bright with too much Christmas fare and wine. Better to let him doze off his bad temper alone. When the boys came in from their party, he'd be back to his old self. His eyes lit up with pride when he saw them together.

Poor man had journeyed north for a break from war talk and planning; all he wanted was his paper, a good book and plenty to smoke and drink. He'd taken the boys out for long hikes. A house full of men could be lonely for a mother at times, however much they gave her loving presents and praise. Sometimes she sensed he was relieved she was out of his hair in London, glad she was up north so he could keep his own hours in peace.

She had bred him sons, however late in life, ensuring the family name into the next generation. Her duty was done. He slept in the dressing room in the single bed most nights – his snoring would upset her, he apologised – hardly bothering her with any physical affection. She guessed he was getting that elsewhere. He hadn't meant to hurt her but his indifference and short fuse stung just the same.

They had had the usual Christmas ceremonies: church at midnight, a delightful Christmas tree in the hall, a long walk after an enormous luncheon, lots of visitors bringing gifts and gossip. The house was trimmed discreetly with holly and ivy, berried garlands up the spiral staircase. There was even a dusting of snow like a Christmas card scene on Christmas morning. The vicar had complained over mulled wine about the chapel rowdies waking them at dawn.

'I can't bear religious enthusiasts,' Charles sympathised. 'But I suppose we ought to be grateful that our local workers are singing from a hymn sheet rather than a striker's ballot paper.' They all laughed.

She'd bought the boys new dinner suits and they looked so handsome together, so grown up. They could pass for eighteen, they were so tall and strong. It was alarming.

What if war came? Should she go to London or stay here? Her place was close to her boys and the village where she would be expected to take some leadership in parochial matters. She would see that no son of hers would be allowed to slip underage into the forces, cadet or not! Plenty of time for them to enlist should such a time come.

Oh, why did such thoughts have to sour their festivities? Charles's warning, like Angus's recent fits, hung heavy on her heart. Surely the Royal Navy would make enough noise to see off the Kaiser's affectations? Suddenly she was not looking forward to 1914.

Guy and Angus joined the crowd gathered in Elm Tree Square outside the Hart's Head for the traditional send-off to the Boxing Day meet. The snow had come to nothing and the ground was sure enough for a full hunt. Hounds were wagging their tails ready for the off, horses snorting breath and dumping manure for the allotment holders already waiting with buckets at the ready. A crowd of spectators and followers were assembled on the pavement, watching the colourful spectacle of masters in their scarlet coats, ladies in veiled black top hats and riding habits, younger riders in tweed hacking jackets and jodhpurs circling round with their ponies; a magnificent turnout. It was going to be a brilliant meet.

Guy's eyes searched through the crowd to see if Selma Bartley had bothered to see them off but the door of the forge was shut, with no sign of life from the cottage. Perhaps they were visiting or out walking, as was the custom in the village on this holiday.

He'd never been interested in girls before. It wasn't encouraged even to flirt with the maids in school. There were careful articles in his *Boys' Herald* about gentlemanly behaviour towards the weaker sex and such rot. He just thought it was a shame that boys and girls couldn't be friends, brothers and sisters, and equals. Why couldn't you

51

talk to a girl without sniggers from chums? Funny, though, when he looked at Selma, all he saw were those huge chocolate-brown eyes and smiling face, and how her wet shirt clung to her body when she had stood out of the beck after the accident. A strange yearning churned him up inside at the memory.

It was not as if he didn't meet pretty girls at the family gatherings, girls all buttoned up with frills and ruffles, and simpering glances in his direction.

Selma was different, full of life and fun. He'd once watched her leap onto one of the horses grazing in the paddock waiting to be shod. She would make a fearless horsewoman, confident and yet gentle at the same time. That talent was innate; riding skills could be taught but not that sense of oneness with your mount. The Bartley boys too were skilled with the farm horses, leading the huge beasts, checking their forelocks, calming them down. It was a pity that none of them had the use of a horse to exercise.

Perhaps it was that tomboy bit of Selma he was attracted to. How he'd love to lend her Jemima, Mother's chestnut, which she hardly rode, but he knew it wouldn't be proper to single her out. The Bartleys and Cantrells didn't mix socially and it would be taken amiss if they did. Pity, he sighed as he searched the crowd again. Riding high it was so easy to look down on villagers as if you were somehow above them.

Then he saw her watching him from the corner of Prospect Row, almost hidden. She was wearing a bright scarlet beret and scarf over her usual winter coat. He gave a short wave so as not to embarrass her and she smiled back mouthing 'Good luck'. How he wished he could ask her to come and join them. Now the landlord was carrying a tray full of stirrup cups. Soon the hunting horn would round up the stragglers for the off; the hounds were champing for the chase.

Guy had promised his mother to keep an eye on Angus, but he was already ahead with Father in his scarlet jacket. Angus got very stroppy if he thought they were mollycoddling him and refused to discuss his last fit in the school changing rooms.

Guy took one final look but Selma had disappeared. It was sad that there were two villages in Sharland divided by an invisible bridge. On one side were the House and church, the vicarage, the public school and the gentleman farmers' estates, on the other side were millworkers' cottages, the chapel and board school and quarrymen's houses. Once a year they met on the cricket pitch and sometimes in the Hart's Head, and that was about it.

As he trotted down towards the river bridge and fields ahead, he thought how it was just like himself and Selma . . . all they could ever do was smile and wave across the yawning divide.

I smile thinking of those horses clattering off from Elm Tree Square all those years ago. Horses . . . horses, always horses close to my heart. I'd watched the Boxing Day meets since I was nobbut a child, little knowing this would be the last gathering before war came and things were never the same. Besides, how do you ever forget the day you first fell in love?

I can see him now resplendent in jodhpurs and hard hat on his mount, giving me that precious grin of recognition and, with it, a spark of knowing flashing between us. How innocent were those stolen glances but how I hugged them to myself for months on end. How I longed to be riding alongside Guy Cantrell as an equal, but knowing this was not how things would ever be in our staid Yorkshire village. The next time we met on horseback, the world was entirely changed . . .

Come on, old girl, concentrate, back to the ceremony. Will that young version of Guy turn up somewhere on the fringes of my vision if I'm patient?

One of the secrets of old age is the people you see that others do not: those long departed gathering in the corners, waiting to welcome you home. But not just yet.

The ceremony's hardly begun but I can still hear hoofs on the trot and remember that awful day they took all our horses to war . . .

4

'They can't take all the horses away! They just can't!' cried Selma, watching the men in khaki leading a line of them roped together like prisoners across the square. 'Dad! Stop them!'

Asa shrugged his shoulders and sucked on his pipe, shaking his head. 'They'll be well looked after if they're doing war work. Don't take on so. The country needs them.'

'But there's Sybil's pony!' She pointed out a sturdy grey belonging to her school friend. 'How can the farmers manage without them? You will have no shoeing . . .' Selma turned indoors, unable to watch this terrible procession, hardly believing what was happening.

In just a few weeks since the Bank Holiday war had been declared, everything was topsy-turvy in the village. The Rifle Association had taken over Colonel Cantrell's bottom field for target practice, there were posters everywhere demanding citizens be on guard for German spies. The railway line was patrolled day and night. The Territorials were making preparations to leave from Sowerthwaite station.

Poor Mr Jerome, the old German photographer, had had his windows smashed and his equipment taken in case he was in league with the enemy. All the talk in school was about the wicked Hun stealing poor little Belgium.

Now the district had to yield up a quota of serviceable animals: hunters, cart horses and drayhorses, ponies. How could the milkman manage without Barney, or Stamper, the coalman's steady Dales horse? They were taking all the beasts she'd known all her life down the road and across the sea to a foreign land. They would be so bewildered and scared. Selma was sobbing as Essie tried to comfort her.

'They're not all gone. Don't fret. Lady Hester's hunter is still in the barn out of the way. It was a good job she was being shoed here but I expect she'll go with Master Guy or Angus before long.'

Selma wept over these dumb beasts that had no say in their fate. Next it would be her brothers and the boys who stood at the notice board regarding Lord Kitchener's big poster: 'Your Country Needs You', his finger pointing accusingly towards her. Well, he wasn't having any of *her* family. They were blacksmiths and farriers; important trades that kept the farm machines at work. Men could volunteer but her dad would have more sense and her brothers were too young. They knew nothing about fighting wars.

Suddenly it felt as if the whole world had gone mad. There were flags and bunting in the streets, and cheering processions as if this was something to shout about. Soon the village horses would pull guns and the guns would be let off and people would be getting killed. All because some duke they had never heard of got shot in a country she couldn't find on the map. Why had they got to get involved? No one had explained it to her satisfaction, not even the Head, Mr Pierce, whom she'd heard was enlisting in the Duke of Wellington's Regiment, the famous 'Havercake lads'.

'Now the army's gone, take Jemima out of the barn and into the paddock, Selma. Keep busy and don't fret is my motto,' Asa smiled. 'Go and take that miserable face into the sunshine. Happen it's time to stop the bullyboys in their tracks and show them what all our King's men can do. Go on . . . wipe yer tears and get a bit of fresh air in your lungs.'

Selma led the tall chestnut mare out into the sunshine. She loved this gentle giant who had carried Guy on her back. The groom would be ages before he came to collect her, and then she remembered that Stanley and the stable boy had enlisted together to go with the horses. There was just the chance that Guy might . . . No, she mustn't hope too much.

The late August afternoon sun beat on her forehead as she led the horse into shade and towards the slate trough where cool fresh water bubbled up from a natural spring. Soon the holidays would be over and she would take her post as proper teaching assistant alongside Marigold. Her brother, Jack, was with the Territorials and she kept boasting about him being the first in West Sharland to take the King's shilling and asking why her brothers weren't in uniform yet.

'You have to be eighteen,' Selma replied.

'Who says?' Marie sneered. 'You don't have to take your birth certificate. No one in Skipton would guess that Newton was underage if he signed on there.'

'He has to help Dad.'

'Frank can do that . . . Anyroad, when the horses go, he'll

57

have nowt to do, my dad says.' There was no arguing with Marie. She was always right, but not this time. It was official. Dad needed an assistant and Frank was only sixteen and not very tall.

The urge to mount Jem was now just too hard to resist. They were old friends and riding bareback was no problem for Selma. 'We'll not let you go with those soldiers,' she whispered in her ear. 'You can hide in our barn any day. Now you and me can have a little trot round the paddock or I can ride you home, if no one comes for you.' Guiding the horse to the mounting block by the gate, she slid onto her velvety back and nuzzled into her mane, kicking with her heels to set Jem on her way. But the mare had other ideas and began to gather speed. Then with a whoosh she jumped the stone wall into the next field with Selma clinging on, hair flying, her face flushed with the fun and freedom of chasing the wind. This horse was no sloth and shot off at speed, cantering across the last of the mown hayfields, frisky, disobedient to Selma's commands. There was nothing to it but to relax and enjoy the bumpy ride, let the horse have her head for a while but what if she got injured and Dad had to get the veterinary out to repair the damage? 'Stop! Who-ah!' Selma dug hard and raised her voice. She pulled hard on the reins and mane to no avail. Then Jemima suddenly halted, jerked and threw Selma to the ground, leaving the horse bolting off out of reach towards the river bank.

Selma lay winded but laughing, smelling the clover, meadowsweet and honey of the scratchy stubble. Another horse was flying across in pursuit. The horseman jumped down and came to her aid.

'Are you all right?' It was Guy, like a knight in shining armour, lifting her up to let her hobble to the shelter of the stone wall. 'She can be a monkey if you don't check her.'

'I'm fine, just my pride hurt. I thought she'd like a genteel little trot but she just decided to let rip. Sorry.'

'Just stay put,' Guy ordered, and he was back on horseback and cantering off in the direction of the far field where the chestnut hunter was casually grazing. He tethered her to his own horse and walked them back.

'No bones broken this end,' Guy laughed. 'I gather your father hid her in the barn when the soldiers came but we have permission to keep her awhile longer. I was coming to collect her.'

'We heard the grooms have enlisted,' Selma said, not believing her luck in having Guy all to herself.

'Lucky blighters! I wish I could go now. They say it'll all be over by Christmas but I hope not. I'll only just be seventeen then and I don't want to miss the show.'

'You make it sound like a firework display. Did you see they took twenty horses?'

Guy nodded. 'Mother is furious. They took the trap ponies . . . One day this old lady will have to do her bit, won't you?' Guy nuzzled the horse. 'I hope she'll come with me when my turn comes.'

'Has the colonel gone to France?' Selma asked, hoping it wasn't a secret.

'He's at HQ with Lord Kitchener, would you believe. Father says it will be a long show and no picnic getting Kaiser Bill's army out of Belgium, though.'

'*Will* you be joining up?' Selma dared to voice the question that had been in her head for days.

'As soon as I can, and Angus too. It should be splendid fun going to France. And your brothers? I know Father expects the village to fill its quota.'

'I hope not . . . they're needed at the forge. Mam'll never let them sign up underage.'

'My mother neither, but everyone has to answer the call as best they can. It's sort of expected at school that the cadets set an example.' His eyes glazed over with pride and determination.

'Why do we have to fight for people we don't know?' Selma said, not convinced.

'Because if the Hun comes here, he might do to our womenfolk what he's done over there. No one is safe from bullyboys. You have to stand up to their threats and show them your fists, stand and be counted. The sooner we go, the sooner they'll be kicked back to Germany where they belong.'

'Everyone's going mad about this war. I don't want you all to go away . . . It'll be a village full of old women and kiddies.'

'I know this is a bally cheek, but if I do enlist would you write to me . . . about the horses and the village and all that stuff? I'd be awfully grateful, but if you think I'm being a bit fast . . . It's not as if we're . . . you know, well . . .' Guy stuttered, his cheeks flushing.

'I'd like that but you'll have to write first so I know where you are,' she replied, trying to keep the excitement out of her voice.

'Try and stop me. I expect we'll be months doing boring training and all that. If you'd like to exercise the horses while I'm away, I'm sure Mother wouldn't mind. You have a way with them, all you Bartleys. Jemima can be a fussy old thing.'

'So I see,' Selma laughed, and then wished she hadn't.

'Ouch! That hurt.' They were nearing the paddock and the final gate through into village view. Selma couldn't stop looking up at her rescuer. 'You won't leave before you say goodbye, will you?'

'It'll be ages yet. We have to go into school until the end of term or Mother will have a blue fit. Once I'm seventeen she can't stop me doing what I want, though. Perhaps we could go for a walk one afternoon soon? We could meet under the river bridge.'

'As if by accident . . .' Selma nodded eagerly. 'That would be the best.' It wouldn't do to blaze their friendship in front of her neighbours. Both of them knew that without having to spell it out.

'What about next Sunday before school starts up?'

Selma smiled and flushed, feeling strange to be agreeing to something both of them knew was breaking some unwritten rule of decorum. But so what, Selma thought. The whole world was breaking rules, storming into a neutral country, ransacking homes. Theirs was a very minor misdemeanour compared to that.

'Is it true what they're saying on the market, Lady Hester?'

Hester turned from her basket of materials in the church hall with impatience. 'What is it now, Doris?' If some of these young mothers spent more time sewing and less time gossiping, they might be able to finish their quota of saddle pads, limb bandages and ambulance cushions for the troops on time. There was a list of knitted comforts for soldiers for Christmas still to do.

'We heard the Hun has poisoned all the black spice in the hedgerows,' Doris replied, and her friends all nodded their heads.

61

'What utter bunkum! The blackberries were all picked ages ago before the first frosts. It's October now, and the crop was poor because of the hot summer, my cook tells me. You mustn't believe such rumours.'

Doris was not to be put down. 'Well, I heard that we mustn't use eau-de-Cologne or eat Battenberg cake. It's unpatriotic, it said in the paper.'

'Then use lavender water and call it marzipan slice, if you must. I don't see how that helps the war effort, but concentrating on your stitches does,' Hester snapped back, tired of their tittle-tattle.

These meetings were a chore but Hester was not one to shirk her duty to the community, though her fingers were raw from the rough cloth. The poor souls at the barricades needed all the help they could get and she was going to make sure West Sharland delivered whatever was asked from the District Ladies Comforts Fund. The older women were no bother, sitting primly in their best hats, thimbles at the ready. It was the young fry – farmers' wives, tradespeople – who were eager to volunteer but not so keen to work. The village was pulling together under her tutelage and the vicar's call to arms. She took back all she had said about his wife, Violet. Mrs Hunt was proving to be indefatigable in chivvying up the congregation. Her son, Arnold, was now serving in France and the news wasn't too good there, judging from his letters home.

Most of the women here had family going to the front. Betty Plimmer's boy, Jack, was the first to enlist when the recruiting sergeant held a parade in Sowerthwaite, the nearest town. Everything was all very satisfactory, according to the local *Gazette*, but Charles hinted it would be a long war and the casualty lists were getting longer.

She was dreading the moment her boys turned seventeen. There was pressure for Sharland pupils to be commissioned, of course. Their training was seen as an advantage, shortening the time for official training. Officers of such stalwart character were needed urgently, but not her sons, not yet.

Angus was bursting with keenness. But what if he had another seizure? She had told Charles to use his influence and get him a home posting, something not too vigorous. He'd just laughed and told her to stop mollycoddling the boy. 'Cantrells go in the thick of it! It's what we're bred to do.'

'But they're so young. Plenty of time after school,' she had argued.

'Fiddlesticks, woman! What sort of chap do you think I am to hold back my sons from glory in the field when I've been round every farm and house in the village making sure all the able bods are rooted out and volunteered into service? I can't let one of my own be seen as a slacker . . .'

In her head she knew he was right, but her heart was fearful. You didn't bring children into the world to be shot to pieces. How could it have come to this?

'Lady Hester, are you feeling unwell?' Violet whispered softly. 'You look as if you've seen a ghost.'

She had been daydreaming again, staring into space, making an utter fool of herself.

'I'm just making lists in my head. So much to do . . . so much to do,' she replied, fooling no one.

'The bell will ring soon,' Violet continued.

At noon every day St Wilfred's church bell tolled the hour to remind the village to halt work, bow and pray for those who were fighting. The room fell silent and afterwards it was time for them to break up for luncheon. For once Hester decided to walk home unaccompanied. Time for some fresh air before afternoon visits began. Her days were so full there was hardly time to change from morning gown to afternoon dress, but duty and standards must be set, war or no. She must fly the flag of confidence, no matter how terrified she was feeling.

Essie paused at her scrubbing when she heard the wall clock strike twelve. 'Lord have mercy on our boys, wherever they may be and give courage to their folks at home,' she prayed. Then she carried on rubbing over the flags on her hands and knees until she saw the shadow fall over her and a pair of size ten boots in front of her nose. The polish on his toecaps made her stomach turn over. She looked up. 'I've done it, Mam. Took the King's shilling. I'm off to war!' he announced, grinning as if it was something to rejoice about.

'Oh, Newton Bartley . . . whatever for? What'll yer dad say? He needs you in the forge.'

'No he doesn't. He's got Frank to pump the bellows. When I told them my trade, they nearly bit my hand off . . . asked if I could ride and I leaped on one of their hosses in one jump to show I was not kidding. It'll be the Artillery or Engineers for me. I might get to work with hosses in the cavalry . . . I won't be in the front line but doing what I'm good at. Don't cry . . . I'll be back.'

Essie couldn't hide her tears. 'Oh, I wish you hadn't . . . but I'm that proud of you, just the same. At least they won't send you abroad until you're nineteen.'

'I told them I was eighteen and a half,' Newt confessed.

'Well, you can just go and untell them. If you don't I

will. You're not eighteen until next March. Don't be in such a hurry to wish your life away.'

'It's my life. I hate it when people eye you up and down in the street for not being in uniform. There's loads of lads joining up together. The colonel's been up and down the streets checking who's joined up. I think one of us should go.'

'But not to please him. Yer dad has already chewed off his ear when he poked his head round the smiddy door. He told him someone had to keep the wheels turning and machinery in fine fettle and the farmers' hosses on the trot. *That's* war work too. The colonel went red in the face and stormed out but yer dad got the last word on't matter.'

'I'm not going to please anyone – or the lassies, before you start – but 'cos I sort of have to . . . to prove to meself that village lads are tough and reliable and stand up for what is right. Don't be mad at me; I'll write to you.'

'You'd better had, young man. When will you tell yer dad?'

Newt looked sheepish. 'Not yet a while. I'll wait until he's cooling off. I don't fancy breaking the news with him with a hammer in his hand.' He grinned and Essie wanted to hug him, her first-born, the daft happorth! He had that stubborn mule Bartley streak in him, a devil to shift. Selma had it too, but Frank was more her own makeup, sensitive and feeling. Essie shivered, knowing this blessed war had just crept through her front door and stolen a son.

Angus and Guy stood in Otley Street outside the Drill Hall in Skipton sizing up the queue, the bustle of lads coming in and out, the giggling girls hanging around the gates waiting for their chaps to come out smiling, waving papers.

'Come on, don't hang about,' Guy said. 'Let's get it over with, we've not got long.'

'Not so fast,' Angus grinned. 'We can have some fun here. I'll go in first and you wait outside . . .'

'What for?'

'You'll see.' Angus disappeared through the arched door while Guy looked to see if there was anyone he recognised. Mother would rant and rave when she found out what they were doing but if they waited any longer the war would be over. Angus reappeared, grinning. 'Your turn, give your initials and wait and see.'

Guy stepped inside and joined the queue. He felt conspicuous in his striped school blazer. He stepped up to the table where the Sergeant Major looked up at him with surprise.

'What've you forgotten, lad . . . changed yer mind? Let's be havin' you! Next.' He ignored Guy and looked to the boy behind.

'Sir, I've come to enlist,' Guy offered.

'Oh, aye? You can't do it twice, laddie. I've got you on the list already. Next!'

'That's not me,' Guy said.

'I'm not deaf dumb and blind . . . stop wasting my time. See this joker out!' A soldier made to manhandle him out of the door. So *that* was Angus's little game.

'Thanks a bundle! They wouldn't take me . . .'

'Don't you think it's better if only one of us goes? Poor Mama will have a fit,' Angus offered.

'Don't be so stupid! You're the one who ought to stay at home, not me.' Guy dragged his brother back into the hall. This time there would be no monkey business. The Sergeant looked up as they both saluted and roared, 'Well, I'll be damned! A right pair of jokers, we have here! We'll soon wipe the smile off your faces . . .'

Selma was busy supervising the junior knitting bee when the noon bell tolled. The children rose, put their hands together and offered a silent prayer. Soon the dinner break would start and she must make sure the knitting was well away from spills and sticky fingers. They were attempting mittens for soldiers. Some of the girls were experts already with knitting needles fixed to their belts, but her boys were all fingers and thumbs even though everyone was taking it as seriously as any eight-year-old could.

The autumn sun beamed down through the high arched school window, dust and chalk motes sparkling in the light, no sound but the clacking of needles and squirming clogs on wooden boards. Barbara Finch had just been sick again and sent home though the smell of vomit and sawdust was still in the air, as was the stink of someone's dirty socks, but for once her thoughts rose above her own knit one, purl one to those afternoon walks with Guy . . .

How many Sundays had they met in secret now? How she longed for that precious moment when she stepped onto the secret path, through the iron gate up onto the scar to avoid the usual Sunday strollers and Sharland scholars, her heart beating fast, anticipating the moment when Guy would step out onto the path ahead of her as if by magic and she could drink him all in, those long striding legs, the sway of his hips, the moment when she caught him up and he looked down at her, inclining his head as if he was appraising her for the first time, smiling with those bluest of eyes, holding out his hand, his long fingers grasping her hand with such warmth and tenderness as they held each other in such a gaze that made Selma feel dizzy. It was as if the whole world stopped for those precious hours when they could lose themselves in each other, holding hands like any courting couple but always with one eye on the horizon in case they were discovered, hands separating as they drew close to the village to go their different paths. Sometimes Guy left Jemima tethered close by and they took turns to ride and walk up to the far ridge from where they could see the whole valley spread out before them.

Last week Guy sat staring out over the hills. He'd just heard that one of his school friends had been killed while on training with live ammunition. His name would be the first Sharlander to go on the Roll of Honour but not the last. Both of them sensed that this war was changing lives for ever and Selma felt a flash of fear that this was only the beginning of things to come. They sat under the shelter of a huge piece of granite rock; an erratic, Guy called it.

Selma noticed how when she talked to him her voice softened and her vowels rounded and deepened away from broad Yorkshire, taking her cue from his own refined accent. They were reading from his pocket Palgrave's Golden Treasury.

'You read so well and with such meaning like an actress,' Guy said.

'I've never been to a proper theatre,' she confessed.

'Then you must go . . . perhaps to Bradford or Leeds on the train.'

'I don't think so . . . we don't go to those places.'

'Not even to Shakespeare? You just have to see one of his plays. School's going to do Hamlet next term but I won't be there.'

'What do you mean?'

68

'I was thinking if we got up a party now, a crowd from the village for a train trip or something, your pa'll know you'd be safe. It'll be fun before I . . .' Guy paused. 'It's no good. I've got something to tell you . . .' He was looking at her with such serious eyes and she knew what was coming.

'Oh no, not you and all? You've never joined up, have you?' Selma's heart sank as Guy winked and smiled.

'Officers can join at seventeen, you know. I can't sit about and do nothing when other chaps are getting on with the job.'

'My brother lied about his age and joined up too and now our Frank is going round with a face like a wet weekend and Dad threatening to chain him to the horse's stall if he does the same. Why do you all want to rush off? Your mother will be as worried as mine is now.' Selma felt sick at this news just when they were getting to know each other. What would happen to their Sunday walks?

'Actually she doesn't know yet. We'll pick our moment but she can't stop us. We can get written permission from Papa if she won't agree. Secretly, she'll be very proud. We'll be in training for months so she'll get used to us being away before we're sent off somewhere.'

'It won't be the same though, will it? I mean our walks and talks . . .' Selma blushed, knowing how much she'd miss them.

'I'll be home on leave,' he offered.

'It won't be the same though, will it?'

'Why not?' He looked puzzled.

'It just won't, I know it. You'll be doing manly things while I'm stuck in school with the baby class to teach.'

'That's important work too,' he said with such a look of tenderness in his eyes. 'I'll be larking about marking time, playing pranks with Angus. It'll be just like school. We have to do our bit.'

'I'll miss you.' Selma felt tears of disappointment rising up as she gazed back at him.

'I'm glad to hear it,' he whispered, his face drawing ever closer so they were almost touching. His lips found hers in a soft kiss and they stared at each other with surprise.

'I'm sorry . . . I've never done this sort of thing before,' Guy apologised but, tipping her chin towards him with his finger, he kissed her again and they clung to each other, breathless.

'Me neither,' Selma whispered. The look between them stirred her to the pit of her stomach as they drew close again, kissing and hugging.

'You are my best girl, Selima Bartley, do you know that? My best girl.'

She drew back, laughing. 'How many others do you have?'

'You know what I mean. Ever since I saw you rescuing my brother . . .'

'Ever since I saw you in that bathing costume,' she giggled. 'But I don't want you to go away . . .'

'I'm here now so let's make hay while the sun shines,' he said, pulling her down onto the grass.

Selma surrendered herself to this delicious moment. There was so much to learn.

'Miss . . . Miss, I dropped a stitch again.' Selma was jolted back to work. No peace for the wicked, she smiled. This secret courtship warmed her heart and fired her resolve. She would not let Guy down with shoddy knitting. 'Come on now, children, winter is upon us and those poor soldiers need warm fingers, not mittens with holes!'

*   *   *

Hester sat bolt upright on the horsehair sofa, one eye on the grandfather clock in the corner of the farmhouse parlour. It had a brass face of some distinction, as did the dark oak furniture with fine pewter plates in racks. In her hand a piece of porcelain of antiquity that unfortunately smelled and tasted of musty damp from the china cabinet. The rounds of the sick and elderly were done and she always finished off at the Pateleys' farm at the top end of the village out on the old high road to Sowerthwaite. It was set back among the trees with a fine view across the valley. Whoever had chosen this site knew his arse from his elbow, as Charles would say.

She smiled, knowing her dutiful day was done and Beaven would be waiting to return her to Waterloo House for tea and hot pikelets dripping with this season's raspberry jam. The fire would be roaring in the morning room; they were setting an example of austerity by having only one fire lit during the week to save fuel.

'How's them young 'uns?' said Emma Pateley, the farmer's maiden sister, who kept home for him now he was widowed.

'Ah, growing up too fast,' Hester offered. 'Still at school, of course – too young yet for any war work.'

'Is that so? But not too young to go a-courtin',' Emma chuckled. 'I seed one of yourn the other day up the far field walking a horse with a girl on its back. A proper knight in shining armour he looked.'

'I'm sure you're mistaken,' Hester protested. 'The boys are busy at school.'

'It were a Sunday afternoon, as I recall; he were on that chestnut mare, fine beast. You were lucky the army didn't get her on a rope. Tall as a spear, fair lad. The girl were dark-haired like that one of Bartleys' as teaches school.

71

You know, the one with the funny name. I'd watch it there. Them chapelgoers can be trouble when crossed. They like to match with their own.'

'I'm sure it won't be one of my boys, Miss Pateley.' Hester felt herself flushing. Emma could be a gossipy old crone but her eyes didn't miss much. The boys, it was true did have free periods on Sunday afternoons but surely one of her children wouldn't make a fool of himself in the village?

'When men and maids meet, there's allus mischief, my lady,' Emma continued, unaware of Hester's discomfort. 'Lads will be lads, and lasses aye let them . . .'

'Thank you for the tea, Miss Pateley, but I must take my leave of you. Things to do in these trying times.'

'I 'eard as how old Jones the plumber's boy copped it last week and him a regular in the army. He's been out there since it began . . . He'll not be the last. My cups are telling me we'll all be wearing black afore the next year's out.'

'Yes, yes, perhaps . . . Now you've got some more wool for the socks. I hear you're one of the best heel turners in the district. We want to send socks, scarves and comforts by the end of next month, parcels for our local boys. I can rely on you?' Hester wagged her finger, desperate for Emma to stop talking.

'I'll do my best. Thank you for calling on a poor old soul as is cut off from the world up here.'

Not so cut off that you can't find gossip, mused Hester as she stepped briskly into the waiting carriage. There was something about the woman's ramblings that unsettled her. Could one of her boys really be making a fool of himself with a village girl? How ridiculous, how stupid, to foul on your own doorstep! How dare he shame the family?

No doubt it would be one of Angus's pranks. He was always up for silliness. Had he no respect for his station in life? Just wait until their next exeat: she'd lay down the law. A liaison with a villager was simply unthinkable.

Guy saw the thunderous look on his mother's face after church and wondered what was up. She'd been acting strange all morning, silent and severe. Had another under gardener left them in the lurch? She plonked down her Prayer Book and her gloves, and pointed the twins into the cold drawing room.

'Inside . . . both of you,' she ordered, out of earshot from Shorrocks, who was hovering by the hall stairs with their coats and hats.

'Now which one of you has been silly enough to pay attention to the Bartley girl?'

Neither of them spoke but stood together to attention while she choked them off.

'Don't look at me, Mother,' said Angus. 'I've not been near the village for ages.' He turned to Guy. 'And Guy's head has been stuck in a poetry book, hasn't it?'

Bless Angus for covering for him, but Guy was not ashamed of his friendship with Selma.

'Don't blame Angus. Selma and I have been walking out, riding Jemima. She's awfully clever, you know, training to be a teacher. You'll like her when you meet her.'

'I have no intention of doing any such thing. At your age, walking out with a blacksmith's daughter and a nonconformist – have you no sense? You should be in school, not gadding about with a girl, giving her false expectations. You are far too young for such matters and there's a war on. Why didn't you tell me this was going on, Angus?' Hester accused.

Angus shrugged his shoulders. 'It's all news to me,' he grinned.

'Have you nothing to say, Guy? Stop grinning at each other like simpletons.'

'Sorry, Mother, but we're not kids any more. We're old enough to volunteer and take up commissions—'

'That's as may be, in good time,' Hester interrupted.

'No time like the present.' Angus threw in his verbal grenade, standing to attention to salute. 'We're soldiers now, all signed on the dotted line.'

'You have done what!' she exploded. 'Behind my back? I forbid it!'

'You can't, Mother. It's done. We'll be off to training camps in the next week or so.'

Guy felt sorry for his mother as he saw her bravado crumple. She sat down, pale-faced, deflated for once, speechless at this news. 'Does your father know about this madness?'

'We'll write to him. It's only what he expects of us.'

'But, Angus, you can't go, not with your recent affliction. You won't pass a medical, not with your history.'

'Don't fuss. I'm fine now. It's going to be such a wheeze. Oh, don't cry, Mother. We'll be fine and they might let us join the same regiment.'

'I see you have got it all worked out behind my back. Does this Miss Bartley know your plans too? I dare say she's behind all this show of gallantry,' Hester said, her lips composed, her arms crossed tightly against her bodice.

'That's not fair. Her brother's going too. *Everyone's* going. You both worked hard enough to make sure half the village boys answered the call to arms.'

'But not my sons, not yet, not my two boys at once. Why can't you wait? There's no hurry,' she pleaded.

'The sooner we leave, the sooner our training begins and the sooner we'll be in action before it all fizzles out. I'd hate to miss it,' Angus added, his eyes bright with fervour. 'Guy will keep an eye on me, won't you?'

'I can't take this in, all this secrecy and I'm the last to know. Why?'

'Because we knew you'd take on so . . . You must let us be like all the others and give us your blessing.' Guy sat down beside her, trying to jolt her out of her maudlin mood. It was not like his mother at all.

'I have a bad feeling about this. It's too soon. What will I do without you?'

'What you've always done: put a brave face to the world and get on with your charity work and church duties, keep the home fires burning, as the song says, and make sure we get clean socks, hankies, some of Cook's marmalade, pipe tobacco and up-to-date newspapers. Don't be sad, be glad that we're old enough to be useful to our country in its hour of need.'

'Oh, Guy, do you realise what you're doing?' She was shaking her head, not looking at them both.

'I'm not rightly sure but all I know is that it must be done now . . . Come on, chop chop, no more moping about. There's the luncheon gong. I hope it's roast lamb. Dry your eyes. We'll get plenty of leave while we're training. Might even get as close as Catterick camp. Buck up, old girl. It's not the end of the world.'

But it is the end of my world, sobbed Hester as she paced the bedroom floor later that night, the gentle tick of the marble clock lagging far behind her own heartbeat. How can I live if anything happens to my sons? No sooner out of the nursery than into school and now into the army, and Guy on the arm of some trollop. She's behind it somewhere. Prim school miss she might appear but there's fire in those dark eyes and she's not getting her claws into my boy.

Hester sat on the window seat, drawing back the brocade curtains to reveal a night sky lit with a thousand stars.

There's one good thing about all this, though, she thought, drying her eyes. Once Guy disappears from the scene, all this mooning about will soon fizzle out. I'll put him in the way of some decent county girls from good families; girls of our own class, not upstarts no better than servants. At least he'll be too busy to satisfy that girl's craving for influence. And as for Angus . . . Hester smiled a knowing smile. There must be ways to make sure he got no further than the medical board. Perhaps she could let Guy go now, but not two, oh dear me, no . . . Angus must stay close by, whatever it took.

First the horses, then the men, and the village fell silent as it went about the daily grind. I sigh, looking around the crowds. Everyone thought it was 'all a bit of a bluff and wouldn't come to owt, as old Dickie Beddows had pronounced. I've not thought of him for years, sitting under the elm on the bench with string tied round the knees of his corduroy breeches, sucking an empty pipe, dispensing his wisdom to those who had the time to listen. But as the months wore on and curtains were closed in respect for some mother's son who was lost in places they couldn't pronounce, even he fell silent.

Then there was the shelling of Hartlepool and the Zeppelin raids that bombed Scarborough and the east coast. Yorkshire was under attack; a terror none of us could understand; little kiddies crushed under bricks, mothers cooking breakfast blasted to eternity. This was no bluff.

How strange that I can recall every detail of that time yet forget what day of the week it is so easily, or what I've had for supper.

Being here brings everything to the fore. Nothing's been lost in the house of my memory. I can walk round its rooms and recall those far-off tumultuous days at will.

The elm tree may have been replaced by a sycamore, the guard railings removed with most of the cobbles, the chapel is now a spacious house, but I can see it all as it once was.

The school is still functioning, with its fine playing field. It was my refuge from all the worries of war and home. Things were never the same when Newt left. Frank took his desertion to heart and wouldn't settle. Oh, Frankland . . .

All the King's horses and all the King's men, couldn't put you together again.

2

DARK DAYS
1915–17

When this lousy war is over, no more soldiering for me,
When I get my civvy clothes on, oh how happy I will be.
No more church parades on Sunday, no more begging
　for a pass.
You can tell the sergeant-major to stick his passes up his
　arse!

Attrib. Joseph Scriven

5

'What's up now, son?' Essie asked, seeing Frank storming out of the forge, flinging off his leather apron in disgust.

'Everything's got to be done his way and I can't stomach no more of it. I never wanted to be his skivvy. It was more to Newt's liking than mine. Nothing I do is ever right.'

'It's just his way, love. He likes things to be right,' Essie tried to explain.

'Right enough will do for me . . . Just 'cos I put the sheep horns on the wrong hook, you'd think the world'd come to an end. He's like a bee stuck down my neck buzzing in my ear. I'm off!'

'Calm down, son. Go and get a brew and I'll have a word with your father.'

'Don't bother. It's not fair, me having to take Newt's place,' Frank muttered, disappearing round the corner just as Asa strode out of the forge.

'Where's he gone now, Mam? Never at hand when he's needed. Pateley's unbroken beast is due any moment and he's a right beggar to shoe. It'll take two of us hold that stag down. I never had to tell our Newt what to do. This one's got his head in the clouds.'

'Don't fuss him, Asa. He's only doing his best but his

81

heart's not in the job. It never was. He's allus hankered after working with horses,' Essie said, trying to smooth over yet another bust-up. Poor Asa was looking greyer round the gills these days with twice as much work, despite fewer horses. Everyone was trying to save their tools, repairing their irons and pots, kettles waiting to be fettled up and wheel rims sorted. Making do and mending was the order of the day; no one wanted to waste precious metals.

In the evening they all had to lend a hand with the allotment patch cut out of their paddock and fenced off from nibbling horses. Potatoes, vegetables, anything to fill the pot had to be weeded, hens in the back yard fed and swill taken to fatten up the shared pig in the stable at the back of the Hart's Head.

How Essie missed her eldest son, with his quiet ways and steadying influence over his brother. Frank was missing him too, them being so close in age, and her heart went out to him. But what could she do? Her free time, such as it was, was taken up with the Chapel Ladies Comfort Guild, who met most afternoons to gather up parcels, knitting and treats.

Selma, though busy with the fundraising concert party as well as the school, drifted round like love's lost dream. She was at that funny stage, betwixt and between girl and woman, mooning over letters from one of the Cantrell boys. What could they make of that friendship? All innocent enough, but they were both far too young to be serious, especially when Lady Hester's disapproval was plain to see.

Last week she'd stopped her pony and trap and almost poked Essie in the ribs with her parasol.

'Is my son still sending billets-doux to your daughter?' she demanded.

Essie smiled. 'They both have a keen interest in poetry, I believe,' she replied, trying to keep a straight face. 'Rather sweet at their tender age.' She was not going to be browbeaten by her imperious tone of voice. 'How are your sons faring with their training?'

'As one would expect of a Cantrell,' came the curt reply. 'But I don't want my son distracted by unsuitable entanglements.'

'Of course not . . . but young people today seem to have minds of their own on such matters,' Essie offered, watching Hester Cantrell puffing herself up with disagreement.

'It is a ridiculous situation. I absolutely forbid it!'

'Really? Forbiddance is usually a great encourager, don't you think?' Essie argued back. 'In my experience it adds a whiff of danger to the whole enterprise.'

Hester stared back at her in disbelief at such a bold riposte. 'I hardly think so. In such times as these there's no room for romantic escapades. This war must be won, and soon.'

'You are so right, Lady Hester, but the world has to keep turning and soldiers will take comfort out of battle . . . Better with their friends than with strangers?' Essie continued

'You chapel folk are mighty sure of your opinions, Mrs Bartley.'

'Thank you.' Essie nodded sweetly. 'I find it best to trust to the good common sense of the young, these days. They are bearing the brunt of our mistakes with their blood. I think we can allow them the freedom to choose how they spend what little leisure they have, don't you?'

Lady Hester sat back in shock, trying to think up some caustic put-down, her lips opening and closing. But nothing came out but, 'Good day.'

Oh heck! I've put the fox in the chicken run, and no mistake, thought Essie but still she'd take nothing back. If young men were risking their lives then they must be given such freedoms as compensation. It was only fair, and that went for Newton as well as the Cantrell twins. This war was turning customs upside down.

What a diabolical cheek! Hester couldn't get over Essie Bartley's impudence. Freedoms indeed! In her day children did what parents commanded and with no argument. The whole world was going mad and all civilities were disappearing fast. Even dressing for dinner in the evening was being slackened in favour of lounge suits in some households. Servants were giving notice to go into factories, making it difficult to find replacements. In fact, on several occasions she'd had to go into the kitchen herself to prepare a cold collation when Cook had her day off. Arkie had upsticked to run some convalescent hospital for wounded soldiers. Shorrocks was marrying her soldier boy in a rush and Hester feared she was already in the family way. Mrs Beck came in each day from the village now to clean and tidy and lay the fires, instead of having a live-in maid. That it should come to this at her age. Where would it all end?

She'd not seen Charles for months, just a fleeting visit when she'd begged him to get Angus a safe job out of the line of fire. Of course he'd laughed away her fears and told her to stop meddling. So far there had been no repetition of Angus's seizures but she worried that it was only a matter of time before another one struck.

All too often now, when she came through the front door into the marble-floored hall, there was only silence to greet

84

her or the chimes of the hour from the drawing-room clock. The silence was deafening, the echo of her shoes on the tiles, the barking of a stable dog somewhere. In the silence of the evening she had time to churn over all the day's incidents, her worries, but no one with whom to share these thoughts.

Occasionally this gloom was lifted by one of Guy's letters that she devoured, trying to hear his voice in her mind.

That was what hurt the most: the fact that the Bartley girl was getting his thoughts, his affection. She received a dutiful page or two but it wasn't enough. She wanted more from him, and as for Angus, he was even worse. How could they be so thoughtless? There was such an empty space where once they'd filled her days.

Was this the pattern for her future: afternoon visits, committees, the occasional fundraising concert breaking up the monotony of her days? To rattle around in this uncomfortable silence, waiting for one of her men to return for a night or two was a daunting prospect.

At least her boys were safe in England. They all planned to meet in London on their next leave. She would go down on the train and they could take in a show. Why did she feel so old and unwanted, though?

'Buck up, Hester,' she said to herself. 'Pour yourself a drink and get your sewing out.'

Damn the bloody sewing, she thought. I want them all back . . . I want my boys back here . . .

Selma caught up with Frank on the High Road out of Sowerthwaite, the winding lane that was a short cut to West Sharland. He was swaying in the breeze and if she didn't know any better, she'd say he was 'market fresh'. But Bartley men were abstainers – or were they? As she drew near she smelled the booze on his breath.

'You can't go home in that state!'

'Leave me alone . . . I've had enough of being bossed about . . . I'm going.'

'Going where?' Selma snapped, and then realised what was coming next. 'You haven't . . .'

'I have. I've joined up this morning and no one can stop me. I'm sick of being the only lad left in our street. I'm sick of being stared at. I can work with horses in the army. They need drivers and good riders.'

'You can't go! Dad needs your help. Don't let him down. Mam'll go spare when she finds out. Honestly, Frank, you can be so selfish!'

'That's right, Selma, be a hedgehog; roll in a ball and get your prickles out. It's all right for you, still in school. Girls have got it made but I'm not staying round here while there's a war on.'

'We're doing our bit too. Look at all the women doing men's jobs – driving horse buses, making shells. There's even a postwoman in Sowerthwaite, and volunteer nurses joining up.' Selma strode on, leaving him behind.

'All right, you've made your point.' Frank sat down by a rock on the verge, his eyes glassy. The drink had got to his legs and he was sobering up in the fresh air.

'I hate the forge, pumping bellows, lighting fires, dunking hot metal, and he's allus preaching at me. When do you ever see him laugh?'

'There's not much to laugh about right now. Even less if you walk out on him. Poor Mam will be frantic with two of you out there.'

86

'I'll be one less mouth to feed, one less shirt to scrub.'

'That's not the point. You're letting them down. Going for a soldier isn't the answer.'

'It is for me. It gets me out of this godforsaken hole!'

'Don't get funny with me, it doesn't suit you.'

'And don't you go telling me what I can or can't do. We all know you've got big ideas ever since you palled up with Cantrell. He'll drop you like hot coals before long,' Frank snapped back.

'It's not like that. We're just friends,' she replied, blushing.

'Pull the other leg. I've seen you put those letters in your bride box.'

'What bride box?' she retorted.

'The little carved chest that belonged to Granny Ackroyd. You keep all your treasures in there.'

'Have you been rooting around in my things?' Her cheeks flamed.

'You've got your prickles out again,' he laughed, and despite herself she joined in

He'd be in a heap of trouble when he got home. One by one they were leaving her. The family would shrink to just three. But he was right to go and do his duty. The women would manage; they had to in school when the male teachers had volunteered. Now they were practising for a big fundraising concert where her infant class would be the star turn. They were making outfits for the infants dressed as bantam soldiers to march across the stage and sing 'It's a Long Way to Tipperary'.

They walked the rest of the way in silence and Selma kept wondering if Frank was having second thoughts about his rash decision. Trouble was, he'd be too proud to admit his mistake. The Bartleys were all stubborn mules. It was bred in the bone but she'd be sure to be out of the house when he broke this news.

Guy sat on the train going south from training camp, staring out of the blackened windows, hoping this family weekend would be a success. In some ways his new life was just the same as boarding school: long route marches, drill, rifle shooting, studying the manual like a textbook, learning to bivouac and do cross-country treks in the dark. There was so much theory to learn on how to train up men to obedience and to give orders and earn respect. Some of his training was obvious and some of it bizarre, but he trusted it was all to get him up to scratch for the purpose. He must lead men into battle, make sure they held the line, encourage and discipline men far older than himself and many more experienced.

Angus was in another battalion, romping away like a pig in muck, according to his scribbled letters. Mother's threatened interference hadn't happened, but Guy was uneasy that his brother had lied about his fitness. They'd had their portraits done in uniform, singly and then together, left and right profiles, head to head as if they were one face looking out. They'd both grown moustaches to make them look older, fair tickly little tufts covering their full lips.

He'd sent a photo to Selma for her opinion and she'd not sent it back. It was good to have a girl to write to. He could let rip and describe all the funny incidents in training, his boredom and impatience to get into action. Her last letter had been full of Frank's defection into the Horse Artillery and how her father was struggling to keep up with his work.

He pulled out his pipe, pondering how he'd cope when

the time came and the barrage exploded over his head. Would he make a tit of himself and funk the whole show, be dismissed to the rear or get cashiered out as a coward? He hoped he'd make a good account of himself and serve his men well.

With all the exercise and good food, he'd filled out, grown an inch or two and found new muscle strength. His mother would see a difference and his father would be proud of them both. They were meeting up for lunch at the Trocadero restaurant and then on to a West End show. Angus was joining them from his base near Aldershot. He'd caught up with Father more than once.

The news from the front was mixed. It didn't take a genius to work out the attrition rate among officers was much higher than in the ranks. The casualty lists in *The Times* made sombre reading but Guy was all the more determined that he would be one of the exceptions to the rule.

Charles Cantrell was waiting in the Long Bar of the Trocadero restaurant in Shaftesbury Avenue. It was full of distinguished men in uniform, and Guy was expecting to see Angus lounging somewhere close by, but his father was alone.

'Good journey, old fellow?' Father smiled, shaking his hand.

'Angus not arrived?'

'Not yet. We'll leave his ticket at the Royalty Theatre, if he's late into town. Mother is shopping, and I've booked a theatre dinner. How're things going?'

They sat huddled in the crush, talking shop. Now he was in the army Guy felt a shift between his father and himself, a loosening of the reins, a relaxation in their chitchat, but still he kept checking his new wristwatch, looking up at the entrance for his brother. Still no sign of him.

'Come on, young man . . . Time to go and find your mama before she buys out Derry and Toms.' So they left the male-only enclave to go to search for his mother but she was already waiting downstairs in the foyer, regal in lilac and grey, her eyes smiling up at them with pride.

'No Angus yet? Oh, I did so want us all to be together.' She paused to look at her son admiringly. 'Guy, you've grown.'

'He's learned to stand up straight at last,' Charles laughed. 'No more slouching around; that's why we chose something frivolous to take our minds off all the doom and gloom. *Charley's Aunt* . . . damn silly play, but you'll enjoy it.'

'You've seen it then?' Guy said. 'Perhaps we should go somewhere else?'

'No, no, chaps in the office gave it the thumbs up. I'm starving. I wonder where Angus has got to this time?'

And on to the Royalty they went but Angus's seat stayed empty all night. Mother kept twitching, wanting to make a telephone call to his barracks, but Father wouldn't hear of it.

It was nearly midnight when the doorbell rang in their apartment in South Kensington. Angus stood there, grinning sheepishly.

'Sorry, folks, my pass was cancelled. I'm on leave tomorrow instead so hitched a lift into town. Better late than never.'

'Thank God for that.' Father ushered him in. 'Now your mother can sleep in peace. She's been pacing the floor, worrying as usual. On the move soon?' he asked.

Angus slouched down in the nearest armchair.

'Something like that . . . going down to Wiltshire for more outdoor stuff. How about you, Guy?'

'Still stuck up north, worst luck.'

'Be patient, the two of you. It's no picnic in France,' Charles butted in, handing Angus a glass of brandy. 'No shifting those Huns from their defences . . . bit of a stalemate all round.' He tapped his nose. 'But you didn't hear it from me. You two are better off here for the time being, believe me.'

'So what's it really like? We've heard some tales as how they are firing gas shells at us now.'

'Shush! Don't let Mother hear you next door. Don't worry, we got the measure of them. Mask drill is the only way. You'll find only the battle teaches you about war. One battle is worth two years' training. But make sure your men get used to covering their faces. Discipline and drill, that's the ticket! Two can play at their dirty game. We'll give them a dose of their own medicine soon enough. Come on then, time for bed, young man. Your mother's got a morning of culture lined up for you both and then I'll meet you for lunch. I've got things to do for Lord Kitchener tomorrow. He asked after you both. He still remembers you in short pants.'

Guy noted his father had changed the subject, but he was tired and Angus looked done in. 'Good night.'

Guy lay listening to the noise of traffic outside, so different from the sounds of the barracks or the near silence of Waterloo, where there was only the rattle of trains in the night and the owl hooting in the ash tree. He felt restless after all that talk about gas masks and shells.

They were kipping down in the dressing room on officers' camp beds in the flat.

'You all right?' Guy called to his brother. He didn't answer at first.

91

'Do you ever wonder if we'll get through this in one piece?' Angus said eventually.

'I don't think about it much, do you?' Guy replied.

'It all seems a bit unreal, all the stuff in the training manual. What if I forget half of it?'

'You won't. That's why they drill us to make sure it's second nature. I don't suppose there's time to think in the thick of it,' Guy added.

'I wish we could have a rehearsal and try it all out first, get used to the noise and the smells, don't you think? Exercises and manoeuvres are all very well but I don't want to make an ass of myself in front of my men. I've never seen a dead man in battle. What if I funk it?'

'Any more headaches?' Guy asked; a coded reference to Angus's fitting episodes.

'No, fit as a fiddle. I reckon it's all behind me now, thank God. I don't fancy missing the show now it's really getting going. Can't wait.'

Guy hoped his brother was telling the truth. But still he was uneasy.

You're getting as bad as Mother, Guy mused. Enjoy this family time. Only God knows when we will all meet up again.

The Bartleys were enjoying having Newton home and Frank returned to the fold from his barracks, resplendent in their uniforms. Essie was fussing over them, while Asa muttered he could do with a hand in the forge.

'If I'd known they were coming together I'd've done some more baking,' Essie said as she beat sugar and butter into a bowl to make a sponge cake for the school concert that evening.

'I'd like to make some cinder toffee,' Selma asked. 'So we can sell it for the Princess Mary's Soldiers' Fund. The boys can take some back with them.' She was so glad to see her brothers back, all the family together. Aunty Ruth and Uncle Sam were coming on the train from Bradford. It would be like old times. If only her father would cheer up and not bang around muttering to himself.

He'd taken Frank's leaving as a desertion. Selma'd never seen him take on so. Now he mumbled, 'I doubt it'll be a picnic out there . . . I've got a bad feeling about it all. It just don't seem right to be fighting other Christian folk. How can the Lord be behind the both of us? It don't make sense. Frank's nobbut a milksop with hardly hair on his chest yet, but I'm the last one as any will listen to in this house these days. He should be here by my side, learning his trade.'

'Now don't go on, Asa, getting yourself worked up about what can't be changed,' Mam was quick to silence him. 'Don't spoil their leave. I'm so proud of the both of them.'

'But they don't know what they're letting themselves in for. They're too young to be let loose on the battlefields. Now I'm wondering if I ought to volunteer myself to keep an eye on them both.'

'At your age? Don't be so daft. You've got your work here.' Selma heard fear in her mother's voice.

Alone in the kitchen, she pulled out the little iron pot they kept for toffee making, gathering the ingredients, measuring the butter and sugar, bicarb of soda at the ready. Everything was spick and span for Aunty Ruth's visit, brasses shining, fire high, table laid. Having company to visit was a highlight, war or not. There was always a welcome for an honoured guest.

She smiled, thinking of Guy's last letter filled with his

trip to London, the shows and musical concert and visit to an art gallery. His world was so different from her own. They didn't have to scrimp and save for every little treat. Lady Hester bought whatever took her fancy but Selma wouldn't swap her family for his starchy one any day.

Tonight her little pupils were going to bring the house down with their drilling and marching antics. The school hall would be packed out and she would be showing off her soldier brothers in uniform. Marigold Plimmer would be making eyes at them; all fluttering eyelashes and simpering little laughs at their jokes but for once, Selma would not begrudge them this attention.

She would write to Guy describing all the details of the fundraising concert and the latest news from West Sharland.

Dearest Guy, she composed in her head, wondering what he looked like in his smart uniform. Are you coming home for Christmas or staying in London? Will we be able to go riding on Jem again? I'm busy with my pupils, dressing them up like soldiers, but I can't get them to march in step. Frank and Newton are here. I do miss you . . . Then the smell of burned sugar hit her nostrils.

Frank and Newt were laughing in the doorway. 'Dolly daydream, wake up, your pan's on fire!'

Liquid toffee spurted over the pan top. The mess was everywhere. Frank went for the water jug and before she could stop him he flung it on the mixture and it exploded in all directions, splattering the range, the clean tablecloth, every nearby surface.

'What did you do that for, you dozy brush?' Selma yelled. She cried tears of rage, trying to wipe up the gunge. The molten toffee was solidifying fast.

In the end it took hours, scouring bits of toffee off the

floor and the walls, the boys laughing at her all the while. She was furious with them but most of all herself. What would Mam say about that sickly smell of burned sugar, and her wasting all that precious food? And all because of Guy . . .

Ever since then just the smell of burned sugar or caramel transports me straight back to that afternoon. There should be an orchestra playing in the background, a soundtrack to such special moments as these. How can a scent open the floodgates of memory to a time and a place so fixed in your heart when your history was in the making?

If only we'd known how precious those few evenings were in the autumn of 1915, when we all gathered for a singsong round the piano, walked over the Ridge to watch the last of the autumn leaves painting the trees, me arguing with my brothers, as we always did about whose turn it was to do the washing up? Then I stood on the platform of Sowerthwaite station waving them off as if we had all the time in the world, as if our lives were secure and unchangeable. If only we knew things in advance . . .

Halcyon days, poets call them, those days of calm before a storm. Now I have little sense of smell with which to taste or enjoy food, but still in my dreams I can recall that scene as if it were yesterday: Newt and Frank on their hands and knees scrubbing for dear life while I brushed the blacking on the grate and tried to hide the evidence, all to no avail. I got such a rocket from Mam for wasting precious sugar and there was no cinder toffee to put in their knapsacks. I sent them on their way to war empty-handed. It still breaks my heart to think how unprepared we all were for what was to follow.

6

Hester felt proud of her effort. A thick bowl of broth, with mutton bones, pearl barley, vegetables chopped and lots of salt and pepper. They were having a penny dinner in the church hall to raise funds for the new Women's Institute. To her surprise she quite enjoyed getting stuck in, wearing a long white apron and a lace-edged cap, while Violet Hunt chatted away about all the things this new society might do to help the war effort.

'We need a committee and you must take the chair, of course, Lady Hester. There are groups springing up all over the district. It's all very exciting.'

Violet was becoming a staunch ally and, for a vicar's wife, most liberal in her views. It was she who suggested it might be politic to invite the chapel women. This was an inter-denominational institution, after all, open to all women, married or single, and a splendid way of galvanising all their working parties into one big effort. Instead of lots of separate meetings in order to publicise all the new directives from the government about saving fuel and food and equipment, they were going to pass on useful tips and skills.

It would give the wives of soldiers something to occupy their evenings after an outbreak of khaki fever in the district and some unfortunate incidents between visiting soldiers and local women.

Hester stirred the soup pan, sniffing the delicious aroma. Who would've thought a year ago she would have to cook some of her own meals, tidy her own room, see to some of her mending and, her most daring venture to date learn to ride a bicycle.

Cycling up and down to the shops with her basket was most invigorating in the fresh air, and once or twice on a bright day she'd ventured further afield, shortening her riding skirts to prevent them catching on the chain. Sometimes down the green lanes with stonewalls enclosing her, she heard the curlew bubbling over the fields as she watched the lambs gambolling, almost forgetting that there was a war on. It was all so peaceful and serene. It was impossible to contemplate that five hundred miles away young men were being killed.

She was getting used to the boys being away now, believing Charles when he'd said that they'd not be shoved across the Channel without proper training. Their letters were brief chatty notes full of a world she hardly knew these days. Hers in return were full of how war was changing her domestic life, how the village community responded to the sad news of boys who would never return home. She told them about Violet's new idea to form the Women's Institute like the ones set up in Canada, which her sister had joined.

But the casualty lists were never far away from everyone's mind. Charles hinted that there was a big push coming when the weather faired up; a push in which her sons would surely be involved. The French were taking a pounding, holding their forts at Verdun against terrible odds and suffering atrocious bombardments, so the paper said.

Keep busy and don't think too much was her maxim now. Fill every day with things to do, shore up the gaps with busyness. The garden was turned over now into one big allotment, and potatoes chitted and planted before the ninth of April, the traditional date for planting here. She'd been on her hands and knees with the best of them now she was down to just one old gardener. Everything was dug over except her rose bed.

There had to be some vision of colour and hope to look forward to, she sighed, noticing, as she returned to her morning room, the postman cycling up the drive. As she saw him pull out a telegram from his bag, she went cold.

Hester made for the drive to meet him. It took every ounce of courage to look nonchalant. Old Coleford, seeing her anxiety, waved the paper jauntily in the air.

'Nowt to worry about, your ladyship. 'Tis only from yer son . . .'

She could feel the weakness of relief seeping into her limbs. It was all she could do not to snatch the paper from his fingers but she stood nodding politely.

'Thank you, Coleford,' she managed to say, before taking it to the bench against the south wall, and tearing it open with shaking fingers: 'Meet me at the station. The four o'clock train. A.'

What a relief. Angus was home on leave!

The news sent her into a flurry of flower arranging, lists for Beaven the coachman to do, engagements to cancel, sending the relief maid upstairs to air his bed. There was a menu to shop for. Angus was coming home. It was going to be just splendid!

The train was late and she was miles too early. Beaven had brought her down in the pony and trap, knowing she was impatient to be on the platform as the steam train chugged slowly into the station. The porter was hovering and the stationmaster fussing with his watch and chain.

Then doors clanged open to disgorge scruffy soldiers, unshaven, weary-faced, in muddy uniforms with kitbags on their shoulders. Boys who had travelled for days to snatch a few hours with their families on leave. Some fell into the waiting arms of their womenfolk. They all looked exhausted.

Then from the first-class compartment she saw Angus step out slowly but not in his uniform, looking ordinary somehow in a long tweed coat, carrying a suitcase. How strange. He was shuffling along like an old man and, to her horror, leaning on a walking stick.

'Angus, darling! What a surprise!' Hester smiled, reaching out to greet him.

'Not now, Mother. Let's get out of here.' He didn't look her in the face but shuffled over the railway bridge and out through the station gate into the trap, pulling his trilby over his face. He didn't speak all the way home, but sat sullen, staring out into the dusky night.

Hester could hardly breathe with the shock. What on earth was going on?

Once through the hall, Angus plonked his case down and went straight to his room. She followed him up slowly, fearing the worst. Had he been cashiered out of the army for a scandal, failed his examination, found wanting in leadership? What had Angus been up to and why had Charles not warned her of this disgrace?

Opening the door, she found her son sitting on the bed, sobbing, shaking with distress like a little boy.

'Angus! Pull yourself together and give me some explanation,' she ordered, knowing she must be hard to bring him out of this childish display of emotion.

'I had another bloody fit, didn't I, right in front of everyone on parade when we were standing to attention. It's when I get that smell . . . like iron filings, a metal iron smell, and the flashing lights – my fireworks, I call them – and the next thing I wake up in the hospital ward and they were prodding and poking and asking questions. I made a right tit of myself again. Why? It's not fair just when we were shipping off to France. It's just not fair. I'm going to miss it all, discharged on medical grounds as unfit for service,' he grimaced. 'All I ever wanted to do is taken from me and now I'm useless and there's nothing wrong with me. Not even a bloody war wound to show . . . How can I ever show my face again? They'll think I'm a conchie or a coward.' He flung himself down on the counterpane. 'Just leave me alone . . .'

Hester didn't know what to say to comfort him when all she was feeling was relief that one of her boys was not to be going to the slaughter fields. One day he would thank them for saving his life but now he was in the throes of frustration.

She summoned Dr Mackenzie. They needed a proper explanation of all this.

'In the wars again, young man?' he said, offering his hand in sympathy, but Hester was in no mood for small talk.

'What is epilepsy? There has to be a cure for this

complaint, surely? We must find one of the best doctors—'
Hester started but Angus interrupted.

'You've got to let them find me a job for the war effort.
Anywhere . . . I can't not be part of the show!'

The doctor sat down, trying to make sense of the distress
in the room.

'Calm down, young man. I don't suppose you told them
anything before, did you, at the first medical, about those
school fits?'

'What do you take me for? Of course not. I've been a
year in training and no bother. Then this, out of the blue!
The headaches come and go and I have been struggling to
concentrate. Sometimes I go a bit blank for a few seconds
but I can cover it up. I was doing perfectly fine but now
I'm a freak! They say I'm an epileptic. What sort of condition
is that?'

Mackenzie hesitated. 'It's a serious condition. There are
those who suggest you might be better off in a special
hospital . . . It can get worse . . . or there's always the hope
that it settles down and you never have another one.'

'No one's putting me into some loony bin. If I can't do
my job at the moment I'll rest up here until I can be cured,'
Angus pleaded, pacing the floor in agitation.

Mackenzie shook his head and glanced at Hester. 'You
have to understand, laddie, there's no permanent cure for
your condition, but some pills might calm it down.'

'Give them to me,' Angus said. 'Then I can carry on.'

'I'm sorry, but the medical officers are right. You are a
risk to your men, with this condition. You might collapse
under battle strain. Better to stop now before you do damage.'

Hester watched him dismiss her son's career with a wave
of his hand. Angus was distraught at his honest assessment.

'How can I live after this? I'll have to go away. I don't want the world knowing I'm a nutcase.'

'We'll do no such thing,' said Hester. 'You have the certificates to prove your discharge. We'll find you something to do here. What's needed now is peace and quiet to settle whatever this is and we'll get a second opinion from Harley Street. Isn't that right, Doctor?' She turned to Mackenzie with a sigh.

He nodded in agreement. 'There are other things you can do for the war effort,' he offered, more in hope than certainty.

'Like what?'

'We'll think of something. Hiding away here is pointless. You can rest and be useful in the community. Young men are in short supply. It's not what you wanted, but the alternative is unthinkable.' The doctor leaned across to offer a supportive pat on the arm.

Angus made for the door. 'I'd rather stay indoors and out of sight. I'm tired. I don't want any supper. I'm not hungry.'

It was like dealing with a truculent child, but his distress was real enough. 'Have you told your brother?' Hester asked, sensing Angus would hate to be seen as the lesser of the two, unable to be alongside him when he went abroad.

'No, nor Father yet. I can't bear to think of Guy going and not me. I don't want them to see me like this in civvies again. What am I going to do? It feels I've been given a life sentence. I'm not like other men, am I?'

'Enough! You'll change your clothes, wash your face and we'll dine as usual. Life goes on without us and this isn't the end of the world for you.'

Mackenzie stood up to leave. 'Think on, young man,

you're alive when others have gone west. We'll find you something useful to do. No one will berate you for being ill.'

'But I'm not sick! You're not listening. There's nothing wrong with me but these stupid fainting fits. Oh, why me?'

Hester paused to answer his pain as best she could. She wanted to enfold him in her arms but he would only push her away. 'Your child is your child all your life, Doctor,' she sighed. 'When they hurt, you hurt too.'

He nodded in sympathy. 'Never a truer word, Lady Hester.' He turned to Angus. 'You must play this ball where it's landed. This epilepsy is your battlefield now and you mustn't let it take over your life. We must deal with it as best we can, but now is not the time to argue. You're home and it's time to rest and regroup and think out a strategy like your Father does. There must be a way forward, given time. *Nil desperandum* – don't despair. There are other ways to serve than rattling a sabre.'

Angus ignored his departure. Hester saw the doctor to the door, leaving her son to compose himself. Suddenly her ordered world was turned upside down by his return. Her selfish prayer had been answered, but this wish fulfilled gave no satisfaction at all.

Essie didn't like the sound of Newton's war. His letters came in muddy-fingered clumps – when they came at all. His soldiering was hard, from her reading of his comments. He was busy fettling up gunmetal and horse tackle and delivering wire to the front-line troops. It had been a harsh winter and now his section was supporting the French troops at a place close to Verdun, if the papers were to be believed. He sounded cheerful enough but little phrases kept spearing her mind.

'It's a bit hellish here, and you have to watch your head from sausage bombs and shrapnel. The other chaps are grand,' he said. He'd palled up with a lad from Bingley called Archie Spensley. The villages in France were all in ruins and his food rations sounded boring, tins of Maconochie stew and hard biscuits. The French soldiers had hot meals and were treated much better, he complained: 'You wouldn't feed the dog on what we get.' But she wasn't worried.

It was Frank who was causing her anxiety; he had got in bother for upsetting some officer with cheek. This captain wasn't treating his horse right and Frank had showed his disapproval, which got him on a charge. Frank had always been for his horses. He wouldn't stand any cruelty but he was young and brash, none too keen to hold his tongue.

She had joined this new Women's Institute as a distraction as well as to do her bit. They sang the National Anthem, they had talks on cookery and other women's matters, and sometimes held little competitions for baking and flower arranging, which was fun. It made a change from chapel and the usual chores. But she was worried about Asa struggling to cope on his own. She did what she could in the forge but the heat inside made her wheeze and cough so she couldn't stay in long.

Selma was looking after the veg plot and exercising the horses, still writing to the young Cantrell boy, whose brother was back home now on health grounds. Betty Plimmer said he looked perfectly fit to her when he rode out on his mother's horse. Lady Hester was busy trying to get him fitted up at Sharland School as an instructor for the officer cadets or something. It was all very mysterious. Ethel at the post office hinted he might have got a girl into trouble somewhere. Trust the village gossips to make two and two into five.

Essie tried to keep herself away from tittle-tattle. If they talked about others, they'd talk about you behind your back, she'd worked that out long ago. Better to keep private stuff in the family, and if it made her seem standoffish then so be it.

She was walking up the street when she saw Coleford approaching Prospect Row. Her heart began to thud as he moved closer to their houses. Who was it this time? Jack Plimmer from the Hart's Head?

She scurried home, trying not to look where Coleford was going as she overtook him. He parked his bicycle by the stone wall and bent over to tie his shoe lace and smiled. Phew! Another false alarm. Praise the Lord!

She made for the snicket at the side of the cottage to let herself in the back door, leaving the gate open, and then she turned to see the old man hovering behind her holding an official brown envelope in his hand. The look on his face said it all. She cranked up a grimace of a smile as if he might perhaps move on to another door. Perhaps he didn't have the right address. But she knew, deep in her gut she knew the envelope was for them.

'Mrs Bartley,' he whispered.

'Aye, it's our turn then,' was all she could manage as she turned her back on him and made for the safety of her kitchen. Her hands were shaking and wouldn't open the door properly. The envelope lay burning a hole in the table for hours until Asa came in. She nodded in its direction, unable to speak. He wiped his hands and tore the envelope, read the page, looked up at her shaking his head as if all the sorrows of the world were contained in those sad eyes.

'He's gone missing. Our Newton's missing, presumed killed.' He sat down, his head in his hands. 'I don't understand. We had a letter only the other day. My son . . .'

Asa walked back to his workshop, his shoulders bowed. Essie walked down the path to the open gate and out onto the lane and stared up at the green hills. How could her son be lost and her not know it? How could her lovely lad be so far away from her and she not sense he'd gone from her? While she was sitting, chattering away, he was lying somewhere, unseeing. They got things wrong sometimes, she thought. She would not close the front room curtains yet a while . . . not until the others knew. How on earth was she going to tell Selma?

Selma couldn't believe she'd never see her brother again. He was only missing in action, Mam said. There was hope, however small. So at first she refused to go into black clothes. Frank was not even allowed home from France on compassionate leave. Perhaps he knew more than he was letting on, but he was in the north somewhere far away from Newt's regiment. She managed to go to school in a dream, trying not to show her true feelings. Children didn't want to see suffering faces. Her brother, said the pastor, was in a better place now. Dad nodded but said nothing as neighbours called with their little gifts of kindness: buns, pastries and vegetables. As if any of them wanted to eat at such a time. Everything stuck like pebbles in her throat. Mam just stared at Newton's portrait and insisted the gate be kept open at the back just in case. 'You never know . . . he might be trying to find his way home,' she kept whispering.

But it was Archie Spensley's letter a week later that shattered all their illusions.

Dear family,

    I am sad to have to write to you that your son and my dear friend, Newton, is no more. We chummed up straight away in Halifax and he was highly regarded as a conscientious worker and a good Christian. I shall miss his cheery company. We are greatly troubled by enemy fire in this district, which damaged our guns with shells and fragments. Your son was going forward to do a repair. There was another bombardment and I never saw him again. Be assured he would not have suffered and would want you to know you were ever in his thoughts.

    May God bless all of you in your darkest hour, may He show you every mercy.

    Yours sincerely,

    Private Archibald Spensley

Suddenly, Selma's parents looked old, weary and bent with sorrow. If only there was something she could do to lighten their load. Without the boys' help Dad was sinking under a pile of unfinished orders. If only Frank could be made to come home like Angus Cantrell, who was hanging about the Hart's Head like a knotless thread. She knew Guy was anxious to hear if she'd seen him but she was no tale-teller and said nothing to worry him.

Angus looked able-bodied enough to give a helping hand if he had a mind to it but such an impertinent request was out of the question. Lady Hester would never condone such lowly employment.

They held a simple memorial service and sang Newton's favourite hymn, 'Who would true valour see, Let him come hither'. She tried to sing but the words collapsed in her throat. She didn't hear the pastor's oration. She was living in a sort of dream. It wasn't real because they had no body to bury, just a flag draped around the portrait he'd had taken in his uniform when he first volunteered. There were only old men and Angus Cantrell and his mother. He looked so like his brother and her heart ached at the sight of his tall frame and broad shoulders. Those who had already lost sons shielded her parents with loving concern. They had been admitted to a club whose entrance fee was young blood; a club no one wanted to join.

How hard it was for women to sit on the sidelines watching their loved ones fall down like skittles. Then, in the stillness of the chapel, an idea came into Selma's head – an arrow-sharp idea.

If men were absent then the women must do their work – not just the easy stuff, but the hard stuff too, the heavy jobs, the dangerous skills. It was the least they could do. Why hadn't she thought of it before?

'Don't be silly, you can't be a blacksmith! It's heavy work,' said her father on hearing her bright idea the next day.

'Why not? I can help, hold things steady, I can learn. I've watched enough times,' Selma argued as she and her parents sat hugging the fire.

'But what about your schooling? We signed for you to be a teaching assistant . . .'

'This is wartime. I'm needed at home. Dad needs someone by his side to run errands. We might find a young

108

boy to train up until Frank comes back, but in the meantime it's what Newt would want me to do,' Selma added.

Asa stared into the fire, scratching his head. 'Who's put this idea in your head? Not you, Essie?'

'Nowt to do with me. She's thought this one up herself. It's not women's work but someone has to do it, I suppose.'

'Neither is ploughing or making shells or driving steam engines, but there are girls out there doing that. I'll give it a go . . . I'm strong,' Selma said, sensing their opposition weakening.

'I don't know, love. What'll folk say of me, letting you hammer out their metalwork?'

'They'll not bother as long as their stuff is repaired. You can't do everything yourself. It's worth a try. I haven't settled to sitting in school all day. It's not right. Not now.'

'But your hands . . . there's splashes and it's dangerous.'

'I know you'll show me the right way to go about things. I can wear leather gloves and an apron.'

'It's a big step and a sacrifice,' Mam sighed.

'But it's nothing to the sacrifice Newton's had to make,' Selma replied.

They fell silent. There was no answering that.

7

Guy hung over the side of the troopship watching Southampton fading into the distance Their embarkation procedure had taken ages. The big push was rumoured to be beginning. There were rumours of a sea battle too but he'd taken comfort from seeing the destroyer forging through the waves ahead of them, leading them southwards towards the French coast.

It was hard not to feel excited to be going abroad at long last, though guilty that he was leaving his family behind in the throes of despair. Angus had not written a word to him about his mysterious discharge but he had had a long explanation from Mother about how the doctor in Harley Street had prescribed heavy sedation, and how Angus must be monitored. She was fussing over her son and Angus was no doubt hating every minute of it, but at least he had a part-time job in the school.

Guy could sense, in the lack of letters, his brother's resentment and fury that he was thwarted by these fits while Guy was now free to pursue his career unhindered. But he promised himself that he would write to Angus as much detail as he could so he could share this experience, even if second-hand, every step of the way.

Selma's sad letter also disturbed him with news of Newton's death and her decision to go into the forge – as an apprentice, of all things. In truth, he was a little shocked at such drastic action. How could a slip of a girl do such heavy work? Surely it was no place for a woman, but she seemed determined to settle down and make the best of it. What a wonderful girl she was: brave, determined; admirable in every way.

Nearly two years of war and still no end in sight. If the rumour mill was to be believed, things were going to hot up soon to shake the stalemate in the northern trenches and his troops were going to be part of some great push forward so he couldn't wait to be in the thick of it. The Yorkshires had trained for just such a battle and he felt proud to be leading his men. The sooner they shunted the Hun eastwards, the sooner he could get back and sort out things with Angus. Selma's other brother would relieve her and they would all get on with their normal lives.

The funny thing was that life in the regiment now seemed his normal life and it was just like school in so many ways, with its traditions and its rules; a world within another world, running on its own tramlines . . .

Now all their training was going to be tested in the heat of battle. He only hoped his courage wouldn't fail when push came to shove.

'Lieutenant Cantrell, sir.' His reverie was interrupted by a saluting NCO. 'Trouble in the hold, sir. Young Bostock's gone berserk, sir. He's in a right state . . . says he'll never see his kiddies again and that we're all going to go west.'

The last thing they needed was someone putting the wind up the troops, Guy thought.

'Bring him up into the fresh air and I'll have a word.'

Private Bostock was an orderly, a useful chap, not usually a worry guts, and it was not like him to be in a panic.

Minutes later, the private was marched before him, saluting and looking flustered.

'What's going on? Didn't expect you to get the wind up!' Guy tried to look stern though the man's distress was obvious.

'I hate water, sir. I can't stand the rocking and rolling. I'm a dalesman. The sea puts the fear of God in me, sir . . . get a bad feeling inside. Makes me legs go funny, dizzy, like, and I see things,' said the private, trying not to shake.

'What things?' Guy demanded.

'I looked round at my mates, sir. I got a bad feeling . . . None of us'll make it back. They were in the ground in pieces . . . it was like Hell. None of us will make it back home in one piece . . .'

'Enough of this! We can't have you mouthing this sort of funk. It's bad for morale. Nerves are a funny thing. If you've time to get so worked up about nothing then you can do a job for me on deck. I want all this list checked over, every item ticked and when you've done it once you can do it again. See to it right away!'

'Yes, thank you, sir.'

'Dismissed.' Guy hoped he'd done the right thing. Separating a doom-and-gloom merchant from the others was essential. Morale was everything, and his own job was to instil confidence and trust, even if Bostock's words had chilled his own blood. Was he right? Would any of them ever see Southampton dock again?

Another market day again, and there was a queue of traps drawn by horses to be shod. It was Selma's job to make a list and see that they were attended to in turn. The fire had been lit early and needed watching; she was getting used to the acrid smoke, the heat and the routine now. But there was still so much to learn, stuff she'd never noticed before. And how her shoulders ached at the end of the day. But this morning, she dared to put on a pair of Frank's old work breeches, thick wool drabs that fell down almost to her ankles. Skirts were too dangerous and cumbersome. But what would her father say?

Girls who wore trousers were considered fast a few years ago. Surely war had put an end to that. 'I hope Dad'll not be shocked by my new costume?' she had whispered to her mother, blushing.

'To the pure, all things are pure. There's no shame in sensible clothing as long as you don't make a habit of it outside,' Essie had replied

Asa never even noticed her new garb. He was too busy getting ready to receive one of Pateley's horses; a right sparky stallion.

'Now don't get windy of this beast. He'll sense you're new to the job and try it on. We'll put a rope round his neck and bring in Mam to put a rope round the back legs so the fetlocks are drawn in . . . He'll soon go down and know who is boss in here, and while we're at it I want all the tools to hand and then when job's done you'll get on with making stamps to mark the sheep horns . . . Oh, and there's a horse coming in that's knock-kneed and needs special shoes. How are we off for Stockton Tar?'

Selma sighed. 'It's on the shelf. There's a tin of salve, half full,' she said. It was going to be another long day.

After a few weeks the novelty of sacrificing her career had faded into the grim reality of life as a blacksmith's apprentice. Even she had to admit she didn't have the physical strength and, willing as she was, there was so much lifting and dunking and hammering and setting. Her muscles were hardening under the regular strain of this daily grind and she was constantly hungry.

None of them had any appetite for weeks after the news of Newton's death, but gradually life went on, and other casualties were lost and black clothes became as common as closed curtains at the windows and memorial services in the chapel. There was not a single cottage spared some tragic news. The vicar lost his son and he and his wife went into deep mourning like the rest.

There was shock at first that a young woman would do such a job, important as it was, but there had been women blacksmiths before, usually widows who carried on their husbands' work with help. Soon enough, when the farmers came into the forge they ignored Selma as if she wasn't hovering holding reins, massaging nervous horses, her hair piled up high under a makeshift tea cosy of a hat with just a few straggles remaining visible. She looked like any small farmer's boy.

Marigold had stared at her with pity and horror the other day. 'You've ruined your figure and those hands. You must be mad to give up teaching for this! You'd never catch me . . .' Marigold was good at shooting off with her mouth and thinking afterwards. She'd soon forgotten her flirtation with Newt and was now writing to a boy from Sowerthwaite who'd taken her fancy.

Selma didn't mind what people thought, knowing Newton would be proud of her efforts. Frank wrote scrappy letters about being in charge of some officers' horses in the cavalry. She'd hoped he'd ask to be returned home but that wasn't going to happen now so she'd just better get on with the job and try not to make a hash of it.

The only joy of her week was when Guy's letters plopped on the doormat. He wrote pages of news about his life. They were exercising by the coast and once he'd sent her a postcard of Rouen Cathedral. He had a way of describing his men and their funny antics that made her laugh out loud. How the little orderly Bostock had become his batman and how he could read teacups like a woman, but still lost all his pay playing cards. She was glad he couldn't see her looking such a scruff but this was her uniform now.

Then sometimes she'd catch a glimpse of herself in the mirror on the dressing table and see the state of her dishevelled hair and the iron dust ingrained on her cheeks, and she'd want to cry. How sick she was of this war and what it was doing to people all over the country. A brave face was expected, even if it was getting harder to pin it on each day.

Her father was snappy to work with, silent, lost in his tasks. Sometimes, he barked orders at her as if she should know already what was expected. When she didn't drill the square hole to the exact measurement, he snatched it off her to do it himself, making it plain she was a poor substitute for his son.

She cursed Frank for shirking his duty even though she knew he was only doing service as he thought fit. It was all so confusing. Everything was upside down, and she was afraid.

They were so cut off in the village. News, when it came, was days late and they only had the local newspaper accounts to rely on. They were filled with noises of far-off sea battles, of gallant local boys fighting on the front. But the sad lists

115

told another story that didn't add up to all this talk of victory. No one really knew what was happening out there and even Guy was careful how he phrased things. He'd had his first taste of battle and being under fire, and his pencil-scribbled words were sobering.

We are going through the mincer, a hundred of my men gone west already and not much to show for it, I'm afraid. I have to write these ghastly letters to mothers who will hate me for ever for giving them such terrible news. We spend days on the march, while in the distance great shells are blasting some other poor chaps to smithereens. It is hard to believe it is spring with fields full of blossom to the rear. Then as you get near to the front everything is blasted into a brown soup of mud and sludge, broken-off trees and ruined billets, where we smoke and chat, enjoying the peace and quiet until another great blast from the German guns sends us running for cover like the huge rats we see everywhere.

I am so filthy, with a host of living creatures taking residence in the seams of my jackets and trousers. Bostock is doing his best to keep me half decent, nicking them off with a lighted candle. Mother would disown me if she saw the state of me, but mud is a great leveller and I am no better than the men I serve, a hardy loyal bunch of chaps. I have to inspect their feet each evening and make them change their socks or their toes will get in the most appalling mess. So keep the ladies of West Sharland knitting socks. When it is really wet afoot I wear three or four pairs at a time.

116

When night falls it gives me pleasure to look up at the stars to relive those rides out over the Ridge in the sunshine together with old Jemima, knowing that nothing can now touch our green and pleasant land if we stand firm. It makes me feel a bit mushy at times to think of such beauty in this awful terrain.

Be brave, little friend, and keep your letters coming. I laughed thinking about how Elvie Best sang a whole solo out of tune at your Brave Belgium Funds Concert and everyone trying not to laugh and clapping to get her off stage and she thinking she was wanted for an encore and you having to suffer it all over again. You and all you stand for are what keeps me sane.

Your dearest friend, Guy

Selma shared his letters with no one. They were a precious link with his terrible world. Every night she looked up at the night sky, trying to imagine Guy in his trench, pacing the duckboards, shepherding his troops, sitting curled up writing to her, thinking about her and looking up at the same stars. His letters gave her the strength to suffer her father's frustration and bad temper.

'Pull yourself together, Bartley,' she said. 'You've got it easy. Go and do your duty and stop moaning. You must fight your war with a hammer and anvil, not a rifle. So go to it.

Hester had to admit having Angus at home wasn't quite the joy she had hoped for. It wasn't as if he didn't get up to do his drilling stint at Sharland School with cool efficiency. He took no prisoners, according to the head's wife, Maud. He would stand no indiscipline in the ranks or sloppy marching. But they were boys, not troops, and some-times he bawled them out in such a rage that he was becoming very unpopular and there were complaints from parents.

Not ever being part of the farmers' boys or the village lads, he was trying hard to mix and had started to frequent the Hart's Head, giving them his opinions on how the war was faring and how it should be won. He'd got into a fight one evening when the publican's son, Jack Plimmer, back on leave, told him to shut up and put his money where his mouth was, that he was sick of armchair soldiers who never even crossed the Channel . . . There'd been a scrap and Angus had been banned for causing a fracas.

Angus was becoming like a bear with a sore head when Guy's letters arrived; reading them and then tossing them away. 'It's not fair. I'm a useless ornament stuck here!' The more upset he got the more frequent were his fitting episodes, and Dr Mac was summoned to give him sedation.

'Yon laddie's just feeling sorry for himself. Find him some tough work to keep his mind from all this self-pitying. He'll find a way through. God gives the back for the burden. Just give him time.'

That did not go down well with either of them, but Hester set him to garden tasks. Then she sent him down to Charles, to the flat in London, but the colonel was preparing to go north with Lord Kitchener on some hush-hush task and didn't give the boy much time. Angus came back even more miserable than before and considerably more restless. He'd even reapplied for another medical, only to be discharged once more.

Hester confided her worries to Violet Hunt, who since Arnold's death had shrunk into an old woman overnight.

Only her duty at the Women's Institute meetings and her Sunday school teaching had kept her from total collapse. It was pitiable to see such a strong woman brought so low, making Hester feel how lucky she was to have even one of her sons close but things could not go on. If only there was something they could do.

It was Lady Bellerby at one of their morning sewing bees who gave her an idea.

'We've opened our home up for wounded officers as a temporary hospital: somewhere with country air to help them to convalesce quicker, quiet with gardens, where boys can relax and regroup. I know they are looking for suitable billets with spare rooms, and they provide the nurses and staff. To tell the truth it's been a godsend to keep the old ship afloat. You wouldn't have to do the nursing but just provide a suitable space . . . Waterloo House would be ideal, not too big and close to the station for visitors and that sort of thing. You must be rattling round like peas in a drum with just the two of you and Charles off on his jaunts with Lord Kitchener.' Once Daphne Bellerby was in full flow there was no halting her. 'Now isn't he a one-man battleship, a marvellous example to us all? Cometh the hour, cometh the man . . . You must be so proud that Charles is by his side.'

Hester nodded, thinking that this suggestion might just help Angus to get things in perspective when he saw men far worse off than himself. He could talk army talk amongst fellow officers. Was he not in some ways as wounded as they were? It was worth taking the matter further but then came the thought of strangers roaming over Waterloo House. But, she reasoned, officers were gentleman and would honour her home, and the authorities would bring

119

much-needed staff to cook meals and take care of the grounds. Perhaps Daphne was right to suggest they were living in a resource that might help the war effort.

Spring in the Dales was now at its most beautiful; the lush green of the beech leaves, the pink confetti of bird cherry blossom. Nature didn't know there was a war on and put on its annual display of hedgerow flowers, mountain poppies, woodland purple orchids, the scents of bluebells in May bringing colour, hope and renewal. How could a spirit not be lifted in such a place? The aromas from her rose garden in the summer would be another calming influence with views to lift the dullest of spirits. Even the Hart's Head could provide some jollity. Was this the answer to her prayers? Perhaps even the peace and quiet of a humble village setting like Sharland might play its part in winning the war.

Essie was paying a rare visit to see her sister, Ruth, who lived on the outskirts of Bradford. She couldn't recall the last time she'd made the effort to catch the train south but this was Asa's treat to lift her flagging spirits and to celebrate her fortieth birthday. They were going to have tea in town and then go to a matinée; all Ruth's treat, and it was such a beautiful June day when even the chimneys and mills and the dark streets shone in a midsummer glow. She was wearing her best grey frock with a black armband sewn onto the sleeve for Newton's sake. Selma had padded out her hair in the fashion, and her best black straw was perched on the top.

But she could hardly muster any enthusiasm. She still couldn't believe Newt wouldn't come home again. It was as if he was still over there somewhere. How she longed to hear her son's voice again.

Molly Forster had whispered one morning in chapel that she'd been to see a woman in Sowerthwaite who regularly communicated with the dear departed. It had given her comfort to know that her son, Cyril, was happy beyond this veil of tears. The lady described him and said he was watching over her and he'd called her mum. Molly strained to hear his voice but Martha Holbeck said only those God had chosen to be His channels could hear the words.

Essie didn't know what to make of this. She was not sure Asa would approve, not to mention Pastor Rathbone, but Molly seemed the better for it and had started coming back to the Women's Institute again. When women started mixing in company it was a good sign.

They'd had a talk on rearing poultry and rabbits for the pot, and demonstrations on using potatoes as a flour substitute to save the British wheat supply. Someone brought a knitting machine that could churn out balaclavas and socks like a factory and they were taking it in turns to master the technique. Then there was the lady Liberal politician whom Mrs Hunt brought along, who talked about how having the Vote would make a difference to their lives, how it was important that their voices were heard by the elected government. Essie had just wanted to shout, 'Stop this bloody war before anyone else gets hurt!'

Everyone was talking about some big sea battle in the North Sea and a lot of ships sunk, more lives lost, but the navy had repelled the enemy at Jutland bank. She thought of all those men at the bottom of the sea and the afternoon flew by. How quickly she'd forgotten the time, what with the scones and jam tea and the tour around Ruth's grey brick semidetached villa with its parlour and dining room, and a little kitchen with a gas cooker, and inside toilet.

Ruth and Sam lived such a contented life, with no kiddies to mess the floors or worry about. It felt a silent empty space, all neatly fenced off with not a thing out of place. Funny how Essie didn't envy her sister her pretty home one jot. Children had not been given to them and this was what they got in their place, she reckoned.

Ruth had bought her a new blouse with pintucks in lilac cotton, and a pretty knitted cardigan ready for Selma's birthday in August.

Sam Broadbent was busy in the mill, checking wools for quality and sorting it into grades. He was short-staffed for all he was looking prosperous. They had lost so many young men to the Forces. Already, he wondered if the trade would ever recover. Some of his German colleagues had been imprisoned for a while and were now leaving in droves – many for America, taking their skills and money with them. Bradford was busy making uniforms and cloth; another world away from Sharland: faster, slicker with trams and traffic noise and smoke, and she was longing for the train to head north, back to where she felt most at home.

It wasn't as if Ruth made her feel like a country mouse. It was that she was invisible and uncomfortable in such a strange space.

Sam got the latest news in the *Telegraph* each day. Ruth had gone worldly with her wealth, for all she still attended chapel. There were the temptations of cinemas and theatres open every day except Sunday, public houses on every street corner, and the smell of fresh fish and chip vans. The mills towered over her, making Essie feel small and insignificant, but wherever she turned she saw the same sad faces and widows' weeds.

They were saying their goodbyes through the carriage

windows when a man rushed into the vacant seat, waving a newspaper. 'Have you heard? Isn't it terrible?' No one spoke as he waved a page in the air. 'Lord Kitchener's dead . . . blown up . . . at the bottom of the sea!'

The woman opposite Essie crossed herself in shock. 'The war is lost then,' she cried. 'What will become of us?'

Secure in his audience, the young man began to read it aloud. 'The known facts are that his ship struck a mine off Scotland. They abandoned ship . . . six hundred and fifty dead. His lordship was amongst them. It was a dark and stormy night with terrible cries heard from the lifeboats. Only a handful made it alive to the rocks. There will be an inquiry into what happened . . .'

This news silenced everyone as the train steamed out of the station. Essie shivered. Lord Kitchener – he that had taken her sons away from her – Lord Kitchener, the Minister for War, lost at sea. Then she remembered where she'd heard his name recently: from the lips of Lady Hester Cantrell at the last WI meeting. Wasn't her husband one of his . . . ?

In the drawing room of Waterloo House, a chaplain Hester had never seen before was making sympathetic noises that floated over her like smoke. A senior officer accompanying him had come up from London on the morning train to give her the details of this most terrible of tragedies.

Angus sat holding her hand, frozen by the shock of his father's death but trying to ask sensible questions. Hester couldn't speak, just nodded, observing the open and shutting lips as if in some silent dream. *This is not real. This is just some nightmare.* But the instinct of years kicked in and she received their condolences like a true officer's wife, with dignity and courtesy, sitting ramrod straight in her black bombazine dress that needed its beadwork repairing.

She was a widow now. Charles lay at the bottom of Scapa Flow; a sailor's, not a soldier's, death. How strange . . . Were his last thoughts of them or of panic for breath as the waters closed over his head?

'Is there no hope of other survivors?' she asked, knowing that lifeboats could be cast adrift many miles. She thought about the *Titanic* disaster.

'It was a terrible night, Lady Hester. The lifeboats were smashed to pieces by heavy seas and the explosion was midship. The *Hampshire* sank in minutes. Only twelve men have survived, reaching the shore in the lifeboats. The wind and the cold took its toll. The waters round to the Brough of Birsay are treacherous.'

'What were they doing going out on a night like that? Stupid to set off into a storm,' Angus asked angrily.

'You might well ask . . . but we only know that they were on their way to Archangel for some negotiations with the highest Russian officials. The German navy had left mines around Scapa Flow but they were undetected. It was all a terrible coincidence. Had they not turned back because of the storm . . . Had the weather not been so inclement . . . We shall never know.'

Hester didn't want to hear any more of their commiserations. Nothing would bring her husband home again. Their life was changed for ever by this sickening news. And Guy was going into battle even as they spoke.

'Thank you for telling me all this in person. No letter or telegram can ever convey such bad news but I would appreciate being left now to consider all this with my son.'

'Of course, Lady Hester,' said the chaplain. 'There will

be a memorial service in London in due course, but we will keep you informed of any other developments, should they arise.'

'Thank you,' she said, rising, her knees shaking. 'Angus will see you to the door.' She flopped down again, suddenly exhausted by the images in her head: the crashing waves, the broken ship, the scrabble for lifeboats, the cries of the injured and the fear of the doomed men as they wrapped their cork vests over themselves in hope of a rescue. It must have been chaos. There was never any hope.

Oh, Charles, to have drowned in an undignified scramble for safety whilst trying to get Lord Kitchener into a lifeboat. They had survived the explosion, but not the savage seas.

How she needed to weep at such scenes but not a tear would fall. She just felt numb inside. Never to see him again or hear that loud booming voice . . . Theirs was never a romantic passion, but there was respect and friendship, a steady sort of married love. For the past years they had lived separate lives, joined mostly by concern for the boys, but she would not wish that sort of death on anyone. Just when they were looking forward to a more settled way of life in retirement, along came war, and now this.

'Oh, Charles,' that was all she kept repeating. His voice rang in her ears and she shut her eyes and saw him resplendent in his dress uniform. His tall elegant figure with those long legs, 'Give 'em hell' Cantrell, poor, poor Charles, food for the fishes at the bottom of the sea.

Stop this! Hester drew herself together into an effort to get out of the room. There was only one place of consolation for her and that was the walled garden, where the first of the June roses was already opening its buds in the sunshine.

It would be good for just the two of them to have a few hours to themselves before the news drifted through the village and all the formal acts of mourning would begin, a few hours to sit in peace and look out over the Ridge. 'I will lift up mine eyes unto the hills: from whence cometh my help.'

Just to feast on the fresh green of the fells was soothing and with it came a relief of sorts. *I am now as everyone else, a war widow. We have had our quota of suffering, like Violet; the odds have been satisfied.* And to her horror she secretly sighed with relief at the thought that this meant Guy would be spared.

Guy had never received so many letters of sympathy from strangers, from his old headmaster and the vicar, from officers who had served with Charles Cantrell in the past. With every post there were more and more tributes to his father; tributes that gave him fresh insight into his father's army career, his friendships, his club associates, and even one from a lady who claimed to be her father's special friend, a Mrs Amy Trickett from Balham Common. So many tributes from people he'd never met. His mother wrote a terse note telling him his father would want him to do his duty and how proud he was to have him serving in the Yorkshires. Angus wrote that the Village had sent wreaths and attended the church memorial service in droves. It was a splendid occasion with hymns and readings, but strange because there was no burial or coffin, just a picture of Father with a laurel wreath round it like a frame.

Mama was holding up and talking about opening a wing of Waterloo for wounded officers, and she was keeping so busy she kept falling asleep at the oddest times like between the entrée and the dessert, or while she was sitting doing her infernal sewing. Angus was going to oversee all the new arrangements.

I wish we could exchange places. I'd rather be with you any day.

They say they can hear the Allied guns across the Channel in London on a clear day, so you're the 'Give 'em hell' Cantrell now. Go to it and good luck.

Selma's letter was short and simple. She sent pressed flowers from the hay meadows, asking if they were the same as in the French fields. She'd drawn a sketch of the Ridge with Jemima in the foreground and enclosed a copy of the memorial service for him to treasure. How strange that he didn't feel anything much, just numbness.

His father's death was a keen quick end. Now Guy was seeing so much death that was anything but: men hanging on the wire in agony, blown apart. Stomach wounds were the worst, with entrails spilling out and poor beggars pleading to be put down like wounded horses, endless crying for help in no man's land, he listening as the cries for mothers got weaker and more spaced apart. It was a living hell, and there was more to come.

West Sharland was another planet away from this shit hole. No wonder he could read things and not feel emotion, as if he were floating above it all into another world. Sometimes he feared he would end up a dithering idiot, but he must stay strong for his men.

On the first day of the Big Push they'd gone over the top after the bombardment expecting there would be nothing but wasteland between them and the German trenches. The wire would be flattened with such great gaps so they could run through. But it was a hopeless fiasco. They were hit by machine-gun fire and he'd watched men mown down and not get up and waited for something to explode inside him. There were bodies sleeping in the fields as if they were sunbathing, others alive, twitching, begging for water, calling to their comrades. But they moved on like automatons. He was no longer afraid, as if every one of his senses was alert to danger, eyes, ears, muscles tensed up for a fight.

The devastation got worse, and they didn't get far in no man's land before there was no recourse but to turn back while thousands lay piled high in the sunshine, never to return. All this slaughter for a few yards of territory, and then, under cover of darkness, he and his party crawled over the top to collect the dead or the few wounded still breathing.

What a shambles! What a terrible waste of life and limb! He couldn't believe he'd made it so far, and with this standoff came a terrible shaking fear that the next time over would bring his last moment alive on this earth.

What an act it was to stay calm, fighting the urge to sweat and pant, trying to look full of confidence, knowing his men were eyeing his every move in the dugout. They would take their lead from his demeanour. Hidden from view he felt that first courage leaching away, felt his resolve weakening, his hands shaking with fear.

I don't want to die yet. I don't want to end up like these grinning skulls sticking out in the shell holes, picked clean by rats; these shiny long white faces staring, accusing with hollows for eyes. His dreams were full of dancing skeletons and rats the size of moggies.

No one had warned him that in battle he'd be out on all fours in the mud, dragging bodies back to dig shallow graves, taking off identity tags, making lists of names and numbers, ferreting through bloody clothes for letters and remains, writing letters to widows, letters to strangers. This was not the sort of boy heroics he had been expecting and all his childish hopes of glory died in seconds on the poppy fields of the Somme in those first few days of action. Now he knew what his father meant about two hours of battle being worth two years of training.

In those first weeks of July, the sense of desolation grew as one by one his officer chums were blown up or just simply disappeared. He felt their loss more than that of his own father. Over the months they'd all become his family more than his own and that made him feel sick with guilt. Now they were lying in shallow graves while his remaining company was living a gypsy life, scavenging for cover and food until the mess wagons arrived with supplies for their platoons.

After battle there was always plenty to eat, for more than half his men were gone but their rations still kept coming and must be shared out. Feet must be inspected, wounds examined, charges of ill discipline dealt with on the spot. There was no let-up, and all the time he must look as if this fiasco was just a minor blip in the battle plan and encourage them on to the next fight.

There were hints he'd be made captain, for who else was left to do the job? He was one of only a handful of officers living, already on borrowed time.

Then the blessed order to fall back into the reserve line

came, and then further back for some rest. That was the worst time: behind the lines, with time to think about all of the responsibility left on his shoulders, the huge losses, where they would be sent next, how to wind down for a few days in the *estaminet* without the smoke and noise and thunder in his ears.

Guy lay back in a haystack, utterly exhausted, weary of all the nonsense and futility of trying to shift the Hun from their trenches. It was backwards and forwards like some dance of death, and for what . . . a few yards of territory?

Perhaps there was a bigger plan at work but he didn't know what it was. His job was to obey orders, not to question them.

Then he was ordered to HQ, and his first thought was, what have I done wrong now?

'Cantrell.'

'Yes, sir.'

'At ease! You're off, so get your kit.'

'Off where, sir?'

'Spot of leave . . . orders from above . . . Your father was with Lord Kitchener?'

'Yes, sir, he was.'

'Bad show . . . Ten days' leave. Don't just stand there. Get your kit. Just time to catch the hospital train . . .'

'But, sir, my men . . . There're others who've been out longer . . .'

'Orders, Cantrell. Just go. You can argue the toss when you return.'

'Sir!' he saluted briskly, not believing what he was hearing. He was going home to Yorkshire, leaving this hellhole and going north out of the fray. Suddenly he felt very unsure. He wanted to stay where he was with his shaken men.

It felt like desertion, and he didn't deserve leave. He'd achieved nothing. How could he bugger off without a by-your-leave? But orders were orders and who was he to question them?

He should feel overjoyed at this release but then why was he feeling so afraid?

8

Hester was busy overseeing the preparation of bedrooms for the first contingent of wounded officers. The iron beds arrived by lorry and she'd got Mrs Beck from the village to clean out the large bedrooms, ready to receive them.

Since the Battle of the Somme, as the papers called it, there was a rush to equip private homes with beds, and Waterloo House was assigned a voluntary auxiliary nurse and an orderly to prepare the hygiene routines. There was a cook and assistant, so the servants' rooms in the attic had to be cleared out.

Suddenly her home wasn't her own. The staff were taking over. Angus kept out of the way, happy to drive Charles's car to fetch supplies or see to the horses.

Hester felt so bone weary at the end of the day, no time to enjoy cooked meals or anything much but her garden chores. Here she could find some peace and quiet from all the bustle and gardening kept her from worrying about Guy.

Not a word from him this week. Not since the Big Push had fizzled out and the terrible realisation that most of the Sowerthwaite Pals had been killed in the first wave of battle. All those brave local boys, school friends, members of the football and cricket teams, lines of them massacred. The whole town and the villages surrounding were in mourning. Young men at the peak of health and vigour gone for ever. Who would take their place? What would become of their wives and sweethearts? It made her own loss bearable in so far as Charles had had a good life, had travelled the world and seen his boys grow to manhood.

What gaps would *these* men leave when war was over?

Not a word from Guy, but bad news travelled fast from France. The military post was most efficient. Why, only the other day, the first poor Mrs Marshbank knew that her son was fatally wounded was when a letter of condolence came from a fellow soldier and this before she even got an official form!

When Hester looked at Angus she could see Guy in so many ways, which was always a comfort. But still, it was not like her son not to write. Perhaps the girl in the village, the Bartley girl, might have received word. Time to make a detour from her errands and humble herself by visiting the forge.

Hester had to admit she seemed a spirited sort of filly and her mother was a willing horse in the Women's Institute these days. But assistant teacher and Sunday school teacher she might be, she still was not one of their sort. She may not know anything either, but it was worth a try.

Selma was busy stoking the fire. They'd had a delivery of coal and she was covered in dust and muck. June had been a busy month, with grinding and sharpening the sheep shears for clipping time. Now it was time to see to scythes and hay forks and repairs to mowing machines for hay-timing. Even a blacksmith had his own seasonal rhythm.

133

Horses always needed good shoes for the jobs ahead. There were the usual queues to be seen to.

Over the last months, Selma felt her muscles sharpening, her calloused hands hardening up, her shoulders broadening, and after an incident with a spark in her long hair, she'd pleaded to have her hair bobbed short. She was sick of the smell of singed hair. In her breeches and her collarless shirt, she felt like a boy but this was her job and she was sticking to it; feeble as she was when it came to the real heavy work. Now they were that thronged with comings and goings, she didn't know the day of the week, or the hour, so when she saw the figure standing in the doorway she ignored him.

'We're closed!' she shouted, not looking up – even a blacksmith had to eat – but the man didn't move.

'Is Selima in the house?' he asked, and she looked up.

'Who's asking?'

'Tell her Guy is home on leave . . .' He took off his army cap.

Her eyes stared at the silhouette in the doorway and she felt herself blush. He didn't recognise her under all this dirt and mucky clothing.

'You just told her!' she called back, smiling, pulling off her hat to release her bobbed hair. 'You're home!'

'Selma, I'm so sorry . . . I thought . . .' Guy stammered.

'I know what I look like. I should have warned you, you don't wear skirts in a forge!' She paused, embarrassed. 'There's no other way, as you can see, to stay safe. How lovely to see you safe and sound. There's been such terrible losses around here.'

'I know. I heard about the Pals brigade.'

'I was at school with so many of them. But enough

134

sadness, this is just brilliant . . . what a wonderful surprise. If only I'd known, I'd have tried not to give you such a fright!'

Guy was staring at her in all her mucky glory, while her father hovered by the back door observing them both.

'Back from the wars then, Mr Cantrell,' he said. 'One of the few left. This one's my right-hand help now . . . doing champion for a girl. Might I add, not of our choosing. This is not work for women, but as the boys were desperate for glory, beggars can't be choosers.'

'Dad!' All his compliments vanished in his last sentence but she knew he was teasing.

'I say as I find.' Asa Bartley stood firm.

'I think it is rather splendid for her to volunteer . . . and I'm none too clean myself.'

He looked marvellous to her. Selma wanted her dad to disappear, but he stood there staring at them both while she couldn't take her eyes off Guy. He had grown so tall, so thin and gaunt in the cheeks, even more like his brother than before. He looked worn out, and his eyes were tired.

'I can't believe you're here. I got your last letter only yesterday. It sounded terrible. Your mother must be so relieved to see you,' she added.

'She doesn't know yet,' he replied.

'What doesn't she know?' Selma saw his mother standing in the doorway, staring at the scene before her and looking at Selma in fury.

'I just called on the off chance, Miss Bartley, that you might have had word from Guy, but I see you have already renewed your acquaintance in person . . .' She was staring in disbelief at Selma's outfit now. 'I thought you were teaching school.'

'I was, but my father needed a boy,' she stuttered, not sure whether to bob a curtsy or not.

'Well, he certainly has made one of you, I see. I didn't expect my son to arrive unannounced but you obviously have first call on his attention.'

'I wanted to surprise you,' Guy replied, now looking awkward.

'You certainly did that, my son,' said his mother sharply.

But her father intervened. 'You must be thankful that the Lord has brought him home in one piece,' he said, which didn't help the situation at all.

Hester Cantrell drew herself up to her full height, bristling at his impudence. 'Thank you, I don't need telling what is between me and my maker, Mr Bartley. Come along, Guy. Angus will want to know you're back. Good day to you both,' she said pulling Guy's arm.

He smiled and looked sheepish. Perhaps later, his eyes were pleading. Now was not the time for any showdown. He had come to Selma first and that must be enough for now.

'How long have you got?' Selma could not resist this most important of questions as he turned to leave.

'Just five days,' he whispered. 'It takes so long to get here, Selma.'

Only five days of leave . . . after all this time, and his mother and brother desperate for him after their sad loss. She mustn't be selfish, but just to see him standing there, smiling at her . . . Oh, Guy, please come back before you go, she sighed. Any crumb of his company would do.

Guy was so confused by the sight of Selma standing like a soldier in trousers, her dark hair cropped, her brown eyes flashing, caught like rabbit in a Very light. Dear Selma, he hadn't realised how physically he was attracted to her until now, and then for poor Mother to come in, all guns blazing. This was not how it was supposed to be, this unexpected homecoming. Already he felt like a stranger in a foreign land where roses bloomed and green fields were undamaged, no wooden crosses nor bloated horseflesh rotting by the roadside, and cottages standing, not stoved in by shells.

England was going on undisturbed, with stations full of weary soldiers like himself staggering home with dead eyes, uniforms covered in lice. He had dreamed of this moment for so long and now it felt awkward and unreal. His world was back there in the trenches with his men, with Bostock fussing over him and HQ breathing down his neck.

For the first time he felt nervous as they drove up to Waterloo House. It wasn't true that everything was unchanged; even Selma had cut her hair. There were vegetables growing on verges and in parks, and even in the gardens here. Everyone seemed to be wearing black, and there were queues for food in the shops. This was a different sort of war.

'I'd better warn you,' said Mother, 'we've made a few changes. I've got a contingent of six officers coming any day and the whole house is turned upside down to accommodate them. But after your father . . . well, it seemed the right thing to do. I wasn't expecting you, so we've made no extra provisions. If only you'd written earlier.'

'I'm sorry, I should have sent a telegram.'

'And scared the wits out of me? No, this is a wonderful surprise – even if we're to come second after that girl.'

'Selma – she has a name, Mother.'

'Whatever . . . The war has done her no favours, coarsened her looks – and short hair!'

137

'But she's doing her war service as she thinks fit. What have you got against her?' He was not going to be bullied by these cutting remarks, not when he had been through such hell.

'Oh, Guy, as if I have to explain that . . . She's not your type, no refinements at all.'

'But I like Selma, I always have. She's a lovely girl and writes funny letters.'

'I'm sure she does, to entrap you into some engagement. A girl like that wants to better herself, that's all. She's not for you, son,' said his mother, staring up at him with steel in her eyes.

'I'll choose who is or isn't for me. Don't tell me how to spend my time. I may not have much of it left,' he replied, staring away into the distance to the green open spaces he loved so much.

'Guy, please, don't talk like that! We've had our loss. You will live, but not to . . . Have your fling if you must. Get all this youthful lust out of your system, but don't tie yourself in knots to the first pretty girl who flashes her eyes in your direction. Take a mother's warning. Look, there's Angus. Go and give him a surprise and we'll talk no more about this. Don't let's quarrel on your leave. I'll get Cook to make a wonderful supper this evening.'

But Guy wasn't hungry any more.

Oh, Guy, Guy, don't waste your time courting when we have seen so little of you.

Hester didn't want to let him out of her sight now he was here, to have him breathing the same air, smiling, looking so young and handsome and alive when there was nothing but doom and gloom all around. He lit up her life with his grin and his mischievous blue eyes, her beautiful boy, and she could forgive him for taking a peek at the girl from the forge who was stealing his heart – for the moment.

What on earth could he see in such a common trollop? She was a disgrace to her fair sex, war work or not. How could he waste precious time on such a creature?

If he wanted girls she would rustle up a few beauties, nice gals, not village harpies. Even Dr Mac's two daughters would be a better substitute than that girl.

He'd got only a few days and she'd make sure he didn't spend another minute with that Bartley brat. He would only make trouble for himself there if he did.

All she could think of was, would Guy call back? Would he risk his mother's wrath and visit again? As the hours of that first day ticked by Selma felt an excruciating panic and anguish. What if he went back without seeing her, without a chance for them just to talk?

Outside, the summer days were flying by. It didn't last long in these parts. There had been some wet weeks but now the sunshine was beautiful. The swallows were darting overhead and swifts circling high, the smell of fresh-cut hay scenting the air. Their time was so short, and there was nothing she could do but agonise.

Now was the busiest time for the blacksmith, with haymaking in full swing. Broken tools needed fettling up and she couldn't just down her work and meander off in the direction of Waterloo House on the off chance, however much she wanted to.

Mam could read her agitation. 'Don't worry,' she said. 'If I read that young man, he won't leave without saying goodbye to his friends. Your dad told me his ma weren't right pleased with him for calling on you first. She's going to have to learn to let go, is that one. Isn't it enough she's got one of them twins by her side already?'

'But I looked such a fright, he didn't recognise me!'

'Take yerself off for a dip in the river, a bit of a paddle. You can rinse the dust out of your hair. I'm getting to like that bob now. It shines like a conker when it's washed.'

Her father, however, was agitated, watching her for any slackening of pace. 'You're too young for walking out yet. And I wouldn't go looking in that direction. Toffs stick with their own, as a general rule, so don't get your hopes up. He's a soldier on leave. I've heard tales of what they can get up to. No girl of mine is going to be mucked about, gentleman or not. He's a man now, with a man's needs, no doubt. You must remember who you are, young lady; chapel born and bred . . . far too young to be wed, but his mother will make sure he never puts a ring on your finger, if I know her sort.'

'It's not like that . . . we're just good friends, pen pals,' she argued, knowing that this was not strictly true.

'That's all right then, isn't it?'

Why was everyone going on about it as if there could ever be a future between the two of them? It wasn't that she didn't feel something much more. When he had stood there in his uniform she wanted to fling herself into his arms.

All those letters and feelings shared, all the personal stuff they'd written, the things he'd told her about his fears and nightmares. He had drawn them so close. She wanted to see Guy again, but what if he didn't call?

*　　*　　*

140

Guy wanted to slip away after supper, back down to the village to see Selma. He'd brought her a little gift in his kitbag, some French perfume in a pretty bottle.

But Angus was exhausting, pumping him dry with questions and his own theories on the war. He was so desperate to know what was going on but Guy was in no mood for going over the realities of his soldiering. He felt protective of his family, not wanting them to know just how awful it was out there, especially for the lower ranks. His brother was hanging on his every word as if it were gospel and sadly Guy felt the difference between them had grown with every day he'd been away. He felt as old as the hills, while Angus was little more than a schoolboy with all his ideals intact, untempered by battle.

He'd made plans for them both to go out hiking tomorrow. 'There's this spiffing pothole over the Ridge with a fantastic open cave. Let's go and explore,' Angus said, but Guy was noncommittal. Mother was arranging a farewell soiree with some of the Bellerby clan, which sounded utterly boring – listening to ladies warbling at the piano and having to make polite conversation. Even she was sucking out all his energy, fussing about the state of his uniform. It had been sent to the laundry to be defumigated and steamed back into shape. She was appalled at the state of his back from the bites and scratching, insisting he bathe in Jeyes fluid and burn his underwear. Now he just wanted to be left alone to sleep off this dreadful hangover of guilt that he was living in comfort while his men were out there. Here he was drinking Pouilly-Fuissé with fresh trout and garden vegetables, raspberries and cream, while they were dining on bully beef and hard biscuits.

The house was looking like a boarding school dorm with a line of beds all made up for the poor sods in convalescence. Part of him envied their chance to gaze out over the hills. The other part of him was wondering what had happened to his company. Had they gone back into the reserve line? Would they be dispersed to make up the numbers in other companies? But most of all, he just ached to see Selma again, ached for a woman's touch, the tenderness of young arms. He was a man with a man's feelings rising in his body. He didn't want to leave this earth without even kissing her lips, without making love. He didn't want to die a virgin.

There were brothels officers could use if they needed to relieve themselves but he was squeamish and didn't want to catch a disease. Battle fatigue stifled any urge in that direction for him, in any case. He just wanted the real thing: the loving of a genuine girl. He was sure Selma felt the same. He'd seen that look in her eyes when he left the forge. She wanted him as much as he wanted her and there wasn't much time. He *had* to see her again.

Right now, he felt like knocking on her cottage door and demanding to take her out for the evening but it was late and not proper. But if he wrote her a note? It would be like old times up on the Ridge, riding out together as if this war had never happened. Surely no one could begrudge him some time alone with his friend, his *girlfriend*? It didn't matter what Mother thought. He was going to follow his heart's desire.

How time flew when you were in fear of your life in battle, and now on this leave it was also fleeing too quickly. How he wanted time to stretch out endlessly. So he must take control, make it happen, or the chance would drift away and he'd be on that ship back to Calais, perhaps never to return . . .

Guy was waiting outside the forge at the end of her afternoon shift. The sun was still high in the sky and he had Jemima saddled up.

'I've told your mother I'm taking you for a picnic,' he said with a grin. 'She doesn't mind.'

'But I mind, dressed like this,' Selma croaked, squirming with pleasure at seeing him. 'Give me five minutes to change.' She dashed to the cottage.

Asa Bartley, meanwhile, glowered at Guy. 'You might think you can get round her mother but I'm another kettle of fish, young man. So don't go a-putting silly ideas in her head. You'll be off tomorrow, she has to live in this village.'

'Mr Bartley, Selma will be treated as any young lady – with the utmost respect.' Guy was blushing at the bluntness of his suggestion.

'That's all right then. Just have her back before dark. I don't want tongues wagging.'

Selma had overheard this exchange on her return. She'd swapped her forge garb for her best cotton dress and her new birthday cardigan.

'Take no notice of him,' she whispered. 'Bye, Dad!'

'We're just going over the Ridge for old times' sake, Mr Bartley. And thank you for letting Selma ride with me.'

'Don't thank me. If it were up to me . . . Nay, but she knows what I think. It's her mother's doing. You have to thank her. She's got a soft heart in these matters.' Asa fobbed them off with a wave of his hand. 'Be off with you and mind what I said. What'll I tell her ladyship if she sends out a search party?'

'Just tell her truth,' said Guy. 'She'll understand,' he lied. His mother would be livid, jealous, but he didn't care. It was *his* leave.

They sat on the top of the Ridge munching cucumber and salmon sandwiches with the crusts cut off. Beside Selma sat a bowl of strawberries and slices of the lightest sponge cake. Guy had given her the perfume and the scent was perfect.

But there was no container in the world big enough to bottle up this afternoon: this surprise, the perfect weather, the warmth of the sun in her face, the view down the valley and Guy's arm round her shoulder. They had shared the ride and strolled and talked and laughed and teased each other.

For as long as she lived, she sensed, this might be one of the best afternoons of her life. It was so romantic, so precious, everything she could have dreamed of, except that this would be the one and only chance for them to be alone. Lady Hester would see to that. This was their moment and Selma was not going to waste a minute of it thinking about the opposition or the war that was keeping them apart. It was far away over the hills in another country.

Guy lay back, smiling, his arms over his head. 'You can't beat Yorkshire on a day like this,' he said. 'Shall we stop the clock, right here, right now?'

'I wish . . .' Selma sighed, lying back, staring at him, smiling.

'What do you wish?' he asked.

'I wish I could speak more like you and dress like a proper lady so when you looked at me you didn't see my dirty fingernails and rough hands.'

'Stop right here!' Guy put his finger on her lips. 'You are perfect to me as you are so don't spoil the moment.' He leaned over and kissed her on the lips, a gentle kiss filled with promise. Then he held her close, crushing his body onto hers with an urgency and hardness he'd never done before. 'Selma, I just want to love you and hold you.'

'I know, I want you too,' she whispered, giving into his passionate feelings. Then Guy's hand moved across her breast and down to her thighs. She felt a flicker of fear and uncertainty. She suddenly had a vision of a stallion serving a mare. There was no shame in that but she felt a stab of fear now. Things were moving too fast, and she wasn't ready yet.

'No! I'm not sure . . .' She turned her head from his embrace, suddenly cold, alert and afraid.

'But, Selma, you've no idea how long I've waited for this moment. I just want us to be as close as a man can be to a woman.' He was groaning, lost in his own passion, but Selma pushed him away.

'You know, it's not right. I promised my dad . . . I'd not bring shame to the family. I'm not ready yet . . . it's too soon.'

'Sorry,' Guy was fumbling with his clothes. 'I didn't think . . . I thought you wanted the same. You see, there's so little time.' His voice was far away as if he was in some dream world of his own. 'I obviously got it all wrong, forgive me.' He sat up, not looking at her, and Selma felt sick.

'It's been so lovely. It's just . . . I'm still young, a bit young for all that,' she tried explaining, hoping he could see her dilemma. She hadn't washed, her underwear was shabby and no one had ever seen her naked. How could she explain without hurting his feelings?

'Of course, I understand. Think nothing of it,' he replied, but he still didn't look at her.

This was terrible, the worst of misunderstandings. He was expecting her to make love, while she was content with a kiss and a cuddle. Suddenly she felt so silly and naïve, raw and unsophisticated, and all she could think to say was, 'I'm not that sort of girl. Just because I'm a blacksmith's daughter doesn't mean I'm easy like that. You are the only lad I've ever kissed. I'm just not ready.' She knew they weren't the right words.

'So you keep saying. Message received and understood,' he snapped.

'Now you are cross with me. I've spoiled everything.'

'Don't be silly, of course not. Just a little misunderstanding, that's all . . . Come on, I promised to get you home before dark. Up we get. You were right to be cautious. It's just I haven't got much time.'

'What do you mean?' she said.

'Well, once I go back to the front, who knows what will happen to me?'

'Oh, please don't say that. You didn't come up here just to have your way with me in case you never got another chance, did you?'

'No, of course not. How could you even think that? But when you're going into battle you take your chances when you can.'

'I see . . . So I'm one of your chances then, am I?' Selma retorted angrily.

'No. I'm not making myself clear.' Guy paused to look down at her, a flash of anger in his eyes.

'No, you're not.' Selma returned a hard look.

'Oh, forget it.'

Guy stormed off with Jemima while Selma followed, sick at heart. They walked down the hill in silence, each lost in their own thoughts.

If only you could have waited a few more days so I could get used to the idea but you pounced on me. She felt the salt of the tears dripping down her cheeks. Tomorrow he'd be gone and probably never speak to her again.

You absolute chump, you've ruined everything now, upset her feelings, rushed things too much. Why couldn't you hold back a second, do a recce, test the waters instead of thinking with your dick?

Guy escorted her back to the cottage, leaving her at the gate. 'Look here,' he spluttered. 'I've messed things up between us, haven't I? Sorry old thing.'

'I'm sorry for not coming up to scratch,' Selma stuttered. 'It's not that I don't feel the same but . . .'

'Say no more. I don't want us to part on bad terms. You will keep on writing? I didn't mean to hurt you.' The thought of not having her letters to look forward too was unbearable.

'Of course I will, and thank you for the lovely picnic. It was very thoughtful and just perfect.' Now she was being polite and that made things even worse. 'Until I spoiled things.'

No one spoke, each desperately trying to end on a hopeful note. Selma reached up and kissed him. 'Safe journey and I will pray for your safe return. Nothing has changed . . . I promise.' She smiled that wonderful dark-eyed flash of mischief. If only it were so, he sighed.

He walked back uphill to Waterloo with this maelstrom of feelings tumbling in his head. Of course he'd taken his chance selfishly. He didn't want her prayers, he wanted her body to possess for a few minutes of oblivion, just in case . . .

147

This need had overridden his common sense, his gentleman's reserve, and he felt ashamed. Now he must face the wrath of his mother and brother, who would feel neglected in favour of another.

The sooner he went back to the front the better. He was out of touch with civilian life here. Time to pack up his troubles in the old kitbag and march.

I shiver even now at the thought of that last meeting. There are some moments in life when you wish you could turn back the clock with the wisdom of hindsight and reshape, rework the past into something more beautiful and romantic, into passionate scenes from a famous film: the beach scene in From Here to Eternity, *which shocked everyone, or Scarlett's surrender to Rhett Butler in* Gone With the Wind.

Youngsters would laugh at our coyness today, this inbuilt sense of what was right and wrong instilled early. I was a country girl and knew the score: how pregnant girls were dealt with if no one supported them. It was the workhouse or the asylum.

I made a choice that afternoon and wondered ever after if that decision set in motion the chain of events that followed. So many years ago and still the pain of pulling his body from mine stings me. If only I'd known what was in store for all of us. First love cuts the deepest, they say, and I've carried that scar all my life.

9

The arrival of the wounded officers brought new life to Waterloo House, the corridors full of tobacco smoke, the piano tinkling at all hours. Angus was busy ministering to their every need, listening to their stories, copying their lingo. Angus was useful and content, despite his disability.

At his insistence Hester had framed his discharge certificate to prove he was no malingerer. Perhaps on one of his bad days, they might unfortunately see for themselves what ailed him and that he was in no fit state to take command. But so far his health was excellent.

The arrival of the men had taken Hester's mind from Guy's sudden departure. They had exchanged words over the Bartley girl but for some reason he didn't dismiss her usual objections.

'I expect you're right, Mother, as usual. Perhaps we're not suited. Perhaps she is too young, but just cut it out,' he'd barked.

He'd never used slang before and he had been downright rude, turning his back on her when she expressed her disappointment that he'd not turned up when Daphne brought over her lovely nieces, Clarice and Marianne, to play tennis.

Now he was back and for once his letters were more cheery, as if he was glad to return to the thick of it.

> For the first time I met a village face in the middle
> of a march on the road to —. In all that mud and
> chaos, would you believe, there was Frank Bartley,
> of all people, riding out with an officer of horse.
> They'd been in the thick of it and he looked
> exhausted but cheerful. Of course we can't fraternise
> but he recognised me and nodded and saluted. He
> wouldn't know that I'd just come back from
> England . . . funny old world. This is the first time
> that it's happened.

What did she want to know that for? What was it to her that he'd met yet another Bartley brat? Guy was changing, growing away from her, hardening. She could see more of Charles in him recently.

Hester looked around her now. It had been a good suggestion of Daphne's to open the house. Its aspect and its gardens and the surroundings lent themselves to healing.

There was no one too hideously deformed or injured or limbless, but some of them shook for no reason at all, calling out in the middle of the night, walking in their sleep. Some took themselves off on long walks and all of them drank like fish. She got to know their families and their sweethearts, nice girls with gracious manners. Why couldn't Guy turn his attention to girls like these, from good homes? Even Angus was taking an interest, flirting with sisters and pretty wives. It was quite endearing except when she thought of his condition.

He'll not make much of a husband, she mused, but we're

all doing our duty now. The war has come to my door and I have answered the call. The house is warm and provisions good, all is as it should be and yet – why do I feel a constant sense of unease? Have I done enough to keep bad fortune at bay? Surely this war can't go on for much longer?

She would never relax her guard until Guy came home safe and for good.

Guy couldn't believe how quickly he had settled back. It was a relief to see his company had not been disbanded. But many of the old faces had vanished and the new raw recruits needed taking in hand and firming up. They needed a constant show of his confidence but at the first stand to, the old familiar twitches and shakes had made him blush with shame. Once over the top, it was strange. There was so much to do just staying alive. Funny how the old panic seemed to evaporate when death was all around. It would be so easy to drift into danger. He couldn't understand how calm he felt, making sure his men were safe and following orders. If he focused on them he felt no fear, if death came, it came. It was long overdue.

What troubled him most was that strange encounter with Frank Bartley on the road north of Peronne, the last person he expected to see. There had been some shelling and a group of horses had taken the brunt of it. He'd seen a lad kneeling down, watching his dead officer's horse trapped under debris, torn by shrapnel and dying. The boy was weeping, wanting someone to put it out of its misery and Guy, being first on the scene, took his pistol and shot it.

'Bloody Hun!' screamed the boy. He stood motionless, pointing his finger in the direction of the guns like a statue, transfixed. That's when Guy recognised him.

'Frank – Frank Bartley?' he whispered.

But the lad wasn't moving, unable to answer or do anything but stare ahead with such hatred in his eyes. He was frozen to the spot, uncomprehending.

'Bartley!' shouted the next officer in charge. 'Move along!'

But still the private didn't move and Guy sensed trouble. Here was a boy at the end of his rope, ready to wander off in a dazed condition and in danger of a serious charge of disobedience. He was quick to his defence.

'If everyone cared for their animals like this chap and showed such fury towards the enemy, we'd soon be winning the war,' Guy offered. 'Young Bartley here . . . he's from my own village and saved my brother's life once. Good man all round but looks to me as if he needs to stand down and rest up.' Guy patted Frank on the shoulder.

Taking his cue from these words, the officer nodded. 'Fall back . . . go and get a cup of tea then,' he ordered. 'Bit of a mouth on him, that one, but you're right, he cares more for the horses than any of the other men. Melody was one of his favourites. This bloody war! No horse can fight the gun in this mud. Their days are numbered, what?'

'You may be right there,' Guy replied. They saluted and rode on as Frank was guided down the line for a rest, still staring back at the horse. How could he tell Selma what he had just witnessed? Frank was in big trouble, of that he was certain.

The chapel harvest supper was in full swing, tables laden with apples, pears, quinces, bowls of blackberries and fresh cream. All the vegetables dug up made a colourful display around the chapel windowsills and the smells were tempting. Sugar had been saved to make jams and chutneys. Bottles of fruit like shining jewels, ruby, gold, amber and amethyst, lined up for the auction later, along with fresh eggs from ducks and hens. There was even a few bowls of hazelnuts and sweet chestnuts. From the mill owner, Mr Best's, walled garden and greenhouse came plums and grapes and other exotics, which Selma eyed with longing.

She loved harvest home and a chance for a bit of a shindig with the Sunday school scholars, the last remnant of her former teaching role. There was talk of cancelling the event this year for lack of produce, and no one was in the mood for jollity, but Pastor Rathbone insisted that the Lord be honoured for His bountiful goodness.

'Seedtime and harvest never faileth and the earth's riches are for us to garner. We have to be grateful,' he had said. 'Trust in His mercy.'

Now, after the service, it was time for the supper and Mam had baked apple pies by the dozen as well as cooking potatoes in the big forge fire until they were golden and crisp. There were jugs of elderberry cordial that would warm the throats for a singsong, and Selma and her Sunday school pupils promised to provide a little entertainment; some sketches that were simple to do but funny.

She had to stay busy so as not to think too much about letting Guy down with her prudishness. How could she have been such a fool as to let him go back to war without showing him how much she loved him?

His letters still came on cue and they tried to pretend she hadn't rebuffed him with gossip and news. He was relieved his batman, Bostock, was still safe but disappointed that he had been assigned to someone else. Then there was the intriguing note that he may have seen her brother on the road one evening. He sounded glad to be back with his men.

'Miss . . . Miss, please is it time for us to do a sketch yet?' said Polly Askew.

'In a minute. Wait while the tables are cleared away and the auction of produce begins,' she replied.

This was when everyone bid against each other for jars and fruit, eggs, hoping to raise a goodly sum towards The Soldiers' and Sailors' Comforts Fund.

Pennies, sixpences, shillings and sometimes if it was a special item, the odd ten shilling note, were bid. Even the leftover pies were offered until all that was left were bags of carrots and parsnips, a moth-eaten cauliflower or two and bags of windfall cooking apples.

Every year it was the same familiar routine, war or no war, and that was a comfort somehow.

Selma borrowed a sheet and a lantern and then dimmed the gaslights from the schoolroom to create a shadow picture behind a white screen.

'Doctor, Doctor, my throat hurts.' Polly Askew went behind the sheet to be examined and Selma opened up her mouth and pulled out a hairbrush, throwing it over the curtain for the audience to see. Out came Polly: 'That feels better.' Off she went and next Jimmy Cowgill stepped up on the platform behind the sheet.

'Doctor, Doctor, my belly aches.'

'Lie down on the bench then,' Selma ordered, bringing out a pair of sheep shears and waving them about so everyone laughed, and then a hammer, banging it down and pulling out a line of mock sausages on a string to more laughter, and then a stick with a string, with which she pretended to sew him.

Jimmy staggered out, rubbing his stomach. 'Eeh, that's better!' he said, and everyone applauded. Selma liked making them laugh. The old ones were always the best. So they managed six little items and then Elvie Best stood up and everyone groaned. Being the mill owner's daughter she had to have her hearing. But after a few bars of her rendition of Bless This House everyone was ready for home.

Things were hotting up again. Guy had watched the great tanks rolling forth like giant iron monsters. It was slow progress but capturing the village of Thiepval inch by inch was a start. They were making headway, the infantry had followed behind in hope of a breakthrough, but the rain and the mud swallowed up any advantage. The Germans were in no mood to retreat so it was stalemate again.

How far away home seemed now. Selma's letters were full of harvest home and frolics. The only harvest he could see was one of torn flesh and bones, chunks of metal and machinery. His new recruits were proving a windy lot and needed chivvying into position in the observation posts.

He had tried to instil the need for foot care and gas mask training, something now routine to the veteran troops, but no one wanted to struggle to cover themselves with those old choking gas masks. He had hated feeling trapped inside such a small place, but now he had the Small Box Respirator, with hose pipes attached, round his chest and a breathing tube and eye mask. This was better, but relatively untested. Worst of all now was the continuous mud and duckboard tracks. It was like wading through thick brown gruel, up to the waist at times, a slow squelching progress and what came rising up out of its bowels was a very hell itself: bodies, helmets, limbs. Sometimes, he felt his spirit just leaching away into a dull stupor of aching cold, a miserable depression that he knew it would be fatal to show.

Did everybody in war have a personal account of courage . . . courage that could be quickly spent up in conditions like these? Day by day he felt his account dwindling; soon he'd be overdrawn if he didn't buck himself up. It was an effort to be the last man seen to duck into a dugout when the shells came over, just to prove to his men he could take it.

Tonight just putting one foot in front of the other was enough as he waded from the forward observation post. He was trying hard to find something to put his weight on, and dusk was approaching. Then he stumbled, losing most of his equipment into this brown soup, fumbling, cursing to high heaven. He ferreted around, trying to retrieve his gas mask bits when he sniffed that old familiar, peppery pineapple smell and saw the green cloud drifting in his direction.

Damn and blast, they'd sent over a gas shell and bits of his SBR were lost in the mire. 'Gas! Gas!' someone was shouting as he struggled away from the nauseating cloud, with so little protection. Terror of its effects forced his limbs into action, pushing through the gloop, but with each laboured breath he was feeling more wretched and floundering, knowing now that one careless slip might cost him his life. Without gas protection, he couldn't last long.

'Come on, sir.' He felt himself manhandled into a dugout tunnel, through the thick gas curtain, but his throat and his eyes were burning. 'Don't scratch your eyes, sir, and keep coughing it out . . .' Someone tied his hands to stop him tearing at his throat.

So was this it, death by stealth in the sodden mud? Not

in some heroic battle but lying in this fetid hole, struggling for breath, gasping at his burning throat, cursing like fury. This was not how it should be.

Someone was bandaging his eyes with a wet cloth to soothe them. He wanted to scream in agony but not a sound could he make as he gasped for air, utterly useless now, a burden to his men. What an example, mud-coated and writhing with not a bloody mark on him!

The journey to the clearing station was like some nightmare. His head felt as if it was going to explode and he cried out, but nothing would come. He had seen enough men die from chlorine gas, a slow lingering death. His chances were slim, even though his exposure was not long enough to kill him outright.

With each stumbling jolt through the trench, coughing and spluttering, he felt the darkness enclosing him. How could he have been so stupid as to lose part of his SBR? What a waste of all his training, to peg out for want of a breathing tube. But as he grew weaker, he sighed in resignation, thinking how death no longer seemed an agony of panic. He had no strength left to fight. It was as if he was in some strange dreamlike journey. So this is it, your time to go. Don't fight it, give in to the bastard, he's bigger than you.

Hester was doing her rounds like the Lady of the Lamp. She liked to see the men tucked in, and the house put to bed. Its smells had changed from garden fragrances to carbolic Lysol, a hospital smell. How eight men could make so much work and smoke so much tobacco and make so much noise was beyond her.

They came in quiet enough, subdued, full of their

ailments but day by day got stronger, noisier and more demanding, with loud patrician voices calling for their batmen and orderlies, and Angus scuttling around at their beck and call.

It was pathetic to see him so grateful, so eager to please but, so far so good, he'd not had a fit in months. Perhaps a miracle was happening and he was returning to normal, but it was still early days, too soon to hope. If he remained stable he would want to go before another army medical tribunal.

She found him pacing up and down the drawing room like an agitated horse, back and forth, on his face a look of anguish.

'What ever is the matter?'

'I don't know. Something is wrong – I can feel it.'

She had spoken too soon. He was working up to one of his turns again.

'Have you taken your pills?'

'Of course, but I can smell pear drops up my nose, a strong smell of pear drops, and my head aches . . . I've been doing so well. I feel sick,' he groaned, looking pale.

'Then go to bed. I'll ask the nurse to come and look at you.' She felt his forehead. 'You're hot. Perhaps you have a fever coming on.'

'Don't fuss . . . I just feel odd. It came on suddenly. One minute I was chatting to old Smithers in the dorm, and then I started to feel sick and shivery. My head feels tight as a drum. I thought I might be in for another bloody turn but this feels different.'

'Angus, don't swear!'

'Sorry, Mother, but I feel so wretched. I wanted to read that spiffing book Smithers lent me, *The Thirty-Nine Steps*.

All the men are talking about it but now my eyes are itchy and sore. My throat hurts. I hope it isn't catching.'

'Just go to bed and it will pass. I'll keep an eye on things.' Hester felt sick seeing his crumpled face. It didn't pay to anticipate, to plan ahead. Just when she thought everything was settled, Angus goes down with an infection – or worse. When was she ever going to find some peace in these wretched times?

Guy had no recollection of how he arrived at the military hospital near Etaples. Only that every breath was agony, that his eyes were bandaged for a while, that his head was bursting like a shell into his ear drum, that he was so weak he couldn't lift his head, that every movement was agony, and his chest was so tight he was sure someone had bound it with wire. Why was he here?

'Had a lucky escape there, Cantrell,' someone said, and he was aware of a brass hat with many pips leaning over him, breathing whisky fumes. 'You'll live.'

Guy tried to speak, but nothing came out. He tried to nod and open his mouth but his lips were burned.

'Got a dose of chlorine gas inside your lungs but you will live to fight again. The doctor says in a couple of months we'll have you storming the barricades. What?'

Guy tried to form a smile but his face was too sore. What was this brigadier on about? Chlorine . . . what chlorine? Then he recalled that dreadful green cloud enveloping him as he stood trapped in the mud. Who had saved him? Bostock? Was he alive? A vision of the mud and him floundering took his breath away and he started to choke with fear. Would he ever walk again? He felt so feeble, so raw and at the mercy of nurses and orderlies and now some

159

officer chivvying him up. Leave me in peace, he sighed and turned to face the wall.

He remembered drifting away from hell on that stretcher, and then he'd heard a voice in his head calling him back, shouting his name. 'Come on, Guy, don't leave us . . . Guy, wake up!' It was Angus's voice. How the blazes! It must have been one of those strange dreams. He wanted to sleep but Angus kept shouting his name. It was as unreal as this man standing over him. But how could Angus know what was happening here except for that connection he'd always felt with his twin brother? It was something he'd never spoken to anybody about, not even Angus.

Had they got the dreaded telegram? Did they know where he was? Would this mean he'd got a Blighty? He hoped not. All he wanted was to be back with his company, back into the fray. This was not how it was meant to be at all. But for the moment he knew he'd not be going further than this iron bed.

Why had he not died on that stretcher like so many others? Nothing made any sense any more.

Selma was at Battys, the Sowerthwaite grocer's shop, queuing patiently in line for the chance of dried fruit. Mother was insistent that she must get her supplies in for Christmas baking, war or not. There would be a plum pudding of sorts and spiced cake, and now that these goods were in short supply Selma was making sure that they got their allowance.

They were lucky in the country to have a ready supply of eggs and milk, fresh fruit and vegetables, and the Bartleys had been packaging eggs down the railway line to Aunty Ruth in Bradford.

Every spare bit of ground was now sprouting leeks, winter cabbages, kale and boxes of chicory salad hidden in sand. The field mushrooms had been good this year and they'd taken to drying them off and stringing them up along with apple rings. Mushroom soup was one of Selma's favourites and she could now make it as well as her mam.

Someone was poring over the *Gazette* in front of her, raking through the casualty lists, every known name commented upon while others in the queue joined in sympathy. A weary acceptance of death and mutilation was creeping over the area, numbing them. It was no longer a shock to hear that so-and-so's brother had 'gone west'.

'Shame about young Cantrell,' said the woman. 'Lady Hester has had her share and no mistake, and now her son.'

Selma went cold. Had she heard right? Guy? She edged closer, trying to sound casual. 'Who was that you just mentioned?' she asked the unknown woman in the black crocheted shawl and pokey bonnet.

The woman turned, eyeing her up and down. 'No one you'd be knowing, love. One of Lady Hester Cantrell's sons.'

'Dead?' Selma asked, her stomach churning .

'Not yet . . . gassed, it says here. I dunno, rich and poor alike, we're all getting our bellyful and no mistake.' The woman turned back to chat to the others about the price of butter. 'Some of them farmers are charging a pretty penny . . .'

Selma stepped back in shock. She couldn't think of anything but this awful news. She wanted to run, to find out if it were true. But she had to stand there at her post for Mam's sake. It was only last week that she'd had a cheery letter from Guy all about these newfangled tanks and how they kept breaking down and were like sitting ducks once the Hun set his big guns on them. Where was he? She must find out. Perhaps she could ask for the right address. Would Lady Hester speak to her? Perhaps Mam might find out from the Women's Institute meeting. Surely they sent officers' parents to their bedsides if things were really bad. That she *did* know.

Oh, Guy . . . all this time you've been ill and I never knew, she thought in anguish. Why has no one said anything to me?

She knew the answer to that one: she didn't exist as far as the Cantrell family were concerned. She was just a village girl he wrote to as a friend. She didn't count in their eyes, but if only they knew how close she felt to him, how much she loved him; her first and only beau. How could they be so cruel as to keep her in ignorance?

But think on, she sighed. They too are anxious, too shocked, too busy making plans to bother with other people. Just be patient, send them a letter of concern. Do things properly and they will respond. Some way or another she would find his address. She was not going to desert him when he needed her most. No one at Waterloo House was going to shut her out.

Come back, Guy! Come back to me . . .

Hester was busy packing for their journey to London. Guy had been transferred to the First London General Hospital for further investigation. He was off the immediate danger list. She'd pulled every official string to find out how he was progressing. She wanted him seen by London chest specialists so anything that might give him a fighting chance of survival could be started.

162

The telegram had come swiftly but Angus had not been shocked. 'It wasn't me, Mother, it was Guy . . . Suddenly I just knew something was wrong with one of us and it wasn't me for a change.'

Sometimes he talked such rot but she humoured him and told him to oversee the houseguests while she was away. Her first priority was Guy. He was going to live. To recover. However long it took. The sooner she visited him the sooner she could take control. Then she'd bring him home for fresh air and rest. He was never going back to those slaughter fields if she had a hand in things.

Hadn't she suffered enough, sacrificed her husband and now her son to this horrible war, and for what? She felt like a tigress protecting her cub. The Cantrell name still had some clout in military circles. All that mattered was his recovery.

Her first instinct was to shoo out all those noisy men from her home to pave the way for Guy's return. He would need peace and quiet and rest, not smoke-filled rooms. There was just so much to think about but first she must open up Charles's flat and live there until Guy was fit to return. She was not going to let him out of her sight until she could see some progress; nothing and no one must interfere with her mission, not least that Bartley brat. How dare she write fishing for his new address?

If he'd wanted her to write he'd have sent a card himself. There were nurses to do that sort of thing. Oh, no, better to prune that little fortune-hunter to size and nip out any further connection for both their sakes.

As the weeks went by Guy felt himself getting stronger, his breathing less laboured. His eyes were healing well and he began to taste a little more food. Mother came every visiting hour, bringing in fresh fruit, newspapers, fussing over him like a baby , anxious to discuss his progress with any man in a white coat.

He knew all the medical terms now, how his larynx and his pharynx were healing. His bronchial pneumonia had peaked and was fading fast. He had survived the crisis that killed so many in the first few days after a gas attack. His general fitness had fought on his side and now he was attempting to walk a little, but the breathlessness was scary.

He had tried to read the books Angus sent and received many well-wishes, but nothing from Selma so far, which hurt him at first until he rationalised that her letters were probably drifting all over France in search of him. His thoughts were like wheels spinning, not gripping anything much. They said the pleurisy would take a long time to heal so no exertions for weeks to come. Was he going to end up like a blob of jelly?

Everyone seemed pleased with his progress, though.

'They thought they might lose you, darling,' his mother said. 'But we Cantrells are made to last . . . But no more soldiering for you, young man. You've done your bit.'

He let her rant on about his war being over. He would be given ample time to recover and then examined for full fitness. He knew the pack drill: a spell of retraining somewhere in England and then patched up to be sent back to France. Experienced officers were too thin on the ground now to be released. The army owned him, no matter what his mother might think, and this war was far from over.

He was not ready to give up on it either. Better to let Mother have her way for a while, nurse him back to fitness if the officials sent him north. He'd have preferred to stay in London, closer to the heart of things, but he was in no fit condition to do anything much now but lie back.

This idleness couldn't last, even if he'd slept better than for ages. What was happening over there? He was desperate for news. Angus was coming down soon. That would be something to look forward to. Mother could be exhausting, with her enthusiasms, her enquiries into his every bowel movement. Angus would be fun and he wanted to thank him for saving his life. For he was certain it was his voice that kept him from drifting away into the final sleep.

Selma walked up to the stables at Waterloo on the pretext that she had carrots and apples for the horses. She had promised Guy she'd make a fuss of old Jemima, who was getting on in years but still had a glint of interest in her eye when she saw her arrive.

'Here you are, old girl . . . Guy sends his love to you. He's getting better, just you wait and see . . . Then he'll come and ride you again over the Ridge.' She was leaning over the stable half-door stroking the velvety skin when Angus walked into the courtyard and announced himself.

'I just came to see Jem. I promised Guy.'

'I know.'

'How's he doing?'

'Fine, Mother's with him in London.'

'Will you be visiting soon?'

'Going down on Friday to relieve her.'

'Will you give him this from the Village . . . it's a greetings card.'

'Of course. Who's it from, did you say?'

Selma blushed. 'All of us who know him. We just wanted

him to know we were thinking about him and hoping he will get well soon.'

It was, of course, an out-and-out lie. Inside the envelope everything was from her, but it was the only way she knew to bypass Hester Cantrell.

Angus wouldn't mind being a postman. He wasn't bothered either way, she sensed. Besides, he owed her one, or at least he owed Frank a favour; a favour he'd never publicly acknowledged. 'I'll see he gets it.'

'So which hospital is it then?' she asked, hoping for a clue, but he sidestepped it neatly.

'Not sure . . . a temporary one . . . in a college, I think. You know they open and close them after each big push . . . He'll be moved again.'

'When do you think he'll be sent back?'

'Not ever, if my mother has anything to do with it. But it's early days, and he has been rather poorly, you know.'

'We guessed as much.'

'Nearly died, but came back from the brink.'

'Praise the Lord!' she answered.

'Just so,' he replied. 'Must get on, things to do. You will shut the gate, won't you, when you leave?' Angus turned away from her.

He was as stuffy and awkward as Guy was warm and casual, but seeing him in the flesh was always a comfort, for it gave her a glimpse of Guy fit and well. He'd taken her card and she was sure he'd deliver it.

If only things could be different between them. Instead of this polite and strained communication Angus could be their ally. All that mattered was that Guy was on the mend and perhaps she might see him again soon and then she would give herself to him body and soul.

166

He was never going through the agonies of the past few months again, no matter what the preachers said. Love between a man and a woman was sacred and holy whether there was a wedding ring or not. Like animals, humans had instincts that shouldn't be denied, and more than ever before Guy needed her. She'd not be letting him down this time, whatever the cost.

Loving someone, she was beginning to understand, had a price. It meant risk and sacrifice. Distance and absence from Guy had made her love even stronger now. He had to know she was praying for his recovery.

10

Waterloo House was looking festive in its red and white and green, all the holly garlands with lush berries decorating the staircase, the Christmas tree freshly cut from the wood by the river, bedecked with tiny candles and baubles. It had snowed just enough to give the grounds a dusting like sugar. Hester was so excited that Guy would be home for Christmas, that both her boys would be by her side to face this first one without Charles. She could hardly wait to see the back of this dreadful year.

Guy was recovered enough to travel north on condition he slept with windows open night and day, no matter what the temperature. His chest was to be checked regularly and his fluid diet maintained to help alleviate the terrible effects of gas on his stomach and lungs.

She had sent Beaven to drive Guy home. He was not to be subjected to a train journey and the germs lurking amongst the dirty soldiers at the crowded stations.

Her officers had all gone home for the season, much to her relief, and she was in no hurry for them to return while Guy was on extended leave. It was going to be wonderful to be together at last. And no expense was being spared to give them the best Christmas they could possibly have.

He was still weak, and his first medical examiner had agreed that he needed extra recovery time.

'They can't mean to send him back,' Hester screamed at Dr Mac when he called in with Angus's prescription.

'He's a lucky young laddie and his body will recover given time,' he offered, seeing her concern.

'But what about the next time? He might not be so lucky.'

'Try not to fret. We'll take care of him, see that we build up his vital organs with rest and fresh air. But mind to keep him away from sickness and he'll be fine. It'll be good for young Angus to have his brother's company. He's been a different chap since you took in those officers, and you all deserve a bit of respite. You've not had far to find your sorrows this year,' said the doctor.

'Yes, well, yes,' Hester dismissed his sympathy. It didn't do to let people see your weakness but she must be charitable, this being the season of goodwill to all men.

'You'll be having a wee soiree?' he continued, fishing for an invitation, no doubt.

'But as you said, there's to be no mixing amongst the village, just in case,' Hester replied, ushering him towards the door. 'I hope you have a good celebration,' she ended, pointing to the door again.

'The same to you all, and may yer lum aye reek!' He laughed.

'I beg your pardon, what language is that?'

'Scots, Lady Hester. May you have good fortune in 1917.'

'Thank you, I will see to it that we do. Nineteen sixteen has not been one of our better years.'

169

Now she must go and wrap presents for the boys: a pair of binoculars each and some leather journals, a smart Thresher and Glenny trench coat for Guy, and a fine Harris tweed hacking jacket for Angus and another of the John Buchan novels he was so fond of. It was as if they were little boys again.

She couldn't wait for the festivities to begin: the Midnight vigil on Christmas Eve, the Belfield soiree at the Brooklyn. They were going to Daphne Bellerby's Boxing Day dinner. There would be lots of lovely gals for the boys to dance with. No more cavorting with local girls. She was going to launch her handsome sons into the county and see what beauties they could ensnare. It was going to be such fun.

Guy slept most of the journey up the Great North Road, though Beaven had to stop to mend punctures; only four in total. Guy had to stay in the car. He was useless at lifting anything and the chill air caught his chest. He was sick of this damn weakness in his lungs. Every exertion was an effort. He had to admit the last medical had been a farce and he'd hardly passed anything, but red tape meant it had to be attended.

As he stared at the brown earth and big skies of Lincolnshire, he felt his excitement mounting. He couldn't wait to see the hills again, the green Dales, where the air was crisp and sharp and tasted of peat.

In his pocket was Selma's last letter, full of concern. Angus had delivered the village card not knowing it was from her alone. No one had let her know of his injuries and he was furious with Mother for being such a stubborn stickler. Now he was coming home, and he was going to see Selma somehow, even if he had to crawl on his hands and knees to get to her.

They stopped at The George in Stamford, to take lunch and freshen up, and to find a garage and fill up the petrol cans just in case there was a shortage further north. Guy just wished he felt stronger to stand up to Mother over her absolute refusal to accept Selma. He feared he was going to have to do something drastic to make her see sense, to break free of her stranglehold over his private life.

Bless her, those first early visits were comforting and gave him the courage to survive the pain, the choking and the weakness. But then she started to give orders to the nurses and he could see the looks of relief after she'd gone. He was embarrassed to be thought of as a mother's boy.

None of them understood the horrors he had endured. How could they imagine what it was like out there, the sufferings of his fellow soldiers? He was ashamed of the treatment he got as a priority, the comforts he was receiving, the privileges that came with rank. He was going home now knowing other poor sods were having to live through another cold winter in the trenches, fingers and toes frozen to the marrow, the threat of gas shells and everyone nailed down until the spring. He had got off lightly, and he knew it wasn't fair.

It was dusk when they approached the High Road leading out from Sowerthwaite to his village and the warmth of his fireside, his eyes straining to see in the darkness with only the side lamps for guidance. A lone figure was trudging uphill, a slow familiar shape of a soldier with his gun slung over his shoulder. His cap was softened to show he had been in action, his shoulders were slumped with tiredness. Probably walking from the station to give his family a

171

wonderful surprise. In the shadows he looked for all the world like the last man at his post, lost in his thoughts, unaware of the motor behind him.

'Stop the car, Beaven!' Guy ordered. Officer or no, no man should have to walk on by as he rolled past in comfort and style. 'Hop in, young man,' he called from the back seat. 'We can take you as far as West Sharland.'

'Thanks, sir,' said the breathless voice as he was saluted. Their eyes met. It was Frank Bartley, last seen in distress on the road from Peronne all those months ago. The boy stared back at him. 'That were a Christian act and no mistake. Thought I'd never get back, I'm that whacked.'

'Do they know you're coming home?' Guy asked.

'No . . . thought I'd give them a surprise, but the boat was slow and the train was that thronged. But I'm here now. I'm much obliged.'

'Don't mention it. Things going well with your company?' He didn't want to ask him how long his leave was, knowing no soldier wanted reminding he'd only have a few days before turning back south again. Leave was leave, no matter if you lived in the back of beyond or close to the Kent coast. Everyone got the same amount.

'I'd like to thank you, sir, for what you did back in France . . . I were in a right state. They gave me two days' rest, just the ticket.'

'Forget it . . . It's another world out there, so don't expect much sympathy from folks here. They haven't a clue.'

'My first leave in years,' Frank sighed as the car drew up to the village square. 'Drop us off here. It'll be good to walk the last few yards. I am much obliged to you, Captain Cantrell. Merry Christmas!'

Guy watched him gathering himself together, his shoulders pushed back, his step brisk. He was going to put on a brave show; they all did. No point in burdening families with all that horror and uncertainty. You pinned on your cheerful smile like the song: 'Pack up your troubles in your old kitbag and smile, smile, smile.'

He whistled the tune to himself. They all did it, made light of things. It was the only way to survive.

Essie was hard at her chores. It was time for the Christmas clean, and while Asa and Selma were busy in the forge, she wanted to get all the brasses polished in the front parlour. They would light a fire and have a singsong round the piano, and perhaps ask a few neighbours in for a bit of Christmas cheer and a slice of her Christmas loaf.

She heard the latch dropping. 'Is that you, love? Kettle's on the hob . . . fetch us a brew,' she shouted into the living room.

'One sugar or two?' Essie froze at the sound of a man's voice. She dropped her polishing rag and ran into the room to see her son standing there, pink-faced, bright eyes shining.

'Oh, Frankland Bartley, you gave me such a fright. I don't believe it! Let me look at you, you devil, you . . . not giving us word. God be praised, what a Christmas gift is this . . . better than anything boxed up. How you've grown! But you look pinched in the face, sit down, sit down! Wait till your dad sees you're home.'

Her son plonked himself on the nearest chair, staring round the room with pleasure. 'I have dreamed of this return . . . It's grand to be back.'

Selma burst through the door in all her muck and glory, her breeches covered in dust and her jumper in holes, a flat cap on her head. She took it all in at once. 'Frank!' she shouted, and he stared back at her in disbelief.

'Look what the wind's blown in,' said Essie, beaming.

'You never told me you'd changed into a boy. God Almighty, Selma, what have they done to you?'

'None of that, son. She's taken your place, as well you know. Don't tease her. She had to change her clothes and her hair for this job but she's still our bonnie lass!'

'Look at you . . . all the way from France. How did you get here?'

'With my own two feet,' Frank laughed. 'I've not grown wings yet, but I'm working on it. It took a train, a boat, another train and an angel on four wheels. I got a lift up the lane. You'll never guess who . . .'

'Go on . . .'

'Captain Cantrell. He stopped for me,' Frank said.

'A right gentleman is that one,' said Essie.

'He's only about the same age as you, you know. You make him sound like an old man,' Selma added.

'Officers are officers, a different breed, but he's a good 'un, a proper gent, and he asked after you all.'

'We'd heard he'd been gassed and in hospital for months. Is he well?'

'I couldn't see in the back but his voice were croaky.'

'He's a friend of your sister. They've been riding out together and sending letters,' Essie couldn't resist.

'Mam!' Selma was blushing.

'Let's get the soup pot warmed up and some bread on the table. You must be starving.'

'I am that. I can't tell you how much I've been looking

174

forward to coming back. But I must warn you, I am in need of a damn good scrub.'

'Language, Frank . . . you're not in the barracks now. We'll get the zinc tub down and boil the kettle. I'll light the copper and boil up your clothes in the morning. This is just champion, an answer to prayer,' said Essie, wanting to hug him.

The door opened and Asa stood smiling at the scene before him. 'Well, I'll be beggared. Who have we here? Bring out the fatted calf, Mam. The prodigal has returned. Tidings of comfort and joy, and no mistake.'

It was going to be the best Christmas ever.

He's home, Selma sighed, but it wasn't her brother she was thinking about. A mile up the road Guy was resting, and somewhere, sometime, they'd meet up again.

Frank had slept solid for nearly two days and nights. No one spoke about Newton. They wanted nothing to spoil his fleeting visit, but she noticed when anyone asked him questions about his war he swiftly changed the subject: 'I'm on holiday. So don't remind me.'

On Christmas Day he refused to go to church with them. 'I'm not much for God-bothering these days,' he said defiantly.

Asa was shocked. 'While you are under my roof, you will honour the season, young man. So put your uniform on.'

Frank stood firm. 'Sorry, Dad, but we have to differ. If I'm old enough to fight and die for my country, I'm old enough to make up my own mind on such matters as what I believe. Nothing that preacher can rant about hellfire and damnation can match what I've seen out there . . . nothing! It don't make sense. You will know what the

175

Germans wear on their belt buckles: "Gott mit uns" or "God with mittens", we say . . . "God with us", it means. He thinks God Almighty is on his side and we think He is on ours but I've seen such things as makes you wonder where the hell He is in no man's land.' Frank began to shake and Selma took his arm.

'Don't take on. It's just that Dad's that proud you're back, he wants to show you off. Just come and sing a few carols with us today. That won't break your principles. It is the season of goodwill to all men.'

'Oh, aye . . . what about the poor beasts of the fields who are out there in the mud with hardly any proper rations, frozen solid. It's so cruel. I hate to see our horses suffer as they do. They've done nothing to deserve all of it. I came home to see you lot, not be paraded round like a dray horse on gala day.'

'You've made your point,' Dad replied, stepping back for once. 'Never let it be said I had to force one of mine into chapel, but I am disappointed.'

Frank ignored him. 'I need to go out for a walk, for some fresh air. I'll stay back and bank up the fire and keep an eye on things for you. I'll sing you a few trench hymns but you won't like them . . . There's this one to the tune of "What a friend we have in Jesus". "When this lowsy war is over, no more soldiering for me . . ."'

'That's enough, son,' said Asa. 'I don't think I want to hear any more of that.'

At chapel his absence was noted. Everyone asked after him at the end of the service and Essie made excuses about him being tired and needing to rest up.

Frank had changed, hardened; his eyes were like flints when he was roused. In some lights he looked an old man hunched by the fire, staring into the flames, lost in his own world.

'Penny for them,' Selma asked.

'Not worth a farthing, love,' he replied. 'I feel strange being back like a visitor in my own house.'

'Are you still with Captain Richards?'

'Nah, he was killed ages ago. I'm driving ammo wagons now.'

'Is that dangerous?'

'What do you think?'

'Does Mam know?'

'Don't say owt, she'll only worry. It's not a bad job, mostly behind the lines. But those bloody howitzers take no prisoners. One stray John Jackson lands on our head and we're mincemeat. It's a wonder there are any horses left. I'd really like to work in the Veterinary Corps, putting them back to health, not taking them out to be blown to bits. Sorry, no more war talk. So what's all this about you and Cantrell? Mam says you've been walking out with him on his last leave.'

'We've been writing to each other for ages but I expect he's busy with Christmas parties and his family. You know his father was lost with Lord Kitchener?'

'I did hear . . . Funny how our paths keep crossing at the Foss, then in France and then him giving me a lift. How's the other one?'

'Angus? He was discharged from the army on medical grounds. He's had bad fits, but he's helping run the officers' hospital at Waterloo House.'

'You don't fancy him, then? They're as alike as two peas.'

'No, not at all. He's quite different, always hanging round the pub – even got banned once – buys drinks but nobody talks to him much.'

'How do you know? Been sneaking into the Hart's Head of a night?'

'Marigold tells me; she misses nothing.'

'She wouldn't, that nosy body,' Frank winked. 'I heard she's one who follows anything in khaki. I hope you're not doing the same.'

'I'm spoken for,' Selma whispered.

'Has he said anything?'

'No, not yet, but we're getting there.'

'Getting where?' Mam was standing in the doorway, listening.

'Nothing,' Selma blushed, feeling hot. Guy had not even called on them yet so why she was saying such things she didn't know. It was tempting fate.

'What do you mean, you gave Frank Bartley a lift? Didn't I tell you not to mix with riffraff? Now look at you, with a cold, and if that goes on your chest . . . Honestly, Guy, you are so wayward. Beaven has told me it was you who made him stop.'

'I need some fresh air, not to sit mollycoddled round the fire like an invalid in a Bath chair. I'm fine, nothing a brisk walk won't cure.'

'Then Angus will go with you, just in case.'

'Just in case of what? A chap needs his own company once in a while, don't you think? You've paraded me round the drawing rooms of Sowerthwaite, introduced me to all the bright young things you could muster. Don't think I don't know what you're up to, and no, I haven't seen one to compare with Miss Bartley for intelligence, and good looks. And yes, I will be calling on her when I am feeling a bit stronger, but a tour around the grounds is all I can manage at the moment. Please don't go on about it; my mind is made up. I shall call on her father and make my intentions plain.'

'Guy, I absolutely forbid it! You are not even of age. It is a ridiculous idea. You will embarrass us all. There is no bridge between them and us. It is impossible. I think you've taken leave of your senses again. If only your father was here to guide,' Hester fretted.

'I'm not ungrateful for all you've done. But life is short, and who knows what will happen next? I just want to be able to enjoy what little time is left with Selma by my side. Father would understand, after all, he didn't exactly live like a monk when he was away, did he?'

'How dare you say such things? I don't want to hear another word on the matter. If you go ahead with this ridiculous scheme, I shall take legal measures: nothing will come to you until you are thirty and I will change my will. You will not defy me in this!'

'Be that as it may, Mother, I've got my officer's pay . . .'

'That won't go far to pay your present mess bills and equipment. I had hoped you would grow out of such fancies.'

'And you tried to make sure Selma wouldn't write to me, refusing to give her my address or my news. She found out in a shop queue. I feel ashamed of you.'

'I'm doing this for the best. Believe me, you'll thank me one day.' His mother was standing face to face with him, practically spitting out the words.

Guy stormed out, banging the drawing-room door. His chest was feeling tight now, and then he started to cough and couldn't stop.

* * *

Hester took one look at him and ordered him to bed, hot and flustered at his defiance. She was concerned about his fitness, as was Dr Mac when he examined him later. There was no way Guy was going to be fit to return after Christmas. Getting worked up about a village girl wasn't going to help either.

She'd put him in the front guest room with the best view and the large open window where the westerly could blow in and give him fresh air. She plumped up his pillows to keep him upright, relieved that his cold would confine him to bed again and out of harm's way. And Selma's.

Having her sons to herself was the best Yuletide present, and if she could get him to stay longer, she might persuade him to stop this infatuation with the blacksmith's daughter. What on earth had she got to offer him? She was peasant stock – good childbearing hips, no doubt, but he was still too young to be making love to girls. He was still her little boy and needed protecting.

Time to do another tidy-up herself. She was getting used to doing menial jobs now that the daily help had left. That it should come to this. Opening Angus's room door she thought she saw Guy admiring himself in the long dressing mirror, in his full uniform. 'You should be in bed!' she ordered and then realised she'd just taken Guy a jug of water. There was a roar of laughter. 'Fooled you!' Angus grinned under the cap.

'Oh, you gave me a fright! What on earth are you dressed up like that for?'

'Just trying it on for size. Don't I look the part? No one could tell the difference.'

'Take it off at once. It's just been cleaned. Honestly, Angus,

180

you are the limit, and poor Guy coughing up his guts across the corridor . . .'

'Makes you think, though, doesn't it? I mean, no one would know, would they, if I turned up as Guy Cantrell. Even our initials are the same.'

'Turn up where?' she asked, puzzled.

'At his medical . . . to give him a few more weeks' grace with you. He's bound to be put on light duties or retraining. I could cover for him. What a hoot! No one can tell us apart.'

'Angus, you would be impersonating another officer. Guy would never allow it. You don't know a thing about his men or his duties out there. It's a ridiculous idea. Take those clothes off at once. Where do you think up such schemes?' Hester could feel her heart thudding.

'Don't you think it makes some sense . . . just for a week or two? I've been right for months. Anyone can see Guy needs more time.'

'The army will see to that and extend his convalescence.'

'But this way I get a proper shot at the job. I'm sick of seeing silly schoolboys in the OTC going off to war when I should be out there. This way I can have my turn and prove that I'm as good as anybody.'

'Is this what it's all about, jealousy of your brother? Oh, grow up and face the facts. You are a liability now.'

'No I'm not and I know how you want Guy to be home to rest here. This way we both get what we want.'

'Guy would never agree,' said Hester, hesitating now.

'Why should he know? We could say I'd gone to London on business. Dr Mac will give a report saying Guy's too sick to attend, and by the time he recovers I'll be back and we can swap back. Then I can tell him the truth, if needs be.'

'It would never work. It's madness. We can't take risks with his work.'

'What work? He'd not last a week in the trenches or on a route march. Think of this as saving his life, letting him off the hook a while longer. Don't I deserve a chance to prove myself?'

'But, Angus, your fits could return at any time and you need your medication.'

'I'll make sure I take plenty of supplies. I'll be fine. Think about it. We could all benefit, especially Guy. He's my twin; I don't want harm to come to him, not after Father.'

'Just take the uniform off. Give me time to think this over. If I thought you could pull it off for a week or so . . . Guy would be court-martialled if it ever came to light.'

'It won't be for that long . . . it'll be such fun,' Angus grinned.

'War isn't *fun*. Surely you realise that by now?' Hester said, seeing the mischief sparkling in his eyes.

Angus was crazy to think up such a scheme, but it did have a few points in its favour. It would give her time to nurture and time to keep Guy away from making a fool of himself with that girl. This way he would not be able to leave the house. She could keep him safe from the guns and the trenches before another injury could claim her precious son. Only Angus would be taking a risk too . . . brave boy. He so wanted to be part of the fighting army. She could see where desperation, boredom, envy and curiosity had brought him to such a suggestion, but it was still madness, a crazy madness.

'Isn't it time you saw to the horses? Put Guy's uniform away or, better still, give it to me. I think we'd better forget this conversation. He won't have to face another medical for a week or two yet.'

'But, Mother, it makes sense . . .'

'No matter. I'll have that uniform now.' Then she paused, suddenly having another idea. 'On the other hand, there is one thing you can do for me. Something just as important, but not a word to Guy. This is between you, me and the wallpaper.'

Essie, Asa and Selma were standing on the windy platform at Sowerthwaite, the chill breeze whipping their heavy skirts and coats, tearing at their hats. Frank was standing shivering, waiting for the down train to Leeds to carry him back to barracks and back on to France. None of them felt like speaking. His leave had been so short and over so soon.

Parting was not for cowards, but Essie insisted they all come to wave him off. 'You've got some brass in your pocket, son,' said Asa, palming some coins into his hand with a wink.

'Thanks, Dad.'

'You will write to us, keep us in touch?' said Essie, holding him in a vicelike grip of loving concern and trying not to cry.

'I'll do my best.' Her son's grey eyes were blank and unreadable. So much left unsaid between them. Now he looked so young and yet old at the same time, her heart trembled that this might be the last time ever. But she pushed away the thought. 'Oh, Frank, you will be careful? No more trouble, promise? Just do your job.'

'Don't worry, Mam, I'll be a good wheelbarrow and go wherever I'm pushed, I promise,' he laughed, and gave Selma a brotherly bear hug. 'Next time I come home, I expect you to be a Lady Muck in your finery, a captain's girl, no less. Who would have thought it?'

'Don't be daft . . .'

'I hear he's still not very well and confined to bed. So Mrs Beck says, who does for them. He's got a right bad chest from the gas and he won't be going back for a while. So plenty of time convalescing,' Essie winked, and they all laughed.

'That's officers for you. They live by different rules, but Cantrell is a good one, as I said. He stood up for me when I was in a spot of bother.'

'You never said!' Selma snapped.

'You never asked . . . Here's the train coming. Cheery-bye . . . no tears. So don't hang about,' Frank shouted, picking up his rifle and his kitbag. 'I'll not be looking back.' And he walked away from them.

'Oh, son . . .' Essie's tears began to flow.

'Come on, owd lass.' Asa guided her through the gate but Selma stood defiant.

'What did he mean, Guy helping him out of bother?'

'Come on, do what you're told for once. The fire will need banking up, so it's back to work,' her father ordered.

When they got back to the forge Essie saw the familiar outline of Jemima and the uniformed figure of Guy Cantrell waiting outside the closed forge door, pacing up and down.

'I've been waiting ages . . . Where have you been?' he barked to Asa, ignoring the women by his side.

'Seeing off our son to war at the station,' Essie replied, puzzled by the coolness of his attitude, surprised he was out of bed.

'Jemima has lost a shoe again. I don't think you put the

last one on properly, Mr Bartley. Lady Hester is not best pleased.'

Asa hurried to set up his stall and Selma hung back to talk to Guy.

He raised his cap. 'Good afternoon, Miss Bartley.'

'Are you feeling better? We heard you were confined to bed.'

'As you see, I'm fine. This village makes gossip where there is none,' he replied. 'You had a pleasant Christmas, I gather? So your brother has gone. I shan't be far behind.'

There was an awkward pause as the two youngsters stared at each other, Selma hesitant and Guy looking decidedly uneasy. 'I'll leave Jemima in your capable hands, Miss Bartley. Beaven will call back later for her. Must dash, things to do . . .' Then he turned on his heel, striding back towards Waterloo House without a backward glance.

Her daughter had been publicly put down and ignored as if she were a stranger and Essie didn't know what to make of this sudden coolness. 'Well, that was a turn-up,' she said, looking to Asa and trying not to see Selma's distress.

'That's gentry folk for you: pick you up and drop you like a hot coals.'

Both of them watched Selma backing out of the forge into the cottage to change. Essie made to go after her but Asa held her back.

'Let her be a few moments. She'll need to deal with this by herself, but I've seen another side to that young man, Essie. Officer or no, that were a right poor show of manners and no mistake.'

* * *

185

Stunned by the sight of Guy on his high horse, peering down at her as if she was a nobody, Selma couldn't believe what had just happened. She'd never seen him so cold and imperious so cruel. He knew what it was like to say farewell to a soldier on leave. He knew Dad's shoeing was the best in the district. He had looked down his nose at them as if they were dirt. It didn't make sense.

They hadn't quarrelled, yet he hadn't made an effort to visit them and he looked pretty fit to her as he'd marched up that hill at a fair lick, not like the invalid they had been led to believe he was.

Was it all a pack of lies? Was he just avoiding her? No mention of their letter writing. She so wanted to know how he had helped Frank. He'd only mentioned he'd seen him in passing.

She sat on her bed trying to make sense of this puzzle; all those little dreams of courtship, country rides and walking out in public, crumpled and crushed by this one encounter. He had snubbed her in front of her parents. You couldn't get a better message than that, she sighed, and felt sick.

What had happened to change his attitude? Was it something she'd said? Was it something she had done or not done? Was it because of Frank, being a lowly private? Was it because Lady Hester had made her views plain or was he just being cruel to be kind, knowing there was no future in this romance?

In one fell blow he'd dashed all her hopes, cutting off their friendship as if it were of no importance. But one thing was certain: Captain Cantrell had had a change of heart.

Her virtue was safe. Obviously he had found romance

elsewhere with one of his own kind over Christmas. She was now surplus to requirements, yesterday's girl, and it hurt. Oh, how it hurt to be dumped from the warmth of their friendship and intimacy into this wintry chill of rejection.

11

Guy looked out of the window across the park up to the hills. The chill wind in his face was bracing. Storm clouds were darkening the sky and snow feathers floated down. He had slept for days and sensed his pleurisy was lifting. He could breathe deeper and there was a surge of energy in his limbs. Today he would get up and ride down to the forge to see Selma at long last. He had been confined to bed for so much of his leave, fit for nothing. But all the rest was at last having an effect.

He slid out of bed and put on his thick dressing gown and tweed slippers. The fire was crackling and soon Angus would be bringing in breakfast, but Guy wanted to be up and doing. Being an invalid was tedious and he must make an effort to strengthen his muscles. It worried him that he was forgetting the war, getting too used to civilian life, to a soft bed and hot meals. It wasn't right to be lounging about when others were soldiering on.

Angus and his mother were in the hallway chatting, but their conversation stopped when he reached the bottom of the stairs.

'Guy, what are you doing out of bed?' Hester demanded.

'Time to be stretching my legs. I'm getting cabin fever up there.'

'But it's too soon. You need to rest up today.'

'I *need* some fresh air.'

'Look outside . . . it's snowing hard. The sky is full of lead. No point in undoing all my good work by catching a chill.'

'Stop fussing, you two. Anyone would think you wanted me to stay sick.' Guy realised it wasn't in fact too far from the truth; they liked to have him where they could see him. 'I have to go back to my company soon.'

'Plenty of time for that in due course.' Mother dismissed his arguments.

'But I've got another medical in a week. They'll only put me on light duties so I'll still be somewhere in this country. You'll be sick of the sight of me. I'm starving – is that bacon and eggs I can smell?'

'Light gruel and egg flip for you,' Angus laughed. 'You know what the doctor said.'

'Bugger Dr Mac! I need bacon and eggs, toast and jam. How can I build up my strength on slops?'

'He's definitely better, Mother.' Angus was grinning. 'He'll make that medical board yet.'

'Any letters?'

Guy could see Mother hesitating. 'Just bills and postcards, nothing for you to worry about . . . Oh, and Daphne said Caroline Pointer was much taken with you at the Boxing Day dinner.'

'Don't start that again. I'm going to see Selma today. Beaven can drive me there.'

'Not in this weather he won't, and you're not fit to walk there and back. Plenty of time for that later.'

'You've changed your tune,' Guy said suspiciously. 'Shall I ask her for tea then?'

'Just let's enjoy being together before the house fills up with invalids again. Another day or two won't do any harm, will it? I thought we could try that new card game Captain Fielding taught us after supper.'

What could he do but give in? They were right. It was foul outside and going to get worse. No sense in getting a chill. And he didn't want Selma trekking in these conditions. Better to wait a few more days and build up his strength. He wanted Selma to see him strong, not as an invalid. Bless his mother, for all her fussing she did have his best interests at heart.

Hester was woken by a terrible dream. She was on a station platform waiting for a train, a train that took aeons to arrive and when it did it steamed past, leaving her stranded. She could see Charles, Angus and Guy hanging out of the window, frantically waving. But she couldn't get on the train as it flashed past and when she ran out of the station to find Beaven and the car, he was driving away down the road without her. So she went to the omnibus park. But she had no handbag and so no taxi fare. She woke in a sweat.

How had she ever considered going along with Angus's crazy scheme? It was ridiculous to hold on to Guy and prevent him doing his duty. Besides, Angus would be a hindrance and a liability to fighting men. He had neither the stamina nor the experience. He might put them all in danger. It was a silly childish dream, well meant but unworthy of her ever having discussed it. And as for the other business with the Bartley girl . . . It was for Guy's own good. Angus had done what Guy would never do without

190

a murmur. Guy was too soft-hearted to let her down. His brother had done it at a stroke, so at least the uniform had come in useful there.

It was good to see Guy on the mend. The Yorkshire Dales air was working its magic and filling his lungs with goodness. She must not be selfish. In the morning she would make Angus know the score and insist he forget his silly notion. He would still be useful when they opened the home again. He must learn to be content doing his service here, learning the ropes of running Waterloo House. There would be plenty to keep him occupied.

She tried to get back to sleep but her mind was racing. She rose early in the winter light. The sky after the heavy snow was pigeon grey, the beautiful scene outside her window delightful, the boughs arched over with frozen snow making her pause. She peered through the frost to admire the view and saw a line of footsteps making their way out of the long drive.

It was too early for any deliveries and the footprints were going in the direction of the gate. Curious. Smiling, she opened Guy's door and heard him snoring; his window was wide open with flakes of snow on the windowsill. She peered in at Angus – her precious boys all under one roof – but his bed was empty . Her heart jumped a beat.

The dressing table was emptied of its silver jars, combs and brushes. The room looked quite bare. Then she rushed into Guy's old bedroom at the back. His uniform was gone, his shoes, his new trench coat. Everything he had arrived with had gone. Angus had taken his uniform: a quiet but public exit. Unbeknown to her, making no farewells, he'd switched his life for Guy's and now it was too late to follow him. She knew he'd gone for the milk train at six o'clock.

While she was dreaming that awful dream he'd sneaked off.

Hester fell on his bed in a faint. *What am I going to tell Guy? God in heaven, what have we done?*

The snow fell over the village for days on end until the lanes were blocked with drifts swirling into sculptures like ice-cream cones, decorating the roofs with icicle daggers, stonewalls hidden under drifts and sheep trapped on the moors. Everyone was slithering over the cobbles until Asa Bartley threw out cinders and ash, helping Prospect Row to cut itself out of the drifts. There would be no farm work, so Selma had even more time to brood over Guy's desertion as she helped her father mend kettle spouts, fire irons, bucket handles and fenders; all the small jobs saved for bad weather. At least she stayed warm in the forge. Mam popped in with mugs full of hot broth.

'What a blow-in. This will last for days, will this,' commented Asa.

'I wish it would thaw,' Selma sighed, feeling trapped.

'Don't you go wishing your life away. The nights are pulling out now so be glad of that.'

Selma felt a restlessness she'd never known before. For as far back as she could recall Guy's letters were a fixed point in her week. She'd loved taking herself off to a quiet corner to read them over and over before replying. Now he had gone without a by-your-leave. He had been seen by one of the farmers' wives before the big snow at Sowerthwaite station, getting into a first-class carriage. No one missed anything in West Sharland. What had gone wrong? It must be her fault. She was obviously too common and looked a mess.

Don't keep going over it again, she chided herself, trying to concentrate on the job in hand. But her mind was spinning and she dropped the mould and it banged and caught her on the shin. Asa yelled at her and she burst into tears. It was not the sting or the shock of the bruise, it was pure misery overcoming her. Misery bound up tight inside so no one could see.

'Go home and get yourself sorted. I can't have you here as useless as a treacle glove! Pull yourself together and stop moping over that boy. It wasn't meant to be. Better to find out now than later. There's plenty of chapel boys who would give you their last pear drop if you put on a dress and smiled in their direction. Go on. Tell your mam to make use of you . . . you're no use to me here!'

She limped back, looking up at the purple sky, full of flakes, sick of the stuff, too old for sledging. If only she'd stayed on at school. Marigold Plimmer was taking classes now.

Then she noticed the feathery flakes getting bigger. Fat flakes were wet flakes, and that meant a thaw was on its way. About time, she sighed. Then she might get on with life without constantly looking across from the forge door in case Guy was riding past. Perhaps he'd only gone for some training. He might come home again.

'Where's Angus?' said Guy.

'He's gone to London on business for me. He has to earn his keep,' said Hester, bustling around him. 'I hope you're not thinking of getting up in this chill.'

'He never said he was going away. He could have posted some letters for me. It's been nearly a week.'

'Angus does have his own life to lead,' Hester snapped back.

193

'I'm not criticising, just surprised. It was very sudden, and in this weather . . . when's he coming back?'

'Just concentrate on getting yourself better. I'm not your brother's keeper. He left you his Buchans to read. You enjoy them in peace and quiet, because it won't last. I expect we will have some more young men to contend with soon.'

'I'm looking forward to meeting them,' Guy replied.

'Well, then, just rest and relax. Everything is under control,' Hester answered, knowing everything was far from it. She'd not slept in a week, wondering where Angus was, praying he would write to put her mind at rest. But not a word from him. She was frantic with worry.

What a foolhardy scheme this was, and now having to keep Guy out of the picture was so important. He must know nothing of this or he would be implicated. As the days went on, she felt more and more this was all her doing. She should have whipped the uniform away when she saw how Angus's fevered brain was working, instead of colluding with him in that little charade at the forge.

If Guy took himself down to the village and called on the Bartleys the game would be up and the girl would know that it couldn't possibly have been him on the horse. *You went too far there, Hester, a big mistake . . . Guy would never forgive you if he knew. Time enough to put matters right when Gus returns, and this whole silly prank will be behind us. Guy will understand, perhaps even see the funny side of it all.*

Not many men had a willing double to stand in for them. But she still felt uneasy that Angus had been away so long with not a word. He was going too far keeping her in the dark, and them both having to deceive his brother.

Guy was getting stronger by the day and she couldn't

keep him confined to bed for much longer. If he was up and about he'd start looking for his uniform, asking awkward questions, and she would be put in the most appalling position.

Oh, where are you, Angus? Why don't you write? What can I do to hold time still?

Then, she had the most devilish of ideas. Desperate times called for desperate measures. There was one way she could keep them all safe for the time being Had she got the courage to do it?

You are your father's daughter, she thought, drawing herself up to her full height. We were bred to take control. What you are about to do will be done for the good of everyone. Surely a mother has to do what she can to save her sons when they are in danger?

Guy was enjoying *The Thirty-Nine Steps*. He'd missed reading at the front. The novel rattled along at a good pace, but his eyes were heavy and blurred from reading too long. He rose to go to the bathroom and the room spun round as if he were going to faint. So he aimed at the commode and crawled back into bed. Mother was right. It was too soon. There had been a few turns lately and he seemed to be sleeping more than his fair share.

It felt as if the whole world was drifting away from him into a warm haze of contentment, where nothing mattered much. The fact that Angus hadn't returned, the fact that Mother was looking strained and had cancelled having more of the wounded officers to convalesce, the fact that he had missed his medical board didn't seem to matter much. No doubt Dr Mac had confirmed his relapse, as he couldn't be absent without leave. It was all drifting away and he was relieved not to have to think about anything much. His appetite had faded, and he existed on malted milky drinks that Mother sent up at regular intervals to keep up his strength, such as it was.

Funny how he didn't know which day of the week it was or what was happening in the outside world. The snow had thawed and the sky was blue. He could see snowdrops out on the one part of the lawn that wasn't dug up, purple crocuses feeling their way under the trees. It was almost spring. How time was flying by. Even his befuddled brain knew he'd been home for months but was no stronger for it. Sometimes it was hard to recall even who he was.

Perhaps it was the long-term effects of the gas but something nagged at him. He'd been doing so well but it was time to call in Dr Mackenzie again. His breathing was better, and his throat; only his legs were all wobbly with lack of use. He must make an effort to exercise them or they wouldn't obey him at all.

God forgive me for what I am doing, prayed Hester, on her knees in the empty church. But what else could she do? Where did she turn now? Burning in her pocket was a letter from Angus at long last. With what relief she had seen his scrawly handwriting on the envelope, and then with what horror had she read its contents.

Dear Mother,

All has gone to plan, in fact better than I first thought. I turned up at the board and went through the usual checks, which thankfully I'm very familiar with from times past. Passed fit with flying colours. In fact, they remarked on how well I'd recovered from the gas. But they decided, in their wisdom, to send me for some special retraining – near Selby, would you believe – a hush-hush training camp for special trench warfare manoeuvres. The officers here are a ripping lot. I find myself back at school with a load of chaps going through the basics, mostly wounded; such a jolly bunch, no problems. Yes, I am fine and enjoying myself so much. I'm going to stick around until the next leave comes up.

I hope Guy forgives me but I deserve a crack at the target, a chance to be another 'Give 'em hell' Cantrell. Don't be angry. Guy can have more time with you. I want to make you both proud of me. It really is for the best, you know. I'm learning so much here. I have all Guy's old letters and photos to study so if they send me overseas I know who is who in his company. But the chances are that I'll be deployed to another company altogether, in a place where no one will know which Cantrell they're getting. So don't worry, after weeks of practice I can do Guy's signature like my own. If I don't recognise anyone I'll just say it was the shell shock and my memory is a bit wobbly.

Don't be cross with me for doing this off my own bat. I guessed you might change your mind and forbid it but what's done is done now.

Your loving son,

G. A. C. Cantrell.

P.S. You should have given us different initials!

So he wasn't coming back. He was taking his chance and he was in dire trouble if found out. You stupid, stupid boy, she cried, don't you realise what we've done and now I am

197

drugging my own son to keep him from knowing the truth, taking risks with his health all for the good of the Cantrell name. Your father would be appalled, after all we have endured, that it has come to this.

'Is everything all right, Lady Hester?' whispered the timid voice of Violet Hunt, the vicar's wife. She had come to strip the altar cloth before Lent began. 'Did I disturb you?'

'No, I'm just leaving. I just wanted a little time . . .' She rose up from her knees, feeling foolish. Violet meant well but she was always prying.

'I have disturbed you, I'm sorry. Is Guy recovered and safe?'

'Yes, he is safe, he's gone back, but Gus hasn't been himself lately – you know how it is?'

'Perhaps it'll all be over this year. It has been so long and everyone is weary for peace. There are so many empty pews,' Violet sighed, looking around her.

Hester couldn't wait to escape from those grey anxious eyes. If you only knew what I'd done, she thought, you wouldn't be so sympathetic. I am a monster but I am the mother of sons and I am doing it for the best and now it's all going wrong – so very wrong.

There was one thing she could put right, though. Better to tell the truth and be damned than to keep on deceiving Guy, tricking him. But she was afraid of the look in his eye if she told him about Angus. Better to let things be for the moment. When the time was right she would confess all and put herself at his mercy. While there was still a chance that Angus might return, better to keep quiet.

'Master Angus, it's Dr Mac to see you . . . He said that you'd sent a note and the mistress is out; shall I be letting him up to your room?'

Why was Mrs Beck calling him Angus? He was so befuddled, forgetting in one of his better moments he'd sent a note to Mill House for the doctor to call. He wanted to check that his absence from the medical board had been covered.

'Send him up,' he said, trying to straighten himself as well as his head. He smelled unwashed, wearing Angus's striped pyjamas, for some reason, and in his bedroom too. How had he got there? He couldn't recall any of it. It didn't make sense.

'Now then, young man, you look a bit worse for wear. No more turns?'

Turns? What was he talking about?

'I'm not getting any stronger . . . I feel so weak and wobbly.'

'You must have taken too much sedation. I told Lady Hester to go easy on the bottle. Have you been drinking?' Out came the instruments from his bag.

'Chance would be a fine thing, but I'm not on any medication. Can you sound out my chest?'

'Certainly, but it's always been your strong point.' He put the stethoscope on Guy's chest and then lifted it up and looked at him. 'Have you had a cold? It's a bit rattly. Did Captain Guy get off before the snow?' he asked.

'Angus went off to London. We've not seen sight nor sound of him since.'

The doctor was looking at him strangely. 'We *are* off today, aren't we? I think I'd better have a word with your mother. She must let me sort out the right dosage in future.'

'You did inform them about my medical board examination?' Guy asked. 'The one I didn't make because of all this.'

'I'm sorry, I'm not with you, old chap. What medical?'

'Oh, come on, Dr Mackenzie. I've been on extended leave for months. This can't go on, but these fuzzy heads of mine . . .'

'Look, Angus, you're not making sense!'

'And you're not making any sense either. This is *Guy* Cantrell you're speaking to, not Angus. I sent for you to check me over.'

'I see.' The doctor got up from the bed and looked around him. 'I *did* get a note from Guy, but the captain left weeks ago. And this is Angus's room – are you playing games with me? You are a wee bit old for pranks and I'm a busy man.'

'For goodness' sake, I'm Guy, not Angus. Can't you tell, man?'

'There's only one way to find out,' said the doctor, leaning over him and yanking up his blond forelock to reveal his forehead.

'Blood and sand, you're right! There's no scar! I'm sorry, Captain Cantrell, I don't understand. We all thought—'

'Never mind what you thought,' Guy interrupted him, 'what the bloody hell is going on? Can someone please explain?'

'I'm awfully sorry, I haven't a clue, but I'm sure your mother will have an answer. The sooner you're up and moving about, the better, in my opinion. Back to the open window for you and some fresh air. We'll get you back on your feet in no time. If I didn't know better I'd say you were in drink but your breath doesn't smell.' He was shining his torch into Guy's eyes. 'So that's it! You have a habit?'

'What habit?'

'Oh, don't come the innocent with me. Lots of lads have recourse to it to steady their nerves; no one wants a windy officer,' said the doctor. 'I don't blame you, but you can get addicted to the stuff. Starts off with a wee tincture or two and then the effect wears off, so it's a little bit more. You shouldn't be doing it, not with your condition. It can affect the heart.'

'Talk sense, man!' Guy could feel his head busting with frustration.

'Your pupils are distended. You've been taking laudanum or some other potion; all the signs are there.'

'I beg your pardon, I've never resorted to such drugs in my life.'

'Don't deny it, laddie. There's no shame in it after what you've been through. Stronger men than you have cracked under the strain. We all need our crutches. Mine happens to be a bottle of good malt whisky.' The doctor smiled, patting his arm indulgently as if he were a naughty child. 'Better to be out in the open about it and then we can help you through it. No use trying to cover it up.'

Guy was furious. 'I don't know where you got this notion, but I've been bedridden for weeks. This is outrageous.'

'I'm sorry you can't see it my way, but you're on a path to destruction if you carry on this caper. No wonder you can't walk in a straight line. You have to face your fears, not hide from them in a bottle. I took you to be a hero, Guy, not a coward,' said the doctor, peering over his spectacles at him.

'Get out of here! I won't have you making such accusations. Get out!'

'I'm going, laddie, but you know where I am if you need me. There's no shame in asking for help. Admission is the first step to recovery. Chew on that if you can. I'll not be troubling you further.'

Guy sank back exhausted. What on earth was going on? And why did they all think that he had left? Why had Dr Mac thought he was Angus, and what was his mother's part in all this? A sudden sickening dread filled his stomach and he rushed to retch into the chamber pot. It was a chilling thought, which wouldn't go away.

Hester heard Guy struggling down the stairs, the noise of his cursing having woken her from her dozing in the drawing room. 'Come and sit by the fire,' she ordered, but he was staring at her with eyes aflame.

'What the hell do you think you're playing at?' he demanded.

She looked up, surprised. 'Guy?'

'Or should you be calling me, Angus, like Mrs Beck does every time I see her, or like Dr Mac did when he called in this afternoon?'

'You called in Mackenzie?'

'Tell me what's going on. What have you done to me over these past weeks? What have you popped in my nightcap?'

She was stunned by his outburst.

'Don't deny it.'

Hester remained silent, not knowing what to say. 'I just wanted you to sleep well,' she offered eventually.

'You wanted me out of the way. Where is Angus?'

'In London, as I said,' she replied, feeling her heart thumping.

'Then, fetch me my uniform. I'm leaving!' Guy replied.

'No, darling, not yet. You're not well enough.'

'Stop mollycoddling me! Where is my bloody uniform? It's not in my room. For goodness' sake, Mother, tell me the truth!'

202

'Shush, someone will hear!'

'I don't care if the whole wide world hears what's been going on.'

Hester felt her legs trembling with fear as she began to speak. 'Now, you had better stay calm. No point in getting worked up,' she said, rising slowly to go to the writing bureau, handing him Angus's letters with shaking hands. 'Angus thought he was helping, so don't judge him too harshly.'

Guy read the contents, and his face hardened like granite, his eyes like steel. His breathing came in rasps. 'He's taken my place, by God! Impersonating an officer – has he no sense? It's a capital offence . . . he must be out of his mind to play such a trick. I must get back and see if I can limit the damage—'

She interrupted him in full flow. 'You can't. He's being transferred to France. He passed his training. He'll be out there within days. It's too late.' She handed him another letter. Guy read it and threw it across the room. The look he gave her chilled her to the very core.

'And as for you, how could you collude in this? How could you let him do this? I don't know what to say . . . My own mother giving me doping medicine. Knowing full well . . . Now Dr Mac thinks I have an addiction!'

'I'm sorry.' She couldn't look at him.

'Sorry is not enough. Do you know what you've done? Do you know what you might have set in motion? If Angus has a bad turn, if he fails his men . . . you will be responsible for the deaths of scores of brave soldiers under his command.'

'You must understand, I didn't go along with it. I went to tell him to give me the uniform back but he'd already gone. He so desperately wants to prove himself. He's your twin – he wants to be like you in every way.'

'Lord give me strength! We have separate lives to live. He is not me, nor I him. You must have encouraged him in some way. I'll never forgive you for what you've done . . . never!' He stormed out of the drawing room.

Hester ran after him. 'If you have an ounce of family honour, please don't give him away now. Don't disgrace your father's name. What he did was wrong and what I've done to you was too, but you are my sons. I would never do anything to hurt my boys. You're my life's work, my world, don't give him away.' Hester was pleading with him, holding her hands out in supplication, but he turned his back on her.

'I don't believe this,' he shouted, shaking with rage. 'How can your love be so sick and manipulating as to control and trap me into colluding with your schemes? I don't know what to say to you. You're not the mother I knew or respected. What in hell did you hope to gain from letting him take my place?'

'He promised it was just for a week or two to give you time to recover fully,' she pleaded, hoping he would understand. 'We thought—'

'We thought . . . we thought. What about me? Don't you think I had a right to my own life? Do you think I like being stuck here, an invalid, cosseted in this cocoon until I thought I was going mad? I'm going to tell Selma all about this.' He made for the front door.

'You can't, Guy. If you do, you will kill your brother. He took his leave of her weeks ago. It was all very formal, and there's been no contact since. I did it for the best.' She saw the look of pure hatred flashing over his face.

204

'You selfish old woman! You let him go to her; I can only imagine what was said. You disgust me. Get out of my sight!'

'My son, my darling, I did it for the best. A mother has an instinct for these things.'

'Go away. Leave me alone and don't even attempt to give me food or drink again. From this moment on I will feed myself.'

Hester turned back. The room was a blur, her tears blinding her.

What on earth have I done?

Guy paced around the walled garden, trying to collect his jumbled thoughts. He felt sick and trembly at the horror of what he had just heard, and with the certain knowledge that he too was trapped in this web of deceit. If he denounced his brother, what would happen to Angus?

Of course he understood why Angus would want to have a go, but to take such a risk . . . His brother had no idea what life was really like in France. What if he was put in command too soon, taken straight up to the front without preparation? How would he face the shelling and bombardments when most raw recruits, officers or no, were terrified out of their wits? His nerves wouldn't hold up for long before he made a show of himself and funked it. Officers who were weak or bullies often never made it out of no man's land. Sometimes they were found with bullets in their backs; British bullets.

I have to go out there and rescue him was Guy's first instinct, but common sense told him that it was already hopeless. He would have to wait until he came back, then no one would know the truth. It would be ages before he was entitled to another home leave.

He sat on a stone bench, feeling his world had collapsed. What would Father have said? How could he rescue the family honour? As for his mother, he didn't understand, but one thing was certain: he was not going to stay another night with her. He didn't trust her not to lock his door. This farcical charade of making out to the servants that he was Angus must stop. He'd never felt so alone, and to know she'd cut him off from Selma . . .

But she was right. If he contacted her who knew where it might end? A village has a thousand eyes. There would be speculation that might jeopardise his brother's life. He mustn't take that risk.

For all his stupidity, Angus was his other half. But just now this knowledge hung heavy. He was feeling peculiar, his body and mind in a mess after weeks of medication he had never truly needed.

There was only one person now to whom he could turn, but to do that he must play along with these wiles a little longer, change his clothes, pack a bag, throw himself on the mercy of Dr Mackenzie. He must admit an addiction and ask him for the name of a private clinic where he could shake the dust of Waterloo House off his feet. Mother could stew in her own juices with this one. He would not wait until Angus saw fit to resume his rightful place.

He looked up at the old house with sadness. He'd been so happy here as a boy, but now it was tainted with deceit and treachery. Let Mother rattle round in it on her own for a while and feel the icy chill of both their absence. She had brought it all on herself. He wouldn't trust her word again.

Now it was time to find a new billet. Guy Cantrell didn't exist here, nor Angus neither. Time to find a new name, a new identity and a new hiding place. He would not be taking his brother's name. He wanted to go far away from this cursed place to lick his wounds. If your family betrays you who else can you trust?

Hester paced from room to room, opening and shutting doors, tidying up any sign of clutter, busying herself as if there was a purpose to each day. Dr Mac's words were ringing in her ears.

'Of course, that young man will do fine now he's got a place where there is no temptation. They'll clear out his system with hot baths and a good regime of sleep and exercise. It's a pity he was allowed to get in such a state in the first place, Lady Hester. Going through the withdrawal of sedation is never easy, but he is young and determined to get back on the straight and narrow. But what is puzzling me is how he got hold of the stuff in the first place. It's not as if I'm in the habit of prescribing such drugs. But then I suppose plenty of apothecary shops will deliver to the door. Did you not notice anything?'

Hester shrugged. 'The youth of today are a law unto themselves,' she replied, not looking him in the face.

'But what also puzzles me is how Captain Guy is still here, but everyone was calling him Master Angus. He was troubled by that too. I had to look for the scar to convince myself that it was the case. Where is Angus? Is he well?'

'Well enough, the last letter I had from London,' she lied.

'I'm glad to hear it. For a moment there I thought he might have played some silly prank on the lot of us. If I thought that were so I would have to report it to the authorities, knowing what I do about his condition.'

'I'm sure you would, but enough of this nonsense. Angus is safe in London. Guy is in the clinic. You will have his address?' she asked, anxious to put things right.

'Ha-ha! Patient confidentiality, your ladyship . . . I'm not at liberty to reveal that without his permission.'

'Oh, come now, I'm his mother!' she snapped.

The man paused, peering at her over his spectacles. 'Aye . . . I know that but I'm still wondering just what your part has been in all this chicanery, Lady Hester.'

'How dare you suggest that I would be a party to—'

'Of course not,' he said hurriedly. 'What mother would do such a terrible thing to her boys? It's a mystery to me.' He paused by the door. 'By the bye, there's a new chappie in Sowerthwaite taking up medical practice, looking to build up his list of patients. I was just wondering under the circumstances whether it wouldn't be better for you to consult him in the future. He would be grateful for your patronage.'

The cheek of that jumped-up Scot, to dismiss her as if she was some common or garden patient. He knew . . . he had guessed the shameful knowledge that tore at her gut.

You have to live with this for the rest of your life.

At least Angus didn't know what misery she was suffering. He was too busy fulfilling his dream. Perhaps he would make them proud. Perhaps it was his time to shine. That was a crumb of comfort to cling on to.

For the moment she didn't want to see anyone but found solace in her garden. Her back was aching, her fingers numb from weeding and hoeing down the rows. She was safe from

208

scrutiny behind the high walls. There would be no letters from Guy. He wanted no contact.

Here among the evergreen shrubbery she could weep for all her mistakes, the stupid deception. There was no one to blame but herself. But a colonel's wife knew that tactical retreat wasn't a battle lost . . . not yet. If only one could turn the clock back . . . How was she ever going to put things right?

If only. If only I'd known what was going on at this time, but Waterloo House was its own kingdom behind those great stone walls and imposing gates No one called there without an invitation and in the following months Lady Hester went a bit peculiar, as they said back then. She kept herself to herself, cut herself off from the village so no one knew about the estrangement. Except that Master Angus had gone away for treatment at some spa, it was rumoured, and Captain Guy was back at the front fully recovered from his wounds.

I received no letters but had long since given up hope of any coming. Frank was not much of a scribbler so news was always stale. That year, 1917, was hard for the troops and the losses continued. Little did we know what a terrible burden was to drop on us from a great height, which even now is clouded in mystery, lost in the archives of military records; a burden to tear out the very roots of my life in West Sharland, breaking the bonds of our family for ever, an event that has cast a shadow down each generation in turn.

12

There was great excitement in the village about the annual Easter egg rolling. The pace egg decorating and the chapel ramble to Bolton Abbey. Spring had come in all its glory to the Dales, with its yellow and white hedgerows, the garlicky smell of ramsons, the chatter of birdsong and promise of sunshine. Everything was fresh, and a crop of new lambs were in the fields like little blobs of cotton wool, all reminding Selma that life went on, no matter how miserable she was feeling inside.

She must get used to the idea of Guy having gone from her life. Marigold kept asking her to go dancing at the farm hops but she just wasn't in the mood to get her feet trodden on by boys in hobnail boots. Her parents wouldn't approve anyway; they would rather she joined the choir and keep with her own chapel crowd.

'You're such a spoilsport, not going to the cinema or dancing. Where's the fun in singing hymns all day? You're fast becoming an old maid, stuck in that forge or on a chapel pew,' Marigold protested.

'All in good time. I'm too young for romancing.'

'You'd better get your skates on. There won't be many lads left at the rate they're being killed off,' came the reply. Marigold could be a right little ray of sunshine sometimes, Selma thought.

'I'll let you marry my brother, Jack, if you like. He's still going strong, although I don't fancy your Frank much. He's too young for me. He'd smell of horse manure all day. Have you heard from him?'

'Not for a while, he's driving ammunition wagons – or at least he was.' They'd not heard a word in weeks.

'What about your fancy captain? We didn't see him at your door over Christmas.'

'Leave it off, Marie, it's none of your business. Come and give me a hand with bringing in this coal.'

'Not on your life with my clean dress on. How you can stand such a mucky job . . . ? Be seeing you.'

Not if I can help it, Selma muttered, having decided weeks ago she didn't care overmuch for Marigold Plimmer any more. She had the knack of making her feel small, poured cold water over her ideas, and Jack was a foul-mouthed oaf who always pinched her bottom when no one was looking. She'd rather stay single for ever than marry him.

She was still scuttling up the delivery of coal when the postman passed by, wheeling his bike. He took off his cap.

'I think you'd better go home, love. There's bad news, I fear, come to your door.'

Selma rubbed her hands on her breeches and made for the back gate. She could hear Mam's wailing and stood there, not wanting to go in. If she didn't go in, she wouldn't hear and it wouldn't be real.

Steeling herself, Selma entered the house. The dreaded

211

brown envelope was lying on the floor, and Mam was sobbing, while Dad was reading the notice over and over again.

He looked up. 'News travels fast, then. It just says Frank died of wounds two weeks ago and is buried at Poperinge. Where the heck is that?'

No one spoke; they just sat huddled together.

'I'll make another brew,' Selma offered eventually, too shocked to cry.

'I am sick of brews. I need something stronger,' sobbed Essie, fishing in her pocket for a hanky.

'Now, don't start that caper. Just give her another cup with plenty of sugar in it. Two sons gone west . . . two sons given up to the war machine, and for what? This scrap of paper that tells you nothing.'

'We'll get more letters soon like we did when Newton died. They were a right comfort to us. We'll soon know more. His officer will write like Captain Guy used to do,' Selma suggested, but her mother wasn't listening.

'I thought he was safe with them horses. They don't put them in the front line, do they?'

'I'm not sure it's not that sort of battle these days,' Dad replied gravely. 'No one is safe from big guns or carrying ammunition up to the front. Close the curtains, lass, and lock the door. Let's keep it to ourselves awhile longer.'

'I can't seem to see straight,' Mam cried, rubbing her eyes. 'It's the shock. You think everything is going well and then the Lord beats us on the back with the stick. What is it He's playing at?'

Mam wasn't making much sense, rocking backwards and forwards hugging herself. Selma didn't know what to say to either of them. There were just the three of them now.

212

She couldn't bear the stuffy atmosphere, this fug of gloom. How could Frank be gone? It was only a few months since he had been here, playing the fool, helping in the forge each morning. Now there was no one left to take over her place. She would be stuck for life in that forge like a prisoner in chains.

It was a selfish thought but she couldn't help it. It wasn't fair. Why them? Why Frank? What had he done to deserve to die but be daft enough to serve his King and Country? She wanted to stamp her feet like a child, but then she saw her mother's tear-stained face, her crumpled shoulders. Time to see to the living, not the dead.

Essie was relieved to see the prompt obituary in the *Gazette* with a picture of Frank in his army uniform.

Driver Frankland Walter Bartley of the Field Artillery, has died of wounds in action on the Western front, the official intimation to that effect being received by Mr and Mrs Asa Bartley who reside at Forge Cottage, Prospect Row in West Sharland.

Driver Bartley is their second son to be lost in France. He joined the army at 17 and has seen a great deal of service in the war front. He was connected to West Sharland chapel and was held in high esteem by all who knew him. Much sympathy is felt for his parents and his sister on this sad loss.

The windowsills were filled with fresh flowers, late daffodils and gillyflowers from neighbours. Their tins were filled with other people's baking, their mantelpiece filled with condolences. Essie was trying to pick up the threads and keep going, but it was hard with no proper details of where her son fell. Then, when letters began to appear with army post-marks, she felt a relief. What made her pick up one before the rest, she'd never know, but it was a bulky package and looked official. This would be a comfort to read, a solace in this terrible time.

She read the first typed letter, not understanding a single word. Something about a court martial and only the barest sentences, a note from a padre called the Reverend Thomas Mulcaster.

It is a burden for me to have to send what must be your son's last letter home after the sentence of death was confirmed on him. In his final hours he rose to the very bravest conduct in facing his punishment with dignity, cheerfulness and courage. I will pray for you at this difficult time . . .

The letter slipped from her hand. A sentence of death? Not Frank, never in this world! Had he murdered someone? Inside the package was another letter, in a familiar scrawl. Her hands were shaking as she read each sentence slowly, over and over, trying to take it in.

Dear Mam and Dad,
    I hope by now you will have had the news. I have to leave you all. I am sorry for the trouble I will cause. My hand is shaking as I write goodbye.
    Tomorrow I will have to face the firing squad. You see, I did something very wrong. I was provoked but what I did carries a heavy penalty.
    I am not alone now, the padre is with me tonight,

but I should like you to write to him back as he has
been very kind. I leave all my effects to you. Will
you give Selma my best wishes for the future and
half the monies owing to me. Please don't tell her
what I did. I am sorry for bringing shame to your
door this way.

If only her captain would have spoke up for me
things might have been different. There were other
things against me. It must be God's will that I must go.

This is all I can put down on paper. I never were
one for words.

God bless and protect you all.

Your loving son,

Frankland

Essie gripped the paper, shoving her fist in her mouth to stop
the screams. What did this mean? The burden of all this
terrible knowledge ripped through her. She staggered over to
the slop sink and vomited just as Asa came through the door.

He stared at her ashen face. 'What's brought this on?' he
said in his usual gruff voice.

She pointed to the letter. 'Read them, both of them, but
not a word to Selma. What's been going on? What did he do
to deserve this? And what was all that about Captain Guy?'

Hester saw the obituary in the newspaper and shuddered;
another village boy lost but not how it appeared in print.
She combed another account of his demise. It was sitting
on her lap, a letter that gave her no pleasure to read. She
would make sure no other person would ever read it if
she was to keep the family name intact.

Dearest Mother,

This has been the toughest month yet, but I'm still holding up and I've got a splendid troop of men.

Just thought I'd warn you. News has no doubt broken about Frank Bartley and how he died, but I'm afraid it wasn't quite as simple as you will have been told. There was a court martial. He went berserk over some incident in a stable, so I heard. Of course, he was charged and sent to a field general court. He pleaded guilty, the evidence was overwhelming and not a very edifying occasion. But the poor chap tried to stick up for himself saying there was provocation, but without a prisoner's friend to defend him he made a pig's ear of it.

All soldiers know the score. Disobedience is next to mutiny and carries the death penalty so his fate was sealed, but he had the cheek to ask Guy to be a character witness, to give a testimonial. I was out at the front and didn't really know the form on this one so I didn't attend.

How was I to give him a good word? Hardly knew the chap and neither did Guy, except through his sister and that wasn't relevant, so I wrote what I could, not realising that written testimony didn't count. Not that anyone could make any difference, his own field service record told volumes. There were several serious charges of indiscipline, giving cheek to superiors, etc.

There's no stomach for this behaviour when everyone has to muck in under terrible conditions. So he was sentenced according to the military law and details of each firing squad goes down the line as a warning. I'm told he made a good end.

Hope the truth doesn't get round the village. It's the family I feel sorry for. Gives us all a bad name.

I don't think you'd better tell Guy. Tell him I'm due leave soon, if I can wangle it. He deserves every medal he can get, surviving so long in this hellhole. It's no cakewalk. I have trouble sleeping and the conditions defy description, but I am fine.

All the best,

G.A.C.

PS. I could do with more socks and lice powder.

Oh, Angus, you stupid boy, Hester sighed. How could you forget it was the Bartley boys who saved your life all those years ago? How could you imagine that word won't get out about how a Cantrell refused to speak up for one of his villagers?

How immature his letters sounded. Strangely, he was enjoying this war in his own irresponsible way. Did he never stop to think of anyone but himself? It was time he was told a truth or two to put him straight. At least a mother could chastise her son, make him see that this charade must end sooner rather than later. Hadn't he done enough damage?

They were quiet in the forge on market day, no horseshoes to repair, no visitors. It ought to have been their busiest of times with sheep shears to be reground and sharpened and fettled but there was nothing doing.

'It's like a Sunday,' Selma mumbled.

'Aye, but happen it'll come busy while dinner,' said her father.

But even then there was no business to speak of, and she was sent home.

Since the memorial service in the chapel they'd not had many visitors, nobody was speaking to them much. Her mother had stopped going to the women's meeting, preferring to sit at home, pinched and shrunken, lost in her own thoughts.

Something was amiss. Whenever Selma tried to mention Frank, she was rebuffed. 'Not now . . . not yet,' was the only reply. Selma didn't understand why this mourning was so different from Newton's, this wall of silence growing around them.

Then funny things started happening. There was a small fire in the back garden shed, dog muck was chucked outside their door. One morning she went up to the allotment to pick peas and found all the pea sticks removed and the peas trampled on as if a flock of sheep had been let loose onto their plot. Who's doing this? she asked, but met with only a shrug of shoulders and blank faces from her parents.

Then one day, when she was on the bus to Sowerthwaite, she sensed people were pointing her out, nudging each other and eyeing her up in a strange way. Marigold Plimmer passed her by in the street with her nose in the air. Where once there was warmth in the chapel greetings, now there was a distinct coolness.

One Sunday afternoon she found she had no pupils in her class. So she went to the superintendent to ask where they all were and he shook his head. 'It's summer, the children are tempted by the open fields. Perhaps we can start your class up again in the autumn.' But other classes were full.

What have I done? she thought, sniffing her armpits to see if she smelled ripe. Had she grown horns overnight? There was no solace to be had at home. Sadness lingered there like smoke, hovering up on the ceiling. Her parents began to look old and grey and lost for words, bickering at each other over silly things and whispering in corners where once they all talked and laughed round the kitchen table.

One evening, when they heard a brick thrown into the parlour window, cracking it from end to end, she'd jumped up in anger. 'What *is* going on?' she demanded. 'I'm fed up of all this silence and nobody speaking to us. Are we in trouble? Do we owe money?'

Her dad was quick to reassure her. 'Nowt like that, love, just a little disagreement . . . local politics and such stuff . . .'

'But our window's been smashed.'

'Just little toerags up to mischief. Think nothing of it,' he replied, but his eyes told another story. 'Put the kettle on. Your mam and me have something to tell you.'

'We're leaving the smithy?' she asked, sensing change in the air.

'Now why should I do that?' He smiled a weary smile. 'How would you like to go and visit Aunty Ruth and Uncle Sam in Bradford?'

'For a holiday?'

'Not exactly. A bit of a longer visit, a change of scene,' her mother added.

'You mean leave Forge Cottage? But Dad needs me.'

'Not at the moment while things are quiet. Do you good, a change of air, and you could be helpful to Aunty Ruth in the house. You've allus wanted to travel.'

'But not to Bradford. To London . . . to York, maybe, but *Bradford*? Do I have to go?'

'We think it is for the best. You've been a good help in the forge, but it's not suitable for you in the long term . . .' Her mother's hands were shaking as she sipped her tea.

'Am I not good enough?'

'Nay, lass, it's not that. Things are just different now. We may have to sell up if it doesn't improve. So time to take stock. You know you'll be very welcome with Sam and Ruth. They make a big fuss of you.'

'I don't want to go. I'm needed here if there's trouble.'

'We think it best,' they said in unison.

'Why? What have I done to be sent away?' She felt the tears coming that had been threatening.

'Look, Selma, you have done nowt wrong, none of us has. Always remember that. It's just . . . things are difficult and I'd rather you had a break from this village, full of gossips and small minds. Go and get a chance to better yourself.' Asa wasn't looking her in the eye and his voice was trembling. 'Just you trust in a father's good intention and a mother's love. We'll manage fine, the two of us. Besides, lots of girls your age go into the city for jobs.'

'I'm not a town girl, never have been!' she snapped back.

'So now's your chance to sample it.'

'You're not listening, I don't want to,' she insisted.

'You'll do as you're told, lass. We mean what we say. It's for your own good. One day perhaps you'll understand the reasons. We only want what's best for you, love.'

There was no standing against the two of them when they held a united front. One of them she might have wheedled into submission, but not two of them. Even she knew when she was defeated. There was no gainsaying this decision. For whatever reason, they wanted her out of the way. Things were going on that she didn't understand but one way or another she would find out.

*　*　*

Guy woke from his dozing, hearing that blessed tune going round and round in his head of 'If You Were the Only Girl in the World.'

Someone in the day room had been playing it repeatedly: a young second lieutenant from the dragoons, who sat rocking back and forth listening to it, his ear right up into the trumpet of the phonograph. It was pitiable to see a young boy so shaken up with nerves.

Guy was getting used to being in Holt Park sanatorium, with its nauseous smells and noisy neighbours, who screamed and shouted for their mothers in the night. There were old men wandering up and down with their pyjama bottoms round their ankles, confused eyes like glassy pebbles.

At least he was in the private wing. God help the poor souls locked up in the open wards. He had his own room overlooking the park. It was not far from the town of Warrington; a barracklike institution with turrets and battlements, trying to pretend it was anything other than a lunatic asylum.

He was miles away from Yorkshire, but not far from smoking chimneys and factory smells, with a tincture of open sea in the air when the wind was keen.

Dr Mac had arranged his stay discreetly, admitting Guy under the name of Charles West. They'd cleaned him out of all the poison in his system after some terrible nights of nightmares when he shook and grew agitated. They put him into a deep sleep and he woke up feeling more like his old self, his mind back on its tram tracks. He felt a fraud for taking up a bed but reasoned he was better off here, having time to think what to do next.

When he thought of Waterloo he thought only of the misery of the past year since his father had drowned at sea.

221

The thought that he was a deserter shook him to his core. If Angus was exposed as an impostor, the charge would be laid at his own door for aiding and abetting the deception. Once he knew the truth he must be considered to be in collusion with them both, however unwillingly. What on earth could he do to salvage the situation?

He'd kept thinking about his brother. Where was he? They'd never been out of touch for so long. He couldn't get the thought out of his mind that he might not see Angus again. That fear kept him awake at night until he had no choice but to write to him, sending the letter to be forwarded on. It could do no harm. He needed to express his fears and feelings on paper; his fury at being deceived, his anger at Angus for taking such risks with his own health, with the other men. He had lost him his chance of happiness with Selma. Angus was weak to let Mother twist him to suit her own purposes. He wanted him to know what a monster she had become, how cloying her love was for them. He never wanted to see her again.

'She has ruined both our lives by allowing you to play this part. I'm writing this to bring you to your senses. For God's sake come home before it is all too late!' he advised.

In the middle of the night he unlocked his leather writing case and poured his heart onto the page, addressed his own name in blocked letters and took it to the lodge gate first thing for the porter to post.

Only then could he sit in the sunshine and relax. It felt like a weight off his mind. Angus would read it and understand the concern behind his harsh words.

Guy didn't mind having no visitors. It gave him time to read and build his strength in the gymnasium. He made up a foursome in the evenings with three officers who were in Holt Park for drying out, but somehow they always managed to produce some spirit out of the air or their hot-water bottles. They had accepted his own story and shared some of their hairy experiences in that offhand, black-humoured way he knew so well. They were all old men before their time, who had found the last dregs of their courage in the bottom of one glass too many.

Two weeks into the cure, Elliot-Jones was reading yesterday's *Times* and bemoaning the huge casualty lists.

'Another crop for the worms!' he sighed. 'A place called Passchendaele . . . anyone know it? Another push in the mud gone wrong . . . a pile of chaps from your neck of the woods, West.' He flung across the pages in Guy's direction.

Guy was in no mind to read them but the instinct of curiosity got the better of him; great columns of names and one or two he recognised until one name hit him between the eyes. Captain Guy Arthur Charles Cantrell, missing presumed killed. He started to shake and dropped the paper.

'You all right? Someone you know bought it?' said Britton.

Guy couldn't speak. Shock froze his tongue, his mouth went dry and the sides of his vision blurred into a cloud. Somehow he nodded.

'Sorry, old chap . . . bad luck,' offered Anderson, getting out of his chair to fetch his stick. 'What you need is a tot of brandy to steady the nerves.' Out of his stick handle he produced a secret silver flask. 'Get that down you . . . You never get used to it. How they expect us to go back into that shithole without this ammunition, buggers me. Go and have a bawl out in private. The doc says it helps, but I haven't got a tear left.'

Guy stumbled back to his room and stared out of the

window in disbelief. Angus was dead. He knew what missing in action meant: blown up, lost in no man's land with no body parts recognisable, sunk deep into the mud, trodden underfoot to emerge, months later, as rotten meat.

Angus, you got your desperate glory, he sobbed. How can you not exist any more? The ties that had bound them in the womb were severed. How had he not known? Why had he not felt his death as Angus had felt his wounds?

Now he was utterly alone in the world. If Angus had stayed safe, would it have been his *own* fate? Why did he keep on living?

He hugged this pain and, later, the guilty realisation that he was free. Guy Cantrell no longer existed. Only Charles West did, free to go where he pleased, no longer a condemned man.

He couldn't re-enlist – that was courting danger – but there were other services to join. Let no man say he was deserting his country. As a voluntary patient he was free to walk away now any time. Liverpool wasn't far away. What better place than a seaport to disappear, to reinvent himself?

How could he be thinking such selfish thoughts when his brother lay broken? How could he harden his heart against his grieving mother? But that was for her to live with, not him. He would write to Dr Mackenzie to find out more details and give him warning that he would not return as Angus.

He was an orphan now, full of guilt that he had written such a harsh letter to his twin. From now on he would look after himself, live as he pleased, beholden to no one, not even Selma.

She could be no more than a figure of his innocent imagination. This had to be a clean break from all that had gone before: no looking back at what might have been. There was nothing for him in West Sharland now but bad memories and there was no law that said he must return.

He would mourn his brother in private. For the rest of his life he'd feel the loss of him but Angus died while living out his dream. Charles West must take his chance and live for both of them now.

3

NEW WORLDS
1917–1932

There's a long, long trail a-winding
Into the land of my dreams,
Where nightingales are singing
And a white moon beams.

Stoddart King, 1915

13

It took all of Hester's strength to dig the hole in the back of the rose border, a hole deep enough to bury Angus's bloodstained uniform that had arrived in a brown paper parcel like laundry from Sowerthwaite two weeks after the telegram.

She'd opened the paper not knowing the horrors within. The stench of mud. stale blood and dampness made her gag with revulsion. This was no living smell but the smell of death and destruction.

His trousers and jacket were ripped apart, a sleeve and leg were missing. Mercifully no underclothes were returned but she could imagine the state of him torn apart, bleeding. Her mind refused to accept the rest.

His cap was caked in sweat and blood, battered. How dare they send such obscenities to a family? Only his belt and his badge remained intact. She would keep them and the letters, of course.

My beautiful sons destroyed, she wept, not wanting to look at the crumpled uniform but unable to tear her eyes from it; Guy's uniform in fact. There was no glory in battle only bloodied broken limbs, sinews and such suffering. Were his thoughts of her when he lay dying in the mud? Now she was putting the cloth to rot in the soil where it belonged. She would plant roses one day in this sacred spot.

She sat nursing his wallet, cradling it, looking into the dark earth. With Angus's terrible loss at the Second Battle of Ypres in the summer of 1917 any hope of a reconciliation with Guy was now out of the question. With her son's death, her whole family had collapsed into the Passchendaele mud.

Angus's personal effects had been sent on ahead with a letter of condolence from his senior officer. In her worst moments, she'd pondered if her own letter, giving him a dressing down and telling him that Guy had disappeared, might have contributed to his recklessness.

She knew the officer's words off by heart.

Dear Lady Cantrell
    It is never easy to write such a letter to the parent of a fellow officer but you will want to know that your son was a first-rate chap, a crack shot and a good example to his men. I never saw him flinch before them. He knew his duty and volunteered to go on a listening patrol in no man's land. It takes a special courage to face the unknown in the darkness but Guy was determined to see it through no matter what the danger. The loss of such a courageous young man is grievous to all of us. Conditions were too treacherous for us to retrieve his remains but some of his men went out later to bring him back.
    He was given a military funeral with a firing party and buried with honour. I hope this is of comfort to you and his twin brother . . .

The padre who wrote had also sent some last effects among which was Guy's own letter from his hospital, pulling no punches in its anger and frustration, telling him exactly what had gone on at Waterloo House, and how he was now incarcerated at Holt Park under an assumed name. The humiliation of that visit still stung in her chest like a knife wound.

She had taken the first train to Warrington and a cab to the hospital, full of hope that the dreadful news she was to impart would somehow bring Guy back to his senses. The two of them must stand together, prop each other up in grief, find strength to face the future. She was even prepared not to blow his cover and call him by his new name.

She stood in the secretarial office and gave her name and demanded to see her son immediately. The slip of a secretary eyed her up and down, told her to take a seat and shouted to a porter.

'Have we got a West in the private wing? His grandma's come to see him!'

Hester blushed at this insult. *Do I look so old?* There was no mirror to confirm that she had aged over the past year, stooped by grief, drained by wearing black. She waited until her back ached on the hard chair.

A doctor came rushing past and stopped. 'Ah, hah! You want young West? Done a bunk, dear lady, walked out one fine morning and not been seen since. Had some bad news in the family and thought it was time he got back into the fray . . . Sorry to disappoint but he was doing well enough. Would you like a cup of tea? You look as if you need it.'

How could he be so cheery, so unconcerned, so brisk and she so woebegone by this news? Somehow Guy had found out about Angus. Perhaps he was on his way back home? She must turn round and retrace her journey to Sharland in the hope that he was returning as she dearly hoped. She had waited weeks for his return. Now he was lost too and it was all her fault.

There was another fear haunting her sleep. Had they both driven Angus over the top? Had Guy's angry letter and her complaint made him even more reckless? She hoped Guy never found out that his brother had let down Frank Bartley. Now so many doubts and fears raged in her brain like a fever. She had to know.

She had to know that Angus was safe somewhere. How could he leave this life without saying goodbye? What if he thought she was still angry at him? He needed to know she begged his forgiveness if her letter had disturbed him enough to try to prove himself again. Had he sought his own death in this way? No, no! That was too terrible to think about. She had to know he was safe. There was only one way to find out.

Hester waited until it was dark before she quietly drew up the car in Sowerthwaite town square. She walked through the side streets, early for her appointment. She didn't want anyone to know her business in such a dismal area of the market town. Her face was veiled in black netting, her beaver coat hung shapeless over her shrunken shoulders. She drifted like a black shadow between the high stone walls of the alley leading to Bond End Row.

The recommendation had come accidentally from her cleaner who'd heard that Martha Holbeck gave a good reading of cards and was well used in the district.

Hester fought her conscience for nights on end. Was this witchcraft at work? But what was the harm in giving it a chance? Only desperation would have driven her to this. She had to know.

The back door was open and she was to wait on a wooden chair at the kitchen table until a bell rang. The note's instructions had been precise. There would be other clients inside not wishing to be seen.

The paraffin lamp glimmered on the scrubbed deal table. At least the woman kept a clean house. It was a plain working man's cottage and she thought of the famous song 'Keep the Home Fires Burning'.

The sadness of her own loss choked her for a second and she wanted to run back into the darkness. But having come so far . . . Now, her gloved hands were restless and her button boot heel tapped on the stone floor in agitation. Then she heard voices and farewells, and to her surprise a woman opened the door.

'I've left my gamp in the back.' Into the room rushed Essie Bartley, who looked at her, nodded, grabbed the umbrella and fled.

She had aged ten years, her face lined with sorrow, her hair almost white. Hester could feel her cheeks stinging with embarrassment. Did the Bartleys know? Did they know it was her son who had not given testimony to their son's good character? Did they know how he had really died and why?

In those brief seconds of their encounter she saw only the familiar face of another brokenhearted mother like herself, another bereaved soul. Violet had whispered that there was trouble in the village; Jack Plimmer had come back on leave with rumours about the Bartley boy being shot at dawn for desertion or perhaps cowardice. No one would believe it at first, Frank being such a lively lad, but then letters came from sons who told a similar tale and the village had been split in two over the matter. The churches were ready to believe Jack Plimmer's version, while the chapel folk now wouldn't have a word said against the Bartleys.

Just one glimpse of the utter exhaustion on that woman's face blew away years of dismissing her and her family as mere tradespeople with whom she had nothing in common. What courage it must take to stay and face all that calumny with dignity. Then there was the daughter, who Violet said had gone to stay with relatives and to work in Bradford.

So I needn't have worried about that romance after all, Hester sighed. If only she'd not interfered and let things be, Guy would have gone back, leaving Angus at home, and Selma would have left anyway. Things would have taken their own course.

'Lady Hester, please step this way. I hope I've not kept you waiting but, as you see, there are many like yourself in need of the strength to keep going.'

Hester stepped into the tiny cottage parlour. It smelled of beeswax polish and fresh lavender. There were crocheted lace valances at the window and a thick velour curtain, the colour of dried blood, which the woman quickly drew across. A small round table stood in front of the fire but the room was cool; there was almost a chill in the air Hester sensed she was in the presence of a decent soul.

The first thing she noticed were her ice-blue eyes with the dark circles around the blue, piercing eyes fringed with black lashes: Irish eyes that seemed to look into her very soul. It was hard to hold her gaze.

'Let me say from the start, I am not a fortune-teller wanting silver. The gift of knowledge that I have comes from on high. I was born with a seeing eye and it must be used only for God's glory. I am at the mercy of the will of our great Creator. What I reveal comes from His realms of glory. It is to Him that you must make account. Let me also say what's spoken here is between ourselves and not to be talked about to others. How may I help you?'

All Hester's doubts leached away, replaced with a surge of relief. Here was a safe place.

'I have a son who is no longer with us. I have to know he is safe,' Hester said.

'You have two sons, each the half of the other. Don't worry, your twins are well known in the district but one is safe, the other has passed over.'

'That is what I just said.' This was not impressive.

Martha Holbeck closed her eyes, took a deep breath and opened them again, piercing Hester with a stare that felt like an arrow's dart. 'There is a cloud of mist round your head, a cloud of anger and sad disappointments all mixed up together. I'm not sure . . .'

Martha closed her eyes again and breathed in deeply, muttering as if in prayer.

'The son you have lost is not the one who stands in heavenly light. He is safe now. What I see is the one in life in danger. There is sea and a ship faraway—'

Hester cut her off. 'It's not him I'm worried about. It's my son who died in battle. Did *he* suffer?'

'I have no message for you on that score but I sense he is content to be now, where he is. It's the other half of him who is far from you. There was anger and a falling out?'

Was she fishing for information? 'Thank you, if that is all. What do I owe you?' Hester made to gather herself to leave the room.

'There's no charge for the gift, but donations are welcome. I am getting a strong feeling of distance . . . an ocean of distance between the living and the dead. You must not worry. What was done in war and love will one day be put right in peacetime; ties broken will be bound together one day. Forgiveness, hope and justice . . . Why am I getting those words? Justice for someone wronged. You must help put justice back where it belongs and with it will come forgiveness.'

'You are talking in riddles, woman,' Hester protested.

'But this is what you must hear. I can only speak what has been given to me. These are not my words.'

Hester wanted to run from the room. These were not the words of consolation she was expecting but challenging accusations. Had Martha Holbeck somehow guessed what had happened between them all?

'Don't worry. It's always hard the first time,' Martha said gently. 'Don't expect to understand everything. But write this down before you go, as a reminder, and one day perhaps it will all make sense. You have an important role to play in something that will be revealed in the fullness of time. That's my humble understanding of the matter. The rest is veiled from my eyes.'

'I'm not sure you have helped me very much, Mrs Holbeck,' Hester said stiffly.

'I'm sorry about that, but we are all here to help each other, Lady Hester, high or low. It is in the helping that your peace will be found.'

'I will see myself out. I bid you good night. I won't be returning,' Hester said as she stumbled out of the front door into the summer evening. The stars were already high in the ink-blue sky.

What was there of comfort in the words she'd dutifully written down? Guy was out there . . . at sea, in danger? What did that mean, all that stuff about justice? She felt cheated. Martha's words had brought only confusion and despair.

Essie walked back from the town in the darkness. The silence around her was soothing to her aching heart. To have seen that woman sitting in Martha's kitchen . . . She could scarce believe it, but then, like so many others Lady Hester had lost her son. It was only to be expected she wanted contact with him now her other son had left the district too, just as Selma had been exiled to Bradford.

How she missed her daughter's cheery presence, but she must honour Frank's request that Selma be spared the disgrace of his execution. She would never forget the hurt look in her daughter's eyes as she was bundled on the down train out of harm's way. There was no choice since those horrible anonymous letters arrived, accusing them of harbouring a coward and a deserter, the shunnings in the street every day as if they were now strangers to be avoided. Asa's work was drying up; just a few outlying farmers who came in, as usual, but once they were put in the picture at the Hart's Head, they too soon stopped their custom.

The Lord had been merciful and there were other more comforting letters from Frank's comrades; one in particular that she kept in her Bible. It told a very different story about how Frank died.

Her son was no coward. He had stood his ground, lost his temper and paid heavily for it. But the hardest part was knowing that Captain Cantrell had not given a testimonial on his behalf. She didn't understand, but the soldiers were in no position to say anything. They were lucky to know anything at all. The official notification was so brief. There would be no medals or further pay. Frank no longer existed and this public disgrace couldn't be hidden for long once the rumour mill got to work. She was glad Selma would be shielded from it. Ruth had been sworn to secrecy.

As she trudged uphill, under the night sky, she paused to look at its dark beauty. A dog fox barked, sheep were bleating out on the moor.

Martha had sensed her anguish, pouring her a glass of something gingery and soothing to ease her churning stomach.

'Where is my lad?' she had whispered.

'He's close by, Essie, very close. You'll feel his spirit with you always. He loved you very much. His last thoughts were of you.'

'But is he at peace?'

'He will be when things are made right.'

'What things?'

'When what is right and just comes to pass. Hold these words to your heart. One day all shall be well and all manner of things shall be well.'

'You're not making sense to me,' Essie had sobbed.

'Be patient. Frank is close by. He will comfort you.'

As she ironed these words over and over her mind, trying to flatten them into some shape for future comfort, she felt such sadness. 'All my sons gone and my daughter exiled – how do we live with this?' she had cried out.

'One day at a time, Essie. Put one foot in front of the other. You will survive this just one day at a time,' Martha had comforted her.

As she took the steep path towards West Sharland now,

she sensed she wasn't alone. For a second she felt fear and she turned round. 'I know you're there!' she shouted. 'Stop mucking about!'

There was nobody there, but in the gloom she thought she saw a figure walking ahead. A solitary shape, trudging in front of her, shoulders stooped.

'No moon tonight, but such stars,' she called out.

The figure didn't stop. It kept on walking, lost in its own thoughts.

Just somebody else who thought a Bartley were a bad lot she thought. When she came to the first crossroads in the village, she'd soon see who it was ignoring her. The figure marched ahead and she followed behind, out of puff, trying to keep up with him. Then she stopped for breath, looking up, blinking, and the figure had vanished into thin air. There was no gate or lane end, there was no one there. At least he hadn't turned round and cursed her. She was getting used to that when drunks came out of the pub to pee up the back lane outside their entrance, making it reek.

How were they going to manage if their trade entirely dried up? Sell up, get jobs in a factory? Perhaps she could go back into service? In the darkness the future looked so bleak and uncertain, but she must try to keep Martha's sayings in her heart.

All shall be well and all manner of things shall be well. How could that be? Their lives were broken, the family lost.

Selma peered out of her bedroom window over a dusty privet hedge and a line of washing down below. Above her, slate roofs and blackened chimneys, dark stone houses glowered, but in the distance, a mystic outline of hills cheered her soul. Would she ever get used to the blackened stone and the clutter of houses, the rattle of the trams up and down the Main Road? She felt she was drowning in a torrent of misery, utterly wretched at being forced into this strange city.

It wasn't as if Sam and Ruth weren't kindness itself. Her bedroom was small but cosy, with a rag rug to warm her toes, a fireplace, a little bookshelf and chest of drawers, even a tiny writing bureau to write from, but who was there to write to now?

Marigold had made it plain that her absence would not be missed: 'I'm not surprised you're going away. I wouldn't be in a hurry to get back.'

'But why? What have I done?' Selma had asked, determined to get some answers.

'It's not my place to tell you what I'm sure you already know. We don't want traitors in this village.'

'Traitor? Who's a traitor,' she had asked but Marigold had just sniffed and walked away.

Selma had run home to ask her mother. 'Why are we traitors?'

'Take no notice, love. No one's a traitor. The villagers make the usual two and two into five. Bartleys have every reason to hold their heads up. We stand for what is right.'

Mother hadn't made sense, but something had made her parents want her out of the way. It was the first thing she'd asked Aunty Ruth after she'd arrived: 'Why am I here?'

'Because it's time you sampled a bit of city life after all that hard work. We want to make a lady of you, open your eyes, widen your horizons.' Ruth had bustled round her, not pausing for breath. 'First, though, I'm going to take you into town to buy some dresses for church, and show you how to catch a tram. Show you all our grand buildings.

Then we'll go to the market in Kirkgate and Swan Arcade, and for walks in Lister Park to hear the brass bands. You will love it all.'

They were living in one of the outlying suburbs. Not quite as grand as Heaton Park, where the rich wool merchants had their mansions, those great stone palaces with turrets and iron gates, but in a neat avenue of semi-detached villas with snug rooms and gas mantles that flickered a warm light. They had a large marble fireplace that Alice, the maid, who slept in the attic bedroom, kept banked up night and day.

Ruth was one for tidiness and housework, everything having its place, or covered from the coal dust with crocheted doilies and antimacassars. She was so proud of all her ornaments in the china cabinet: shepherdesses and pretty cups and saucers. Her wedding china was for display only. The windows of the parlour were draped with lace and then surrounded with velvet curtains the colour of treacle, fringed with gold braid.

They were attenders at the Wesleyan Chapel, a barn of a bricked church with a gallery above and the mighty organ in the middle. It was a much freer congregation than Selma was used to, who wore bright hats and cheerful smiles despite so many of them being in mourning. There was a tennis court within the grounds, a room that doubled up for concert parties, Sunday school and public meetings. It was all very different from Sharland chapel.

Some Sundays they entertained visiting preachers with vast high teas on the dining table, white tablecloths laden with home baking and pots of tea. Aunty Ruth worked them all hard when company was expected.

Uncle Sam spent his week in the wool sorter's office,

241

grading wool, and promised to give Selma a tour of the mill. He sang in the chapel choir in a deep baritone. They were trying so hard to make her welcome but she was missing the intimacy of the village, her tiny room, the horses in the field, even her old life in the forge. There was too much time to brood. She needed to make herself useful. But no one would want a female blacksmith's apprentice round here. There were plenty of jobs in the woollen mills or shops, but the idea of them scared her. Aunty Ruth could see she was pining.

'I know it's hard, but it is for the best. Your mam wants to give you a fresh start.'

'Why?' Selma saw the flustered look on Ruth's face.

'That business with the officer chappie . . . It hurt your mother to see you pulled down, but we mustn't speak ill of the dead, I suppose.'

'What do you mean?' Selma said, feeling her heart beat fast.

'I thought you knew? It was in the *Yorkshire Post*. The captain was killed. Your mother wrote to tell me . . . I'm sorry, didn't they tell you?'

Selma was stunned, shaking her head, trying not to cry. 'Nobody tells me anything,' she snapped. 'I don't believe it. Guy dead?'

'I'm afraid so, after Passchendaele. There's been a lot round here made widows. Oh, love, she knew you were that fond of him. Happen this was one way she could soften the blow. It's a good job you're down here. It'll give you a chance to meet other young people like yourself and put it behind you.'

'So they've sent me here to find a husband?' Selma was shaking. 'Why must I have to be kept in the dark since

242

Frank died? There's been something going on. Have we done something wrong?'

'I'll fetch you a cup of tea. It's the shock. I'm sorry to break such bad news. I know you were very pally. I can't believe your mother didn't tell you anything.'

'I thought we were more than pen pals, but then he turned up one day and it was like he was a different person, looking down his nose at us from a great height. It just wasn't like him and now he's dead and I never got to say goodbye. Jemima will miss him so.' Selma was choking with emotion.

'Who's Jemima?' asked Ruth

'His favourite horse, the one the army didn't take because we hid her. We used to ride out over the Ridge. She once threw me in the field and Guy raced after her to rein her in. Are you sure it's him? He has a twin brother, the one that Frank and Newt saved from the Foss.'

'Oh, yes, we know all about that. It seems everyone has forgotten about *that* fact. Poor Frank, it didn't help him, did it?'

'What do you mean?' Selma asked.

Ruth blanched. 'Take no notice of me wittering on . . . Sit down and have a drink and some shortcake with real butter in it.'

'I'm not hungry, thank you.' All she wanted to do was to be alone.

'Please yourself, but don't go mithering. Sounds as if that young man weren't worth much.'

How could she say that? She didn't know the real Guy; the kind and loving Guy. How could they brush his death off as if it were nothing? All her secret hopes had gone; those silly fantasies of coming here to better herself, to go

243

back home and woo him back to her side, dashed with one terrible sentence.

She sobbed on her bed.

Oh, Guy, we had so little time and you had such a short life, no more cantering on Jemima, no late nights under the stars or falling in love. Your life's been mown down like grass in the field.

She felt such a wave of sadness gripping at her throat. Life would never be the same again.

14

Guy was woken in the bunkhouse by the fleabites itching on his legs. He was living on the south side of Halifax, Nova Scotia, where they had volunteered to escort the horses from out of town back to the ship. It had been a restless night, and he was hung over from a night in the bars along the harbour. The crew of SS *Santa Philomena* were celebrating crossing the Atlantic safely, zigzagging away from the threat of submarines and travelling in a convoy. Their escort had brought them safely into Bedford Basin, an ideal anchorage to assemble the return convoy back to France.

They'd been given leave to lower themselves down and head for the darkness of Halifax. The place was packed with sailors and crews and cargo waiting to be loaded, and ladies willing to take every penny off them for their favours.

Guy lay back, thinking what a different world he had discovered when he'd signed on in Liverpool dock in the merchant navy. It had been a terrible year for the merchant ships. Back in October on the Scandinavian run, their escort was destroyed and the *Mary Rose* and *Strongbow* were sunk in the North Sea. It was whispered that London was now

245

down to six weeks' supply of food if the Atlantic convoys didn't get through.

When he'd left Holt Park he'd taken a train straight to Liverpool Lime Street, determined to carry on in His Majesty's service. He spun some tale of having been ill and robbed of all his baggage, his papers stolen, signing himself on as Charles Arthur West, and took the first job offered as a humble deckhand.

'You don't look like a deckhand to me.' The officer had eyed him with suspicion.

'I've been ill; the fresh air will do me good,' Guy said, trying to flatten his vowels and disguise his pukka accent. The man looked at him with surprise. It took an officer to know one but he shrugged his shoulders. 'Here are your papers then.'

It was simple. They were desperate. *He* was desperate, and now he trawled up and down the Atlantic crossing, earning his sea legs the hard way, no longer a first tripper but a hardened sea dog. When they found he was good with horses he was relieved of some of his chores and sent below to help calm the poor beasts being enlisted for France. It was a smelly stable, and the horses were nervous, kicking out, but, packed together, their own herd mentality seemed to bring a measure of calm. But sometimes he could have done with Frank Bartley's gentling hand on the poor beasts.

The crew were a tough no-nonsense lot of scousers, men like the rank and file of his own soldiers, salt-of-the-earth types. They were curious why he was putting himself in danger, with only rough seas and fog as their friends.

He tried to make out he was a Yorkshireman craving adventure, wounded in the chest and discharged on medical grounds.

He knew most of them thought he was on the run: 'Did you get a girl into trouble?' 'Is her father after you with a shot gun?' He laughed and let them think what they liked. He was happy to be as far away as he could from all the terrible mess in Europe. He was no deserter. This was as dangerous a job as any he had done over there but the change of tactics to herding ships together in a convoy seemed to be keeping the wolves at bay.

It was rumoured that their next cargo would be troops from the eastern seaboard of the States: soldiers bound for France, instead of horses, and that America was on the move now, mobilising for war. In that were the seeds of hope. More fresh soldiers to the slaughter, he sighed, but Allied forces would outnumber the opposition soon, and then this war might just end.

Suddenly the whole earth shook, the bunk rocked as an explosion like nothing Guy had ever heard since the one at Messines Ridge in 1916 blasted him onto the floor. What the hell was that? He'd ducked instinctively, holding his ears as a series of explosions like huge guns ripped through the air.

'It's coming from the harbour. The Germans are shelling Halifax! Bloody hell, run for cover!' one of the mates ordered.

'Get the horses back. Cover their heads . . . They'll be terrified!' Guy issued orders in the old way as a pall of black billowing smoke suddenly darkened the morning sky. This was no ordinary shellfire, the huge cloud of smoke and dust rose high and then a terrible rain of shrapnel began to fall. Those who had helmets covered themselves from the deluge. Others were not so lucky and screamed as the hot metal pierced them.

'The horses . . . we must stop them stampeding!'

No one was listening to Guy, too busy trying to find cover. The smell was choking and Guy felt the tension closing his chest. He must find air. They were south of the city, out of range of the first explosions. What had happened to the *Philomena* and to the poor sods in the harbour or those still on board? 'We must see to the horses, and then go and give a hand. It looks as if the whole town is on fire. They'll need our help,' he shouted, trying to round up the fleeing crew.

He might not understand what was happening up there but it was serious, and many must have been killed in the blast. 'Come on, chaps . . . we must help,' he yelled. 'There's women and children trapped out there.'

No one was prepared for what they saw through the smoke and flames. A whole side of the harbour was flattened. Not a building standing. It was like a scene from Dante's *Inferno*: charred corpses everywhere, children wandering in what was left of their streets, wide-eyed with terror, horses gutted. Such a terrible vision of innocent slaughter Guy never wanted to see in his life again. Sickened but determined, he forced the rest of his crewmates further down town to see the damage, to gather up all the children they could.

Then, as they got nearer, they saw all the wooden buildings were on fire and high on Citadel Hill, crowds were gathering, screaming at the furnace creeping ever towards them.

'What's happened?' Guy kept asking, but no one knew for certain: two ships had collided in the Narrows and blown up, was one version; a submarine torpedoed the harbour, another. Someone said it was a Zeppelin bombing

Halifax, and there was a great wave of shock that had rocked every ship to the north in terror.

Guy felt helpless. Damn and blast this war. These were civilians, innocent women and children going about their daily business. Now, even on the outskirts, there was not a home standing. Fires were smouldering and there was nothing much the survivors could do but organise themselves into rescue parties to dig out those still trapped and find water to put out the fires.

The town was full of men in uniform; those still able-bodied enough to help did their bit. But when rumour came that the naval magazine might blow at the barracks, it fired up more terror as crowds rushed for cover.

Guy stood firm against this tide of panic. 'We must move in, chaps,' he ordered, thinking on his feet, giving instructions, assessing the danger. He had to move forward and help in any way possible. Their own ship would be blasted out the water by now, stricken and unfit to use. They were stranded with their terrified cargo until help came. 'Shift your arses, make yourselves useful! We can't stand here and watch Halifax burn!' he yelled.

The magazine didn't blow because hundreds of volunteers like him slowly dismantled the ammunition dump, lifting, loading, unloading and throwing anything that might explode into the harbour.

To make matters much worse, that night it snowed incessantly, covering all the broken homes and streets with huge drifts. People took makeshift shelter where they could, in any building still standing, churches, barns, even in tents, frozen to the bone in the terrible blizzard. This was the final deathblow on the stricken town, but the fires were doused.

Guy was exhausted. Every sinew in his body ached as the crew spent the night comforting the horses. It was going to be a long night. At least they were warm, but his eyes were stinging with the smoke and heat, and his body sickened by all the terrible sights he had seen. This destruction was worse than in the trenches. How strange that, once again, he had survived when by rights he should be at the bottom of the sea. He didn't understand why he was being allowed to live on when so many innocents had died. Had they not been punished enough without the blizzard's cruel blow?

For as long as he lived he would never forget 6 December 1917. When was all this suffering going to end? For the first time in months, he thought of his mother alone for Christmas and felt a pang of sorrow for her. Just for a second, he also thought about Selma and Angus and West Sharland. But all he wanted to do was sleep.

Hester watched the village muster its venom against the Bartley family, some cool and distant, others downright vicious. It was common knowledge now that the boy had been shot at dawn. But Angus's part in the tragedy would never be known. She would have to live with her own role in bringing this about for the rest of her life. This shameful knowledge gnawed away at her stomach alongside Guy's desertion, breaking her heart. Was there no way to put things right? She didn't know if Guy was alive or dead, and it was as much as she could do to face each day alone in the family house. There were no more officers to nurse. Only the garden was her solace as she began to take back the vegetables into rose beds and shrubbery once more. The horses had gone, just old Jemima left as a reminder of Guy, and she was looking old and weary, like herself.

She had a servant or two but little company. The Hunts had taken up a new parish, and there was now a young curate in charge, a puny weakling with flat feet who had dodged conscription, she surmised.

Martha Holbeck's words kept worrying at her: an injustice to be righted. She kept both the boys' rooms just as they had left them. She couldn't bear to see them cleaned out and emptied, unable to face the desolation of cold lifeless bedrooms. She felt as if she was half living. What was there left for her now?

Beaven knocked on the scullery door to say Jemima was limping and needed a shoe again and should he take her to the blacksmith in Sowerthwaite.

'What's wrong with Bartley? He's my tenant.'

'I just wondered, ma'am, if you wanted me to go there,' came the cautious reply.

'How can my rent be paid for if he has no custom? Take her down and leave her there.'

'Yes, ma'am,' he replied.

'And you can take the firearms from the dining room. The clasp has gone. Tell him there is no rush.'

If her horse was seen in the paddock it would be noticed and word would get around that the lady of the manor was in no mood to abandon a good workman, whatever the circumstances. This silliness had gone on for too long. They may be on the other side of the social fence but the Bartleys were honest people. They were not responsible for their son's behaviour, not like herself. Perhaps this gesture might help them over a difficult time and ensure they didn't fall behind with their rent. What if they did? Would she have the heart to throw them out of their cottage? How she prayed it would never come to that.

*　　*　　*

251

Ruth had persuaded Selma's parents to come to see them over the New Year, but only Essie turned up, looking harassed in her black coat and a felt hat. She wore no other colour and Selma felt a flicker of shame at the sight of her rough boots and her shabby three-quarter coat. The broken veins in her cheeks were like red ink marks on white paper. Mam wore a weary look of resignation. She was here out of duty, not desire.

Since she had settled with Ruth Selma was getting used to Bradford life and all the attractions a bustling city had to offer. They had gone to a real pantomime and to the moving pictures, to a musical concert at St George's Hall and to the Wesleyan Amateur Operatic Society's production of *The Arcadians*.

There was so much to tell her mother about her new position as companion nursemaid to a young girl down the Avenue, Lisa Greenwood. Lisa had started at the High School for Girls as a day pupil, while her father was at work in Leeds University. It was Selma's job to meet her from school, cook her a simple meal and see that she did her studies until he returned home.

It was a bit of a shock at first to realise they were German born. The first Germans she'd ever met. But Mr Greenwood didn't have horns coming out of his ears. In fact, he was quite old with grey hair and a moustache; a professor of textile technology in Leeds, a learned man with a kindly twinkle in his eye. Lisa's name was really Elise Grunwald, but they'd changed it by deed poll to sound more English. She was a remarkable girl, old for her age. Her mother had died when she was small. Lisa was clever and played the piano and violin. She and her father spoke German to each other in private but always chattered away in her schoolgirl

English to Selma. The house was full of books and Selma was free to take anything off the shelves. She fancied the picture books full of paintings and sculptures the best.

Rose Villa was just like Aunty Ruth's house from the outside but inside it was cluttered, with dark heavy furniture, framed pictures on the walls, a jumble of papers, instruments and books and the smell of rich cigar smoke.

Professor Greenwood had been sent into a camp for German nationals at the beginning of the war and Lisa was farmed out amongst the neighbours until Uncle Sam and some important people spoke up for him and they were all reunited.

Parent and child were very close in a way she'd never seen before. They laughed and discussed, argued on points of order, nit-picking until her ears were aching. The professor talked to Lisa as if she were an adult, not a child, but also realised there were some things in the home that needed a more female influence.

'Make sure she doesn't become too blue a stocking,' he would joke. Selma wasn't sure what he meant.

They went to the theatre at the weekends and kept themselves busy on Sundays entertaining other German friends. They didn't go to church. 'I have not found one church that can answer all my questions,' Lisa's father explained.

They never talked about the war's progress or about their family. He had chosen to stay on in England and was cut off from his own kin.

There was a picture of Lisa's mother in a silver frame. She had a strong face, like Lisa, fair, blue-eyed with strong cheekbones and a long nose. Not pretty but striking in a different way.

Selma often wondered how she was being paid to do

such an interesting job. There was so much to tell her mother but she didn't seem interested in her new exciting world.

Ruth had made one of her special high teas. They had had to queue for bread flour and fancy pies, but made a trifle and sponge cake with borrowed eggs. Mum hardly did justice to all this effort. In the months since Frank's death she'd grown thin.

'How are things with Asa?' Ruth asked. 'Has business picked up?'

'Aye, it has, surprisingly. Her ladyship has deemed to honour us with her patronage. She keeps bringing in regular bits and pieces and now her tenant farmers have brought themselves down off the tops to do the same. Asa is busy enough and now he's leading his Bible class again, and thinking of training up as a preacher. His head's stuck in his Bible commentary book and we have a new preacher now, but his sermons are not much to my liking: lots of flowery sentences with not much meat in them. He is one that likes the sound of his own voice. There's been a falling-off in attendance,' she replied.

'Are you still in that WI? I hear they've got groups all over the country now,' Ruth asked, trying to pull Essie out of her mood.

'No, I don't go now not after . . . well, you know, I haven't got time.'

'You must make the effort,' Ruth said briskly before swiftly changing the subject. 'So what do you think of our Selma? Isn't she a fancy piece these days?'

Essie looked her daughter up and down. 'But I'm surprised she's not still in mourning. It's been only nine months.'

'Talk to me direct, Mam. I am here! I did wear it up until

the New Year. But Aunty suggested I lighten up a bit. I have this job to do now.'

'So I hear, but a girl of eleven is surely too old for a nursemaid,' her mother sniffed.

'She has no mother and the professor works long hours. I'm going to join the Wesleyan Players. They're doing a pierrot show and I might get a turn.'

'You soon forgot yer chapel ways. Dad'll be most disappointed if you do.'

'Come on, Essie, she's only young once,' Ruth protested. 'Give her a chance to meet people her own age. What's the harm in that?'

Mam looked up. 'I'm not hanging together very well, am I? You do as you see fit, Selma. I don't know what's got into the world. What have we to show for this war but blood, sweat and tears? I'm that strung out, what with Asa being so thin and worn out, a puff of wind would blow him over.' Essie paused to look around the room with a sigh. 'You've got it real nice, Ruth. Mind you, you always did have a good eye, and it's as well to know that Selma has a good home, if anything happens to us.'

Ruth was having none of it. 'Nothing's going to happen, Essie, so stop this sorry talk. We wanted you here to give you a treat, not a talking to . . .'

'A change is as good as a rest, they say, but I never did stand easy under chimneys and mills with all that soot and smoke. But I suppose it has its compensation, and you have done me proud, both of you, with this fine spread.' She smiled weakly. 'But excuse me if I have little appetite. I can't seem to taste my food these days. It stays in a lump down my throat and I can hardly swallow it. Sometimes I feel as if it'll choke me.'

'You should see the doctor,' Ruth urged anxiously.

'I'm not foiling out good brass for him to tell me what I already know. I'm that choked inside. It must be the time of life.'

'What time?' Selma asked.

'Never you mind, but Ruth knows what I mean. If it's not one thing it's another.'

Selma was secretly relieved when they waved Essie off in the late afternoon. It had not been a good visit, and soon it would be her turn to go back home. But she hoped not for a while. Much as she loved her family she wasn't sure she wanted to return just yet. Bradford was fast becoming her home.

Essie first noticed the little shrine in Elm Tree Square weeks ago: a wooden cross on which were a few bunches of flowers and a Union Jack, messages with names pinned onto it. But as the summer of 1918 drew to a close, the flowers faded and the notes blew away. Everyone was talking about a peace settlement coming soon. Not that they talked about it to her.

That first wave of anger against the Bartleys, those impulsive acts of vandalism, broken windows and hate messages had stopped, to be replaced by a cool silence. Cold shouldering was far worse in many ways, the whispering behind her back whenever she passed. It made it hard to sit on the bus and she took to walking the two miles into Sowerthwaite just to avoid it. She often looked for the strange figure in the mist but it never appeared again.

The only person who bothered to be civil to them both was their landlady, who took to calling in person to bring repairs to Asa. She too had aged in the past few years, wearing deepest black at all times, her cheeks sunken, dark circles under her eyes. She looked as if she was in need of a good meal or two.

Essie recognised what it was like to be stuck in a grief that never left her. Asa said it was ungodly to take on so. He just kept his head down and took his solace in delivering sermons in the outlying chapels, riding out on a spare horse into the Dales and returning often soaked through, tired, but with a fire in his eyes. His faith was his great comfort. It was no longer hers. She wanted to stand up and argue with the new pastor. What did he know of the suffering that clung to her guts, squeezing all the joy out of her life: the joy of seeing spring lambs, the meadows full of flowers waving through the hay, cornflowers, pink corncockle, clovers, yellow rattle or the autumn colours and leaf fall? Everything around her looked a dull grey sludge, and when peace finally came and the streets were full of bunting and flags and dancing outside the Hart's Head, she stayed inside and wept.

What were they dancing for? What had been gained but a load of pain? Who was there left to come back here? Would Selma ever leave Ruth's comfortable billet to be a blacksmith's daughter again? She doubted it.

'Don't take on so,' Asa said, trying to bring some solace. 'We have our Selma safe. The rest was the Lord's will.'

'What do you mean, the Lord's will? To have my boy tied to a post and shot like an animal? How can you stand in that pulpit and talk about the Lord's will? All those young men slaughtered, and for what? When are you going to face up to what He's done to us, instead of all this pious talk?'

'Now, Essie, don't get angry.'

257

'Why shouldn't I be angry? What was done to Frank wasn't right. It wasn't just. I want answers, proper answers.'

'It doesn't do to stir up trouble. We have to live here now.'

She looked up at him with scorn. 'What's happened to you? You've lost your bite.' She stared again with contempt, and then with fear. He looked so tired, so done in. 'I'm sorry. That was unkind. You do as you think best. We have to eat.'

'I keep my thoughts for my prayers, much of it best left unsaid, but bitterness is like an acid, it burns away old metal, given time. Don't give in to bitterness. We can't change what has happened to Newton or Frank. They won't come home like a fair few other village boys, but we will always remember their sacrifice.' He started to cough.

The singing and dancing, the celebration services and pageants went on all through those cold November weeks. But then a few wounded soldiers trickled home and letters came that one or two had fallen for a bad dose of influenza in hospital and they'd not be coming home again.

The sickness started in dribs and drabs at first. Asa was preaching in chapels once full, but now half empty. Soon, it seemed half the village were coughing and spluttering. The church bell was tolling as young and old succumbed to this terrible affliction.

When her husband took to his bed Essie knew real fear as she watched him burning up and shaking, his body limp and his breathing so bad she sent for Dr Mac, who didn't look too good himself.

'Keep him warm and lots of drinks down him. The fever will take its course, one way or another.' That was when she sent for Selma, only to receive a telegram from Ruth to say Selma and Sam were both down with the flu and she was feeling badly herself.

There was no time to dwell on this cruel twist of fate. Asa was delirious with fever, his handsome face now sunken and grey. She sat with him night and day, willing him to fight, but his body was too weak. She read him whole passages of the Psalms at his request, begged him to sip on the cup with the spout, gave him brandy disguised as cocoa, which he enjoyed. But then his breathing became so laboured that she knew his heart was giving out.

'You can't do this to me!' she screamed. 'Take my sons and then my husband. You can't do this to me, cruel God.' She had never felt such hatred and anger in all her life. But it was all to no avail.

Asa slipped from her quietly one evening while she was dozing. She woke and his hand was as cold as the chill and the frost on the panes of window glass. She was utterly broken and wishing that she too would be stricken with the same. Why was she still fit and strong? Why did she have only snuffling cold? Why was the better half of them taken?

She laid him out as only she knew how. With tenderness she washed him, combing his tousled hair, shaving him so he looked dignified in death. She closed the curtains and sat waiting for the carpenter to call.

It was two days before he came to measure up, two days with no visitors but the pastor, who made arrangements for the funeral.

Ruth wrote to say that Selma and Sam were on the mend but Professor Greenwood had died in the night and poor Lisa was distraught. Selma would be too weak to attend her own father's funeral but Ruth would try to come herself.

What will happen to me now? Essie cried into her pillow. How can I live? How can I pay the rent with only a widow's pension to fall back on? Black thoughts swirled in her mind like smoke. The utter desolation of this cruel fate overwhelmed her tough spirit. She hadn't strength left even to think.

There was a modest turn out for Asa's funeral but few of the other villagers who spoke to them dared to risk attending for fear of infection. Her husband was lowered into the hard ground in the corner of St Wilfred's that was the enclave of the chapel attenders: 'Hellfire Corner' – they'd once joked about its nickname.

It was hard to mouth his favourite hymns, to listen to his friends making pious praises over him. 'You know nowt!' she wanted to scream. 'You have no idea how his sons' deaths had broken his spirit, weakened his body. He bore it all uncomplaining, carried his sorrows on his back like a cross until he cracked.'

When God sent this plague to punish this wicked world, it struck at random, good and evil alike, soldiers, civilians, doctors and nurses, innocent children, rich and poor.

How could she believe in such a creator ever again?

This is the last time I'll darken these doors with my shadow, she mused. Pulpit words would hold no sway over her again. She stood as the rain beat down on her coat, watching Asa sliding into the earth for ever. Her only comfort was the knowledge that he wasn't there. That was just the shell of him. She'd laid out enough folk to know that when the breath left the body, the soul flew out too. That was why she always opened the window to set it free.

What shall I do now? she cried. Where do I go from here?'

The answer came slowly as week after week people knocked on her door to ask her to lay out their dead. Since she had survived this 'Spanish Flu', as they were calling it now, she was a good omen. Her services were in demand and the coins slipped to her were never refused. This was how she would survive until Selma came home again. Together they would make their way forward.

15

'What shall I do, Aunty Ruth? I don't want to go back to West Sharland. Lisa needs me now more than ever. I can't let her down.' Selma had woken from her sick bed to find the whole world changed. Her father was dead and buried, and now Ruth was recovering from the same ailment. Selma was running the household and that of Professor Greenwood. Poor Lisa was distraught. Selma was nursing her back to strength as if she were her little sister at the same time as grieving for her dead dad.

'You owe it to your mother, but you must do what you think fit by Miss Lisa, poor lamb without a soul in the world. Your mother can manage a while longer, I'm sure, but she will expect you to return,' Ruth replied.

'But I want to stay here. I like Bradford now. I didn't at first. I wish Mam could come and share my room,' Selma said.

'That's not a good idea and you know it. Much as I love my sister, it wouldn't work. Chalk and cheese we allus have been. You must go and pay your respects. I'll have Lisa here for Christmas . . . The first Christmas of peace and everyone too ill to enjoy it, I reckon.'

Ruth was right. Selma was being selfish as usual, but she

262

couldn't leave Lisa for long, knowing she was an orphan. Professor Greenwood had begged her to stay with her and see that she was taken care of. There was money and instructions with his lawyer if anything happened. He'd made plans but didn't say what they were. But she owed Mam her services too. This flu had ravaged town and country alike: shops, banks, trams, schools closed with staff stricken, and the poor soldiers limping home to face yet more sickness and danger.

As she packed her bag full of spare tins of food, she sighed knowing she'd be missing the Christmas pierrot show. She'd auditioned for a part in a sketch and did a funny song dressing up as a blacksmith with a sooty face.

Everyone had laughed and clapped and asked her to join the concert party. It comprised mostly women, of course, but they made her welcome and soon she was attending rehearsals, making friends. The influenza had ruined everything. It was weeks since those trips out to Ilkley Moor and Shipley Glen, teas in cafés and the tram home. It had helped her forget all the past troubles in the village – and Guy. Now returning home would bring everything back.

Duty called and she felt ashamed that she resented having to interrupt her own plans to help out in Mam's hour of need. She was going back with a bad grace and she prayed it wouldn't show.

'We are going to have to do something about that shrine growing on Elm Tree Square. It's getting so gaudy and unsightly,' said Hester at the parish meeting. 'It's just getting out of hand.'

'Our people,' said the chairman, Ebenezer Best, 'just want to remember their loved ones. It's only natural they want a focal point. We were thinking of making up a roll of honour for our Sunday school scholars, listing all those who served,' he added.

'St Wilfred's will want to do the same – something suitable for the church wall – but we need legal permission, a faculty from the Dioceses in due course,' said the vicar, not wanting to be outdone. 'We want something tasteful, not sentimental messages. I agree with Lady Hester that it does look a mess,' he continued.

'Perhaps then, it is time to think of something suitable for the whole village: a public war memorial. There have been suggestions, since the Cenotaph is being built in London, that other towns may want to do the same.'

'There'll have to be a central committee then,' said Hester, foreseeing all sorts of complications. 'But I'm sure it's too early to be thinking of such commemorations.'

'It's never too early to honour our fallen heroes,' remarked Mr Plimmer.

'So it's just the dead or will it be a muster list of all who served?' someone suggested.

'That's not necessary. Think of all those names to fit on,' said another.

'You're not going to put names on the memorial, surely?' said Hester. 'That's never been done before.'

'I think you'll find it has in some towns.'

'I don't think so,' Hester argued.

'Can you both address the chair?' shouted Mr Best. 'You see what I mean . . . it's going to take a lot of thinking out.'

'Will we have to pay or will the government pay for it?' asked Mr Plimmer. 'I'm not forking out for some plaque on a church wall I'll never see.'

'At this early stage we will have to take advice. We must

264

make our memorial appropriate to the size of our community, take everyone's wishes into account,' said the chairman.

'If their idea of a memorial is anything like that muddle in the square, I'm not sure it's in the right place,' Hester added, not wishing to be thwarted.

'I think we will have to form a subcommittee. Views must be minuted and done properly and if we are going to have to shell out from the parish, then others must be co-opted onto it.'

'Is that necessary?' Hester protested. She'd hoped they'd all agreed to demolish the wooden shrine, put up some stone obelisk and leave it at that.

'Lady Hester, this is far too important a monument to be rushed into. Future generations will look at it and learn.'

'Perhaps we ought to have a fund-raising event and put up railings to replace them as have been taken for salvage. Railings round the elm tree and a bench would do the trick,' a man from the back row suggested.

'We could open a bit of a field as the kiddies play park,' said someone else

'What's that got to do with our fallen heroes?' yelled Mr Plimmer.

'If you're going down that route, we need some lavatories in the reading room,' said Miss Barnes, the new schoolmistress.

'Gentlemen, ladies, please order! A committee will need to look into all these suggestions. Shall we vote on this matter and get on with the rest of business or shall we be still here in the morning?' Ebenezer Best as usual had the last word.

The motion to form a committee was seconded and voted through. Hester was determined that she would sit on this committee and ensure that it was to her liking. She was, after all, a patron of St Wilfred's, which would give her a say in what went on there, but the thought of names going on a plaque troubled her. How could she make sure both of her sons were honoured for their sacrifice? And what about the Bartley boy?

The forge had closed since Asa's death. Somehow Essie Bartley had managed to pay her rent on the due day but it was only a matter of time before she too would struggle. Hester felt a wave of pity for that isolated woman. She had never returned to the Women's Institute meetings, nor now went to chapel, it was rumoured.

If only there was something she could do to make amends to help her through this bad patch. But one look at those fierce dark eyes and she knew this proud woman would suffer shame and want before she'd ask for help.

Hester wasn't going to let her end up in the workhouse. Where was the daughter when she needed her? It really wasn't her responsibility. The two women were strangers in many ways. But something must be done and she was going to have to make the first move.

If Guy had had his way, by now they might have been related by marriage. If only Hester knew where he was. She had hoped now the war was over he would have made contact by postcard. But each day the post brought no news.

Oh, what do you expect, postcards from the dead? That was what hit her hard. His name on the memorial would be a lie and Angus, who had died in his place, would never get what was due to him either. It was all such a terrible mess. What on earth was she going to do?

*　*　*

Essie hardly recognised her own daughter. She looked that smart in her short skirt and posh little hat, her hair bobbed and sleek as she marched across the station bridge, waving and smiling. Her heart sank when she noticed Selma had brought only a small leather case. Not big enough to mean she was coming home for good.

'Well, what a picture you make! Ruth must have kitted you out,' she said, forcing a smile to her lips.

'No, I bought them myself. Do like my new coat?'

'Very swish,' Essie said, knowing her older shabby grey tweed was threadbare.

'Shall we wait for a bus?' Selma asked.

'What's wrong with Shanks's pony?'

'My new shoes won't stand it,' she laughed, pointing to neat little court shoes.

'I forgot you're a town girl now,' Essie quipped, half joking.

'Just you wait. I've got such news. Can I treat you to tea at Bowskills bakery?' Selma offered.

'Why do you want to pay those prices for summat as I can make for nothing, Selma Bartley? You'd need a magnifying glass to find a currant in their fruit scones!'

'This is a treat for you, Mam . . . afternoon tea in a café.'

'Wasted on me, lass. Let's get home and put the kettle on the hob and have a good chinwag. I want to know all about things and you could do with fattening up. Plus I thought you'd want to go and see your father's grave,' she added.

'All in good time, Mam. It's on my agenda.'

'Agenda? What's one of those when it's at home? Where do you get such words?'

'From Lisa – she's a walking dictionary. I've been reading

267

her schoolbooks too. Do you know, she knows Latin and French and she's only twelve, and there's German, of course.'

'Why does she want to speak that language?'

'Didn't I tell you she was German? Her father came from Munich long before the war.'

Essie was not impressed. 'What was he doing here, a spy?'

'Don't be so small-minded, not all Germans are spies. He's been here for years.'

Essie couldn't understand Selma's breathless enthusiasm over Miss Lisa's world of art and music; a world away from the village school and the forge. But she held her tongue and let the girl rattle on. It was lovely just to see her bright face in front of her.

They arrived back home and Selma looked around the room. 'I never realised how small our cottage is,' she said.

'Big enough to raise a family and big enough to rattle around on my own,' Essie replied. 'It may not be Ruth's palace but it kept you warm and dry on many a stormy night, or have you forgotten already?'

'I didn't mean . . . Don't take on. I'm just observing, that's all. Lisa says observation is important if you want to look and learn.'

'This Lisa seems full of herself.'

'That's not fair. She's just lost her father and been ill.'

'Sit down, yer tea's mashed. We need to put some flesh on those bones. You look half starved.'

'No, I'm not, it's the look – the streamlined look, Lisa calls it.'

Essie had had enough. 'Lisa, Lisa – haven't you got a thought in your own head?' Selma had changed into a dizzy, flighty young woman and Essie didn't like what she was seeing. 'You've not asked once how things are here for me,' she chided.

'West Sharland is pickled in aspic, Aunty Ruth says. It'll never change: pretty, hard-working, everything as it always was,' she replied, looking around her.

'Do you really think so? You have been away a long time. After four years of war nothing is the same. Half of the men never came home. The forge is closed, and now some man from Sowerthwaite wants to fettle up motor cars in there. It's full of wheels and banging all hours . . . He's dug a pit into the floor. I don't know what's come over folk.'

'You've got to go with the times, Mam, or they will leave you behind. What else is fresh?'

'They want to put up some memorial statue for the soldiers, but no one can agree on what. There'll be names round the bottom of it.'

'That'll be nice for you to see our Newt and Frank's on it.'

'Will it now? I'd rather have them here. I'd rather be washing their shirts than walking past their names every day,' Essie snapped. It was quite plain that no one would be putting Frank's name on any plaque after what had happened, but Selma didn't know the details and never would from Essie's lips.

'The war's over now. Time to get on with things. Which brings me to the most exciting news. I'm going to America,' Selma announced as coolly as if she was going for the bus.

Essie thought she'd heard wrong. 'Who's going to America?'

'When Professor Greenwood was sick, he wrote to his brother who lives across on the west coast in Los Angeles. Isn't that a beautiful name? Lisa says it means the angels.'

'Get on with it,' Essie snapped, feeling sick.

'We had a visit from the lawyer in Bradford, who said her father had written a will leaving money for Lisa and her companion – that's me – to go on a ship to New York and then across by train to deliver Lisa to her uncle Cornelius Grunwald . . .'

'When is all this going to happen?'

'As soon as it can be arranged. Can you believe it, I'm going on a ship to the New World?'

'How long are you going to stay and who will bring you back? You can't come back alone.'

'We've not got that far. I might find work out there. It's where they make moving pictures for the cinema. Fancy me bumping into Mary Pickford or John Barrymore!'

'And who are they when they're at home?' sniffed Essie.

'Mam, don't be so slow . . . they're famous film stars.'

'I've never heard of them.'

'You should go to the Picturedrome in Sowerthwaite.'

'Whatever for?'

'Where's your sense of fun? The war's over. We have to put it behind us now and move on.'

'How can you put what's happened behind you? Have you forgotten we've lost all our men? Your dad's hardly cold in his grave and you act as if nothing has happened. I am hanging on here by my fingernails to pay the rent. I was hoping that you'd be coming home—'

Selma interrupted, 'Don't worry, I'll send you money. I'll be getting a wage. It's going to be such fun. We've been reading up on what we can see in New York. I can't believe it's going to happen to me. You wouldn't want me to miss such an opportunity, would you?'

Essie was struck dumb by Selma's bombshell. Here she was thinking her daughter would come home and settle back into village life after eighteen months away. Now in front of her was this giddy girl, dressed up like a doll with not a thought in her head but her own selfish plans to go halfway across the world to see film stars with a German's daughter, for goodness' sake.

'Drink your tea and calm down. Are you sure you're doing the right thing, rushing off into the wilderness at the beck and call of some young lass you hardly know? What if she tires of your company? How will you get back home?'

'You were the one who told me I had to go to Bradford and take my chance there, and I have. There's a whole new world outside this village. Look, I'll always be grateful that you and Dad let me leave,' she continued softly, 'but I can't settle back here. It would drive me crazy. You'll be all right without me, won't you?'

This was the moment when Essie could tell her how lonely she was, explain about Frank, put her into the true picture of what had happened since Frank was shot. If she told her all this, she could make her daughter stay. But one look into those bright, eager eyes, full of hope and excitement, and she knew she couldn't spoil her big adventure.

'The grass isn't always greener over the fence, lass. You think on. I'll manage fine on my own. I have a little rent from the forge to tide me over. You go off on your travels and send me postcards. As long as I know you're safe, I'll be content.' She lied with conviction, looking down so Selma couldn't see the tears in her eyes. 'I expect you've lots to do.'

'You're right there: documents, a passport. I came for my birth certificate and I need a reference on my photograph. I thought Dr Mackenzie or Mr Best might sign them. It has to be someone important.' Then she paused. 'I heard about Guy Cantrell from Aunty Ruth. Why didn't you tell me first?'

'I thought it was best left unsaid. Then slipped my mind, what with your father—'

'Did his brother ever come back here?' Selma interrupted.

'No one has heard from him for years. There was a big falling out at Waterloo House, they say. But Lady Hester is not as haughty as she once was.'

'She put the spoke in the wheel of Guy and me,' Selma said with obvious bitterness. 'Serves her right!'

'Perhaps it was for the best but, let me tell you, it was her as kept Asa in work when no one else bothered. I have to thank her for that and so must you. Now she lives alone, like me.'

'You will manage after I'm gone?' Selma said, drawing her chair closer 'You will get out more? I never understood why the village took against us.'

'All that's past history, all dead and buried now. I do a bit of sitting in, laying out. I keep busy. But promise to write regular or I will worry.'

'I promise, honest, you'll be the first to know all there is to know.' Selma jumped up. 'I'm going to go and tell Dad, if you don't mind, on my own. He'd want to know.'

Essie sat staring into the flames, unable to speak. Her heart was so full. One by one they'd all gone. Selma living in Bradford was one thing, halfway across the world was quite another. But there was no stopping her. Essie could read the raw determined look in her eyes. She had Asa's dark eyes like nuggets of coal. She was so like him in many ways.

'Your children are only lent for a season,' she once heard her own mother say, years ago, 'and they must go their own gait.'

Essie had never wandered far from her own fireside, but for one second she envied the chances her daughter was getting.

'Let her go . . . She'll find her own way back one day. All manner of things shall be well.' Where did those words come from?

'Is that you, Asa?' She turned, half expecting him to be standing in the doorway, his black eyes flashing. The door was ajar, but no one was there. But she felt his presence as surely as if he was sitting by her side. How could she ever roam far from here while his spirit was watching over her? She smiled through the tears. 'Thanks, love, I needed that.'

The graveyard across the square holds them both now. I never got to see my mother in good health again. It took a child of my own to make me realise what a gift she had given me in that precious week I spent with her.

When you are young you are thoughtless, wrapped up in your own world. You don't think of the hurt you cause others by your selfish actions.

I deserted my mother in favour of a stranger's child. I wanted adventure I wanted to travel and to leave behind this mundane world of sad memories. I didn't think of her feeling rejected, losing me as she had lost all the rest of us. I just wanted to get away.

She let me go without protest because she loved me, and only wanted my happiness. She let me go to give me the freedom to be myself. She protected me from the shadows in the family, covered up her grief and loneliness and pain. I didn't see behind her farewell tears or realise that I might never see her like this again.

All the secrets in the family were hidden from me for good reason. Had I known what I know now, would I have ever left West Sharland? What a different life I might have lived, and these children and grandchildren by my side would have had no existence.

Some say, what is meant for you will not go past you, what comes round goes round until its perpetual motion finds a resting place. Now, I return to where I began, and at last there is peace in this remembering.

16

Guy signed on another term after the war ended. He was in no mood to return to England. What was there for him there but deceit and investigation? His only contact was with Dr Mac, who wrote amusing letters, keeping him informed about the doings of his village. Over the years he had become a friend, and his letters reminded Guy of Selma's with their funny little stories. He had gleaned from them that Selma's father had died and the forge had turned into a garage for motor cars. Selma was living in Bradford and not expected to return. His own mother was battling on with some committee work and in good enough health. Wasn't it about time he sent her a postcard on the principle of forgive and forget, Mac said.

You can stuff that for a game of soldiers! He wanted no reminders of home. He was too busy roaming all over the world on passenger liners. His days as a deckhand were long gone. He played deck quoits with pretty girls, drank like a fish, spent his money in ports east and west. He was beholden to no one but himself, and that suited him just fine.

He picked up his mail in Boston after returning a cargo of wounded American soldiers too sick to be sent straight back after the war. Some were prisoners of war and shell-shocked. It was one of the sadder crossings he had made and he spent time with those who were put on deck for fresh air. There were several sea burials aboard the *Regina*. How sad to be so close to home, and yet not make it back. How cruel! He kept thinking of one particular soldier, Zack, an infantryman – 'a dough boy' – from Pennsylvania, who had struggled to fight off the effects of his wounds, until infection gradually overwhelmed his body.

'I have to get home and make my peace with my folks,' he whispered. 'They don't know, nothing much. I ran away. They don't hold with fighting, being plain Mennonite folk. I was one until I became a soldier. Now I ain't going to make it . . .'

Guy protested, 'Shush . . .'

'No, I know it in my bones but I need to make my peace. Can you fetch some paper and write it down for me?'

'Sure,' Guy nodded, having done this many times over the years. But by the blue tinge on Zack's lips, he knew he must be quick.

SS *Regina*

Dear Folks,

We were not much for putting pen to paper so my buddy here is putting my last thoughts to you. You were right as you always were, war is a terrible waste. All that is left in France at the end are great monuments to destruction, broken homesteads, barren fields and sad pieces of ruined lives. Now it's over, and I hope never again. We fought to kill, to

276

maim and destroy; everything that is against your faith.

Some of us will come back home to be with our folks, but not me. I won't be making it back to you.

Forgive my disobedience. I should have listened to Pa and followed the Ordnung as he ordered, but I wanted to see this old world for myself and I have . . . It ain't much to write home about, except for the kindness of strangers.

I don't want to enter life eternal knowing that we are not at one with each other. I got my taste of worldly freedom, and now it is bitter on my tongue. May I have in death what was denied in life – your blessing, Pa

Your loving son,
Zacharias Yoder

Guy read it back to him with tears in his own eyes. Here was another son, estranged from his family. He thought about Angus, defying his mother, and then he folded the letter gently and turned to ask for the address from a Red Cross nurse, but Zack had already drifted back into unconsciousness and wasn't likely to return. He called for help and to find someone who would give him the address.

They buried Zack at sea, and when Guy reached the port of Boston, Massachusetts, he collected his own post, such as it was, a long letter from Dr Mac. He stuck it in his pocket to read later.

He sat in a bar gazing out over the harbour, thinking about young Zack not much younger than himself. Then he opened Mac's letter.

There is such a hullabaloo in the village about the proposed war memorial statue. No one can agree on which design and now it must be funded from public subscription. No one can agree about that either. Everyone is up in arms, no pun intended. Then there is the delicate matter of whether Frank Bartley's name can be added to the roll of honour. As you could imagine the village is divided.

There are those who think a man executed for disobedience should never be honoured alongside those considered heroes, like Captain Guy Cantrell. Oh, what a tangled web we weave . . .

These sentences leaped out at Guy. Frank shot at dawn? What had happened? The last he knew was that he was in one of the artillery regiments and that Angus had joined them. What on earth had happened? Poor Selma and her family. He could just imagine the response in the village to that scurrilous news.

He'd known of military executions but, thank God, was never present at one himself. Had Angus been present? Did he have to witness such an awful event? He had to know.

There was only one way to find out – by swallowing his pride and writing to his mother. Young Frank was never a coward but he was near the edge that day on the road to Peronne. Had something happened?

Guy ordered another bottle of whisky and settled down in a corner to drown his sorrows in the bottom of a glass.

It was good to get the garden back into shape again, although Hester had to do most of it herself. There were no young gardeners willing to take up the challenge. She was making plans for a new herbaceous border. There was such talk in the Royal Horticultural Society magazine about the designs of Gertrude Jekyll and descriptions of her lush and flowing palette of colours with rippling perennials for every season. She rather fancied having a go herself.

The staff was now down to a minimum and she was back to using the kitchen herself except when she entertained, which was rare these days.

This business of a memorial was causing such a stir in the village. The new chapel pastor, Fanshawe, wanted all serving men to be honoured, dead or alive, on a scroll. Only the dead would be carved on the monument with their ranks, ages, regiments and dates of death.

Then there were those who wanted no rank to be mentioned, or a statue, but a useful building to be dedicated to the fallen. She had argued they already had a church, a chapel and men's reading room and parish room-cum-village hall and the children's swing park. What else could they possibly want? She wasn't going to fork out for such unnecessary extravagance.

Then someone suggested an annual scholarship for a pupil to go to Sharland School. They were making their own elaborate arrangements to honour their former pupils, which was another matter. Looming over it all was Frank Bartley's omission from the memorial. It had split the village since persistent rumours that he had been wrongly executed. Some said that he was as much a victim of war as anyone else and ought to be honoured, but others would have no truck with his inclusion under any circumstances.

It had raised such a furore at the last committee meeting, she'd been tempted to walk out, if only her family weren't implicated in so many ways. It made Angus's lack of action so much worse. Perhaps if he had intervened . . .

She must bear the knowledge that the wrong Cantrell might be etched in stone for eternity and once done could never be put right.

Every night, she prayed that Guy would make his peace with her, let her know how he was faring. She could then tell him how sorry she was and how much she wanted to be reconciled.

As if in answer to all these supplications, one morning George the postman brought a letter to the door. 'From foreign parts is this, Lady Hester.' He gave her the letter, hovering over her, curious to see who it was from, but she smiled and closed the door, her heart racing. She'd know that writing anywhere.

It has come at last. Thank you. Thank you. She noticed the American stamp and made up a cup of precious Earl Grey tea as a treat and sat down to savour the envelope, slitting it open with her silver paper knife.

Mother,

I feel it is time that I gave you news of my life. I enlisted into the merchant navy under an assumed name. I served on the Atlantic convoys and signed on for further trips to see the world. I have had many adventures and met interesting people of all nations.

But the real reason for my writing is this. It has come to my notice that Frank Bartley was executed after a court martial in 1917 and that this has caused problems for his family. I gather that the village cannot decide about his name on the memorial. I strongly believe his name must be honoured there.

I hope you were doing all to support the family in their quest for justice. I have heard about summary executions at the front and know many were rushed affairs with not all the prisoners adequately defended. Did he have a prisoner's friend to speak for him? Did Angus mention anything before his death?

It troubles me that I was not able to write in his defence as he was a good lad and dedicated to his horses' welfare when many were not. He gave Angus a chance of life when he could have drowned. It therefore behoves us to take up his defence and find the true facts of this case.

I am well here. I don't know how long I shall stay at sea. America is a land of opportunity. I may explore the States, but I don't intend to return to England. Here, I can be who I choose to be with no questions asked. You may reply to the poste restante address here. I would appreciate an early response.

G. A. C.

Hester laid down the paper with a sigh. A cool formal letter of enquiry. It was only to be expected, after all this time. He'd not asked about her welfare. He had not shown any softening of his anger towards her.

He was expecting a prompt reply but what could she say but more lies and half-truths to put his mind at rest. Should she tell him the shocking truth?

At least this was a chink of light in the shutter. He had written, risked his address, and she already knew his assumed name from the clinic. She would write to Mr Charles West and tell him just what he wanted to know, whether it was to his liking or not. She owed him the truth: no more shielding the dead. It made no difference now to Angus or Frank Bartley and she cursed the day those boys had met at the Foss and their lives became inextricably linked.

If Guy saw her honesty, and if she made a promise to help Mrs Bartley get some justice for her son, perhaps then mother and son could be reconciled. She could make her own passage to America and visit him, make peace.

'Justice . . . to right an injustice' – where had she heard those words before? In the back of her mind rose that misty night all those years ago, when she had gone to visit Martha Holbeck in secret. 'You have to right an injustice.' She hadn't understood then but she did now.

If she befriended Essie Bartley, she might melt Guy's frozen heart.

Hester sat down at the bureau and wrote the most important letter of her life.

Selma hung over the side of the SS *Carmania*, savouring every last second, breathing in the seaweed smoky air of the Liverpool dock. In a week's time she'd arrive in the New World. She felt the breeze whipping round her and shivered with excitement. It was really happening. The luggage was safe in their smart second-class cabin. She stared up at the grey stone buildings of the city; towering blocks of offices, such grandeur on the waterfront, and then at the gunmetal sea that was to carry them so far. She'd never seen the sea before – park lakes and rivers, nothing bigger – and now she was going to cross an entire ocean.

Somewhere amongst the crowds were Aunty Ruth and Uncle Sam waving a farewell with white handkerchiefs. She wanted Mam to be with them but she refused, saying she'd not want to make a show of herself. They had said their farewells on Sowerthwaite station instead and she could still feel those trembling hands and see those eyes full of emotion.

'Don't forget where you come from, Selma. There's always a bed waiting for your return, and don't wed the first man who asks you. I know you'll cope, but don't forget you're a Yorkshire lass, so no fancy American talk.'

She had cried all the way back to Bradford, tears of guilt, excitement and relief all at the same time.

Now the moment had come and Lisa was clinging onto her arm, almost falling over the rails in an effort to make one last farewell. The girl darted a look of fear, as the horn blew from the two funnels. 'It won't sink, will it?' she cried. No one would ever forget the fate of the *Titanic* eight years before.

'Not a chance . . . looks as if it's been done up with fresh paint and a fancy rigout. We're going to have such a time, so wipe your eyes.'

'What if my uncle doesn't like me and sends me back?'

'Now stop this mithering and let's go exploring. Did you see those ladies in their fur coats and hats coming up the gangplank to first class? I expect they're dripping with jewels.'

Selma didn't want to waste a minute. She wanted to breathe in everything along the Mersey: the tugboats, the ferries, the barges and the grey warships docked. When will I see this again? she sighed. Who will I be then?

Her new life was beginning right here on the ship. She drew in a breath of satisfaction. This time next week they'd be in America.

*   *   *

283

Guy sat watching the ships docking in the harbour. He loved to see them as specks on the horizon drawing ever closer, turning in with a flurry of ropes and carts on the dockside, waiting for the loading to begin, the gangplank coming down and a stream of passengers pouring out, some carrying bundles and children into waiting cars and taxis. Who were they? Where had they come from?

He was putting off the moment when he would have to open his mother's letter addressed to him in his now familiar name.

He laughed, catching himself in a chandler's window. She wouldn't recognise Charlie West, his hair bleached white from salt and sun, his reddish beard making him look more like a Viking raider than the former officer and gentleman. His hands were calloused with rope burns and the wind, his breath smelled of stale bourbon, his lips cracked with tobacco smoke like an old sea dog.

What was he hoping for from her reply? At best nothing but the usual gossip, a list of society weddings, may be a few pleasantries and small talk. What lay between them now was an ocean of mistrust, disappointment and frustration.

If only Angus hadn't been such a rash fool, but after nearly three years Guy still keenly felt the loss of that other half of himself. But he only had to look in a mirror to know what his brother might have looked like now, seasoned by war and weariness.

Guy knew he'd toughened up himself, drunk too much, made use of dubious women who prowled the docks. They gave him a quick release from the tension that never went away. How long could he keep up this crisscrossing of oceans? Sometimes he had to force his muscles to crank into gear and give him the impetus to keep going.

The thought of a desk job didn't appeal – never had – not after the trenches and the convoys. He needed an outdoor life. He rather fancied himself as a cowboy out west riding the range . . . Open the damn thing, he scolded himself. But he needed another glass for courage before he did. He signalled to the barman.

Waterloo House.

My dear boy,

At last you write to me with news. I can scarcely believe such adventures. I hope you are not tiring yourself out too much. Don't punish your body.

As for the request for information about Frank Bartley, I will leave it to Angus's letter to put you in the picture. He wrote to me shortly before his death, telling me about the sad affair. Apparently you were called on for a character testimony, but Angus, being unaware of its importance, and forgetting that the Bartley boy once saved his life, let the matter slide until it was too late. The soldier's own poor field service record went against him in the end. So don't blame your brother for his ignorance and forgetfulness, as I did. I fear it may have contributed to his own reckless pursuit of some desperate quest for glory, which ultimately led to his death.

Information is scarce on the trial of the Bartley boy. These things are not for public consumption, but there have been rumblings in the press lately about the execution of soldiers at the front and inquiries are to be held.

Be that as it may, I will do my utmost to see that his name is cut into the monument. If and when it is ever erected. It is too early yet for any major decision. The grief of us who are bereaved is too raw for any enthusiasm for memorials. Doubtless they will follow in good time.

I hope you will continue to correspond with me, if only occasionally. A mother never means to hurt her offspring, but when she does she must expect the hand that fed to be bitten hard and must bear the pain.

Your ever loving
Mother

Guy read it over again, feeling sick, angry and sad at the same time. He slipped the letter into his inside pocket and to his surprise pulled out another one. It was addressed to Izaak Yoder. It was Zack's last letter and still no address written on it, as he had promised.

Those poor folks would think their son had died unrepentant. Guy slumped back and ordered another whisky. He was exhausted by his mother's news. What must Selma think of him now? His family had let everyone down, his honour was besmirched and no mistake. Now he just wanted to drink himself into oblivion, knowing tomorrow he must start another journey. At least there was one honourable thing he could still do.

As the ship made its way into New York harbour, Selma and Lisa strained to see the great skyline coming into view.

'Pinch me!' Lisa screamed. 'Am I dreaming? Look, the Statue of Liberty. It's huge, and that's Ellis Island where the steerage passengers must pass through.'

'Do we have to go there too?' Selma shivered, seeing the austere buildings in the middle of the bay.

'No, we've done ours, signed all those papers; where we came from, where we are going and our new address. We'll just dock and go through customs.'

'How do you know all this?'

'Didn't you read the pamphlet? Honestly, Selma, or should I call you Selima? I didn't know that was your real name.'

'Did they mind you being a Elise Grunwald?' Selma asked, her eyes fixed on the harbour coming into view.

'No one batted an eyelid. My papers are in order. Look . . . there's where we dock, do you think my cousins are waiting? I've only got an old photograph of Heinz and Sarah. I hope they come. There's so much I want to see before we catch the train west.'

Selma was feeling queasy at the thought of meeting strangers. There was no one in this whole country she knew, no relatives. Suddenly she felt very alone. Her job was to protect the professor's daughter, and here she was feeling that Lisa was looking after *her*. They had had such fun on the ship, dining, playing games, parading on deck – people watching, Lisa called it – making up stories about the other passengers: who was eloping, who was going to start a farm, who was running away with a bag full of banknotes.

They had lived in tiers on the ship and they were in the middle tier, comfortable in their cabin. Selma knew there were hundreds living rough down below in steerage; a different world altogether, just as their deck was separated from the first class passengers above. Now rich or poor, they'd all arrived safely, and the real adventure was beginning.

How could it not feel like a fresh start? The terrible war

287

was over and the sickness that followed it was abating. Now she must read up about New York. She didn't want to miss a moment of life in this exciting city.

As they passed through the terminal, Selma stared at the uniforms and heard loud voices speaking in a strange twang. She saw black-skinned porters with big eyes and flashing teeth. Everything was so brash, loud and large. You could fit two Sharlands into the dockside alone.

Hold your head up high and look confident, even if you don't feel it, she urged herself. This is your job so do it as best you can. Look for those faces in the crowd. Lisa was clinging on to her arm. 'Can you see them?' she croaked. 'I can't . . . Oh, what are we going to do?'

Selma's Yorkshire grit took over. 'Wait and see who comes to us,' she said, her eyes searching a sea of faces. Then she saw a placard held high: 'Grunwald'. 'Look over there. Wave and smile, Lisa. They've come for you.'

Suddenly a young man with a moustache and bowler hat and a pretty young woman in a fur coat and cloth hat emerged from the crowd.

'Elise, is that you? I'm Sarah, your cousin, and this is my husband, Heinz Berger. Welcome to New York!' They rattled forth in German and then in English, 'And you must be Miss Bartley. Welcome. Come, we've got a taxi. You must be tired and hungry.'

'Where is Uncle Cornelius?' Lisa asked.

'Business, I'm afraid, but your aunt Pearl has written to say everything is prepared for you over there. We thought you'd like a few days here to see the sights and go shopping.'

'Spiffing,' Lisa smiled. 'Come on, Selima, let's get going. Where do we start?'

In the days that followed Selma hardly had time to draw

breath as Sarah marched them all over the city, through Central Park, down to the great art museums, up and down Madison and Fifth Avenues to window-shop and browse around the great department stores. It made the Bradford shops seem like village stalls. The girls were dwarfed by the tall, grey buildings towering above them; skyscrapers, they called them. How on earth could anyone clean all those windows? They were treated to a cinema show in Times Square where Lillian Gish starred in a dramatic tale of a country girl seduced by a wicked man. It was so melo-dramatic Selma cried with relief when it all ended happily.

Each night Sarah's cook placed meals on the table such as pasta and cooked meats she'd never experienced before, spicy hot chillies, mustards and sweet relishes, spaghetti like wriggling worms with meat sauces and wonderful dark pop that tasted sweet and fizzy.

They lived in a terrace of tall brown houses with steps leading from the pavement that they called sidewalks, and dustbins they called garbage cans. The streets were full of people rushing to offices and shops in short skirts. It was a different world, and this was only the beginning. Soon they would go on a steam train taking them right across the country; a week on a train to another big city where Lisa would be meeting her father's brother, and starting a new life out West. That's when Selma's own journey would end.

It would be time for her to turn back or stay on. But what was she going to do out there alone? Her future was uncertain, but one thing was sure: this was a land for young people, a land where no one cared who you were or where you came from, a land of opportunity. Surely there was a place for her in such an amazing country.

*   *   *

289

Guy drank his way down the eastern seaboard of America from Boston through to New York and New Jersey, drifting further south in a haze of bourbon and beer. He saw it as a sort of vacation from everything to do with war, his brother's death, his English life, but his accent always betrayed his roots and drew attention.

In his head he was on a mission to find the Yoders of Pennsylvania and give them the letter he'd kept so long. But he was finding Pennsylvania was a large state, and Yoder was a common name in places.

His only clue was that Zack had said they were plain folk, which in his ignorance he'd thought meant simple country people. Then he discovered that this meant they belonged to some religious group. They were Puritans of German origin, who lived in districts together separated by their dress, customs, language and religion from the rest of the people. But, to add to this confusion, there were many such groups all over the state.

For weeks on end, he hitched rides on trucks and wagons, jumping on rail trucks, living rough by the road, dossing around but always asking if there were plain folk in this township.

As weeks turned into months his clothes became filthy, his beard matted and his scalp scratched until even the fleas deserted him. It reminded him of life in the trenches, cold, hungry, living by his wits, working a day here or there just to fuel his throat. He knew he was getting weaker, and he must find a settled place before winter set in. He had walked inland from New Jersey, through Flemington and on towards the Delaware River, over covered bridges. To the south of him was the great city of Philadelphia. If all else failed, he could head there, clean up, sign on again.

But he had no more stomach for seafaring. That part of his life was over.

He couldn't believe he'd reached this level, bogtrotting, as they used to say in Yorkshire, cadging soup and hot drinks in church crypts and hostels with other down-and-out hobos. It was as if his life didn't matter any more. Angus was dead, his family was broken, all that mattered was the next meal, the next drink. Everything of value he possessed was flogged for a few dollars. There was just no point any more, except for the crumpled letter in his pocket. If he could deliver this to its rightful owner then he'd have completed one act of decency in this wasted life. After that he'd take his chance.

He hadn't bothered to reply to his mother or Dr Mac. That part of his life was over, never to return. He felt nothing but itching, chill and a tight chest. All the walking had firmed his leg muscles, but his poor eating had weakened him and he guessed one bad bout of bronchitis would finish him off.

Perhaps he'd end up in some ditch, stiff and cold like the boys in no man's land, their grinning white skulls that haunted his dreams and the rats the size of cats feasting on the rich pickings of the Flanders mud. But not before he found Izaak Yoder.

He did have one piece of luck in a place near Quakertown. He'd gone there because of the name. Even he knew Quakers were plain livers, but no one knew the Yoder family there. A woman in the queue keeping downwind of him suggested he might go further out into a township towards Bethlehem.

'There are plain folk out there, with many farms and churches. You might find who you are looking for around those parts,' she offered. 'They keep themselves to themselves but are good people. May God bless you on your search,' she nodded. It was the first kind word spoken to him for weeks. 'How does a gentle-spoken English boy come to be brought so low? You don't speak like no bum to me.' She pushed a quarter in his hand.

He nodded, not wanting to cry at her compassion. 'I'm not sure, ma'am. But thank you kindly.'

It was too much temptation not to fill his guts with whisky before he set off, but he resisted. He fixed his eyes on the sight of the autumn leaves in the trees ahead, all those gold, crimsons, burnt ochres. It was fine country with white limestone houses that reminded him of Sharland stone. He walked on, hitching a lift towards the wide open farmlands where the red painted Dutch barns dotted the landscape, standing out against the rolling gentle hills.

Everywhere he stopped he asked if Izaak Yoder had a farmstead, but no one knew, until his legs were aching, his back seared with pain and he knew he could go no further.

He stopped at an inn by some crossroads and was sent to the back door and given a cup of soup.

'You'll find the Mennonites over the hill. Yoders aplenty up there, all related. Maybe you'll strike lucky at one of them before sundown, but they ain't folks like us. No drinking . . . no dancing, no fancy clothes, no nothing but praying and hard work, and they don't put up no fight neither. It's against their faith. If they don't know yer folks someone else will. They sit tight together, them and the Amish. Now they're real strict, but they're over Lancaster County way. You could try there too.'

Feeling exhausted, Guy walked down that lone road. He could barely breathe and knew he'd have to stop and find shelter.

He turned off the first track that wound through a copse of pines. He heard a rustling in the undergrowth. Was it deer, turkey or wild dogs? The silence was broken only by the call of something on the hill. There were no lights to guide him, just a total exhaustion as he gathered up dried leaves to make himself a bed, breaking a few branches to cover him. It was still warm and there was a stream gurgling somewhere close by. He was so doggone whacked, all he wanted to do was lie down and never get up again. To be so close and yet so far. If he pegged out someone would find his coat and a letter in his pocket and pass it on. Then this journey and his passing would not have been in vain. Guy sighed. So this is it, the long sleep. Better here than in the bottom of a shell hole at the mercy of the giant rats. He lay back and knew no more.

17

Hester woke from one of her nightmares with a bad feeling in her chest. Was it Guy in danger? Who else was there left to worry about? Was it that awful committee meeting that had caused such a storm in the village the night before when she had said her piece, lost her temper over their shillyshallying about Frank Bartley's name? She had woken in such a sweat and panic. Something was wrong!

'If you think I'm contributing to a monument that honours only those you think suitable, you've another think coming.' She recalled every word. 'This debate has gone on long enough and if we cannot agree on a solution, I suggest we reconvene at a later date when we've all thought about the proposal carefully.

'Mrs Bartley lost two sons. I lost one, as have most people here. We do not know all the circumstances of Frank Bartley's execution, but certain facts are known. Many people in this country are not happy that some of our men met this fate at the hands of their own army. There have been enquiries in Parliament, and until this issue is resolved I think we should wait before condemning this young man to oblivion. I have a son, retired on medical grounds; he should also be on the muster roll of honour. I don't think this is the time or moment to make decisions without all the facts to hand.'

'But Bankwell and Sowerthwaite have plans for their crosses; it's about time we got ours in shape too. It's a disgrace to all those families to have nothing to look at when Armistice Day comes round,' said the treasurer.

'Where are the memorials to Waterloo or Balaclava or Agincourt? It didn't make their sacrifice any the less,' she argued. 'If we put on the names we put on all the names, I say, not a chosen few. There will be no plaque in St Wilfred's without the say-so of the patrons. The chapel can do as it likes. It's the public one in the street that matters. Where is the right place to set it? What is the most dignified design? How much can we raise?'

'Sharland School is putting up wrought-iron gates in memory of its lost boys, and I've heard that they plan to put a bridge over the River Ribble near Settle. Why do we have to do something like everyone else?' asked Ebenezer Best. 'I fear, Lady Hester, your protests keep putting our plans in jeopardy. People are impatient to honour Remembrance Day.'

'So you keep saying, but I say, if they want a two-minute silence, they can keep it in their own houses or go to Sowerthwaite for a ceremony. We either agree or disagree, but don't go half-cock at this project. Better to wait until we are unanimous on the matter.'

Everyone was muttering at her remarks. She was getting so weary of the same old arguments, well aware she was holding up the show with her protests. She was sick of the whole remembrance sentimentality. Why did they need a public statue?

As she lay in bed, thinking it all out, she knew where that anger was coming from: from guilt and shame, fear and regret. The longer she could make them wait the longer she could avoid the constant reminder of her own family's part in the Bartley affair.

Oh, Guy, where are you? Why didn't you write back? What has become of you? Why do I feel you are in need of my prayers? Oh, son, don't waste your life because of all this mess. Find peace and happiness for yourself. Don't give up on life while you have breath in your body.

She was crying again, stupid tears of self-pity. Then another voice boomed in her ear.

'Get a hold of yourself, woman,' she could hear Charles ordering. 'Do your duty. Stop whining over what is lost to you. Just battle on with it!'

Guy blinked, aware that someone was standing over him. It was a boy, barefoot, in dirty denim overalls and shirt, staring at him.

'Englisher?' he said. His dog was standing guard, eyeing Guy with interest. He nodded. How could he tell that without him speaking a word?

'*Kommen sie hier . . .*' the boy pointed to the track. He was speaking some sort of German.

'*Danke, Kamerad,*' Guy replied, not knowing where he was being led but too damp and stiff to care. It was almost dark.

The boy took him down the track, the dog sniffing his heels as he opened the side door of a wooden barn. 'You sleep . . .' There was a bunch of straw in the corner and a horse blanket. Then he pointed to Guy's pockets: 'Lucifer . . . Lucifer.' He wanted matches and Guy ferreted down his pockets to find the last of his strikes.

'Give, please. No lights, no fire,' said the boy. So Guy handed them over.

'*Danke* . . . thank you . . . Yoder?' he asked.

The boy shook his head. 'Clemmer. You sleep here. My father will come.' He closed the door and Guy sat down, not sure what to do next.

A lantern appeared and a man with a full beard and straw hat looked down on him. 'English, you want to rest?'

'Yes, sir,' Guy replied, feeling dirty, smelling to high heaven. 'I have to find Izaak Yoder. I have a letter.' He produced it from his pocket, waving it.

'That can wait. You look sick man to me,' he replied in slow broken English, and he felt Guy's forehead. 'You have fever . . . Here, drink and rest. You will go nowhere . . . sleep. In the morning my wife will see to . . . a wash . . . food.'

Guy had no energy to argue, overwhelmed by the kindness of a hay barn and a bowl of hot soup with rough bread. 'You are German?' he asked.

'No, we be American Mennonites. We live apart and speak the old tongue but English we can understand. You have a name for me?'

'Charles West, from England. I was a soldier. Now I am nothing.'

'Before God, we are all someone. You have travelled a long way to find us?'

'I have a letter for Izaak Yoder. It is important.'

'As I said, it can wait for tomorrow. God give you rest and peace,' said the man as he closed the door. Guy curled up under the blanket, snug and warm.

In the morning, he rose shaking for want of a drink, but strangely rested. Where was he? Somewhere warm and dry and alive, off the beaten track, he remembered with a smile.

The boy brought in a bowl of hot water and a towel and a bit of a soap. 'For you,' he said.

Guy smiled again. 'Thank you. And how do I call you, young man?'

'Simeon Clemmer.'

'Pleased to meet you, Simeon Clemmer.' The boy grinned shyly.

'You come to the house and the kitchen to eat.'

Guy nodded, touched by this hospitality but unnerved to be offered a seat at their table. He was not fit to be seen. 'I need a wash first.' He blushed as the boy looked at his rags with a direct gaze. He was ashamed of his filthy shirt, his unshaven chin, the flea bites on his arms.

Simeon indicated the soap and water, then went to check the stock at the far end of the barn while Guy had his first wash for weeks. 'We have eggs – you are hungry?'

Guy nodded, feeling fresher for the wash, though the grime on the towel was embarrassing. How had he let himself get into this filthy state? He tried to make the best of his old uniform pants, brushing straw from them and stuffing fresh straw into the holes in his boots. How could a British officer, a Sharland School pupil, a colonel's son, have sunk so low?

He stood at the back door, smelling the breakfast cooking, suddenly ravenous. It took him back to village days, when they visited Pinkerton's farm. I wasn't always a tramp begging at back doors, he thought.

A woman opened the door in a long grey dress and white pinafore, her hair scraped back into a tight bun caught in a cap that tied under her chin.

'Mr West, come you in, sit down with us and eat.' Simeon was already seated with a line of small children, all eyeing him with interest. Everything in the kitchen was neat: ordered shelves, clean and very spare, pegs on the walls, wooden chairs; a simple cooking range. These were indeed plain folk.

A plate of ham and eggs was put in front of him and Simeon sat by his side, parents at either end of the table. They fell silent, bowed their heads in prayer for grace and then pounced on their ham and eggs with gusto. There was fresh milk to drink, and bread. Guy had not eaten so well in weeks.

'You asked for Izaak Yoder, what is your business?' asked the man, Hans Clemmer.

'I have a letter, given to me by his son. I promised I would post it but the address got mislaid. Do you know them? I've been searching a long time,' Guy replied.

'He might be known to me. Yoder is a common name amongst us.'

'You can say that again . . .' His cough broke out and his chest was tight with hope that his journey had borne fruit.

'You have travelled far to find him?' Hans's wife asked.

'From Boston.'

'That is far. You are not in work?' she continued

'I was a soldier and then a sailor, but now, I don't know.' They had seen the state of his clothes and his shaking hands.

'His son is well?'

Guy didn't reply. It was not his place to tell a stranger such sad news and yet he must know more. 'You knew him . . . Zacharias?'

'We did know one of that name, but he left our fellowship many years ago. He is not one of us now.'

'I see,' Guy sighed. 'That's a pity. I had hoped—'

'Hans, don't torment the poor boy with what he will not understand. Mr West, when a boy disobeys the orders of our Church he is no longer part of our community. His family

299

must choose also to distance themselves from him or not. That is how we live by our *Ordnung*, the old order. We discipline each other in love. We are not of this world and choose to live apart, as you see. We choose to dress plain and live simply. The Bible tells us this is the right way and we must all obey.'

Guy was feeling hot again, his cheeks flushed. 'I'm sorry. I'm not well. I'd better go . . . I do not want to repay your kindness by bringing sickness to your door.' The room was spinning around him.

'Mr West, you lie down. There is no rush for your mission. Come, we will let you rest, not as an animal in a barn but as a human being who needs clean clothes, a shave and medicine. I think you have come a long way down from where you began in this life. God has brought you to our door for His purpose.'

Guy lay on the bed for days, tossing and turning, crying out to Angus, sweating; the wooden beams across the ceiling spinning round like tops over his head if he raised himself. Someone sponged his face, made him sip warm bitter tea and bathed his limbs, always in silence and always with courtesy, giving him back the dignity he had forgotten.

His old clothes hung on a peg, and bit by bit were replaced by a clean plain shirt, overalls and breeches until one day he sat up hungry, refreshed in his mind, and his chest no longer bound by steel ropes.

The children came in and watched him: twins Melinda and Mary, Simeon and little Menno. Then later a tall man with a striking beard and hat stood over him in a black frock coat.

'Preacher Friesen has come to visit with us. We told him of your journey. He has good news.'

300

'You have found my Yoders?' Guy said.

'On a farm not a few miles up the road. I wanted to check Izaak's son was your Zacharias. His daughter, Rose of Sharon, and his wife, Miriam Zimmermann, confirm this. You could have wandered for years and never found them.'

Guy sank back, relieved that his mission was accomplished. 'I have the letter . . . Do you wish to take it?' He pointed to the envelope.

'No, God brought you all this way. It is for you to put it in his hands. No doubt they will have many questions.'

'You told him I am coming?' Had he broken the sad news?

'No, just to expect a visitor from afar. News travels fast in this community. We do not see many English Englishers,' he said, a twinkle in his eye. 'God must have plans for you. Get your strength back and take your time. He will wait for your visit with a good heart.'

Guy shook his hand, strangely comforted by these words. Plain folk they might be but they had giant hearts, bringing him back from the dead. It would do no harm to rest a while among them and find a way to repay their kindness. For the first time in years, he felt a little of his old self returning, or, at the least, a newer version of himself. Guy Cantrell was dead and buried but Charles West had only just been born.

Selma woke to the rattle of the wheels on the rail track. They had been sleeping in the train for days, travelling across the Midwest States, one by one, going ever westwards, cocooned in their little sleeping compartment, but dining in the open diner, taking in the spectacular scenery from the glass viewing chamber.

How could she describe all the wonders of this journey to her mother back home? She'd sent postcards from New York and Chicago and now she was writing to tell her all about the Greenwood family they would meet in Los Angeles.

Lisa was busy making notes and drawings of the mountain passes and plains from the window, drawing sketches in her journal, chattering about watersheds and river beds with excitement. Selma felt so privileged to have such a wonderful experience.

The more she saw of this country, the more she wondered at its wilderness and open space, the grandeur of the Rocky Mountains. Round every corner was a new vista, rivers as wide as seas, and their fellow passengers were enjoying it all as much as they were, especially the young Scotsman who kept them entertained en route in the evenings.

His name was James Barr, he was twenty-six and off to Los Angeles to find work in the picture industry. He'd been an actor in Glasgow and then in the army. He had the most lilting accent and startling copper hair and chestnut eyes.

Lisa called him their guardian angel. He played a mean game of cards and sang sad folk songs with a funny little pipe. He had latched on to them and when he found out Lisa's uncle was Cornelius Grunwald, he seemed very impressed.

Selma felt he'd singled them out and her in particular, wanting to know all about her life in Bradford and why they were making this epic journey together.

He had been staying in New York, trying to find work in the theatre, but now was searching out west. Every evening she found she was looking forward to seeing his handsome face, making sure her dress was pressed and her stockings straight, her hair neatly waved.

'He's taken a shine to you,' Lisa teased. 'Are you going to kiss him?'

'Don't be daft! I hardly know him,' Selma blushed.

'He likes you, he keeps giving you his foxy stare.'

'No he doesn't.'

'I think he's so handsome . . . He's played in *Hamlet*, you know, and the Scottish play.'

'Well, he would, he's a Scotch man.'

'It's bad luck to call the play *Macbeth*,' Lisa whispered.

'I don't know what you're on about. I'm not one for play-acting,' Selma said, ashamed of her ignorance. 'It wasn't allowed.'

'You are funny. How can anyone not want to see real plays? Daddy and I used to go every week.' Then she fell silent, knowing she'd never see him again.

'It's all make believe,' Selma said kindly. 'Not real life.'

'But it echoes real life . . . beams it back to us so we can understand things better. "Brings a mirror to ourselves," my drama teacher used to say.'

'You talk such rot!'

'No, I don't! Ask James. I've never met a real play-actor before. We'll have to go and see him on the stage. Then you'll know what it's all about.'

Was it possible on this strange journey across the continent that she was allowing herself to open her heart again? When she looked at James, with those dark eyes, her heart flipped a beat. What on earth had they got in common? He rattled on about people and places she'd never heard of and she loved every second of his cheery company. It was such a long time since anyone had paid her such close attention.

Guy's face no longer filled her mind. That was over and gone. Now she must look to her future, take a chance on this unexpected turn-up.

Perhaps when they reached their destination, the test would come. Did he really mean all those compliments or was it all play-acting too? Time would tell if he was sincere. She was no pushover and wouldn't be hurt again.

Lady Hester seemed to fill the front parlour with her presence, sitting down holding her stick like Britannia on her throne.

'What do you think of my proposition?'

Essie was so flummoxed she could hardly speak. 'You want me to come and live in Waterloo . . . in your service? I don't understand. Are you selling my home over my head?'

'Not at all. We don't sell our properties but the young mechanic next door wants to expand his business and needs to be closer to the premises. Cars are the new horses, I'm afraid. I thought you might consider a position away from the village a little more to your liking.'

'Oh, I don't mind the gossips . . . sticks and stones and all that. Words won't harm me. And I don't need charity. I can find summat if you're chucking me out.'

'Don't be so prickly, woman. We may have very different views but you are an honest worker and these days it's hard to find reliable staff. Since the war nobody wants to return to their old posts.'

The compliment was unexpected but Essie still wasn't sure. 'It's not as if I'm not grateful, but I'll have to think it over, write to our Selma in America.' She paused to point out the line of postcards and letters on the mantelpiece. 'She's out west as a lady's companion . . . done well for herself and she's walking out with a young chap from Scotland,' she sighed. 'Trust her to go all that way to meet a kiltie when they are two a penny two hours up the track in Carlisle. But that's young ones for you: go their own way. Is Master Angus still abroad?'

Hester nodded. 'Quite well, thank you. But back to my offer – will you consider it? You haven't been to the WI for months.'

'You know the reason for that. I don't feel comfortable.'

'Nonsense! When you come to work for me, I shall insist we go down there together. That'll soon put a stop to such ignorance,' she said, rising from the button-back chair, her black skirts swishing across the furniture. 'A change will do you good.'

'If you say so,' Essie sighed. Why was the woman doing this? She'd never taken any notice of them before, but she had, much to her surprise, put a word in for Frank's name to be included on the memorial. The decision was delayed on Armistice Day in favour of tolling the church bell at the eleventh hour, one for each of the fallen, twenty-seven tolls so each could stand and remember in his or her own place.

She was a queer old stick in many ways and now she was rattling round in that barn of a house with only a couple of regular staff. Mrs Beck was bad with her rheumatics again and not able to come in each day. Was Lady Hester expecting her to take over her place?

It wasn't as if she was afraid of the hard work, but to have that dragon breathing down her neck giving orders . . . They would have to come to some accommodation. But it did make sense. She was only just scraping by. Selma sent dollars when she could but extra would help.

She had cut herself off from chapel and was in danger

of becoming a bitter old battleaxe. She didn't need to ask anyone's permission to make this move, even if it was just changing one kitchen sink for another. But to leave this place for good? She looked around her. Whyever not? Memories could be taken anywhere when they were rooted into her heart.

As she set about her own chores that day, she felt touched that Lady Hester was singling her out but she guessed the reason why.

Lady Hester knew her son had let their son down and that Angus owed his life to her boys too. Then there was the matter of the romance that Hester had squashed between the two sweethearts. Now *all* the boys were gone. For all her high and mighty ways she was a lonely old woman, just like herself, and for that reason alone she would write a note accepting the position. There was nothing left for her here but reminders of better days.

Guy stood in the large kitchen farmhouse, clutching his dark hat, wondering how he had got to this moment. He was clothed in a sober black coat and trousers that smelled of camphor, and a stiff shirt. His beard was trimmed and his hands were twitching. He needed a drink, but all that was on offer was water. In his pocket was the crumpled letter.

Hans Clemmer guided him in. 'This is the young man who has come from afar, Izaak. He brings news.'

Facing him was a stern-looking man, who towered over him, with a full beard and wearing a checked shirt and trousers ready for the day's work. His wife stood by his side with anxious eyes. Guy was about to break their hearts.

It was one thing writing letters of condolence in the

trenches when you didn't have to face parents in person. Delivering the bad news was quite another.

'Sit down, Englishman.'

Guy was getting used to this formal manner with strangers, their broken English and sudden burst into a language straight out of a German textbook, to his ears.

He told them how he had met Zacharias on board the *Regina*, how sick he was and how he had dictated this letter before he passed away in his sleep.

The woman put her hand to her mouth as he handed over the letter. 'I am sorry,' he said, seeing the pain etched on their faces.

'Your son is your son all his life . . . however far he strays from the track,' Izaak sighed. 'You do not expect to bury your grown-up children, only your babies. He did what he thought was his duty and made his choice. Now he has paid the price. We will read this later,' he said, taking the letter and placing it on the table unopened. 'And you, young man, did you enlist for your country? You'll be marked by your memories? It must be heavy burden to bear, knowing you have killed your fellow men in anger and in cold blood. The Bible says, "Thou shalt not kill . . . Do not be overcome by evil but overcome with good." That is our understanding of Scriptures so we resist the call to arms.'

'Yes,' Guy replied, feeling very weary.

'Come, young man, what are your plans now you have brought this to our door?'

'I have no plans, sir.'

Izaak turned to his wife and back to Guy. 'We have need of a pair of hands to plough the fields and see to the horses. You are welcome to work here until you are given guidance for what is to come. Is that not so, Miriam?'

The woman nodded, looking at Guy over metal-rimmed spectacles.

Hans Clemmer smiled. 'I think Mr West is in need of time to grow fresh skin around himself. I shall leave you in their care. The Lord gives and the Lord takes, brothers. Blessed be his name.'

'Amen,' they all said in unison

It was as if it had all been decided above his head and he hadn't the energy to protest that he must be on his way. Then a girl came running through the door.

'I've finished the milking, Pa,' she rattled in their quaint German. Seeing the stranger, she stopped and bowed her head.

'Rose of Sharon, this is Mr West. He's brought sad news of your brother. Now the Lord has sent him to take his place.'

Her golden hair was plaited over her head, her cap was awry, her dress was grey and white stripes with a grubby pinafore on the top and her feet were bare, but her eyes shone out at Guy like sapphires.

'The Lord be with you, Brother West,' she said in perfect English, and he looked into those shining blue orbs and knew he would not be leaving for a while.

18

The dry searing heat drained Selma of her normal energy, but the luxury of diving into the turquoise-blue-tiled swimming pool was wonderful. The Grunwald residence, Casa Pinto, sprawled over three acres of prime real estate as Cornelius's new wife, Pearl, kept reminding them. Lisa's uncle worked in the big barns they called Hollywood Grange on the outskirts of the sprawling city. He was in the film industry, doing some sort of bookkeeping, Lisa said.

Selma was getting a distinct feeling that she was outstaying her initial welcome and that Pearl was eager to see Lisa settled at the local high school and out of the way. Their arrival had disrupted her routine. She had been a vaudeville artiste, and now ruled their black servants like an Eastern potentate, so the thought of taking on a teenage girl and her companion did not appeal. But she was polite enough when her husband was around.

Cornelius Grunwald was a grizzled fifty-year-old with dark hawk eyes, who seemed to spend most of his time on the telephone or dashing out in his enormous car to meetings with clients, while his wife sunned herself on the terrace, reading magazines and Sears and Roebuck catalogues.

Lisa wouldn't hear of Selma leaving. 'Please don't go and leave me with that crocodile. She smiles and then bites my head off. Poor Uncle Corrie, he wasn't very clever, was he, choosing her after Aunt Minnie?'

'Why?'

'She's a gold digger. I've never seen her do a hand's turn, and you know what they say: all that glitters . . . I don't like her.'

'But she's your aunty now.' They had to be sensible. Lisa must stay here.

'I know, but don't go yet. I'm sure Uncle Corrie will find you somewhere in his office.'

'But I'm not qualified. I'd be hopeless in an office. I can shoe horses and groom them – if we had one, that is.'

'There you go, you've made a job, and you can teach me to ride and Jamie too. He needs to ride well in cowboy pictures. You'd love that.' She winked.

Since their arrival in Hollywood, James was always calling in. He'd found work waiting tables while trying to get auditions. At least Pearl had offered to help him find a decent agent. She was all sweetness and light when he turned up to take Selma out.

Only last week, he dashed round to tell them there was a big party going on in Beverly Hills and they were looking for extra catering staff. So Lisa and Selma were dragooned into service in little black dresses and white lace caps and pinnies to stand at the door and serve fruit cocktails.

Selma nearly dropped her tray when she saw Douglas Fairbanks drift in with Mary Pickford on his arm. Lisa whispered that the actress wasn't his first wife, nor he her first husband. 'They do that a lot – swap wives about. A girl at my school told me she's had three stepfathers already!'

Selma tried not to look shocked but Jamie was trying to circulate and get noticed, tossing his lion's mane of hair, winking at her across the room. She felt protective of him, as if it were her job to make the Grunwalds secure him that first rung on the ladder, but she didn't know the first thing about this mysterious movie world. To her untutored eye the studios looked like a lot of grubby barns huddled together under a brown haze of smog that pricked her eyes and hid the sun.

'Uncle Corrie says you can teach us all to ride,' Lisa shouted. 'And Jamie too!'

Selma's feet were aching, and her jaw too with trying to smile. The room was full of tobacco smoke and the smell of strong spirits and Jamie kept helping himself to half-empty glasses.

'Just a perk of the job . . . come and eat your fill. The girls won't eat in case they get fat and the men are too busy swilling down the booze. Isn't this the place to be seen?'

Selma wasn't so sure. There was a raw hungry look on some of those faces; people smiled with their teeth but not their eyes when they were talking to each other. The waiters were barked at like dogs or else ignored entirely. It felt a million miles away from Sharland gatherings.

True to his word, Uncle Corrie hired some horses and Selma got a chance to show them the basics of how to approach the animal, saddle it up, groom and comb and then sit and ride. She couldn't help showing off, riding bareback and racing off.

Lisa was nervous and stiff but Jamie was impatient, wanting to do everything at once, and kept falling off. He was rough with the horse, who had a will of its own, quick to flare up.

'This is hopeless!'

'Be patient. You need to make a friend of him so it trusts you. They can tell if you are nervous. Don't force it. You have to practise. Black Magic needs to respect you.'

Sometimes she left them to canter over the desert track, her thighs gripping the sides, hair in the wind, at one with the beast, and it brought back those summer days with Guy, making her suddenly homesick for the green hills.

Perhaps it was time to return to England, but she pushed that thought to the back of her mind. Lisa needed a friend and Jamie was becoming more than just one. They were all strangers in a foreign land, clinging together for support.

The poor lad was exhausted, trying to work at anything and everything, turning up for castings – a bar man in a saloon brawl; an extra in a crowd scene – and when there were no castings, he lugged cameras and cases of film to locations. He was on set from seven in the morning until after midnight.

His spare time was spent at the local boxing ring and gymnasium, or midnight training swims in the Grunwalds' pool. He grew his hair like a poet. His idols on set were John Barrymore and Richard Dix. No one bothered about his gingery hair in black-and-white movies – it could be sky blue – and his accent didn't matter either.

Selma felt so proud of his efforts and watched over the weeks as he tamed his impatience and rode so well that he left her standing when they raced on the shoreline.

One night they huddled together on the sand.

'Do you ever think of home, Jamie?' she whispered. 'Scotland and your family?'

He shivered. 'What would I be thinking of that lot for?'

'But your parents . . .' she continued, but he put his fingers over her lips.

312

'What's there to miss? A pa who was gae handy with the leather strap and his wee wifie who got her head bashed if Partick Thistle took a pasting at the football match. It was no picnic growing up with them but I found a way . . . in the army, in the plays. When you act you become another person. I can change my voice and be anybody I choose. When I'm famous I'll have a house like Pearl's, and no more waiting tables . . . another life with a yacht and horses, you'll see.'

'I wish I knew what to do next,' she confessed. 'I'm on borrowed time. One day Lisa will not want me to look after her and Pearl keeps dropping hints that I've outstayed my welcome.'

'You worry too much. You'll get by. Come here and give me a kiss . . . You and me will always be fine, Selma.'

They kissed and cuddled under the stars. It was the most romantic night of her young life. She felt safe, for Jamie was going places and he would let her tag along too. She lay back in his arms, content in this safe haven. Together, everything was possible, together they would make his future happen.

Young love is blind to the pitfalls of passion, the dark alleys where she cats pounce and bite. Love is blind to everything but each dizzy meeting, each kiss, caress, each promise that these feelings will never end.

Jamie and I were soon lovers. This time there was no prudish holding back. No one was there to stop me, no one cared where I was late at night, sneaking out for our secret trysts under the stars.

Oh, those heady nights when clinches turned into careless

lovemaking, snatching moments between shoots and location work. Little did I know the world we were courting was a world full of uncertainties, filled with a colony of rootless insecure actors who spent their lives in constant fear of being typecast, out of the public eye or being upstaged by more beautiful creatures snapping at their heels; a world of bored wives who wooed new flesh to their sides for the excitement of the chase.

We were such innocents abroad, but unknown to me Jamie was learning fast how to hustle and play this game. I should have been his sister, not his wife. By the time I realised that sobering fact, it was far too late to change matters. There was a baby on the way.

Essie stared at the photograph in hurt and unbelief, thinking, I don't believe it! Selma had gone and got herself wed. What was she thinking of and to the Scotch lad, the actor? Look at the two of them, not a penny to rub together and all dolled up like a dish of tripe and onions. She had to sit down, feeling faint.

It was her silver and brass day, and the scullery girl, Maggie, was sitting opposite, eyeing the picture with a sigh. 'He's so handsome!'

'Handsome is as handsome does. Get on with your polishing.'

She'd been shocked at how the place had been let go: dust everywhere, dull brass door knobs, fire irons, dirty curtain linings. Every room needed bottoming out. Lady Hester just didn't see the grime. She needed new spectacles. It was going to take months to put this place in order. Why was it rich folk didn't appreciate what they had?

'Is he a film star? This husband of Selma's,' Maggie asked.

'Hardly that, he's got a part in some Wild West picture. They're going down south to film in the desert and she's going with him.'

'Look at that dress! It's proper lace, and the garden full of flowers. Can you imagine getting married in a garden round here?'

Essie sniffed. She wasn't going to tell Maggie that James Barr was a left-footer, a Catholic, so there was no proper church wedding. Why couldn't they wait and come back home and do it properly? How could these paupers pay their fares back to England?

They did make a handsome couple, though, and Selma looked radiant behind an enormous bunch of roses. Lisa was the bridesmaid in a floral print dress and caped sleeves.

How she missed her daughter's company. She would have loved to be there but she'd have to content herself with buying a pretty frame for the portrait and showing it off. In her heart she ached to have been part of all the preparations and excitement, and to have sized up the groom for herself. But no use getting upset. The deed was done.

Perhaps they would make a trip back here one day and she'd see him for herself.

She'd settled down in Waterloo House better than she'd thought. She had her own bedroom and sitting room on the top floor with a view right over the village out onto the Ridge. A view for all seasons, she smiled, watching the chimney smoke from the village cottages showing which way the wind was blowing.

Sometimes when she prepared Lady Hester's supper,

they would sit down in the kitchen and share a pot of tea. Under all that stiff bravado was a woman of many opinions, who spoke of the old days when her boys were lads with a yearning that matched Essie's exact feelings.

True to her word, she'd insisted Essie go back into the WI. There were new faces among the old, some speakers were interesting, and, worryingly, some were spouting about there being another war coming if they didn't heed what was going on in Germany.

Then Essie thought about Angus, who never wrote home, and how Hester pined for news. What had gone wrong there she'd never know. You didn't ask such personal questions of such a proud lady. There were rumours he'd turned to drink, that he'd gone to Australia in search of gold, that he was in prison, or worse. She kept the boys' rooms as if they were due home any minute: beds aired, floors polished, clothes laundered.

They made Essie shudder, these ghost-filled rooms, empty of all life and warmth, never disturbed; wardrobes full of warm tweeds and suits that would cover the backs of soldiers, out of work, begging at back doors. It was a crying shame.

Lady Hester spent hours in her flower borders, shaping, pruning, planting, lost in her green world. Someone once quipped that ladies of her age went for God or their garden. Essie hadn't time for either.

Asa would be ashamed of her heathen ways. Sunday was her day off and she would read, go for a walk, make sure the luncheon was ready for when Hester came back from church, and then retire to the cane chair by the attic window to write reams to Selma.

In the little silver comforts tin that came with Newton's

effects, she popped in spare coins: threepenny pieces, halfpennies for her holiday fund. One day she'd get herself across that ocean and see this land of plenty for herself.

As the seasons sped past – seed time, haymaking and harvest – Guy found his strength returning. Everyone pulled together on this ninety-acre farm with its small herd of cattle, horses and four grain crops to sow and reap. Their living depended on the whole family working from dawn to dusk. He found their quiet frugal way of life a revelation, such hard labour for little reward. Then when Hans Clemmer's brother's barn caught fire all the farmers in the district left their own work to help rebuild the barn with gifts of wood, nails, food and tools. In a tight community every man was your brother, your friend and your keeper.

They jabbered away in their version of German, they called 'Pennsylvania Dutch' and gradually Guy began to pick up key words – and insults! They absorbed him into their community until it was natural that he began to attend their services in the stone meeting house, sitting on the bench – men on one side, women on the other – so he might catch secret glimpses of Rose of Sharon in her prayer cap and shawl, sitting demurely.

That was a trial, trying to understand preaching in another language, but it didn't matter. These folks preached with their simple lives, their trust in him and shared concern for the sick and the elderly. By American farming standards, many of them were poor smallholders, but what they really had was a peace, contentment and surety about their faith that moved him.

He'd gone to church at school and drumhead parades

in the army, but nothing prepared him for this simple piety. For every aspect of daily life, there was a Bible quote for guidance; their plain clothes set them apart as unworldly. There were no picture houses, theatres, dance halls, speakeasy bars to distract them; just get-togethers in houses, music on the piano, feasts of home cooking when everybody brought something.

Guy knew his motives were clouded by his attraction to Rose. He knew that he must be of their faith to have even a chance of courting her. When he thought of all the women that he had used for pleasure in the past, there was only Selma in the same class as this girl, and she was a girl from his other life: the life that he had put behind him for ever.

Rose stood for everything good about this new life. Here he could forget killing and maiming and the carnage of war. He was dead to that life now, but to prove himself worthy of this prize, he must first take on this way of life, curtail old habits, boozing and worldly pleasures, and enter this serious, sober hard-working community with sincerity.

Had he been sent there to replace Zack? Was it pre-ordained that he should find them and be welcomed into the Yoder farmstead? Did Rose look on him only as a brotherly substitute? There were rituals and customs here he would have to apply, but first he must show willing to take on their beliefs, set his reason and doubting aside and embrace this order as a novice might enter a monastery.

In his heart it was all part of paying back the Yoders for saving his life, giving him clothes, food and shelter when he couldn't earn his keep. Would they risk giving their daughter to him in marriage? Only time would tell.

At first he struggled to keep up with the physical hardships of leading the team of horses with the plough, learning to harvest and to build. He must repay their trust in him. He had come from a different world where everything was done for him: horses groomed, clothes cleaned, food prepared, repairs to wheels and harnesses taken and returned fixed by others. He had been waited on hand and foot as an officer, given privileges, better food, transport, a fine uniform. How would they even contemplate the luxuries he had grown to take for granted?

None of that mattered here. They took as they found and he was doing his best to please. The women worked even harder than the men, sewing, spinning wool, tending flocks of birds, nursing children and old people, baking, preparing for gatherings, making clothes with nothing that made their labours easy except sewing machines, flat irons and iron mangles. The mattresses were stuffed with feathers from birds. The house was bare, swept, mopped, freshened with garden herbs, but no one went hungry, clothes were mended and redarned, put away and then brought out again. He was wearing Zack's cotton bib overalls and knockabout clothes with his one black Sunday suit that had to be let out and reshaped to fit his long legs.

His beard grew thick. He wanted to look just like all the other young men, but it was hard not to stand out.

'How do I join your Church?' he asked Izaak one night after supper.

The man smiled and leaned back on his chair. 'You have to attend meetings, read your Bible, accept the law of Christ, bear each other's burdens and live in peace with all men. You must take membership and communion, be examined and subject to the disciplines of your fellow brothers in Christ. We do accept people of other faiths, so don't look worried: you are halfway there already. I knew the minute

319

you gave me that letter that you were sent to us for a purpose. Be patient. There's no rush in these matters.'

Oh, but there is, Guy sighed, thinking of Rose. I must wed her before some other young buck has the same idea.

Selma threw up all the way down the coast. The heat and the dust and the constant jostling of the train journey made her sick. It was not turning out to be the best of honeymoons. Jamie was full of his part in the Western, nervous that this might be his big break into a junior lead. They'd cast him for his height and brawn, and he looked good on horseback. He was growing a beard that tickled when he kissed her,

The film was called *White Horse Mesa* and it was being made in Arizona, where they had to find five thousand wild horses and Indians in costume, and shoot lots of action shots. The offer couldn't have come at a better time.

'I'm late,' she'd confessed to Jamie one night. 'I think there is a baby coming our way.'

He'd stared at her agape for a second, then burst out laughing. 'I'll have to make an honest woman of you then.' There was no shock, no anger, as if they'd not done anything wrong at all. 'We'll have to get our skates on, I suppose, and find a judge to marry us; in and out in five minutes,' he'd laughed, as if it were all some joke.

'But it's my wedding. We have to do it properly,' she protested.

'You do what you want. I'll turn up and we'll take a few shots for the studio. Buy yourself a new dress, though. I'm sick of seeing that old thing.' He laughed again, not seeing the hurt in her eyes.

'We're going to get married,' she confessed to Lisa, who immediately asked Uncle Corrie for the loan of his garden for the ceremony.

Pearl was no doubt relieved that Selma would be out of their hair and offered to lay on a buffet. 'You must make sure the press get hold of the story. Jamie needs publicity.' The roller coaster was on its way.

They dragged her to a fancy dressmaker in the costume department, who loaned her a lacy concoction with a feather headdress, made from an old garment. Jamie was kitted out in a frock coat and frilly shirt. They looked as if they'd just stepped off a set for a theatrical musical in Broadway.

Selma managed not to throw up in public and the wedding day went perfectly. The portrait was sent to her mother and she kept glancing at her ring finger with pride. No one guessed her condition except perhaps the dressmaker, who had to let out the waist using both seam allowances.

Jamie played his part, dancing with everyone, flirting with Pearl, and made a funny speech about Selma capturing him straight off the Scottish steam ship, which wasn't true, but it got a lot of laughs.

Little did she know she was about to see one of the greatest wonders of the world: the Grand Canyon. They stayed overnight on the South Rim to catch the sunset over the rainbow-coloured rocks. She had never seen anything so wonderful in her life and it made her want to cry at the glory of God's creation.

There was something majestic about the landscape of Arizona, with its red rocks and desert, the ochre and carmine earth, the wonderful trading posts with walls covered in rugs and skins, baskets and jewellery. Outside, Navajo women were weaving rugs with arms jingling with silver and turquoise jewellery.

Jamie bought her a bracelet of turquoise stones and she'd never took it off. In those few hectic weeks when he was always on set, she took a horse and trekked with anyone willing to accompany her, through creeks and sagebrush trails where cactuses towered above her. It was like living in a picture book under an ink-blue sky. It was fairy tale and magic all rolled into one. Was this what her life was going to be like from now on, going to such exotic places?

No, it wasn't. Soon they returned to Jamie's pokey rooms. Selma came down to earth with a bump. How would they fit another person into the apartment? Money was tight and there wasn't any other work on the horizon. This time it was her turn to wait in a diner, where her legs ached in the heat and the body sweat of the men made her want to vomit. While Jamie stood and waited for bit parts or extra work, she kept them in leftovers and free meals, trying not to let her pregnancy show.

When she told Lisa about the baby, she gave a whoop of delight. 'A honeymoon baby, how romantic!' There was no point in disillusioning her. Lisa was going to be far too worldly wise and educated ever to get herself into this mess.

It was only a matter of weeks before Selma realised how feckless Jamie was with money. When he had cash he spent it on stupid things like new shirts or magazines. He'd go out with the crew and ply them with drinks in the hope of catching titbits of gossip about who was filming and casting, and when.

When she complained about them having nothing put by for the baby he turned round and snapped, 'It's your bairn, you see to it. I've got other things to do.'

This was their first real argument and she saw a new side to him. Or had this always been there and she just hadn't noticed?

It was then that she felt utterly alone. The baby was not going to stop his career, of course – that was to be expected – but not even to contribute to its coming was cruel and selfish. Somehow she was going to have to earn extra herself and where better than the Hollywood studios?

If Jamie could be an extra then so could she. Time to sign on and see if they could find her background work. She had grown her hair back long out of economy and put on a firm corset to hide her bump. Taking herself off to the casting offices, she was told to provide photo shots and interviewed.

'You've got a good pioneer face, corsets and shawl work for you, hair scraped back, good fair features . . . you'll do.'

She was given forms to fill in and told to go to the costume bay to be kitted up, take the docket and line up. 'They may want you or not.' On the ticket her name was written as Zelma Barr and she didn't correct it.

It was a long day sitting in the shade, dressed in a crinoline and boots, wig and bonnet, until the director marched up and down picking out extras: 'Yous and yous and yous . . . over there on the street, up and down, walk! Hey, yous,' he pointed to Selma, 'pusha the pram and look as if you mean it.'

Her first job was pushing an old metal pram up and down a main street of a row of wooden shop fronts propped up at the back; back and forth for hours while they took their angle shots and rehearsed the scene. Her back ached with the heat and boredom, but there was a canteen and it saved her cooking on that terrible contraption that passed for a stove.

This was as far away from the Arizona honeymoon as she could imagine but for thirteen dollars a day who was complaining?

Jamie was furious when she told him what she had done.

'You told me to find work.'

'I did not!'

'In so many words, you did. If you won't feed our baby, I will!'

'I didna mean it like that . . . the two of us can't be in the same business.'

'Whyever not? I've nothing else to do. It's come-and-go work . . . but they did say I had the face for it, so as long as they do Wild West pictures someone has to walk the frontier towns looking prim and proper,' she smiled, hoping he'd see the funny side of it all.

'There we'll be, me up one side and you down the other. This isn't quite what I had planned,' he sighed, no longer sulking, which was a relief.

'We ought to think of finding another apartment when junior arrives. There isn't room to swing a cat in here,' Selma said, striking while he was in a good mood.

'My pa and ma raised six weans in a single end . . . in just one room in a tenement,' was his reply.

'Where did you all sleep?'

'Topped and tailed in the dunny in the wall on a mattress, the weans in a cot and my parents in a makeshift bed. A bairn is happy with a bottom drawer for a few months.'

324

Selma didn't want their baby sleeping in the sideboard drawer but needs must. At least she'd got him thinking about the coming event. When he became a father, he'd soon take his responsibilities more seriously. It was then she realised just how little she knew about her husband and how little he knew about her.

Guy stood in wonder watching the scarlet flash of the red cardinal in the bush. The birds here were so bright and colourful, the blue jays and the woodpeckers. The great hawks wheeling in the sky still made him down tools to observe them. He liked to take himself off alone just to think over how much his life was changing.

He was plucking up courage to ask Izaak if he might approach his daughter. Now he had been accepted for membership and adult baptism, taken his first communion and made himself useful on the farm. It was only natural he'd want to settle down into his own family life.

He loved to watch Rose busying herself with her mother, cooking, sewing dresses, making fancy quilts, always on the go. But when he stepped into the room, the air changed, he saw her cheeks flush and she glanced up at him out of the corner of her blue eyes with the briefest hint of a smile.

They needed no excuse to walk the fields together and she asked him about his old life, his family and what England was really like. She couldn't understand how he could leave his country and he found himself talking with nostalgia about Yorkshire and how bits of it were just like here, about Jemima and his brother. How time had stopped for him living there.

'Like you, I don't have a big family, any more. School

and the army were my family too.' She looked perplexed, not understanding any of it. How could he begin to describe his pampered life to a girl whose own education had ended at thirteen? That was when her real education began. She'd been baking bread since she was five, and sewing too.

They came from such different worlds – what did Rose know of his terrible flashbacks when he woke in the night to the sounds of hundreds of men screaming at once, choking for breath because of the explosions in his head, those colours of fire raging around him, orange, yellow swirling flames, the smell of burning flesh and blood in his nostrils that haunted his dreams.

Having known combat, life had a special flavour for him now, which these gentle folk would never know. He yearned to lose himself in simple things with decent people who cared nothing for external wealth and status. His mother would be horrified at his choice of bride, but he had cut her out of his heart. He did not want to examine the power of these feelings towards her, the bitterness and anger. All he wanted was to belong right here, forget what had gone before and start over again.

The delicacy of his request was making him shake, not wanting to do the wrong thing. Would they accept this English Englisher? There was only one way to find out.

After supper, when Izaak was sitting on the porch watching the sun creeping down behind the barn roof, Guy stood cap in hand. 'I have something to say, Brother Izaak,' he stuttered.

The farmer looked up and smiled. 'Feel free, brother.'

'I have a request to ask. I have taken a liking to your daughter. So much so that I would like to settle down with her for the rest of my days if I have your permission.'

'Have you indeed?' Izaak looked up sternly for a second. 'This is serious talk. Do you know what is expected of a man in making such an offer?'

'I'm not sure,' Guy hesitated, feeling this was not going well.

'Let me tell you how it is done, provided she gives her consent. There must be a period of walking out together in public. There must be a period of spiritual preparation, a house has to be built, stocked with all the basic linens, furniture and kitchenware a bride needs to set up her own home. Then there is a ceremony to be undertaken at the right time of the season so many can visit the Homestead, a feast to prepare, and all this must fit around our farm duties. Some have had to wait many years for such a coming together.' Izaak looked up, seeing the disappointment on Guy's face. Then he burst out laughing, 'Sit down, sit down . . . before you fall down. Don't look so flattened. Five years might do it. Did not Jacob wait seven years for his Rachel?'

Guy sighed. Five years was an age at his time of life. 'I was hoping for five months, brother,' he replied.

'Oh, Charles, I'm only teasing. I know how it is between the two of you. Anyone can see the Lord put a fire in both your eyes the moment you met. What took you so long to spit it out?'

Only then did Guy flop down with relief. 'I promise to take care of her.'

'You will cherish each other. That is what marriage means: two horses hitched to the same wagon pulling in the same direction – well, most of the time,' he chuckled. 'You were brought here for a purpose, Charles. Besides, every farm needs new bloodstock if it is to prosper,' he winked. 'Now let's see what the women have to say.'

As if on cue, Miriam and Rose appeared from the doorway, smiling. 'Well, sisters, how say you?'

'It looks as if it's going to be a busy summer and a busy fall this year,' Miriam said. 'November is a good wedding month.'

Rose looked at Guy with such relief and tenderness. He just wanted to get down on his knees and pray, what have I done to deserve such fortune?

19

Selma looked down at her daughter's pink face and cried with relief to see such a perfect baby staring back at her.

Lisa was fussing over the bed. 'She's so beautiful. What will you call her?'

She'd agreed with Jamie that if it was a girl it would be her choice, and his if it was a boy, but he was too busy on location out of town to worry about names.

'I'm going to give her two names,' she smiled. 'Esther, to please my mother and Sharland, after the village where I was born . . . Sharland Esther. What do you think?'

'Ripping!' Lisa said. 'But how will you manage here?' She looked around. 'It doesn't get any bigger, does it?'

They had not made the move she'd hoped for. Money was leaking through their fingers, but Lisa had bought a wicker crib for the baby that would do for a few months. Selma wrote to Jamie hoping he'd be back to help her with little Shari, as she had quickly taken to calling her. But the regular work he was getting with the studios meant he was hardly ever at home.

His new agent, Danny Steel, was hustling hard on his behalf.

Jamie did a good line in mountain men in beaver skins

with long hair and beards. It looked as if she would have to go back to being Zelma Barr, pioneer woman, soon and little Shari might be used as an extra too, if the authorities allowed. She might as well push a pram up and down Frontier Street with a real baby in it, and if she howled, who was to know as there were no sound?

Since their honeymoon, and once her belly began to bloom, there had been no more long trips on location. She made trips to the ocean in the vacations with Lisa, who always plugged the gap that Jamie seemed to leave. Yet Lisa was growing up fast now and had a gang of high school friends. She wanted to go to college to study geography. Selma wasn't looking forward to the time when they must inevitably go their separate ways.

Her new life was like a row of skittles being knocked down: emigrating, marriage, and now a baby. Her Yorkshire roots had been yanked up and transplanted into this dry soil. She wasn't sure they'd struck, and kept thinking of that journey south to Arizona, to those rides in the sagebrush and mesquite, the mountains and canyons that in a strange way felt more like home than here.

'I'll take you there, one day,' she whispered as her baby suckled on her breast. 'You'd like it there. We'll have some ponies to ride.' Tears rolled down her face, tears of pride and sadness. If only Jamie would come home and see his little girl. She wanted them all to be a proper family.

None of this went into the long letter home with the photos of Shari in her Victorian lacy dress and bonnet, the one Selma had borrowed from the costume department for the baby's baptism. Shari had a fuzz of reddy golden hair and dark eyes, an unusual combination. She was her daddy's girl all right. Selma told Mam that she was born premature so as not to raise any suspicions that she was conceived out of wedlock.

As the weeks went by and Jamie didn't rush home but made more and more excuses about new scenes to shoot, a niggling doubt began to grow in her gut that he was going to leave her alone, and that scared her.

Nothing was going to get in the way of his career now it was taking off, especially not a tiny baby. She was on her own now, fending for herself, and there was no choice but to try for work again. They couldn't live on air.

Hester followed the debates in the newspapers with growing interest, knowing there was a movement against capital punishment for men in the Forces. The Labour MP Ernest Thurtle was championing the cause at the National Federation of Discharged Soldiers. There was talk of a bill in Parliament to abolish capital punishment in the military. She tried to broach the subject with Essie but any talk of the war and she clammed shut.

They had never discussed what had really happened to Frank. It was a closed book better not opened if they were to stay on the same side. It was enough that her own stubbornness had persuaded the parish council to adopt the tolling bell on Armistice Day and nothing else. The Church had followed suit, and disaffected villagers had their heroes carved onto the Sowerthwaite Memorial.

This decision was unpopular but occasionally someone sidled up to Hester, after heated discussions, to whisper, 'All or nobody . . . It's got to be right that all those young boys who volunteered or were conscripted, who served their country at a cost to their lives, should be honoured. If some fell short of bravery, it's not up to us to judge.'

Most people knew about the Bartleys saving the Cantrell twin all those years ago. It was a legend much embellished, and for Hester every reminder of it brought such turmoil of emotions. She owed Frank Bartley support.

Essie was proving a loyal servant, diligent to the point of obstinacy, at times. Woe betide her if she messed up her spring cleaning, the rug brushing, the cupboard clearing-outs. Waterloo House sparkled. For one week each year, Essie took the train to her sister's home and from there they took the air at Bridlington or Scarborough for a brief holiday.

How Hester envied Essie those photographs: Selma's wedding portrait and then the birth of her daughter – whoever named a child after a village? But they were Americans now; they did things differently there. She had to admit she was a pretty child with a mop of curls and dark eyes.

There was some mystery about the husband, the one who was in the moving pictures; Big Jim Barr was his stage name. He didn't seem to play much part in the family and now mother and daughter were taking film parts and Essie was saving to make the big journey herself.

But with a downturn in jobs and the current bleak climate, things were looking bad. The war had bankrupted the nation, but all the war machinery still had to be paid for. There was no money for luxuries. Those lost men had left so many gaps. Most of Hester's friends had lost sons and heirs. She had no heirs to look forward to and she was jealous of Essie's one little sparkling grandchild.

She had letters to cherish, which she displayed like medals in the privacy of her rooms. Essie was tactful that way, not rubbing in the fact that Hester's own remaining son was estranged for reasons no one would ever guess.

With each passing month the hope of ever being reconciled was fading. She had no idea where Guy was. All she knew was his false name, Charles Arthur West. Sometimes she caught herself scouring the pages of *The Times*, just in case there was a mention of his name. Not even Essie knew this secret shame. How could she explain that if the war memorial was ever erected, it would have the wrong name at its head?

As months turned into years, the two widows drew closer, more companionable, each within the well-defined roles of mistress or servant until those roles became blurred by familiarity and everyday contact. Essie was never overfamiliar, always correct, but Hester looked forward to their suppers in the kitchen in front of the range, talking over her day's gardening and Essie's adventures into the cookery books. With all those fresh vegetables in the garden and a copy of Mrs Beeton's Book of Household Management, she had become more adventurous in her recipes, always frugal, and making one meal do two days if she could. A variety of meatless dishes suited Hester's frequent dyspepsia and poor appetite.

Common sense told her the house was too large. The stables were now bare, the car had long since been sold for a more modest version that she could drive, should she choose. There was just Maggie and Essie to see to her needs where once there had been half a dozen servants. The washing was laundered in the village, the garden she managed herself, and Beaven came out of retirement to see to the lawns and heavier work.

Some weeks she need never wander out of the gates of

Waterloo unless for matins or evensong – never both; that smacked of religious enthusiasm.

Essie had no truck with church at all. The war business had taken away her faith in the providence of an Almighty. Hester had found it had drawn her closer to a basic trust in the power of Christian love and forgiveness. Was she not a sinner in need of salvation? Had she not fallen short of the great ideal, but was trying to make up for her failings none the less? Every night she prayed that she would see her son again, and know he was well in this world, feel his forgiveness in her heart and find peace at last.

Should it be taking this long? Guy paced around the porch waiting for the cries of a newborn baby. Rose was well attended by the local women, the birth having come earlier than expected, and he feared no one would believe they had not even kissed until the night before the wedding.

He had been so cautious not to offend the family until Rose had dragged him into the garden and set upon him. 'Don't you want to touch me?' she had cried. 'Am I that plain?'

How he had reassured her otherwise with kisses and apologies. He adored her tender kisses, so different from those frantic couplings in port bars after a long sea voyage with women interested only in the content of his wallet for their favours.

Their wedding night was everything he had hoped for, snuggled in their newly built annexe of bedrooms that he knew they were expected to fill to the brim one day. She had given herself to him in love and trust as he took her in his arms and peeled off each layer of pretty clothing, all hand sewn and embellished with fine stitches. They were not old Amish, who wore only plain colours. Mennonites wore brighter garments in fabrics with simple spots and checks, and some even wore worldly outfits, much to the disapproval of the older generation, who frowned on the purchase of tractors and engines and anything that was too modern. Guy didn't mind either way, being too new a member to make any comment. Rose could have worn a flour sack and he would still have thought she looked beautiful.

She had opened herself to him that first time with eagerness and good humour, laughing and teasing his tentative moves. 'I'm not an egg . . . I won't crack!' she had said, pulling him towards her. 'We are married and everything is permitted!'

Now it seemed hours and hours before Miriam rushed down the stairs to put a precious bundle in his arms. 'You have a son, Charles,' she beamed. 'A beautiful son, praise the Lord!'

'Can I go and see her now?' Guy made for the stairs.

'No, not yet. She's not finished yet. We think there's another one on the way, so she mustn't be disturbed.'

'Is she . . . ?' he hardly dare speak at this news.

'She will be fine.'

His son was swaddled in sheets and a pretty patchwork quilt, his eyes peering up at Guy's face, trying to focus. This is my own flesh and blood, made from our bodies, Guy thought, and he felt such a surge of pride and love and tenderness. This tiny mite made him want to cry – and to think there would be two of them. His heart was bursting: another set of twins. Was this his legacy to the Yoders? Double trouble? He was still smiling when Miriam came downstairs, silent and calm as always, but her face was tired.

'You can come now. Rose needs you,' she said, taking the new baby from him, and he tore up the stairs, two at a time, sensing something was wrong. Rose was in trouble. He flung open the door to see her holding the baby. But she didn't smile and her wide eyes held such sadness.

'What's wrong?' he asked.

She held out the bundle, the tiniest of bundles. Inside was a little wax doll, perfect, but with no life in its body.

'He was too small. He couldn't take his first breath. He's perfect, but not ours,' she cried. 'I lost him . . . I was too small to carry them both,' she wept.

The women melted away to leave them to grieve alone. Guy held the baby and cried. What could he say to comfort her?

'We have a son. We mustn't be greedy. One will be enough for me. Let's give this little one a name and christen him right here.'

Rose shook her head. 'We don't christen babies. Baptism is for those old enough to make their own choice. He belongs to God now.'

'But he must have a name,' Guy insisted. 'He'll always be a part of us and little Charlie must know he had a twin brother. I had one too but he was lost in the war.' To his surprise he found himself sobbing, 'He left one morning. I never said goodbye, and he was killed instead of me, Rose.'

'You wait until now to tell me all this? You must have such sadness in your heart. What was his name?'

'Angus . . . Gus.'

'Then we shall name this little one after him, little Gus. He's so perfect, isn't he?'

'How can you stay so calm?' Guy cried.

'I've been spared my first-born and my own life too, so

there'll be others. The Lord chooses who He takes and when. It's pointless arguing with what we cannot change.' With brimming eyes she looked down at the blanket.

However long he lived Guy knew he would never have such an unquestioning faith or such serenity. Her acceptance shamed him but he reasoned she'd been born to such a way of belief and now it repaid her in times of trouble.

Miriam brought the screaming infant back into the room for his first feed. 'Shall I take the other one away?' she whispered.

'No, Charles will see to little Gus. He'll find him a little place to rest.'

Guy left them to women's business, taking Gus to show Izaak, who sighed and pointed out a pretty spot on the slope of the hill set apart. 'We'll put him in there and deep . . . make a bench to remind us. Come on, I'll give you a hand. It's been a long day.'

20

Selma wondered if her ghost would haunt the cardboard
frontier towns that she paced up and down each week.
There were only so many ways to crisscross the background
up and down with a pram, and then later up and down
with a toddling child, whisked away when the bad men
rode into town. Later still, when Shari grew pigtails, Zelma
the extra paraded across the dusty track road holding her
hand: child in a smocked overall and boots, and mother in
her corseted dress that stank of other women's sweat.

Small-budget films used the same extras as a background
over and over again in the same costumes until she felt
those clothes could take themselves for their own walk in
the sun. Shari played the game too. When they were not
being used, she sat reading books while Selma knitted,
sewed, quilted and darned, anything to keep busy. It was
hours of boredom for a few seconds' exposure.

A good extra must blend into the background, look
natural, do the business; chattering, browsing in windows
as if all this make-believe was real life going on.

She was one of their regulars, prompt, reliable and now

338

an old hand. You could spot the new ambitious recruits who tried to steal a scene with a look into the camera when they should be turning away. There were the girls on the make, trying to catch the eye of the director for a better part next time. One or two managed their way into the credits but Selma and Shari were too conscientious to bother any director with uppity antics.

Sometimes Shari got work on her own. She was a pretty, amenable child and the money helped, especially in the lean times. Jamie made enough appearances on screen for Shari to recognise her daddy as he ripped into some Indian brave or fisted a baddie on the chin, riding off into the sunset in a black hot gang of robbers..

When Corrie Grunwald dropped dead in the studio from a heart attack, leaving Pearl a rich widow, she took herself off on a Caribbean cruise and suggested to Lisa that she bring the Barrs in to keep house for her in the staff flat.

Selma didn't need any persuading to leave their humble place in the downtown district for the swish stucco residence in West Hollywood. She wasn't too proud to be in service and the schools would be better for Shari.

The staff quarters were over the garage: a large living room and bathroom, two spacious bedrooms, perfect for the two of them, but Lisa insisted on giving them the run of the whole place, swimming pool and stable when Pearl was away.

Jamie came back, bringing friends who drank and partied and made a mess.

'Why does Daddy not live with us all the time?' Shari asked one day. 'Doesn't he like us very much?'

How could Selma explain his absence from her life?

'Of course he does but he has to work when the studio

wants. He only goes away to bring us all nice things,' Selma replied. That was a lie. Jamie never contributed one cent to Shari's upkeep. Now and again he'd arrive home with a huge Indian doll or pretty bangles and earrings, to the delight of his daughter, who flung herself into his arms and begged him to see her drawings and school books, refusing to settle into bed until he'd read her a story.

They would take a picnic to the beach and look for all the world like a proper family. If only that were true. The last time he'd returned, they'd drunk too much wine and made love. He'd left her with more than kisses and a terrible burning itch in her groin that she had to make an appointment to see the studio doctor about. He'd examined her and asked some searching intimate questions, making her blush as this inquisition.

'You'd better get your husband to call in and see me, the sooner the better,' he said gruffly.

The treatments were expensive and painful and she felt dirty. When she plucked up courage to ask him what was wrong, the doc looked at his desk and shrugged. 'You'd better ask your husband that. If he is your only partner he sure has some explaining to do,' he sighed.

She never asked, she didn't need to. Jamie had given her a dose of something nasty that he'd caught from some cheap starlet on the make, no doubt. She'd guessed he'd been unfaithful for years. She was just another port in a storm, a free billet between castings. It looked good on his studio résumé. *Big Jim Barr at home on the ranch with his lovely wife, Zelma, and their daughter, Sharland.* They had done one shoot on the lawns of Casa Pinto as if it were their home.

As long as things looked good on the surface, that was

all that mattered in movieland. Now she felt dirty and cheap. She was not one of his whores, she was his wife. He'd never come near her again until she knew he was clean.

Sometimes she looked up at the blue sky and endless sun, the white villas, the golden beach, the fancy cars in the driveways, and longed for some old-fashioned rain and snow, grey hills and thick coats and honest Yorkshire values.

Shari would never know another life than this if she didn't make it happen, but how could she change their lives without a steady income? She wanted more for her daughter than tinsel-town glitter.

Selma smiled, knowing now how her mother must have felt when they let her go to Bradford. She'd wanted more for her daughter too, and look where it had landed them both – an ocean apart, a world apart. Perhaps it was time to go home and leave all this behind. Then she thought of Lisa and the horses and the sunshine. Perhaps not.

'We must make preparations for the Eclipse event,' the chairman of the parish council ordered. 'The Dales are expecting an influx of cars and visitors. There's money to be made from car parking and catering. The District has laid down rules that all chimney fires be extinguished overnight to clear the smoke out of the sky in time for the total eclipse moment.

On and on he went about finicky details. The 29 June was going to be the day when the great and good of the country would travel north to observe this momentous event. Sharland's top playing field was considered to be one of the best viewing platforms. Hester yawned.

'We need volunteers to host dignitaries from London and we wondered if you, Lady Hester, might oblige as you did so generously in the war, opening your house and garden to guests.'

I will do no such thing, she mused, but sat silently through the awkward pause.

'Of course we know it is an intrusion on your privacy, ma'am, but we have so often yielded to your wishes in the past. If I could prevail on you for some reciprocity . . .'

The devil, he'd got the measure of her. Tit for tat, in other words. Hester drew in a sharp breath and launched forth. 'I shall have to consult my housekeeper,' she said.

'Essie Bartley won't mind, I'm sure.' The man had the brass cheek to smile in triumph.

'Be that as it may, she deserves the respect of being asked, don't you think?'

That should shut them up, thinking they could wheedle their way into her home. She didn't want strangers in her domain even for one night but she had to set an example, she supposed.

Essie hadn't been well. She'd slowed down, and sometimes she clutched her stomach as if in pain.

'What's the matter?' Hester asked.

'Just a bit of trapped wind . . . too many pickled onions last night. They do repeat so.'

'You must let Dr Mac have a look at you if it doesn't clear up.' Mackenzie of Mill House was still going strong, though ever since their quarrel Hester herself saw Dr Pickles, who always treated her with respect and deference.

'No . . . peppermint lozenges and a cup of fennel tea will sort it out, thank you.'

Hester knew better than to fuss over her but Essie had lost weight and her cheeks were pinched. Was it fair to burden her with extra work?

342

Essie had her own ideas when the request was relayed. 'It'll be grand to open up the house and put a few more living souls in all these rooms. Maggie and me will manage. We can ask in the village for more help. It's going to be quite a do. It said in the *Gazette* that the Prince of Wales may be coming . . . we'll never see the like again in our lifetime. Wait till I tell Selma all the news . . .'

Back and forth over the Atlantic those letters went, full of Shari's doings in school and Big Jim's starring role in *The Westward Run*.

Don't blink or you'll miss us in the trading post scene. I'm the one choosing fabric and Shari is skipping outside, the one with pigtails, but it may end up on the cutting-room floor . . . days of work for nothing but an honest wage.

Essie searched the papers until she found a showing in Keighley so they trekked over there by train to see the film.

Hester had never seen anything so vulgar and garish, and there was no trading post scene. Big Jim hogged the film like a hairy gorilla, making them both want to laugh.

'He's not exactly your Rudi Valentino, is he, and all that make-up on his face. I'll be glad when the talking pictures come in. Voices will make films more exciting, don't you think?' said Essie.

Hester had no opinion one way or another. If she never saw another Wild West shoot-out again it would be no sacrifice, but Essie loved taking herself off for a treat on her night off.

The house endured another of Essie's bottomings out, when Hester was required to put away all her precious bits of porcelain and silver into boxes for safekeeping in the locked cellar.

'You can't be too careful these days,' Essie insisted. 'You have such beautiful china and glass, I wouldn't like to see stuff disappear.'

'But our guests will be people of class,' Hester said.

'Top drawer or not, I don't trust some to help themselves to trinkets. No point in putting temptation in their way, now is there?'

Essie cared about the house as if it were her own. She owned nothing but memories and letters, but polished and cleaned, beat rugs on the washing line as if they were school-boys in need of punishment. She laid out each bedroom, airing the rooms in turn.

One afternoon Hester found her in Guy's old room sitting on the bed. 'I'd like to ask you something.'

'Fire away,' Hester said, not expecting what came next.

'I think it's time Master Guy was laid to rest, and Angus too. Don't you think after all these years it's time to let go of these lifeless things and give them to a good home where they can be used and come back to life again?'

Hester stepped back at the honesty of her appeal and the firm glint in her eyes. 'But they're all I have to remind me . . .'

'Yes, milady, I know, but it's a damn sight more than I will ever have of my boys. They are just things. What you have in your heart can never be taken away . . . your mem-ories of good times. You have photograph albums, your letters. Better to shift them now and make use of the rooms? I'm sure it'll do you good.'

'Who are you to tell me what to do?' Hester snapped, cornered by the suddenness of the onslaught.

'That's unworthy of you. I'm your friend as well as your

servant, I hope. A friend tells the truth, even if it hurts. I just thought this was a good time. I'll allus be grateful you brought me out of the cottage to a new place when I was in need of support. How can I repay you but by being honest back? You have mourned so long as if it was all your doing . . . Don't you think I don't know that your son wasn't there for my son when he was in need of him? Don't you think I know you feel badly for that? But you have made up a hundred times for that omission, giving me a measure of peace and comfort within these walls.'

Hester was winded, flopping down on the bed, trying not to cry. 'How do you live with your pain?' she asked. 'What was done to your son – how do you live with it?'

Essie looked her in the eye and shrugged. 'One day at a time . . . just for this day, I ask for courage to see it through without feeling bitter. I try to recall the happier days: the chara trips, Sunday school concerts, picnics. If I dwell on the other . . . it would have killed me long ago.'

'You make me feel foolish and ashamed. I still have a boy somewhere in the world who hates me.'

'Why do you say that?'

'Because in my possessive love I did a wrong thing and I can't forgive myself for it,' she wept.

'It will come right, just as I know it will come right for my boy. He was no coward. I'm going to show you a letter no living soul has seen but me, not even Asa. It would have broken him.'

Hester watched Essie climb the stairs slowly and pause at the turn to catch her breath. She returned with a letter, much worn with rereading, and pushed it into her hand.

Pulling her glasses from her reticule, Hester read each sentence, hardly breathing until she came to the end. 'Oh, my dear! What a wrong was done. This has to be brought to light . . . such injustice.' Then she recalled Martha Holbeck's words all those years ago. Now I understand what she was talking about, she sighed. Hers was the task of standing up for the Bartley family but first she must repay this trust.

'I'll see if I can find some wicker baskets. Will you make a start in the wardrobe while I clear out these drawers? Perhaps the orphanage could make use of these old toys under the bed. Then we can start on the other room tomorrow.'

Essie smiled and nodded. 'A wise decision.'

Lisa took them both to the great Egyptian palace cinema downtown to see The Jazz Singer with Al Jolson. The musical items were sensational and Selma knew the talkies were here to stay.

Over the past years she'd helped out in prop and costume stores, watching her favourite stars parading onto set. The huge sets held no fear for her now. It was a job like any other and there were always castings to queue for. She was never going to be plucked from obscurity like some of the prettier girls. Her face was too strong and angular, her legs too short and her bust on the flat side, nor did she have that particular allure that the old stars like Vilma Banky and Louise Brooks held.

It was as if they came alive on celluloid, took on a mysterious identity unlike ordinary mortals, which made you believe everything they did on screen. Now even they were cursing the advent of sound, for some of them had squeaky voices with thick accents and some of the men fared even worse. The game had shifted to men with deep husky voices that hinted of seduction, and Big Jim's Glaswegian accent was hard to understand.

Soon he was back in the saddle in buckskin and black sombrero, taking elocution lessons from an ageing English actress to soften his Scots vowels.

They lived apart now. Selma stayed on at Casa Pinto as concierge. Pearl had picked up another rich lover and they seemed to drift around Europe in search of fun and culture, glad to have her villa occupied all year round.

Jamie tried to muscle in when he was broke but Selma insisted Shari was not to be disturbed in her studies. He must find his own rooms. He'd slammed the phone down in temper. Sometimes he was like a truculent child, other times full of impossible schemes. How had she ever thought she'd loved him? That was a lifetime ago and now she was used to fending for them both. Shari was growing up fast and needed new dresses and shoes, which took every penny.

Selma was busy dusting the empty rooms when the doorbell rang. Habit made her open it, expecting it to be Pearl home unexpectedly, barking her orders in that screechy drawl, but it was a boy with a telegram.

'Mrs Barr?'

She nodded and snatched it from his hands. What was wrong? Had Jamie had an accident? She tore it open. The message was stark: 'COME HOME. MOTHER VERY ILL. CANTRELL.'

This was news to Selma. Mam's letters of late had been very cheery, full of village gossip and the WI. Why hadn't she told her? She knew the answer already. Because she'd not want to worry her, being so far away.

It would take weeks to get there, she sighed, but some instinct knew this was not sent lightly. What was she to do?

That was when the panic set in. How could she make such an enormous journey? What about Shari? How could she afford it? There was a little set by for her daughter's education but this was an emergency. Only Lisa would know how to go about it.

Lisa took over all the arrangements, offering to stay with Shari or sneak her into her college. She paid for a flight from San Francisco to New York via Chicago. Then Selma could get the passage back to Southampton and a train back to Yorkshire.

'Don't worry, things have changed since we came out. You'll get back to England in over a week, all being well. Don't worry about anything here. You stay and see to what you must . . .'

Perhaps she ought to damn the expense and take Shari, but Shari was far too excited to be rooming with her idol, Lisa, to worry about missing the journey of a lifetime. She hadn't met her grandmother. She was just a picture in a frame. She'd be fine, but for Selma the thought of leaving her daughter was terrifying, and to be trusting herself to a lump of flying metal even worse. She prayed to every saint under the sun for a safe return. Some of Jamie's popish habits had rubbed off on her after all.

The suddenness of her departure, the rush to get her papers in order and tickets and a suitcase of winter clothes together overrode all her terror of flying.

In the end it all went smoothly, and to watch the land change from desert to mountain, to plains, to lakes and to sea was a wondrous experience for her. The ship home was enormous and she was in the cheapest berth. The sea was rough but bearable, and then she was stood on Southampton Dock, watching soldiers lined up to embark.

It was like old times. She telegraphed ahead to Waterloo to let them know she was on her way.

Only as the train chugged north did she realise that she'd be staying in Waterloo House; the very place where everything had begun with Guy and Frank. A vision of the fierce Lady Cantrell rose up but no longer terrified her. You've been across the world, forged your life. You're as good as her any day. The old order is gone now, she mused, trying to bolster her fears.

How would she find her mother? She must be very ill to call for her like this. In her heart she sensed it was very serious. Oh, why did the train take such an age? She changed at Leeds for the local train and stepped out onto Sowerthwaite station. A flood of memories hit her like a wave, all those farewells made here. Nothing had changed. It still smelled of soot and coal fires, damp leaves, farmyard manure and home. The ten past four bus still ran from the Market Square, and she walked up the hill from West Sharland with trembling legs.

After many time zones and an ocean voyage, she was utterly exhausted. It felt like a dream to be back in England. If only Shari could have come too. She walked up to the main entrance, deliberately making a gesture to her own independence. I'm nobody's servant here, she thought, pulling the bell rope. Then a gaunt figure in black stood assessing her.

'Mrs Barr, at last, you've made it!'

There were no maids hovering. Selma was ushered into the drawing room.

'You're only just in time. Sit down. Your mother is upstairs in bed. Of course, I'd better warn you she's not as you will remember her. I think she's been waiting for your coming.

Dr Mackenzie says she's clung on. We're so pleased to see you've made the journey.'

Was this the same dragon she recalled as a child? She was softer, older and almost gentle. What had happened?

'What's wrong with my mother?' she asked.

'She has a growth in her stomach and it's spread. It's painful so she has to be given painkillers to ease her suffering. She's a very brave woman and took to her bed when I insisted. We have a nurse for her at night. I thought it best to tell you the truth. She pretends it's going to get better but it's just a game we play. It won't be long now. I'm sorry to drag you so far, but I knew you'd want to see her one last time.'

'I'll go up now, if you'll show me.' Selma wanted to face the worst straight away.

'Maggie will put your case in the guest room. You must be exhausted. She will run you a bath, if you wish. Your mother is on the top floor. I wanted to bring her down but she insisted she stayed put. She can be very stubborn. I shall miss her terribly.'

Selma raced up to the attic floor. A fire burned in the bedroom grate and in the middle of a brass-railed bed a little creature peered out with cloudy eyes.

Selma recoiled in shock. Where was her mother? How could this stranger be her? This old lady was all bones and yellowy skin scraped over her sunken cheeks like tissue paper. How could she be her mam?

'Is that you, Selma? You've come . . . I knew you would!'

She rushed to the bed in tears. 'Oh, why didn't you tell me how sick you were? I'd have come sooner.'

'You're here now and that's all that matters . . . still my bonny lass with a face the colour of walnut oil. Let me look at you.'

They sat holding hands, not speaking. Mam had said her piece and lay back exhausted. Lady Hester sent Maggie up with tea and fresh scones. She hadn't tasted real English tea and home baking for years. Mam didn't eat but had a sip of her sleeping juice.

'This will see me into kingdom come and I'll be glad of it. You can have enough of bellyache,' she whispered.

What Selma witnessed next was no mere bellyache. It was a gut-wrenching twisting pain that had Essie curled up thrashing about until it subsided. For all she looked so tiny, her belly was blown up as if there was a huge feather cushion inside.

'Come closer, tell me all your doings. What is my grand-daughter up to now?'

Selma brought out the photographs, and some of her in costume, ones taken on the beach and the family posing outside Casa Pinto. 'What a fancy spread . . . How's that husband of yours?'

'Busy as ever, on his horse in the desert. He loves his little girl,' she lied.

You didn't tell your dying mother that you were living apart and that it had never been much of a marriage from the start. Better to keep such things unsaid.

Her mother kept reaching out for her with a hand that was like a bird's claw in Selma's palm and she wanted to weep. 'You've been treated well, then?' she asked.

'Lady Hester's been a good friend to me. It's been a privilege to work here. Sorrow has softened her. She's made her mistakes, had her hopes dashed. We've rubbed along nicely . . . chalk and cheese like Ruth and me. You will go and stay with her when I'm gone?'

'When you're better we'll both go,' Selma said.

351

'None of that nonsense! Hester likes to play that game. I'm done for. You can't fight this ugly thing. It'll see me out, and when I'm gone take what you want . . . There's a bit of money put by. I was saving to come and visit you but I didn't quite make it, did I?'

'You rest now. I'll have a nap. My head's all over the show . . . It's a different time over there. I'm still on Los Angeles time. I feel I've not slept for days.'

'It's grand to have you home. Go and see your dad. I'll be joining him soon enough.'

'Oh, Mam!'

'My body might be rotting but I've still got all my chairs under the table. I know the score and I can go more peaceful knowing you'll be laying me out. It's all ready in the top drawer: a clean nightie, the pennies for my eyes and the chin bandage, towels. You know what to do and in what order – I've shown you enough times. Now go and get your shuteye. Hester will bring supper. She wants to know about your new life. Her son never writes. I fear he's dead. He did have those terrible fits.'

'I'd forgotten about that.' She'd not thought about Angus Cantrell for years.

'Hester knows all the arrangements when I pass over. Under all that stiff and starch, she's a good egg. If you've got any questions she'll answer them.'

'Questions about what?'

'Just questions. Now go and get some rest.'

'I didn't come here to rest. I came to see you,' Selma protested.

'I know you did, but I need my beauty sleep too and once the juice fades, you'll be wishing you weren't in the same room as me.'

'Not before I thank you for letting me leave when you did all those years ago.'

'I don't need thanking. You've been the best of girls to me. That saying is right, you know. "A man's a son till he gets a wife, a daughter's your daughter all her life." You're a good lass, and if Shari is a chip off the old block, she'll not go wrong in life. Oh, and I must tell you before I ramble off, if you walk up the High Road, look out for our Frank. I've seen him a time or two walking up the lane. He doesn't speak but I think he knows I'm there. His spirit has kept me going, just knowing he's back home where he belongs, but he needs putting to rest, poor lad.'

Poor Mam was rambling in her sleep, Selma mused. Frank on the road to Sowerthwaite? Whatever next? Dad in the forge? Newton at the Foss? They were all dead. Why should Frank be roaming around?

Selma smiled and nodded and tiptoed out of the room. Lady Hester was hovering at the bottom of the stairs, looking anxious. 'How is she?'

'Sleeping, rambling on about Frank on the High Road. I'm so glad you contacted me. How long will she suffer like this? Is there anything the doctor can do?'

'He's doing all he can to ease her pain. That will shorten things, I'm sure. Now go and get some rest while you can.'

Essie tossed and turned to find a comfortable spot, unable to duck the hurricane of pain that swept through her body, curling her into a ball, holding her breath for it to pass. Tonight the sleeping juice couldn't dull the agony. These were not birth pangs thrusting out the new but death throes, cutting the ropes of life, casting her adrift onto a lake of dreams.

They were all there on the bank across the silver ripples. She could see them playing cricket: Asa bowling overarm, Newton keeping wicket as usual, and Frank with his bat, arguing the toss in the stubby field. She wanted to wave and shout, 'I'm coming . . . wait for me, I'll field.'

They looked up and smiled, beckoning her over. She was never one for water but a bit more thrashing and paddling would see her safe to the other side . . .

The funeral was a quiet affair, just a burial in the church-yard. Essie had wanted no religious service. So there was just Ruth and Sam Broadbent, Selma and Hester, Maggie and Mr Hulbert, the coachman, but the vicar hovered in attendance down the path. It seemed a meagre turnout for such a stout-hearted woman, but her sufferings were over, and Hester envied her being at peace.

She invited them all back to Waterloo for a funeral tea. Ruth and Sam wanted to take Selma back to Bradford straight away but she wanted to stay on and sort out her mother's effects.

'I'll come on the train in a few days,' she promised them.

The more Hester saw of Selma, the more she realised what a great mistake she'd made all those years ago. Life in America had given her confidence, and her love for her daughter was obvious. She was curious about the girl's name.

'You called her after this village – how generous after all that happened,' she commented when the visitors had gone. 'Under the circumstances.'

'What do you mean?' Selma replied. 'I have only happy memories of my childhood growing up here. The war changed our lives but the place is still beautiful, and it gives Shari a sense of where she comes from.'

It was then, with a flash of alarm, that Hester realised Selma had no idea what had happened to her brother. Her parents had shielded her from the knowledge as she had tried to shield Guy. Perhaps it was for the best. What she didn't know couldn't hurt – or could it? But how could she fight for the Bartley name on the memorial without some family support? How could this wrong ever be righted? It wasn't her place to open up the terrible secret. Should she interfere and break the news to her. How would Selma take this shock, on top of everything else?

There were the letters, of course, especially the one that Essie had shown her all those years ago. Had she written more to her daughter? Should she warn the girl that there were secrets hidden in those drawers, soften the blow by dropping hints?

Whatever I do will be wrong, she thought. Better to say nothing and let things unfold in the fullness of time. Perhaps Essie had destroyed all the evidence. It would be just like her to take this secret to her grave. Her own wishes must be respected so no more interference. It had cost her both her sons' love and that was a bitter lesson to endure. Leave well alone, you're not family she told herself firmly. You must hang back and trust in Providence to know what is best.

Martha Holbeck's warnings still haunted her but she'd found some peace in befriending Essie. In many ways Essie had given her far more than she deserved in service and loyalty. She sat by the hearth searching the flames for comfort.

I never had a true friend before, one who spoke as she found, took no notice of rank, made me laugh at my own haughty ways. How I'll miss you, Essie. What would you want me to do now? I wish I knew.

21

How could a life come down to this room full of bits and pieces, thought Selma; a wardrobe of shabby tweeds and threadbare clothes, straw hats, warm shirts on hangers, the smell of camphor balls, a drawer of underclothes, well darned, with lavender sachets wrapped carefully around them, vests and corsets, a gold wedding ring, a silver bangle and a rope of cheap beads. There was nothing of value and yet everything held a precious memory for Selma. There was a photograph album in which each postcard from her brothers was neatly labelled with the date, and every letter she'd sent from America wrapped up with satin ribbon. How could she destroy these things or give them away?

What should she take back to Shari? Photographs, the trinket box that belonged to Granny Ackroyd, a little china plate that was a wedding present and the china dogs with cheery faces, which always sat on the mantelpiece, the wooden casket full of letters and Mam's little book of hand-written recipes. The rest, such as it was, could be sent to the poor and needy. Some of the clothes could be used for rag rugs, they were that worn out. Why had she denied herself all these years? In that tin there were pounds that should have been spent on herself.

As she sat among the things around her, Selma felt so alone. *I'm an orphan . . . now there's only Ruth and Sam who knew my family as it once was. The war robbed me of brothers and future sisters-in-law and children and cousins for Shari.*

The war had robbed so many of the future. She packed away everything carefully, wrapping each item as if it were a precious piece of china, checking the shelves and cupboards under the bed until she was certain nothing was left.

The room still had the smell of death in it, even with windows open. Mam had gone and she must leave too. She checked over everything one last time, and it was then that at the back of the drawer she found Mam's old black leather Bible stuffed with cards and letters. It had been gathering dust for years since Mam had gone off chapel in a big way. But it was hers, it must be taken, and now wasn't the time to open it or any of the papers inside. It was too painful and too personal. She didn't want to read her mother's thoughts. It felt like prying into her soul.

Selma looked around the room one last time, then went and put her case on the landing.

This was where Guy had once lived but she couldn't imagine it now. This was where she had struggled as a nervous child while her ladyship gave her the half-guinea. What had happened to those gold coins?

It was all a long time ago, so much had shifted since the war. How different she felt now, knowing that the Bartleys were as good as anyone of rank. It was who you were inside, not what you had, how you lived your life, not how titled you were that mattered. That's why she loved living in America. You could be anything you wanted to be if you tried hard enough.

'I've tidied everything away and taken some souvenirs,' she said at the top of the stairs. 'I hope that's all right.'

'Anything of interest?' said Lady Hester, hovering over her.

'Just letters and bits of memories from the cottage,' Selma replied, holding out her hand in friendship. 'I don't know how to thank you.'

'Is there anything you'd like to ask me, any questions?'

'Funny, Mam said that to me too. "If you've got any questions Lady Hester will answer them." Is there anything I should be knowing, any dark secrets?' She laughed nervously.

Hester didn't smile back. 'I'm here if you need me.'

'I know, and it's such a relief to know too how much you meant to my mother at the end. How can I ever repay you?'

'By thinking kindly of me, whatever happens. We all make mistakes. It's what you do afterwards that counts. A safe journey and keep in touch. Let me know what happens to you both. Take care of Sharland. Enjoy her while she's yours. Childhood is so short and there comes a time when they're gone and you can't change things back. Hulbert will drive you to the station.'

As Selma went to the waiting car she saw the old woman in black standing by the large door, her hand half raised in a wave. What was all that about? It was as if she was trying to warn her: funny old stick! She used to be so tall and daunting and now so frail and uncertain.

Selma made the driver stop by the graveyard for one final farewell to the freshly dug mound. 'I'm off now, Mam, back home. I'll make you proud of us so don't you fret. Cheery-bye!'

She felt village eyes watching from their net curtains but she didn't care. Where were they when the family needed them? She hadn't bothered to go and seek any of them out herself. Marigold Plimmer was still teaching school and looking shrivelled up and mean-faced. She could do without that sort of pal in her life.

Everything was settled, at peace and she could go back with an easy mind. Perhaps one day she'd bring Shari over, but not for an age. There was nothing for them here now but memories.

Miss Heckler stood on the porch as the children lined up to gape at their school teacher coming to their door: Charleson, Lorrie, Kitty, Dorothy and little Joan wondered what they had done wrong.

'Come in,' said Guy, knowing what this was about. Rose brought another cup to the table.

'I can't stop,' Miss Heckler said. 'I just wanted to know if you would like me to move Charlie . . . Charleson up another grade. He is doing so well and I don't want to hold him back in his math . . . if you are agreeable, Brother West and Sister Rose?'

'Sure, that's great, if you think he'll hold his own,' Guy replied. 'He loves his schooling.'

'He's the sort of boy who'll benefit from higher education but I know that's a personal decision for a family and not without sacrifice. Boys are needed on farms, especially in these hard times,' said Miss Heckler.

Guy waved his hand. 'We'll manage, face that when it comes, won't we, Rose? The girls can help him out after school with chores. Thank you for giving us warning.'

The teacher rose. 'I'm so glad you're enthusiastic. In my

experience there's a reluctance to let our brightest pupils go on to higher grades. It means a change of school, of course . . .'

'Of course.' Guy turned to his wife, who had a face like thunder.

'We will discuss this with the family first,' she said.

Miss Heckler backed out, sensing tension. 'I hope I've not brought dissention,' she said. 'Having a brainy child in class sure leavens the dough,' she joked, but Rose did not respond as she shut the door behind her.

'Rose! That was so rude of you. What do you mean?' Guy snapped.

'The boy stays where he is. It doesn't do to favour one over the other. It's not our way. Pa will not hold with sending our boy into a worldly school to better himself.'

'You forget, *I'm* Charlie's pa. Education is a way for him to find his true path in the world.'

'Education is the way out of the community. They leave for college and never come back, or if they do, it's to demand changes and freedoms, unsettling everyone.'

'You can't hold him back,' he argued.

'How can we pay for books and clothes and transport in this depression? There's hardly a cent to spare. You can be so worldly sometimes. He must learn to work within his own kind,' she sighed, not looking at him.

'Doesn't he do that now, ploughing a team of horses since he was nine . . . digging out wells? When I think of my pampered childhood with servants to wait on us. I want my child to be able to do more than read and write. I want him to understand how things are made and how science helps man conquer disease . . .'

'There you go again, forgetting you joined a chosen

360

people, a separate tribe. It is our duty to bring up our children in obedience to the rules, not encourage worldly pursuits.'

'But it is his future not ours here. We have made our choices – shouldn't he be free to experience other things before he makes his?'

'You were happy enough to leave your old life behind and join us, or have you changed your mind now?'

'That was different. There was a war on. I had a good education. It did me no harm,' he argued. This was a side of Rose he'd not seen before.

'It made you into a soldier and brought you low. You were happy to eat dog scraps when I first knew you,' she cornered him.

'This is not like you to throw stuff back at me. What's bugging you?'

'Can't you see I'm afraid? Don't go giving Charlie big ideas, it'll end in tears. Don't forget we've been here before. Look no further than my brother Zack. He was lost to us when he went to war.'

'That won't happen again. I just want Charlie to fulfil the gifts inside him. He's got a mind that is always asking questions and wants answers. I'm not sure he wants to be a farmer.'

'The Lord will decide his path. He must obey the *Ordnung*; obedience to parents' wishes is high in the Ten Commandments. Obedience is the only way to humility and is the path to peace.'

'I don't understand. How can a mother not take pride in having a clever son? Don't you want him to be of use in the world?'

'Growing food, giving to the poor from our surplus is good enough for me.'

When Rose of Sharon got that ornery look on her face there was no shifting her, but he was head of the household and it was his desire to see Charlie educated to a higher standard than the village schoolroom. The Lord had endowed the boy with brains for a purpose. He was his only son. The line of little girls who followed were his joy too but they lived in their mother's domain, kitchen maids and dairy hands. She ruled there.

Izaak would no doubt take him aside in the fields and point out the error of his ways; that he was an offcomer, an Englisher and must learn obedience.

Guy sat alone, knowing that he wasn't giving in on this one. Charlie would go to college no matter what it took. For one fleeting second he contemplated writing to his mother and demanding she send the boy to his own Alma Mater, but then he laughed aloud at such a notion.

Where was the harm in giving his child a chance to open his mind to the joys of learning? It was the least he could do and he would find some way to persuade the Yoders that they must move with the times.

It was a smooth Atlantic crossing. This time Selma felt such a sense of freedom and longing to be going back to the warmth of the Californian sun, to see her daughter's face again and share her grief with Lisa. It was strange that since her mother's death she felt she was her own person, free to take up her life again. Those three precious weeks in Yorkshire convinced her that her own life was no longer there. The past was the past and over with. She had been so lucky to get back in time to say goodbye and to honour her passing. All the little family mementoes were safely packed away and she had time now to stroll on deck and prepare for her return.

She delved into the battered suitcase and pulled out a book, but instead chanced upon her mother's black Bible. Out of it spilled a wodge of letters with army postmarks. Frank and Newton's letters? She didn't want to look at them, but then she saw they weren't in their handwriting. She was curious.

Mam had said she received comforting notes from Frank's pals. It would be nice to read their comments about him, a comfort even. She still felt sad about that last visit home and the silence that followed when she was sent away.

Opening the thickest letter, she decided to go on deck into the sunshine to read them. She found a sheltered deck chair and settled down to the task. What was on those pages made no sense at first. It was all about some court case, but then, as she read her hands turned to ice.

Dear Mr and Mrs Bartley,

I think you ought to know what really happened to your son. It weren't right at all. We had been out with the horses all day, and they were done in and so were we. It was time to put them back in the stable and rub them down and get their tea.

Then our regimental sergeant major came storming in, all guns blazing, saying where the hell have you been and get them horses back out, they're needed!

Frank turned round and said politely, 'But they need to rest up and feed, and we do too.' Which were a mistake.

'Don't you give me cheek, lad. I know your sort, skulking off behind the stalls for a fag, idling . . . get on your way.'

'These horses aren't fit,' Frank said, standing his ground, and I could see him flaring up.

'Shush, Frank,' I said. 'Let him be,' but he were tired and riled and not to be reasoned with. He'd had some bad dos of late.

'Let him take the bloody horses, drive them senseless into the mud but I won't do it. It's not humane what they have to put up with here. They're all God's creatures and can't tell us owt if they suffer,' he said.

'You'll bloody well do what you are told!' came the order.

'Go to hell!' he cursed, and the RSM pulled the cigarette out of his mouth roughly, and that's when Frank punched him hard in the face and swore. We tried to pull him off but he went berserk. Suddenly they were on him and he was marched off on a charge, but he kept lashing out. 'Don't let the buggers get you down!' That was Frank all over, all for his horses, but there weren't anything we could do but obey.

We heard later that he knocked down the second lieutenant and beat him hard. He was a doomed man from that moment on. Perhaps something had snapped, a string cut, a cog in his mind slipped for a second.

By the time he was stood on the mat before the Field Court Martial, he'd regained his composure but the seriousness of the charge washed all the colour from his face, and his past record was against him. You don't strike officers and superiors. It's as bad as mutiny in their eyes. So he was sentenced to

death and had to wait for confirmation from the
bigwigs.

We tried to speak up for him, but that RSM
hated his guts and took delight in goading him. He
was hoping some captain from his village would
speak up for him too but Captain Cantrell, I think
his name was, never came or sent the proper papers,
I'm told, which was a shame. It might have been
different if he had.

It was ordered that some of us would make up
the firing squad but no one volunteered. Frank was
well liked.

We hung about where he was held and the officer
let us talk to him through the window. 'Au revoir,
chum,' I said. It was all I could think of I were that
choked.

Terrible things happen in war, but nothing as
bad as this. I will never forget it as long as I live.
None of us will. It was a despicable act on a good
man.

He was blindfolded at first, his hands tied
together to a post but he stood steady as a rock.
'Take off the blindfold,' he asked. 'I'm not afraid.'
We were made to watch. 'Goodbye, you lot,' he
shouted as if he were going off on leave. The
subaltern was trembling and the firing squad
looked dreadful.

There were a sharp crack of a volley and it were
all over with. Some of the firing squad threw up in
disgust. He was carted off to be buried. We took
some flowers to his grave later – piled high they
were.

That RSM came past and kicked them over with contempt. 'That sort are best forgotten,' he said.

Don't worry, his card's marked, I promise you. We'll get our revenge. That's all I'm saying.

Your son, my pal, was no coward, and as long as I've got breath in my body he will be remembered. He were a brave lad and a credit to you all.

Yours sincerely,

Private Herbert Shackleton

PS. This letter has come via a friend. I didn't want anyone censoring these words. It wasn't right, what happened. It needs seeing to when this lot is over.

The skies darken, the wind whips round my wheelchair as I recall each sentence of that letter by heart. My limbs may be weak but the shock of that discovery still feels like a lead weight tied to them.

My brother was murdered by his own regiment. My brother was executed like a criminal and my parents took this secret to the grave. He waited for Guy to come to his aid and he never did, and I had just spent three weeks under his roof knowing none of this.

It all made sense now. Why I was exiled to Bradford in such a hurry, why dog shit was smeared onto our donkey white front step each morning. Why the window was broken. Everybody had known except me.

How do you live with such knowledge? How do you make it right? What was done to my brother and to others like him was barbaric.

'Vengeance is mine, saith the Lord.'

No, I cried as the icy splinters froze my heart, it will be mine. It was a good job I thought there were no Cantrell twins left in this world or they would have been first on my murderous list.

That was when the icicles pierced my heart with hatred, chilling my respect for my village and country. I'd gone home with love and hope and returned broken, bitter and suspicious. I'm not proud of who I became then.

Buried somewhere in military archives, Frank's case lay forgotten. How could I forgive or forget what the Army did to him? I never wanted to see the Union Jack again.

It still pains me to think of that discovery and the moment when I knew the heavy baton of family responsibility had been passed to me. It was a race I didn't know how to run but knew one day I must finish somehow.

4

THE RETURN
1941 . . .

Over there, over there,
Send the word, send the word over there,
That the Yanks are coming
The Yanks are coming
The drum's rum-tumming evr'ywhere.
So prepare, say a pray'r
Send the word, send the word to beware . . .

George Cohan, 1917

22

December 1941

Charleson West hung over the wireless, grim-faced, not believing this news bulletin. On Sunday morning Pearl Harbor had been bombed. The Japanese attack had destroyed most of the fleet in the harbour and America was now at war. It happened just before the Christmas vacation and he was due home for the festivities, but his heart was heavy at the implications of this attack.

The war in Europe had been going on for two years; cities bombed, armies destroyed. A few of his college friends with British families had rushed to join the RAF squadrons; one of them had been killed already in a training accident. But somehow, it was their war, not his, because he belonged to a Church that believed in non-resistance and pacifism. 'Thou shalt not kill' was the order. But this was different, surely?

His own countrymen were mown down in their beds without warning, his country could be attacked, and his family harmed. Charlie couldn't sit by and do nothing and yet he knew it was not their way of doing things. He realised going home was not going to be easy.

371

Who was there to see his quandary? Not his mother. She was still following the old order in her prayer cape and black bonnet and strict ways. He wished they'd go with the times like many Mennonites who were more progressive in their dealings with the outside world. Even Pa had the use of a pickup car for essential purposes. Many in the congregation wore ordinary everyday clothes, especially the young ones. His sisters made their own pretty dresses and decorated them. He'd been allowed to go to high school and college. His father wanted him to train as a doctor of medicine, but he knew he wasn't cut out for all that blood and gore, but now . . .

There was always tension in college when it came to compulsory military training. He was excused for being a sincere pacifist and given a choice of extra physical jerks or community work to fill that time, but there was something inside him that was more attracted to the military parades, marching to the band and the discipline. He knew it wasn't their way and yet . . .

Christmas at Springville was always a jolly affair. Lots of singing and fellowships, a Christmas tree with handmade decorations, a feast at the table, a chance to catch up with the congregation. But how could they celebrate when their country was in danger? Charleson wondered if any of the other boys were feeling as he did. But as he was one of only a few allowed to go on to further education outside his own community, he reckoned he might be alone in this anxiety. His education had caused tension in the family, and they would be watching for any slackening of his obedience to their way of life. Sometimes he wished he'd not gone away. What you didn't know you didn't miss, but now he had experienced another way of life, some of their old-fashioned ways troubled him.

Guy heard the news at the store in town. He tried to put it to the back of his mind. It was of no consequence to him now since his fighting days were a distant memory but he recalled the Halifax explosion in 1917, and the devastation. He could smell Pearl Harbor, with its burning oil, charred bodies, smoke, chaos and confusion. That vision of hell on earth all those years ago never went away. Some poor mothers' sons lay at the bottom of the sea or trapped in the hold. He kept trying to push it to the back of his mind alongside other matters troubling him.

Rose had never forgiven him for ruling that Charlie would go to college, and the girls too if they wished. He was drawn to the more liberal members of the congregation who were edging closer to the worldly community: sharing with other Churches in community service, in soup kitchens during those terrible years of depression. It made sense to pool resources together.

Rose kept tightly to the old ways. There was a cooling between them, their lovemaking infrequent and unsatisfactory. It was as if joy had flown out of their marriage, and with it laughter and teasing and companionship. Guy kept himself busy with meetings, committees, keeping their farm buildings in repair. Rose kept to the kitchen with Miriam, her aged mother. Isaak had died five years earlier. It was a house of women these days. Charlie was coming home for Christmas and Guy looked forward to those walks around the field with him, a chance to catch up on all his college life, while they sat on Gus's bench.

Gus's bench was close to the little grave of Charlie's twin.

There were two other little mites buried there, who never reached full term and then no more babies came. Guy would sit and survey their land with pride. He'd taken to farming. With Isaak's help he'd learned the best way to make the crops yield well, to choose the best cattle and horses, to follow the rhythm of the seasons. Sometimes he felt so blessed to have found refuge in this community and love after so much despair.

But another war? How could it have happened? Hadn't he fought the war to end all wars? It was rumoured that Germany had found a way to harness labour in the depression, to build fast roads and armament factories, to train up young people to devotion to their country and now Hitler wanted to take over the world. Lust for power, greed for land, hatred of other people's religion . . . It was a sick, sick world and he wanted none of it. How could he turn his back on the sufferings to come?

When he saw his son striding up the lane his heart leaped with pride. Charlie had grown so tall and long-limbed, his fair hair flopping over his forehead as his had done in youth. At least he didn't have to worry about his son being sent off to war. There were whoops of delight as Kitty, Lorrie and Joan ran out to greet him, and Rose walked with outstretched arms to gather him in. Guy looked down from the hillside and grinned to himself. You've got some things right in this life, old man.

He never thought of his own family without wincing at how distanced he had felt from his own father, who was hardly ever there in his childhood, how fussy his mother had been to compensate for that absence. He recalled sharing everything with Angus, until that terrible afternoon at the Foss. There was a dreamlike vagueness about England

and all of his past now. It hardly existed. He didn't talk about it much. It was a foreign country to his children.

All that mattered to him now was sitting in the kitchen together now his backside was freezing on the stone bench. There wasn't a day went by that he didn't thank the Lord for his mercy in giving him a second chance at life.

Sharland Barr rushed out of the college campus, shaking from the terrible news that had flashed on the radio. She'd been late waking up that Sunday morning, as her mother was out on a shoot somewhere. They were at war! No false alarms this time, and all those poor boys in the Pacific Islands. She couldn't believe it. She must do something, sign up as a Red Cross volunteer. How could she sit idly by and do nothing? There had to be a job for her somewhere as a nurse in the army? She'd find something to do. Her college studies could wait. This was too important. But what would Mom say? Difficult to predict since Granny died, she'd not been her cheery self. She came back from England and never mentioned it again. It was like trying to get blood out of a stone. She'd divorced Pa for desertion and concentrated on her own film career.

For someone who hated England she did some mean roles playing British housemaids, serving wenches and anything that required a British accent. She made a living for them both out of bit parts and she'd taken elocution lessons to improve her own accent so she got to play ladies at balls and minor aristocrats. There was nothing in the way of serious acting, just small character parts in some big blockbuster films. She played a widow in black who looked in horror at Scarlett O'Hara's famous widow dancing scene in *Gone with the Wind* and she played a servant in a film about the Brontës. Yet Zelma Barr was best known for her pioneer roles, with a face tough enough to have opened up the West to respectable women.

There'd been just the two of them for so long, and of course Lisa Greenwood, who was a professor in college now and who had a fiancé called Patrick Hamilton the Third, who was already in the navy.

Sometimes, when she was hard up, Shari also did extra work but her auburn hair stood out in colour films and so she toned it down with dye to blend into the background. Acting was not for her at all; not even seeing all those famous stars, jockeying for position on the red carpet, mincing starlets on the arms of old film producers. It was dog eat dog in that business. She'd seen what it'd done to her own pa. He'd been dropped once talkies were established, reduced to bit parts and extras, and he'd drunk his way off too many sets, labelled unreliable, so no agent would then put him on their books. She last heard of him in Las Vegas. She had tried to keep in touch with him but he had drifted out of her life and sometimes it was hard to imagine she'd ever been his golden girl.

Shari sensed everything was changed on that December Sunday morning. The Lockheed aircraft factories would be geared for war machinery. The film board would want patriotic, cheering films to fill the cinemas. Women would have to replace the menfolk in the factories. It was a whole new ball game and she would be part of it too. Wait until Mom found out what was happening – would she want to support the war effort or would she just want to carry on as usual?

Only once, when Shari asked about her uncle and their war, had Mom blown up in anger. 'You were robbed of cousins and family by a wicked war – don't talk to me about that business. The army is fit only for animals. It's a cruel institution. You have no idea what was done under its banner . . .' For a while she'd even wanted her to change her name from Sharland to Esther, for some reason. But Shari was having none of it. Whatever grouse Mom had about her old life in the village in Yorkshire was nothing to do with her so she refused to oblige and it was soon forgotten. Now how would Mom react when she told her that she wanted to join up as a volunteer? Much as she loved her mother it wouldn't matter either way: Shari had made up her mind. She was going to war.

'I've decided to enlist,' Charlie announced calmly after they sat down to supper.

There was silence. His mother rose up from the table and left the room with the girls, unable to control her feelings.

'I know it's not what you preach, Pa, but I can't sit back and do nothing. It just ain't right.'

'You don't know what you're talking about. This isn't some exercise, marching up and down. War is a filthy, nasty business. People get hurt. Have you ever seen a man with his head blown off or trying to hold his guts from spilling on the dirt? It isn't the answer. It wasn't last time. Men died, children died, and for what, I ask myself.'

'So?' Charlie said. 'Nothing stops it happening all over again. London bombed out, France overrun – do we just sit there until Hitler marches through Springville Township?'

'We have our way of doing things, giving support to disasters and famine. You don't have to put on a battledress to be a hero.'

'You did, you went to war once. You must have believed in the cause.'

377

'I don't now. You've no idea what it does to a man.'

'I don't care. I don't want to be a hero, I just want to enlist.'

'You know what'll happen if you do?' Guy bowed his head.

'I'll be shunned, I know. No one will eat with me or invite me to gatherings. I'll have no place in the church service, I'll be disciplined . . . so? I have to do what I think is right,' he argued.

'Why do you have to shame us? Your mother will be heartbroken.'

'My mother has been heartbroken ever since the day Miss Heckler shoved me into the big class. You wanted me to see another way. Much as I love our community, I find their minds so closed and their rules so strict at times. Why can't they move with the times?'

'When I sent you to college, I took a risk. You know how Ma feels. But when it comes to our beliefs – the fundamentals, Charlie – you can't cherry-pick; embracing bits here and dropping bits there . . . It is all or nothing. That is how it is. You'll be brought before the elders and disciplined, as I have been many times for being too worldly – for buying a tractor and then the Ford, for listening to the wireless – but this is a serious decision for all of your family.'

'If the storm troopers beat at your door would you not want to defend us?' Charlie threw up one of the old arguments.

'I would do what was best for your safety, give civil answers . . . render to Caesar what is Caesar's, as we are taught.'

'I don't believe it. If they stole your cattle and insulted your daughters would you stand there and watch? Or does non-resistance mean we surrender everything without a murmur?'

'It won't happen, son.'

'But it's happening all over Europe, to some of Ma's far-flung relatives. What happens to them happens to me. Don't we preach about being each other's keepers? We have to defend the poor, the weak and afflicted wherever they are.' Charlie could feel his cheeks flushing with indignation.

'But not with guns and bombs and bayonets, but with food and medicines and first aid. No one begrudges a pacifist who does such work. There are Quaker non-combatant units who're stretcher bearers and nurses. You could join them.'

Charlie could see the pleading in his father's eyes, the anxious twitch on his cheekbone when he was angry or tense.

'I have to find my own path even if it means leaving here for good,' he said, knowing what a blow he was dealing to his father.

'You will shame us before our brothers, give your mother no peace, and discipline will require us to shut this door in your face. How can I do that to my own son? Don't rush into what you don't know. Think about this.'

'You went to war and killed men, took up arms, why shouldn't I?'

'I knew no better. I was groomed by my family's trad-ition for it. It was the only life I knew but, believe me, we suffered for it. That was my life before Christ entered my heart and changed me. All I feel is shame and regret. War brings out the animal in us not always the human being. You were not brought up to fight—'

'I was brought up to know right from wrong. What

has happened is wrong, and if good men do nothing then evil will take over and destroy this way of life. They will destroy and punish until everyone must live under their rules and under their sword. Do you think for a moment our brothers would be allowed to stay as they are? My mind's made up, I'm not going back to college . . . I'll write and let you know where I am,' Charlie said, close to tears.

'You know we'll not be allowed to read them. Oh, Charlie, don't throw your life away! Don't destroy our family. How am I going to explain this to the girls?'

'Don't worry, I'll love you all, no matter what happens. I know what I'm doing. I feel in my bones it is what I was meant to do . . .'

Charlie bowed his head as his father patted his shoulder with trembling hand.

Rose sobbed until she was exhausted when Charlie left for war. The girls clung to each other. Guy felt such an ache in his side, he thought he'd collapse.

True to the end, the boy stood before the disciplinary committee and argued his case like a lawyer, refusing to back down, and was dismissed.

Everyone looked on the Wests with pity and concern and not a little disappointment.

At the foot-washing service that followed, Guy was humbled as the preacher knelt before him and washed his feet in the bowl as a sign of compassion and acceptance.

What everyone had feared had happened. Too much exposure to worldly company and argument had corrupted his son into disobedience. Straight is the path and narrow the way that leads to salvation, they were taught. Rose blamed Guy not with harsh words but with a stinging silence that was hard to bear.

For the first time in years, Guy felt his unquestioning faith wavering, his loyalties torn. His stomach gave him such pain and bile in his throat. He was not born to this life. Had his old military heritage passed into his blood and through to his son? Was it bred in the bone, this warring urge? Was it all a fault of his own breeding?

For the first time in years, he thought about his own mother's efforts to keep them safe, her desperation to have them close to her side. He knew now what it felt like to lose a child to ideals, to feel the draught of his absence, to yearn to know how he was faring. He didn't know if his own mother was dead or alive, or if Dr Mac was still in West Sharland. Should he make contact, make his peace with her after all this time?

How could it have all gone so wrong? Why don't we understand until it's too late to make amends? How could he survive with such a rock hung round his neck, weighing him down?

Rose was adamant. 'We have no son now. The fields will be ploughed, the harvest reaped, the seasons will turn whether he is here or not. People need corn and milk. We carry on as we have always done for hundreds of years, trusting in the goodness of the Lord that the way of peace is best. You have the girls and friends to help you, and the brethrens' respect. That is surely enough for any man'.

Guy took his straw hat off the peg hook and nodded. How could she be so hard and unfeeling?

Selma knew the film was going to be a hit from the moment William Wyler got hold of Jan Struther's creation, *Mrs Miniver*.

She had to laugh at how British society was portrayed; the genteel English village with thatched cottages with roses everywhere, the cut-glass accents. It was a thousand miles away from the life she had known but she thought about how Lady Hester and her mother had bridged the class gap between them somehow after the Great War. Hollywood had such an unrealistic view of little old England with its quaint locals and funny ways, but it pulled no punches about the way it was suffering under the Luftwaffe.

They were doing the scene in the bombed-out church, being stoical and brave under fire, and Greer Garson doing her upper-crust lady of the manor, but everyone knew her lover was playing her son! She was utterly convincing as the staunch heroine defying the odds as her home was bombed, surviving with the stiff upper lip and Dunkirk spirit that, it was hoped, was going to shock the American public into action.

Selma had a small part in the church scene where the vicar preached a stirring call to arms to the world. It was all good war propaganda for Europe but others in the cast with boys in the Pacific wanted the studio to focus on hitting the Japs, not going to Europe again.

Selma had no feelings either way. She'd seen it all before, her heart sickened by the sight of so many young men in uniform, and now Shari had volunteered for service in the American Red Cross abroad. She was proud but fearful. Lisa said they'd keep the girls safe but if she was posted to London she might be in even worse danger from firebombs.

Lisa was anxious about her fiancé, in the navy. Selma was still living alone in the service flat at Casa Pinto, glad of a bolt hole from the studio set.

Wartime restrictions had hit the studios: no more use of

ironwork; walls must be made of flimsy cotton; nails were to be used sparingly and anything sunk in a battle scene had to be refloated and used again. There were to be few artificial snow scenes as this was wasteful of breakfast cereals. The location work had to be close by and double up for any foreign country needed. There were air-raid shelters and precautions, but everyone seemed to carry on as if the war was a minor inconvenience. Films were good for morale.

Selma tried not to think about England being at war again, tried to keep the ice in her heart against her own people, but the newsreels were heartbreaking. She'd met two little refugees, Cynthia and Mavis, sent by their Jewish parents for safety to relatives who worked in the studios and soon working on set, with their perfect English accents, acting as schoolgirls. She couldn't blame these innocent children for what happened to Frank all those years ago.

There were other residents who fared worse. The American Japanese community was gathered at Santa Anita racetrack as prisoners of war. Soon they were exiled into camps in the valley of the High Sierras out of sight. She had found so many of them kind, quiet, hard-working folk and now they were banished and dismissed as 'the enemy'.

She had written a steaming letter to Aunty Ruth saying she knew now about Frank and what were they going to do about it? They told her that the military death penalty was finally abolished for the sort of offence Frank committed. It had taken ten years of political wrangling and debate. Ruth put her straight in blunt Yorkshire language that she had already written to her MP to protest about her nephew's case.

Don't sit back and sulk, Selma, do something. Write and keep writing! One day the matter will be aired properly. It was Frank's dying wish that you must not be informed. He thought of you so highly. His wishes were honoured at such a cost to Asa and Essie. Don't go blaming anyone else for that!

Some of the anger Selma felt evaporated with this knowledge, but Guy's part in the court martial she would never forget – or Lady Hester's part. She never wrote to her again. She didn't trust herself putting pen to paper.

Everything to do with this matter she kept in a special teak box out of sight from Shari. She was too young to be burdened with such sad facts. Now she was keeping the legacy of silence and shame from Shari, just as had been done to her.

Ruth said there was still no memorial in Elm Tree Square, and now another war was raging who knew when they'd get round to a decision? They might as well wait for extra names to be added.

Selma wrote back to apologise, stuffing the parcel full of tins of salmon and fruit and sweets, cookies, ham and butter. That was something she could do for the Broadbents. They had been so kind in the past and it felt good to be giving something back. Soon she began to collect tins and clothes on a regular basis so they could be parcelled up and sent abroad.

She promised that Shari would look them up if ever she were posted to England. It would be good for her daughter to see the old country in its rough grandeur and muck. Yorkshire was about as far from Mrs Miniver's fake English set as she was from the moon!

23

Charlie spent the long journey across the Atlantic praying that his stomach wouldn't come out of his throat. He'd never retched so much in his life. If this was going to sea you could keep it. Most of his buddies were hanging over the sides as they zigzagged their course, convinced the U-boats would be following alongside ready to pounce on the convoy. They played cards and at first he opted out, trying to keep up old habits from his church life but there wasn't much else to do but pray. You can get mighty holy when there's a wolf pack prowling in search of you.

He'd passed all the exams and aptitude tests. There was a chance for him to go for officer training but as he watched the waves lashing the sides of the ship, spraying him with ice-cold water, he wondered what he'd gone and done in signing up. He could still see his ma's face trying not to cry; hear his father's stricken pleas for him to change his mind. That final view of all he held dear, lost for ever because of his principles.

What a shock army life was: one rule after another, fitness regimes, marching parades, bunking with strangers, and all that lecture stuff on how they must behave towards the British civilians. Don't criticise the King and Queen or say it was us that won the last war. Don't be greedy if you're asked to tea. They will be giving you their rations. Always take something with you, and never talk politics or religion, it is bad form. What would these Brits be like?

He had to remind himself that he was English on his father's side. His family had once lived in Yorkshire and he went to school there at a place called Sharland. That was about all he knew except that his father had a twin brother who died in the war.

For some time he'd been curious about his family history but could never draw Pa out. He'd been in the Merchant Navy but apart from a few details the rest was shrouded in mystery. There was enough, though, to find out a bit more. He had sensed for a long time that Pa was a troubled man before he met the Yoders and joined the Church. There was more to Charles West senior and he meant to find out just what sort of family he came from to satisfy himself once and for all.

He'd devised a way of communication with his parents that they couldn't ignore. He was going to send postcards in envelopes with no message, just pictures unsigned; a gift of pictures so they knew just where he was, even if they couldn't respond. He knew they loved him, and in the end that loving concern would soften them, but it was all too raw and hurtful to them at the moment. So they'd be getting postcards from New York, and whatever port they landed in next, Ireland, Scotland . . . nothing would stop him sending them his love. Even in this disobedience to their rule, he would not be ignored.

Shari sat in the tiny sitting room off Ivy Dene, while Aunty Ruth hovered over her with excitement. 'I can't believe it's you after all these years. So grown up and smart in your uniform . . . We've only had two pictures to go by, haven't we, Sam? You'll have to shout, he's gone quite deaf,' she whispered. 'I don't know who you take after. Not your mother, except you've got her father's black eyes, but that hair, such a colour. I've never seen owt like it . . . like autumn leaves.'

'Maple syrup, my mom calls it. That comes from my dad. He's Scotch like the whisky.'

'We saw the film *Mrs Miniver*. Everyone wept buckets. Not that it looks anything like that round here, of course. I'd have missed Selma if she hadn't told me where to look for her. She's put on a bit of weight since I last saw her.'

'She loves her ice-cream sodas,' Shari said, thinking how cosy it was to be sitting here with someone who knew her own family.

'We've forgotten what they're like, it's been so long. But what can I get you? Some tea?'

'Tea, no milk – that'll be fine.' Shari remembered the instructions and brought out cookies and chocolate as a gift.

'You're lucky it was baking day. I've got some scones with some rhubarb jam, and ginger parkin, and what's all this you've brought?'

'For you and Uncle Sam.' Shari produced some more tins out of her bag.

'There was no need for that, but thank you.' Ruth flushed. 'Your mother's so good to us, but I think a few of her parcels have gone missing at the port. We number our letters now so we can tell if one of the parcels is out of sync.'

'Before I go, I want to see all the family pictures to know who I am on this side of the pond. Mom doesn't tell me much, you know,' Shari laughed. Aunty Ruth was exactly how she'd pictured her, round, warm and neat as a pin.

'Not before we sit down to tea. You have to learn, at four thirty or five we British like to take tea, biscuits, whatever we can scrounge, just to pause and take stock of the day. I got my best china out and washed it especially. Rationing is hard, but it's fair, and I reckon some folks are better fed than they ever were. Whatever we've got, it looks better on a pretty china plate, don't you think? I learned that from my mam.'

'Where was that?' asked Shari.

'In a little village near Settle not far from West Sharland.'

'That's where my name come from. I'll have to see that for myself one day,' Shari replied.

'It's only up the Dale, very pretty. We'll have a run out one day, if we can get some petrol.'

'Petrol?' Sam came alive. 'There's no coupons to be had.'

'Well, we'll borrow some when Shari comes again. You will come again?' urged Ruth.

'Sure, now I've found you folks,' Shari replied.

'We weren't blessed with little ones so we're going to spoil you, young lady. I love to hear you speaking. Straight out of the pictures, you sound. Didn't you fancy being in the pictures yourself?' Ruth asked.

Shari smiled. 'One in the family is enough. No, I love what I'm doing here, and based at a new place that's just opened called the Rainbow Club. We run all the office work upstairs. When the American army arrives or is on the move, the Red Cross isn't far behind with welfare clubs, shows and comforts for our troops.'

'I hope they keep you at the front desk. You'd cheer up any gloom with that big smile of yours. They're lucky to have you.'

'I could have stayed stateside but I felt I wanted to come

over to Europe to do my bit. I gather my uncles did their duty in the last show.'

'Aye, lass, and paid for it. Your poor grandparents never got over it. Your grandfather had the forge in Sharland and he was a blacksmith. It's a garage now. Such a shame it took a war to bring you over here. The last visit was a sad one for your mother. I suppose she told you about it . . . But enough of this. Tell us all about your life in California. It sounds so warm and wonderful, and here is so drab and wet.'

'I don't mind. It's different. I'm getting used to the air. I can see why English girls have such lovely skins. We have so much sun we end up with faces like alligator hide if we don't cover up.'

They chatted and drank tea until Shari was busting. 'Can you show me where Lisa lived? I promised to give her a full account of my visit.'

Ruth pointed up the road to Rose Villa. 'They were a lovely family, the Greenwoods. Is Lisa married yet?'

'Almost. Her fiancé is in the navy.' Shari pulled out a picture of them all lined up on the lawn of Casa Pinto, everyone laughing round the swimming pool.

'Mrs Levine was away, so we got to use the pool. We don't always live in such luxury, though.'

'It makes my poor room look very pokey.'

'You have a home here, Aunty. Pearl has a house. It's mostly empty, full of dust sheets. It's just a shell. Mom has a nice flat, though.'

'You say the nicest things, Sharland. I can see we're going to get along. Make this a home while you're in England. Now we've found you, we'd love to have you stay.'

Shari hugged them both when she left for the station

and the London train. This was what Mom called a real Yorkshire welcome: a crackling fire, a plate of warm biscuits and jam, cake, pots of tea and family chatter. They knew her mother when she was a girl, her grandparents, her great-grandparents the Ackroyds; a whole side of herself she'd never explored until now.

There had only ever been the two of them. She ought to find out about the Barrs in Glasgow. But her father had often painted such a terrible picture about that side of her family. She had no desire to meet the parents who'd made her own pa so feckless and unreliable. This was her first venture north and she liked what she saw. She hoped she could get back for Christmas.

In July 1942 Charlie sent postcards from Liverpool dock and Warrington. How could he describe the broken horrific sight of the bombed city, the grimy docklands, the devastation around him as they disembarked? That was all he could find to show them where he was in the north of England, helping with the transfer from the RAF base at Burtonwood into the United States Army Air Force service centre for US aircraft maintenance and supplies.

It was a huge airfield with thousands of personnel to be housed in Nissen huts alongside the service station. It was like little America on British soil, with their own shops and recreation halls, canteens and baseball teams. He could go for weeks and never hear a British voice except in the canteen or outside the dance hall.

Sometimes he felt like a worker ant scurrying away, but his mechanical expertise was needed. He'd earned his sergeant's stripes and took no cheek from his men. They seemed to respect him because he didn't curse and swear at them, didn't drink or go with women. It just wasn't his way.

He looked at some of those girls hanging round the camp with painted faces and frozen bare legs, eyeing him up with interest. He kept thinking of his sister Lorrie, who was about their age. How would he feel if she was one of them, touting her charms for a pair of nylons?

Men would be men and take their chance if it was offered so blatantly on a plate. But he'd rather go hungry than use a girl and dancing wasn't much his scene either. It wasn't like the sort of barn dance frolics he was used to, more an animalistic sort of mating frenzy. This was when he felt so out of touch with his peers. It was as if he had skipped a whole lusty growing stage. In his Church, courtship was a quiet ordered affair between families, nothing rushed or romantic. He wasn't a regular GI Joe at all. On his leave and twenty-four-hour passes he headed off into the Cheshire countryside to get his bearings, wandering through the ancient towns, admiring the architecture and the churches. That's when he found people suspicious if he asked for postcards, thinking he was spying out the land.

Then one liberty pass he persuaded a friendly mechanic to loan him a Jeep. He was going to head north to the distant hills of Lancashire and see if he could find that school of Pa's. His friend Gary wasn't going to let him out of his sight.

'I'm coming with you, just in case. For a farmer's boy you drive like you have never ridden on four wheels in your life.' Charlie laughed, wondering what Gary Ambler would think if he knew how his father had struggled with his conscience to own a tractor. It was hidden in the barn for days before he dared bring it out and use it.

They took a compass and kept driving north through the grimy cotton towns of Atherton, Leigh, Bolton, Burnley, and onwards to a great town with a castle at the end of the High Street, called Skipton. They stopped to admire the sight and asked directions as there were no signposts to guide them.

It was early winter by now, and cold and snowy on the ground. The hills rose up majestically and the houses were of the same limestone as Springville. By the time they reached Sowerthwaite, it was almost dusk, and they were guided up a narrow lane towards West Sharland.

It was a misty night and Gary was tired. So Charlie took the wheel along the twisting turning lane in the half-light, not knowing where they were going. It was a relief to see a lone figure trudging through the mist in khaki with a gun slung over his shoulder and leather boots and a cap.

As they drew closer to give the soldier a lift, he didn't turn round.

'Look out!' Charlie hooted the horn for the guy to step aside. There wasn't room to squeeze around him. 'Look out, he's right up your ass!' Gary yelled in alarm.

'I know!' Charlie hooted again but the man didn't stop or turn round and Charlie was sweating. He was going to hit him. With a sickening thud of his heart, he braked hard, waiting for the impact.

'The stupid dumb cluck! Are you deaf?' Gary yelled. 'Are you blind?' He poked his head out of the Jeep.

Charlie leaped out to see the damage but there was no one there. No accident, no prostrate body, nothing.

'We did see him, didn't we?'

'Sure as hell we did! He must have jumped in a dyke . . .

Wait till I get my hands on him,' Gary shouted. 'But there's no ditch . . . come out, you jerk, wherever you're hiding.'

They both looked round.

'There's no one here. Come on, it's dark . . .' Charlie got back in the car. 'But we saw a soldier, I'm sure we did. He was walking in front of us . . .'

'We're just tired. Put it down to that . . . Now where the hell are we?' Gary yawned. 'Another fine mess you've got us into . . .'

'I did see someone, I did.' Charlie was unnerved. They were lost up a lane in a strange country and now he'd just seen a ghost. This was not looking good.

Mrs Beck came puffing into the kitchen and plonked her basket onto the table.

'I've just seen a ghost,' she said. 'At least I think it were, but Doreen at the post office said he was just another of them Yanks. Two of them she saw, strolling round the square as bold as brass, asking the way to Sharland School. I hope they weren't spies, after that film we saw last week when the Germans came to a village like ours in disguise.'

She paused turning to Hester. 'Now how are you today, dearie?'

Hester hated being treated like a child. Just because she forgot things, kept having to ask the same questions over and over again, didn't make her stupid. Some days when she woke up it was hard to know what to do next, her mind took hours to crank into gear. Dr Pickles said something about little strokes that slowed her down but she felt perfectly well. There had been one or two falls in the garden, and now she needed a stick to reassure her creaking bones. If this was old age, you can keep it, she sighed. It took up

393

so much of her time just to get dressed and find something she fancied to eat. Nothing tasted the same any more. Sometimes she forgot to eat all day and then felt faint, and Mrs Beck told her off, making her sit down with a sandwich and hot sweetened tea.

Dr Pickles arranged for a family to be billeted on her, but the children were noisy and the woman rushed back to Hull after a few weeks, saying it was too dull in the country and too quiet.

How she missed Essie's company, her calming presence. If only she felt stronger to do things. Now the garden was back to vegetables again, and another war was raging round her but she couldn't be bothered to keep up with events.

She did manage some of the WI work parties when she could remember, but her knitting was slack and she kept dropping stitches. The car was in a stable with the wheels removed. She knew she wasn't fit to drive after she crashed into a wall on the way back from town. She mistakenly thought she'd knocked someone over on the high road and it had shattered her confidence. This was not the old Hester Cantrell, this slow dithery creature.

'Where's the ghost now?' she said, not really understanding the excitement.

'That's what I was going to tell you,' said Mrs Beck as she put the shopping away. 'The tall one looked the spitting image of your boys . . . like they were, of course. I did a double take but he raised his cap and smiled. I can see why the girls like them. They look so snug in their trousers and jackets, so tall and handsome. Now you've got me going on, what shall we do today, bathrooms, upstairs or down?'

'Whatever you like,' Hester said.

'Another bad night again?'

'Never slept a wink, up and down to the lavatory . . . if only I could sleep. I'd be so much better in myself. I don't know what's happening to me. I've become so slow.'

'Just sit where you are. A cup of tea will cheer you up.'

'I wish we had real coffee. What I'd give for a cup of decent Kenyan blend,' she complained. Complaining was something she was still good at.

'We have to make do with what we can get these days. It's Camp coffee or nothing, dearie.'

'Why is that?' Hester was puzzled.

'There is war on, your ladyship . . . I told you yesterday. We've sent Rommel packing in the desert. That's something to be grateful for.'

'Who's Rommel?'

'I told you . . . a German general . . . in the paper, it is. Come on, don't get agitated. It'll all come back to you but you shouldn't be living on your own in this big house. What you need is company, some evacuees or soldiers billeted, a bit of company.'

'I suppose it is rather large, but I could never leave the garden.'

'You've done wonders with it but now it's going to pot for lack of a bit of help. Shall I ask round the village again?' said Mrs Beck.

Hester sipped her tea. It tasted like wet cardboard. What was the point of eating if you had no pleasure in it? At eighty-two years old there wasn't much to look forward to.

'What were those ghosts again?' she asked, knowing it was something to do with her.

'One of them looked just like one of your boys. I never could tell them apart, Master Guy or Master Angus. Like I said, they were on their way up to the big school. Doreen at the post office sent them up there. One of them said his father had been there as a boy.'

'That's nice,' said Hester.

Mrs Beck looked at her again. 'It's not going to be one of your better days, is it, dearie?'

Hester stared blankly into the cup.

Charlie and Gary stood in the corridor speechless at the size of the school. It was like entering some ancient stone fortress set high on the hill overlooking the valley.

The headmaster, Mr Faulds, was a harassed little man brought out of retirement, but courteous enough to the visitors, showing them around the school with pride. 'You say your father attended the school, young man – what dates were those?'

'Before the Great War, I think. His brother died in battle but Pa was in the Merchant Navy. He doesn't talk about it much.'

'None of them does who was there. Let's have a look at the roll of honour . . . his name?'

'Charles Arthur West,' Charlie replied. He'd never seen anything like an English public school before, the oak-panelled classrooms and long libraries of books on shelves, boys in blazers and short grey trousers, hair parted neatly, and that smell of chalk and disinfectant that couldn't mask the sweaty stench of youth. The vaulted roof towered above him like a castle.

'I'm afraid there's no one of that name on our roll of honour,' said the headmaster.

'Hey, didn't you say he was one of twins?' Gary interrupted. 'This is some place to go to school. Mine was a cabin on the prairie.'

'Quite so . . . twins, now that's different. I recall there were a pair. One died but, as I recall, that was Guy Cantrell.' Mr Faulds was pointing to a photograph.

'My God, that could be you, Charlie.' Gary pointed to the portrait.

'Let me go and ask Mrs Southall. She's been here a long time,' said the headmaster.

'It doesn't make sense, but it's Pa all right, or his twin. If this guy died in the war, Pa must be the other one.' Charlie felt a stab of alarm. Perhaps he shouldn't be poking around into Pa's past. He'd left all this behind deliberately. But why?

A middle-aged lady marched in, looking them up and down and then beamed at Charlie as if she knew him.

'You must be Angus's boy. Good heavens, it's like looking at a ghost. Don't look so alarmed. They were good boys. Guy was a captain. He died at Passchendaele. There he is on the memorial roll. Poor Angus was left behind like a knotless thread. He taught here for a while and suffered from bad turns . . . America? My goodness, and now he's sent his son to fight alongside us! That's typical of the Cantrells; a big military family they were, with a proud tradition. His father drowned at the side of Lord Kitchener. Lady Hester has such a burden of grief. She'll be so pleased to see you both.'

'Lady Hester?' Charlie could hardly take this all in.

'Your grandmother who lives outside Sharland village, on the hill in Waterloo House. You can't miss it. What a surprise she's going to get when she sees you.'

'Just a minute,' said the head. 'You said your father's name was Charles West and you are . . . ?'

'Charleson West. That's odd he should change his name.'

397

Charlie sensed a mystery. He nudged Gary. 'There must be an explanation; perhaps the Lady will tell us more.'

'Shall I ring ahead and tell her you're coming? We don't want to shock her. She's quite ancient now,' said Mrs Southall.

'Sure. Can I look at the photograph again?' Charlie asked.

'Come with me. There's a whole wall full of rugby team and cricket team photographs. The boys were good at sport, as I recall.'

'You're kiddin'. My pa would never touch a baseball bat.' Charlie was puzzled.

It was as if a secret door was opening up to a life he knew nothing about. He couldn't take his eyes off the line-ups. The images were clear: two of them, as alike as peas from a pod. He thought of his own twin brother, Gus . . . why, Angus, of course. It made sense. He didn't know what to make of that but suddenly he smiled. 'I know it's an awful cheek but have you such a thing as a postcard I could buy to send to my folks back home? I'd like them to know I've visited here.'

'We've got something even better, young man,' said the school secretary. 'Here's our current brochure, only on wartime paper, of course. Put that in an envelope and tell your father all about your visit. It's always good to meet old pupils' families. It was such a bad time. We lost so many of our brightest pupils, a whole future generation of scholars lost with them. It's grand to see someone who survived and has brought his boy up to fight for the old country.'

If only she knew the truth, Charlie thought.

'How long will you be stopping here? The boys might like to meet some American troops,' she added.

'Oh, we must be going soon, back to base, ma'am,' said Gary hurriedly.

They walked out of the grounds still in shock. 'I think you'd better get down and give this old lady the surprise of her life!'

Charlie said nothing. Was it fair to go behind his father's back? Something must have gone wrong for Pa to change his name and abandon his family. Charlie wasn't sure he wanted to find out just what it was.

Hester was pottering in the garden when she saw the two soldiers strolling up the drive. The Yanks are coming, she smiled thinking of the song: 'Over There, Over There', sung at the end of the war with such gusto that you'd think the Yanks had won the war single-handedly.

She hobbled to see them at closer range, and then stopped in surprise. 'Oh, Guy!' she smiled. 'It's you at long last. What took you so long? Come in . . . come in. Where's Angus?'

The two men stood looking at each other. 'Ma'am, this is Gary Ambler and I'm Charles West . . . They sent me from the school. I think there must have been a mistake. They thought I was your grandson.'

'Grandson? What are you talking about, Guy? Why are you talking like an American film? You've grown so tall, or have I shrunk? There's so much I need to tell you . . . Come in, I'll make you some tea, or would you like sherry?'

'No, ma'am,' said Charlie. 'We're fine. We just wanted to say hello before we made tracks. You are Lady Hester?'

'Of course I am. I'm your mother!'

The young men looked at her and then at each other again.

'Why have you stayed away so long? I wrote to you but you never replied when I told you about Angus and the village boy. I've been waiting so long for you to come back to me. And now you're home for good? Who's your friend?'

'Ma'am, we're soldiers, American soldiers, on a visit to meet with you, but we can't stay long.'

'Oh, don't tease me, darling. I'm not going to let you go after all this time. I'll make up your room and some tea. There's so much we have to say to each other.'

It was so wonderful, seeing Guy so handsome. He'd not aged a scrap in thirty years. He'd been away so long and forgotten all his manners and now had that terrible accent. Amazing, the other one looked a much rougher type. On closer inspection they were both looking at her as if she was not making sense.

'Come and see what I've done in the garden since you left. You shouldn't have sneaked away like a thief in the night. I know Dr Mac put you up to it. I went to the sanatorium and they told me all about you. Mr West, indeed! You didn't have to do that. Cantrell is a fine pedigree. There were generals in your father's family dating back to Waterloo. Where's Angus again? Oh, I forgot, silly me, poor boy was lost in the war. You shouldn't have run away. The boy was only doing his best for us all.' She didn't notice them back, down the drive, waving and then walking away.

'Come back! You've not had your tea,' she cried. 'Don't leave me not when I've found you again, Guy . . . Guy!'

There was no one there and for a moment her mind went blank. 'Did I dream that? Had Guy really come or was it another trick of her mind? But there were two of them. The mist in her muddled head cleared for a second. Yes, two American boys in uniform. If he wasn't her son, who on earth was he?

*　*　*

400

Charlie hardly spoke on the long drive south back to the base at Burtonwood. He was too stunned. Had he dreamed it all? Knocking down the soldier who wasn't there? People smiling at him and welcoming him back to West Sharland as if they knew him, and the school secretary with the team photos of his pa and his brother. Guy and Angus Cantrell, one dead and one still alive. He was so confused he couldn't recall which was which and then that old woman in black thinking he was her son, calling him Guy, pleading with him to stay home. What had happened to his pa that made him change his name and flee his native land?

Anyone could see his grandmother was mad, a pitiable sight, waiting for the son who never came.

Whatever had happened wasn't good news and he didn't know what to make of it, but he did post the school brochure. That would rattle some bones back home. He suddenly felt sick with uncertainty at such discoveries, but one way or another he was going to make his pa face the truth and give him the real story.

Whatever it was, it had driven that old lady crazy. Perhaps he ought to go back again on his own and apologise for their rudeness.

'You OK?' Gary asked.

'Sort of . . . one hell of a crazy day,' Charlie replied.

'That's the first time I've ever heard you swear. I think next time we'll go and see London. Check out the city and have ourselves some fun.'

'You're on!' A trip to London would take his mind off all this mystery. At least in the big city, he wouldn't go bumping into ghosts from the past.

24

It was in the lull between Christmas and New Year that Ruth and Sam took Shari on the train back to her mother's village. They stopped off in Sowerthwaite to find a little café that was open. It had been a cold Christmas and now people were getting into the country to walk and take the air.

Shari was taken with the stone square and fine Georgian buildings. It was just as she had imagined and she bought a postcard to send back to Mom.

They sat on the single-decker bus to West Sharland and Shari posed by the square outside the Hart's Head. There was nothing that said the full name, no road signs or finger-posts. The church bell was tolling and a funeral procession went past slowly. Men stood by the roadside doffing their caps, all the curtains were closed and doors shut in respect. Ruth asked someone whose was the burial.

'Lady Hester from Waterloo House,' came the reply. 'A right cantankerous old beggar who went queer towards the end. They found her in the garden searching for her son, would you believe, and him dead years ago.' The woman paused. 'I mustn't speak ill of the dead . . . Like many others she had her cross to bear, gentry or not.'

Ruth turned to Shari. 'It was the lady who looked after your granny when she fell sick, the one I told you about. She owned the cottages over there that your granddad rented next door to the forge. There was a bit of a romance when your mam was young with one of her son's during the war, but Hester put a stop to that. There was no mixing in those days.'

They watched the procession, the black horses pulling the glass hearse. There weren't many mourners.

'How sad she had no relatives,' murmured Shari.

'That's because there's no one left to mourn her, I expect. Essie once told me Hester was the daughter of an earl; the youngest one and they're all passed on and the title with them. She was a bit of a martinet but your gran spoke highly of her. Gentry or not, that's what we all come to in the end: a box and a few feet of soil. I heard as how Lady Hester stood her ground on some things, all that war memorial business. I see they still haven't erected anything. Happen they'll get round to putting something up now she's gone.'

'What took so long?' Shari said.

'Complications, village politics . . . Come on, let's have a grand tour. There'll be neighbours who still remember your mother. They're getting used to visitors poking round the churchyard, looking for ancestors and relatives.'

Shari tried to imagine her mother as a little girl at school. They visited her grandparents' grave after the burial was finished and the people dispersed. She was introduced to Mrs Beck, the housekeeper, who eyed her up and down with interest.

'Another American visitor,' she smiled. 'We had a couple of GIs the other week. That's what finished off Lady Hester, seeing the lad who reminded her of her lost son. She was convinced he'd come home for good. She dreamed it all, of course. She pined and wouldn't eat and went downhill very fast. So you are Selma's daughter, Essie's granddaughter? I can't say I can see the resemblance. How's your mother shaping in Hollywood? I remember her as a right little tomboy with her brothers.'

'She's still making pictures, under the name of Zelma Barr,' Shari said.

'Well, I never. She was such a one for the horses. Is she famous?'

'Not really, but she still rides horses.'

'Tell her I was asking after her. Her mother was Lady Hester's one true friend in the end. Poor old woman was left with nothing but memories to live on after Essie died, and that's not a good diet for anyone.'

Ruth seemed anxious to get away. 'Come on, Shari, time to make for the bus. I think we've seen all there is to see for today. We don't want you to miss your train back to London.'

Shari took one last look at the freshly dug mound, covered with an expensive wreath. How sad to lie alone in the world with no one to visit your grave, and all because of falling out over a war memorial? What was special about that?

Guy's back ached from all the hoeing and weeding on the farm. They were trying to increase production to help the war effort. The girls were doing their best, but it was now when he could do with his son helping out.

He tried not to think about Charlie too much. They prayed for him every night, of course. The postcards were never displayed, but Rose looked out for their arrival none the less. The school brochure had taken some explaining.

404

Charlie must know everything by now if they had sent him to Waterloo. Well, the truth would come out; it usually did.

He wanted to write a full explanation but hadn't got Charlie's address or his unit. He owed him the truth about why he'd reinvented himself. One night he sat down and confessed everything to Rose too: the whole sorry tale, his mother's part in it, his own shame, and she held him in her arms to reassure him.

'I don't know this Guy Cantrell. All I know is you, Charles. What you were in another life doesn't matter here. That worldly man has gone and Charlie didn't know him either . . . Yet I don't like to think of your mother suffering remorse and having no means to make her peace like my ma and pa with Zack. You must write and give her a chance to hear who you are now. It's only fair. "My son, keep thy father's commandments and forsake not the law of thy mother . . ." She gave you life and loved your brother so don't cast her off in bitterness.'

'But it's been so long. I don't know what to say,' he said, feeling such relief that Rose had been so understanding.

'Just tell her what you told me. Ask about Charlie, see if she met him. Tell her about your family and your new-found faith. Give her hope. I wish you'd told me earlier,' Rose said. 'There's been such a coolness between us because of Charlie. You must have carried all this on your own.'

They clung together with passion for the first time in years. Rose could always surprise him with her generous spirit.

'We ought to write to him. The silence has gone on for months. It doesn't feel right to punish him any longer. He has his own free will. I am beginning to think we've been too hard on the boy,' Guy offered, but Rose shrugged her shoulders.

'That's up to you and your conscience,' she replied. 'Every night, I pray he'll return safe and come back into full fellowship with us, find a good wife within our community and settle down again, but sometimes I am so torn about what is right or not. We have to trust the Bible and its truths for our answers.'

'I suppose so, but never forget the story of the prodigal son who was welcomed home,' Guy offered. 'He's our only boy. He needs to know we still care.'

'Write that letter then. Write both those letters. They're long overdue.'

It was another busy night at the Rainbow Club on the corner of Shaftesbury Avenue, near Piccadilly Circus. It had been raining and the soldiers wanted shelter, a warm meal and some a bed for the night. Saturday nights were usually hectic. There was a sickness bug going round the Red Cross staff so they were short of helpers downstairs. Shari was due another pass but it was cancelled because she was needed. She'd palled up with Deirdre and Pam and they were going as hostesses to the dance in the Rainbow Corner Ballroom.

It was going to be packed and noisy and full of home-sick GIs wanting to jitterbug and jive the night away. Respectable girls were always needed to keep them in line. So much for an early night with a good book to read on her night off, Shari sighed. There was always a gang of boys hanging around Piccadilly Circus, eyeing up the British girls who were hoping to get into the ballroom and pick up someone. The district was notorious for goodtime girls and 'the Piccadilly warriors', out to do business in the local parks.

She could see the desperation in the faces of the soldiers,

bored, lonely and wanting excitement. They'd come over to fight the Nazis not hang around in England in base camps. The Red Cross did their best, providing clubmobiles, dishing donuts and Cokes, magazines and gum around the base camps. Shari was too young to be part of these crews. She worked in the admin office most of the time and had to keep reminding herself, 'They also serve who only stand and wait.'

It was an exciting place, though, since you never knew who would put in an appearance in the club: famous film stars like Clark Gable or band artists like Glenn Miller and Artie Shaw. It was the hub of London life for American troops, despite the raids, and Shari felt safer here than anywhere else. The Red Cross girls were considered little sisters. She was their ginger-nut kid. They were as American as apple pie and soda, a reminder of the women back home, to be treated with respect . . . most of the time.

'Hey, sister, come and shake a leg.' A drunken soldier sidled up, grabbing her hand as they walked towards the dance hall. 'You can be my warm blanket for the night,' he laughed. Shari ignored him.

'Come on, foxy lady, don't be frosty with me. You redheads are always hot for it.'

Deirdre, the tallest of them, pushed Shari forward out of the way of his attention. 'Go boil your head, Private!' she shouted, but the stupid private was too drunk to take no for an answer.

'Don't be a prick tease, you little vixen!'

'Shut it!' Another soldier standing in the shadows stepped forward. 'Would you speak to your sister like that?'

'Who gave you permission to butt in?' The private hadn't seen the young sergeant's stripes.

'I did. Chuck him off the pavement. It's your sort that give us a bad name. Sober up and go find your manners.'

'To hell with you!' The soldier pushed ahead, knocking Shari against the door. This time a bunch of soldiers pounced on him and threw him out onto the pavement.

'I'm sorry, miss,' said the tall blond sergeant. 'Too much whisky . . . where do they get it from?'

'That's OK, Sergeant,' said Shari, brushing down her skirt, eyeing her rescuer with interest. 'It's busy tonight. There's going to be a crush in there.'

'So they tell me. I'm not much of a dancer myself,' he said.

'You've never been to our ballroom?' Shari laughed. 'I think it's about time you learned. We can't have a GI letting the side down. It's all we're famous for. We'll take care of you, won't we, Pam?'

'You bet, soldier. No excuses . . . in you go.' Deirdre grabbed one of his arms and Pam the other. 'Come on in and join the fun.'

Charlie couldn't take his eyes off the red-haired girl with those dark eyes. What a looker! This was going to be so embarrassing. He was getting used to jazz music and all that jigging around but he'd only make a fool of himself and he didn't want to look stupid in her eyes. There was something about that bright smile and laughing face that was like sunshine on a cold rainy night, eyes that lit up his sagging spirits. He was still troubled by that visit to West Sharland.

He'd written to the old lady at Waterloo House, apologising for backing out of her invitation. It had been a stupid thing to do, but he was shocked at her calling him her son.

Then he received a letter from a lawyer in Yorkshire, saying that Lady Cantrell had died suddenly and if he was a relative to get back in touch with them. Did he know the whereabouts of Garth Angus Charles Cantrell, her last known living relative? Charlie didn't know what to make of any of this. Ought he to send the letter to his pa back home?

So he was glad when Gary suggested they make a trip to London. They had walked their feet off in the pouring rain looking at the sights – or what was left of some of them. How did people manage to live normal lives under the grim conditions and the air-raid warnings?

He was shocked at the way some of his fellow GIs were behaving like dogs with local girls in the parks. Even Gary called him a prude and went off in search of his own pleasure, while Charlie had made his way to Rainbow Corner. There was a canteen and a library for troops there, and a chance of a decent meal, but now this had happened. Perhaps he could make a quiet exit. It was all so raucous, but everyone was having fun. The band got his feet tapping. Perhaps if he bought them all a drink it would delay the moment of his shaming. He couldn't dance their way.

'Cokes all round,' he shouted, 'if you find the table.'

'He's going to slink off. Not so fast, buddy. We don't even know your name,' the tall one mouthed.

'Charlie,' he yelled. 'And you?' He was looking at the redhead shyly.

'I'm Shari and this is Pam and Deirdre. We work in the offices at the club.' While Shari was talking someone asked Pam to dance and they drifted off. Deirdre hung around eyeing the crowd until she was whisked away. If he didn't do something soon, Shari would disappear while he got the drinks.

He watched the dancers leaping and leapfrogging and jumping onto each other.

'Don't look so scared,' said Shari. 'It's only the Lindy Hop. There'll be a slow one soon. Have you never really danced before, not even in high school?'

'I've done some barn dancing. I'm sorry . . . if you want to move along, I don't want to tread on your toes.' Better be honest that he was no Fred Astaire

'You're a challenge and I like a challenge,' Shari laughed, and he smiled, knowing it was going to be OK. He must just relax and let himself go.

'You're from the West Coast, right?'

'Los Angeles, and you?'

'From Pennsylvania, Springville, a farm.'

'That explains it then. No dance halls, no jazz, not even in Philadelphia? Then you must be a Quaker, but I thought they—'

'Don't fight. OK, I confess I'm just one of the plain folk. I enlisted against my folks' wishes.' He paused, surprised. 'Why am I telling you all this?'

'Because we're going to be friends, you and me, and the first thing I'm going to do is teach you a slow dance. Listen to the music, put your arm round me like this and we'll set off real slow. Don't worry, it's my job to make strangers feel at home, wherever they come from. Can't have you feeling left out now, can we?'

Charlie smiled and did what he was told. This was going to be one heck of a lesson and he meant to make the most of his teacher's tuition, even if it took all night.

'You made a hit there,' Pam laughed as they were getting ready for bed. 'I love shy guys. There's something so appealing, especially when he looks like a cross between Leslie Howard and Gary Cooper, all mixed up. Where's he from?'

'A farm in the east, somewhere near Delaware River.' Shari was vague; she didn't want to share Charlie's details with anyone. One minute she was fancy-free, one of the girls, the next moment, all she could think of was when she would see him again. He had only a forty-eight-hour pass and he was based up in the north. Chance had brought them together and there was something about his gentle polite manners that disarmed her Hollywood brashness.

They'd danced and laughed over his mistakes, but he was one quick learner and soon he was leading her round the ballroom as if he was born to it. He had rhythm and a natural ear for music. She was going to take him to the museum to hear Dame Myra Hess playing on the piano, if there was a concert on. They were going to walk through all the parks in town. She'd even offered to go to church with him but he said there weren't any of his sort of churches in London so not to worry.

It had taken her by surprise, this sudden flood of attraction to him, a stranger and yet somehow familiar and comfortable to be with, the sort of guy you'd never get tired of talking to. Why was he so different from others she'd met? She just couldn't explain to herself as she lay on her bed, strangely unnerved.

If that drunk hadn't come on heavy, Charlie would never have come to her defence. They would have walked past each other in the dark and never met. Was it fate that brought them together: halfway across the world to this little island, across a whole continent? How strange, how peculiar, how scary. In just a few hours her life had shifted on its axis. Who must she thank for such a miraculous encounter?

'So you met some broad in a dance hall. That's a first for you, preacher boy!' Gary sneered. 'I didn't think you Amish played such tricks.'

'I'm not Amish and Shari is not some broad. She's a Red Cross administrator working in the office. She's been to college. She's wonderful.'

'So what does Little Miss Red Cross see in a dumb ploughboy except the obvious – tall, blond and full of muscle? It's your body she is hankering for. It sure as hell's not your mind.'

'Oh, shut it, Gary. What's bitten you this morning? Didn't you have a good night?'

'You know what, these British girls are pieces of shit . . . pardon my French! This girl comes up to me, all smiles and tits, offering it up on a plate, and takes me to this pub. I buy drinks for her and every goddamn girl in the pub. She goes to the john and then, hey presto, disappears and my wallet's gone walkabout too. I haven't got a dime to my name. So lend me some—'

'Sorry, I'm taking Shari out this morning, meeting her in Trafalgar Square.'

'Then I'll come with you to chaperone you both.'

'Not today. I want her to myself. She's not your type.' Charlie fished in his pocket for a note. 'Here, it's the best I can do. I hope you've still got your liberty pass. I'll meet you back at Euston Station.'

'Thanks, bud, but I'll take the early train. I don't want to cramp your style, but see if your dreamboat has a little sister for next time. I'll take it there'll be a next time?'

'I hope so. It's strange, there was this drunk bothering her and I was passing . . . She has this amazing hair, the colour of maple leaves at fall.'

'Now she's making a poet out of you. This one I have to see for myself: a little Rita Hayworth. They have tempers, redheads. You poor fool, she's hooked you in real good.'

'It's not like that, we're just friends.' Charlie was quick to her defence.

'Don't you feel nothing down your pants, and you a farm boy?'

'We're not all like you. I respect girls. These things take time.'

'Time ain't on our side, Charlie boy! There's a war on somewhere, and one of these days you and I will be heading right there and maybe not coming back. Live for today and to hell with the rest, I say. Give the girl a smacker on the lips. You might never get the chance again.'

Charlie said nothing. It wasn't like that, this wonderful feeling of having met someone special against the odds. It was as if he was meant to be with just this one girl and no other. She was an unexpected gift and he'd treat her like porcelain china, not rough clay. Whatever happened from now on was all part of some plan, but if he didn't get his shoes polished, his tie straightened and his skates on, he was going to be late!

Selma smiled at Shari's letter, full of the meeting with the young Charlie West. It was love at first sight for both of them and they had spent every spare moment of leave together. She'd even taken him up to Bradford to meet Ruth, who also wrote to say the boy was very polite and

413

good-looking, and reminded them of someone but she couldn't think who. He was a farmer's son and they were religious. There'd been a falling-out when he'd enlisted so he didn't talk much about his parents. His father was from Yorkshire, but he didn't say much about that until Shari said she was named after a village called Sharland and Charlie had laughed and said his father went to school there. His name was West and he'd also visited Sharland.

'How we all laughed when he said, "Let's get together and make a village." What a coincidence!'

That puzzled Selma too. Of all the places in such a huge county for them to have connections, but she didn't know any Wests in the village. Maybe they lived further up the Dale.

She was so happy for her daughter but worried with it. What mother didn't feel anxious about a wartime romance? She knew what it was like to be heartbroken by events out of her control and she trusted Shari wouldn't do anything foolish. She hardly knew this young man, respectable or not. They must wait until the war was over before settling down.

Love in a time of war was intense, and soldiers in uniform were so attractive and dashing, emotions ran high. Back home in plainclothes everything was more mundane and humdrum. She couldn't see Shari mucking out on a farm. She wrote back to Shari.

You must find out more about the Wests. If his father went to Sharland School, they must've been wealthy farmers but I've never heard of them.

Don't rush into anything, darling, not like I did

with the first man who showed an interest in me. When I married him I knew none of his funny quirks. Your father was charming too but not good husband material, I'm afraid. The only decent thing he gave me was you!

Send me some photos of you both for my album. Business is brisk here, still churning out happy films to cheer the troops and folks at home. I was background in one of the Bob Hope films with Dorothy Lamour, but now I'm back on Main Street parading up and down in shawl and bonnet. I've had to let the corsets out a notch or two.

Back where I started, but it pays the bills.

We've got a committee together making sure we get donations of clothes and food from the studios to send to 'Bundles For Britain'. I've been telling everyone about the bomb damage and the homeless children, and making sure they know I have a girl serving abroad who has seen it all for herself. Some stars are generous and others I could name are pretty mean monsters. When I think of all the lies that are peddled in these movie magazines about the stars to promote their films, I could tell some real horror stories about them.

Pearl Levine is one of those who needs her eyes opening to what's happening to her race. She's just had a face lift and is covered in bandages and won't go out, so I've cleared out her wardrobe while she's not looking and packaged stuff up. If she sacks me I'll give her a piece of my mind, and I know Lisa will!

Give my love to Ruth and Sam. It was sad about

Lady Hester, I suppose, but I have my reasons for not mourning her passing. Do ask Ruth to put flowers on my parents' grave when she next visits.

Take care of yourself,
Mom

25

Shari lay back in Charlie's arms, contented. If this was married life, it was wonderful: the fusion of their bodies, the deep closeness she felt when they were talking and sharing their different lives. Their marriage had been a spur-of-the-moment decision. They both had to ask permission from their seniors and grabbed a long weekend for their honeymoon. They found a half-bombed church and took their vows with all their friends by their sides. Gary stood up as best man, Pam and Deirdre as her maids; everyone in uniform, no-frills, just little bouquets of flowers for the girls and a special buffet laid on by the Rainbow Club staff. It was wonderful.

There was so little time to be together. Things were hotting up for some big push, the American army was moving down towards the coast, slowly, inexorably trundling towards the Channel and France. Charlie's supply unit was following behind. It was now or never, and they'd taken fate into their own hands.

'How does it feel to be Mrs West?' Charlie whispered into her ear.

417

'I'm getting used to it,' she said, fingering the little gold band they'd found in a pawnbroker's shop window. It was rolled gold and well worn, but she had the idea that it'd been handed down to them with love, and it was a good omen.

'We've got a whole day to ourselves, we ought to go and enjoy it,' he suggested.

'I'm enjoying it here,' she said, snuggling up to him. 'I can't think of anywhere else I'd rather be.'

'Me, neither,' Charlie smiled. 'You know sometimes I wonder if we met in another life. I feel I've always known you. We seem to agree on so many things. Even our names fit together – West Sharland . . . I can't get over that. I told you about the old dame who thought I was her son.'

'And Aunty Ruth said my granny worked for her until she died. It's creepy.'

'Did I tell you, I saw a ghost there? The first time I went there, on the lane. I thought I'd killed a soldier,' Charlie said.

'That's only the drummer boy. Aunty Ruth says he's often seen walking on the lane at dusk. I'm not sure I believe in ghosts.'

'Nor did I, until I saw one. Gary saw him too. Do you think we were both meant to meet up? I hope you've no regrets. It's all been a bit of a rush and not the sort of wedding a girl might dream of.'

'It was perfect and romantic. I'm only following tradition. Mom met my pa on a train going out west.'

'But you said it didn't work out.'

'You're nothing like my pa. No one ever said anything, but the date of my arrival speaks for itself. That's not going to happen to us; I've taken care of that.'

'Pity. If anything happens to me,' Charlie sighed. 'I'd like to think there was a child.'

'Don't say that! Don't even think it. I've learned one thing – that guys who think they're not coming back often don't. I'm only loaning you to the war effort. When we get home stateside we'll have one big party and our folks can meet and celebrate together!'

'Are you always this bossy?' Charlie laughed. 'I don't know what mine will make of all this. They'll love you, but they don't hold with marrying out. I don't want to upset them but I suppose I did that anyway when I enlisted. My pa was in the British Army. I know so little about his life. It's all bricked up inside him, like a walled tower with no door. I know he changed his name. Do you think he did something wrong?'

'Ask him. From what you said about that visit, it must be something to do with that old lady. Have you written to them yet?'

'No, and you?'

'Nope . . . Ma'll be upset she's missed out on things, but it's our life, not theirs. They've had their turn. We don't know what's going to happen in the next few months,' Shari whispered.

'Only that we'll be apart . . . There's so little time.'

'So let's make the most of it right here and now,' Shari smiled, opening up her arms with a grin. 'Come here, soldier, and give me a good time.'

'At your service, ma'am!'

The mysterious package arrived one morning when Guy and his neighbours were busy preparing the farm roof after a bad storm. It was left on the doorstep, while he was at work. It had almost been trodden flat so he took the lantern to the table to open it. It was sealed with wax, and inside was his own letter to Mother returned, opened and resealed with an official stamp.

> We took the liberty of reading this letter to ascertain
> that you must be Garth Angus Charles Cantrell,
> only surviving son of Hester Matilde Cantrell, late
> of Waterloo House, West Sharland in the West
> Riding of Yorkshire.

His mother was dead and she had never got to read his change of heart. He wanted to cry out at the stupidity of waiting so long. There were no tears at this news, just an aching sadness that everyone of his family was gone now.

> If you could send proof of your identity, we will
> in due course take matters further. As regards the
> last will and testament of the aforesaid Lady H.
> M. Cantrell, concerning house, contents, the farm
> estate and other properties, these will be subject
> to probate.
> On all of the above we await your instructions.
> Yours faithfully,
> Messrs Finkel, Boardman and Brown
> Castle House, High Street, Skipton

He shoved the letters into the envelope with a sigh. What was he to do? He had no papers, no identity papers in his own name. Should he pursue the matter, rake up all the past and claim Angus's identity?

'My mother's dead. My letter came too late,' he told Rose. 'You were right, things should have been seen to years ago. Now there's land and property rightly ours, but only if I perjure myself to claim it.'

Rose shrugged. 'Do you want to do that for money?'

'For myself, no; for our children perhaps . . . It would give them a start in life,' he replied.

'How? If the price of this wealth is deception and lies, how can that be good for them? It's against everything we believe in. We can manage without your legacy. We have until now.'

'I know, but what will happen to it all? There are tenants who may depend on us there, not knowing what is to happen to them in cottages and farms.'

'Leave it to the lawyers to devise some plan. It's part of a life you wanted to leave behind, or is the idea of wealth already softening your resolve?' Rose paused. 'Is there any news of Charlie?'

Guy shook his head. Having sent his own letter to find him overseas, he had heard nothing for weeks now. That was worrying too when they'd gotten used to pictures of the Tower of London, Trafalgar Square . . . The last one had come from Somerset and then nothing, but now here was another service envelope with an overseas postmark in strange writing.

He opened it, curious, and a photograph fell out. Charlie was arm in arm with a pretty girl in uniform carrying a bouquet. He pushed the picture over to Rose. 'Better look at that . . . That's why he's not written to us,' he smiled. She took one look and turned it over, shaking her head. Guy picked up the letter.

Dear Mr and Mrs West,

Charlie and I were married in April in London. He is now overseas somewhere in France but he asked me to write to introduce myself to you. My name is Sharland Esther Barr. I am serving with the Red Cross in the capital. We met many months ago and decided we wanted to spend the rest of our lives together. We thought it simplest to marry over here, but hope to meet up with you all when this war ends.

You might like to know that my mother named me after West Sharland, where she was born. Her name was Selma Bartley but she is Mrs Barr, now divorced and living in Hollywood where she works in the film industry. Her father was a blacksmith in the village.

As Charlie said Mr West went to school there, you may have known her family. My grandmother went to work at Waterloo House under the Lady Hester Cantrell, who recently passed away. I have visited the village with my aunt, Ruth Broadbent. It is indeed a beautiful place. I hope you will correspond with me while Charlie is overseas. I am anxious for any news from his family to pass on.

I know you will be surprised at such a letter from a stranger but Charlie entrusted me with keeping in touch with you.

Yours sincerely,
Sharland West

Rose looked up at him, lost for words, 'A wife and an English wife . . . Not one of ours, and now he's in danger. It's just like Zack all over again. History is repeating itself, where will it end?' she cried.

Guy was staring at the girl. 'She's a pretty girl. I didn't recognise her at first. I knew her mother, though. She was my friend, her brothers were the ones who rescued us, and her brother Frank was the one shot; the one I couldn't save. Is this a punishment?' He found he was weeping. 'Will this never end?' He slumped forward. 'I don't know what to do.'

'We keep apart as we always have, and I will write, of course. It's only polite,' said Rose. 'But there will be no meetings, no reunions between us. Charleson has made his choice. He cannot expect us to approve.'

'Don't be so harsh! She's Selma's daughter. We can't turn her from our door, but they must never know about all that sadness.'

'Your identity is safe. It's nobody's business but yours and mine . . . not Charlie's or his wife's. I will write and she needs know nothing more about the connection. It's for the best.'

'But you don't understand. Selma and I were once . . .' he hesitated, not wanting to admit those old feelings.

'You don't need to tell me. I can see it in your eyes. It was a long time ago, and it's nothing to us now.' Rose could turn those sapphire eyes to steel when she chose.

Later that night Guy couldn't sleep. He made an excuse to leave their warm bed to sit out on the veranda, watching the fireflies darting across the yard.

The Lord gives and the Lord takes, he mused. There was no escaping His cunning revenge. So you think you can escape your obligations by burying your head in the sand, Guy Cantrell? Think again. A lot of chickens are coming home to roost in your backyard now. So you'd better build some strong fences to keep them out or gather them in. That's your choice.

*   *   *

423

Selma and Lisa drank a bottle of wine rereading Shari's letter and shoving it back and forward to each other. Lisa's fiancé was missing on board a ship in the Pacific. She was frantic with worry and Selma had been spending time supporting her friend. But now it was her time for comfort.

'How could she do this to me – go and marry the first bloke she met; some guy from Hicksville, a ploughboy? I've never heard of a West in Sharland.'

The photo was grainy and the shadows fell over his face. It was hard to tell what he looked like, just another young soldier, nothing special. Why couldn't they wait? Oh hell, not that again, she wondered. There was no mention of knitting bootees. These modern girls were sensible, but to rush into marriage . . .

Then she burst out laughing. 'Hell's bells! Now I know what my mom felt like when I wrote to her. Lisa, she's gone and done what I did, jumped in with both feet. If she thinks we're going to bring out the fatted calf for her, she's going to regret it, like I did.'

'That's not fair, and you know it. Shari is a bright kid with a loving heart. She's been round the block with some college boys. Trust her to have thought it through,' Lisa said.

'What if there's a baby on the way?'

'What if there is? You coped, didn't you? That's why you got married. I did my sums when Shari was born and she certainly wasn't premature!' Lisa winked at her friend.

'So why all the rush then?' Selma said.

'Oh, come on . . . think about it. The second front's opened up. Shari wants to give him hope; always something to fight for. I wish I'd married Patrick. We were too cautious, and now . . .' Lisa cried. 'What if he's never coming back? How will I survive?'

'You'll find a way. You will get used to it but it hurts like hell.'

'Isn't it about time you found another beau?' Lisa smiled, changing the subject, but Selma shook her head.

'I know it's stupid but I always thought Jamie would come back and settle down or Shari would come home and we'd be a family again. Now she's gone too. I'm too old for that sort of thing.'

'Nonsense! It's never too late to make a life for yourself.'

'Listen to the kettle calling the pot black!'

'It's different for me. While there's life there's always hope . . .'

'I know, I'm sorry, I've drunk too much. Shari's news has unsettled me. It's uncanny her husband having family in the same area as me. I don't know why but I wish I could have met him first. It's just a little too close for comfort, and I can't explain. I suppose I ought to write to his folks and make myself known. If we're going to be related it seems only polite. What on earth am I going to say that would impress them? A divorced, Hollywood extra isn't the ideal ma-in-law.'

'Don't put yourself down, Selma. You're always doing it. I bet they didn't travel half way across the world to make a new life for themselves, forge a career out of nothing and raise a wonderful kid like Shari single-handed and without the benefit of a fancy Sharland School education. You've got nothing to be ashamed of. You're born and bred in Yorkshire: God's own county, as you're always telling everyone here! Sing them your blacksmith's song and show them your mettle. You're as good as anyone else. We'll give

Shari and Charlie a homecoming to remember. Put those yellow ribbons out good and proper. You may have lost a daughter but you've gained a son with the promise of a family to come. Just be thankful for what you have.' Lisa reached out her hand.

Selma smiled. Trust her best and oldest friend to put her straight on matters. She was just being selfish and mean-spirited. Who was she to complain? Her own mother never got the chance to meet her own grandchild. Never got the chance to visit America. Why did she feel so unsettled, as if Shari's wedding had shifted something, stirred her up to face the barrenness of the past few years?

Her own daughter was waiting, worrying for the safety of her new husband as she had once done for her brothers and for Guy Cantrell. It was stirring up all those old feelings again, feelings of injustice, those sad telegrams with bad news, black armbands and mourning posters in windows.

Shari needed her love and support, not her criticism. Life was too short. What could she do to help?

Perhaps she could prepare the ground a little by writing to the West family, or better still, take a trip east and look them up. After all, they were almost one big family now.

It was almost Christmas when Charlie and his supply trucks found themselves bogged down near the Ardennes, stuck in the freezing cold hell of ice and snow. The first he knew that this was no Alpine vacation was when a barrage of German artillery battered them through the forest, turning tree branches into flying scythes. There were sightings of snowmen advancing westwards, crack

426

troops in Alpine suits for perfect camouflage, ghostly figures encircling the 106th Infantry, causing mayhem, confusion and retreat.

They were all caught up in the attack and every man had to defend himself. They were running short of supplies and air support because of the fog. By the middle of December the battle was raging round the hilltop town of Bastogne, and Charlie knew if they didn't hold the town, all would be lost.

Charlie had been right through Europe and seen enough carnage to know what was in store. They'd been caught napping, thinking the enemy was retreating east, going home without a murmur. Now they knew different. Never underestimate a soldier with his back to the wall, but two could play that game. They may not have been the best frontline troops, but the kitchen boys and the mechanics were no pushover either.

He was sick of seeing carpets of frozen corpses, buddies knocked off by snipers and shrapnel. He was weary and scared of what was to come. He was no crack infantryman but once his dander was up he'd found himself cursing like a trooper, grabbing a gun with the best of them and leading his men forward into the worst of it.

He was gutted when Gary got hit, watching the life ebbing away from a tough guy, who had had so much to look forward to in his life. It wouldn't be long before a bullet came with his number on it. He tried to think of Shari and those precious nights in the London hotel on their honeymoon; he thought of Ma and Pa and his sisters, so far away. Pa was right about war. He'd seen it all before in a foxhole in France. Had they learned nothing since then?

Yet this war had to be won, though they weren't doing much of a job here, and the bloody weather didn't help. If only the fog would lift and air support could begin again. He glanced at the paper flyers dropped down on the Third Army, not propaganda, for once, but a prayer from no less a general than Patton himself: a prayer to shift the fog in their favour. Charlie almost laughed at the desperation this was showing.

> Grant us fair weather for battle,
> Graciously hearken to soldiers who call
> Upon thee, that armed with that power
> We may advance from victory to victory.

Where was the Lord in all this? Whose side was he on, if any? Charlie was too tired to think about anything but staying warm and keeping his feet from freezing. It was hard to dig in when the ground was rock hard and covered with snow, and still the barrage came, lifting him off the ground with its impact. All he could do was duck and pray.

When another shell landed close by, he felt nothing, but kept on firing his weapon. Then another one came closer, flinging shrapnel around him. Charlie felt no pain, nothing at first, everything was intact but he couldn't lift his gun and then he saw there was no hand left to do the job. Someone pulled him into the back and pushed him towards the dressing station to get his stump bandaged before he lost too much blood. They gave him morphine and a transfusion and sent him back to an evacuation hospital, knocked him out to clean up the mess.

Charlie woke to a world that looked like a Christmas

card, the telegraph poles outside his window sparkling like tinsel, a forest of Christmas trees, but the snowmen he'd met were storm troopers, their snowballs were grenades and being wet and numb with cold wasn't much fun when you couldn't run home to where a log fire burned and Mom's cookie jar was waiting.

This was no Christmas party. Charlie stared down at his bandaged wound in disbelief. How the hell was he ever going to write home with his left hand?

Dearest Mom,

I wrote before about Charlie's injury. I got to see him in hospital near London and he's in good spirits. I think he's still in shock at losing his right hand. He'll be shipped out eventually to some hospital in California for amputees, but he'll get some leave first.

I'm trying to get leave to be with him. He's being such a brave spirit but his progress is slow and he gets so impatient. He is too proud to write to his parents at the moment so I have told them everything they need to know. It's not the end of the world. It could have been far worse, believe me. You can live with only half an arm and they can do wonders with artificial limbs these days, but it will take time.

It has been a hard few months and the losses from the winter battle they call the Battle of the Bulge have been staggering. But the Germans are routed and racing back home to defend their own territory. It can't be long now. They are exhausted and demoralised. We just have to hang on in there and see it through.

There are so many broken people to mend and the doodlebug rockets have made London a scary place to live. Have you made contact with the Wests like you said? Perhaps when Charlie comes home, we will all meet up together. Thank you for your wonderful parcel. Thank Lisa for the beautiful silk underwear and pretty dress. I shall be so glad to be out of uniform, one day, but for now it is like an armour I wear for protection. When I'm in the street I feel I'm flying the Red Cross flag for humanity and decency and compassion, and so lucky to have Charlie back safe in England for a while.

Your loving Shari

Selma shivered at all this young couple had been through together already. They made her feel ashamed of her easy life so far away from their troubles. A little bit of charity work wasn't enough. She'd not bothered to make the effort to visit the Wests. Her excuse was the journey by train or bus was not absolutely necessary. The posters everywhere demanded sacrifice and savings. Now it was different.

Shari's husband was going to need all the support of his family to overcome this blow. No point on standing on ceremony, the young couple must be welcomed home in style with a party gathering, a reunion. Weren't two families blended into one by this marriage? It was going to be something to look forward to, to plan for, but first she must make the effort to go to Pennsylvania and seek out these elusive Wests.

'The mother is coming to visit with us. She has plans to discuss their return.' Rose read out the letter with a sigh.

'Shall I put her off? It's a long way for her to travel just to be told we're not inclined to rejoice in the same way as she is doing. Charles, are you listening to a word I've said?'

Guy was staring out the window. So it had come, the moment of truth he'd been avoiding for months. 'Oh, let her come and see for herself. We can't put it off. For Charlie's sake, we must make them all welcome.'

Rose had taken Charlie's injury to heart. How would a man without his right hand be able to work the fields or guide horses, build barns or do the necessary repairs, she cried.

Guy tried to explain about artificial limbs and prosthesis, how in the Great War many limbless had found ways of getting round their loss by compensating with other parts of their bodies: toes became fingers, blind men read Braille and wheelchairs became legs.

If only their boy had resisted enlistment. But he was his father's son, and impetuous, just as he himself had been. Now he would know better. He would understand how it felt to look hell in the face and realise there must be another way to keep peace among men. All Guy wanted now was to see his son home safe and well, and to meet the wife who had written to them so graciously, breaking the news of his injury with such delicacy. He liked the sound of Shari West, if her letters were anything to go by.

Rose was jealous that her son had left home so abruptly against their wishes and found a wife for comfort. Rose was hurting at his wounding, angry, shocked and confused. They were going to have to open their hearts to strangers, to English relatives, and he was going to have to face a ghost from his past.

'Let her come, Rose. We can't keep putting this off. We have to make a bridge between us all for the children's sake. What happened in the past between us was none of their doing. Why should they suffer because of my mistakes? It's time I faced Selma Bartley.'

'She may not recognise you after all these years,' Rose said.

'I'm not that decrepit, surely?' he laughed. 'Do I look that old?'

'I won't feed your vanity. I don't want her to steal your heart again.' Rose looked up at him, revealing her fear, and he gathered her into his chest in a bear hug.

'You have filled every crevice in my heart. There's no room for anyone else. We were children then, just sweethearts for a season, just practising being in love.'

'But your mother broke it up so it must have been strong. It didn't run its course. It must still be there somewhere inside you, waiting to come out,' she argued.

'What happened, happened. It brought me here. I've no regrets . . . none at all. Only that it caused Selma pain for a little while. Come on, no more of this talk. Work's got to be done. We don't want Mrs Barr thinking we live in a mess. There's fences to mend and yards to be tidied up!'

Guy was being bright and breezy but, like Rose, he was wishing this visit could be cancelled. He wasn't looking forward to seeing that face from his past again.

Selma's journey took several days, many connections and delays on trains and buses, until her backside ached, her feet swollen with the heat. Now she knew what a real pioneer must have felt like! She could have flown across but wanted to see more of the Midwest states. Lisa offered to come

432

with her for company but she had her college work to prepare and was waiting for more news of Patrick, who was a POW somewhere on a South Pacific island.

She thought of that first overland journey all those years ago when she was so excited and naïve, so full of Jamie Barr. He was last heard of running a bar in Vegas, married to a showgirl there. Why had she never bothered to look for someone else, as Lisa had suggested?

She smiled, thinking about all Pearl Levine's lovers since Corrie died; all those Hollywood liaisons kept secret by the studio executives from their adoring fans, the fake marriages of homosexual stars to please the public. There was so much fakery and illusion in Tinseltown, such a long way from the Yorkshire Dales. What had she lost by going west and staying there?

Perhaps a bit of her true self. She had Shari and Lisa but not a lot else. She'd kept up some horsemanship, loved going to the races and driving around in Lisa's open-top tourer, learning to drive.

She kept returning to Arizona to stake out her claim on the territory round Prescott. She loved its Victorian houses and prim streets. It reminded her of Sowerthwaite, in some strange way. 'If ever I come into money, this is where I'd live,' she told Lisa.

The clothing bank and collections kept her busy supporting the war effort. Looking around the town, with its growing wealth and glamour, she sometimes felt as if she didn't belong here any more. It worried her, as if the gaps in her life were never going to be filled. Would she end up living alone with only her thoughts for company? She wondered what Charlie's parents would be like – solid farm stock, religious by all accounts. She'd have to mind

433

her language with teetotallers and churchgoers, not her type at all these days. But having promised Shari to go and introduce herself, she was keeping to the bargain.

She landed in Philadelphia and caught a bus north through open country, pretty, rolling green hills and lush forests. The colour of stone and earth were so different from California. She could see why the Yorkshire Quakers felt at home and settled around these rivers and creeks all those years ago. There was a horse and buggy waiting for her at the Crossroads Inn to bring her to Springville and the Wests' farmstead.

By this time it was hot, and she was steaming and very tired. As they drew closer to the stop, she glimpsed a man waiting in shirtsleeves, with a large straw hat and a beard. His wife stood in her sky-blue dress with white pinafore, and her hair covered in a white cap with strings tied round. Were they plain folk, Amish, Quakers or what? That's all she needed, she sighed, to be stuck for a week with holy rollers. She was too exhausted to look them in the eye.

'Mrs Barr, Selma Barr?' said the man with the strangest of accents.

She nodded, not looking up into his face. 'Mr and Mrs West, I'm pleased to meet you. Thank you for waiting. Not one thing has left on time since I started out,' she sighed.

'You'll be ready to rest then,' said his wife, smiling. 'Charles will put all your things in the back.'

It was a slow awkward ride through the leafy lanes, trying to make polite conversation with strangers, trying not to show her ignorance of their way of life. It brought back memories of home. She'd not always been a city girl. The scenery was pretty and the shade of the trees welcome. The farmhouse was a wooden slatted salt-box affair with neat glass-panelled windows and a picket fence round a yard full of vegetables. There was something very familiar about the foursquare shape that reminded her of the farms out in the Dales. There were cattle grazing, and in the far meadows she could see horses.

A line of girls stood on the steps waiting to be introduced: Kitty, Lorrie, Joan and Dorothy, all dressed in the same plain frocks, with scrubbed faces, braided hair tied into buns. They had old-fashioned manners, waiting for their parents to take the lead.

All at once Selma felt overdressed in her frilly frock with ruffled sleeves and peep-toe sandals, her hair piled up in pompadour style, her nails coloured bright pink.

Lorrie kept staring at her fingers and back at her hair. They were quiet, polite, shy girls, who disappeared as soon as was respectable to run out into the fields, no doubt to discuss her frivolous outfit.

The shades in the house were down to keep the house cool. She was dying for a smoke but knew that would not be fitting. How on earth was she going to survive here?

'Have you heard any more about your son?' she asked.

'Only what your daughter has been able to tell us. She's been diligent in keeping us in the picture. He'll have to learn to use his left hand, of course,' said Rose.

'When are they coming back home?' she added. There was such a tension in the air and she didn't know what to say next.

'That we don't know, Selma,' said the man quietly, and it was the way he said her name that made her look at him more closely. His hair was bleached white. His beard reddish, his cheeks lined with the sun, but his voice echoed in her head for a second. It wasn't a pure American accent; there was an English vowel or two caught in his speech. Then she recalled he'd gone to Sharland School. Why had she forgotten about that? It was an important connection.

'I gather you're a Yorkshire tyke,' she smiled. 'You went to the public school in my village.'

'I was born in London . . . but I did go there and I lived not far from the forge,' he replied.

'I'm sorry, I don't recall any Wests . . .'

'I wasn't always known by that name,' he replied, staring at her. 'You don't recognise me, do you, Selma, or shall I say, Selima?'

Still, the penny didn't drop as she looked at him blankly.

'Stop teasing her, Charles!' said Rose. 'Mrs Barr, you knew my husband many years ago. Your mother was a friend of his mother, Lady Hester Cantrell.'

'Angus? Not Angus Cantrell? I don't believe it after all these years! We wondered where you were, and you've been hiding away here.' She looked at him again. This was not the haughty young man she recalled, but that was over twenty years ago. 'I hear she's passed away. She was kind to my mother.' How could this man be a Cantrell? On the other side of the world. How odd.

'Your mother was kindness itself to her in her latter years,' he replied.

'And you are well now?' she said, suddenly recalling his fits as a boy.

'Never better. This life suits me. It took a bit of getting used to at first, but Rose and her family made me very welcome.' He smiled at his wife and Selma could see the affection between them.

'I must be dreaming this . . . of all the people in all the world.' Should she break up these cosy reminiscences?

Why should they be sitting there so smugly? Just the sound of that Cantrell name fired up her anger. 'I suppose you heard what happened to my brothers. Your mother must have told you the circumstances of Frank's death. It seems to be common knowledge. He was never a coward or a deserter, but your family did him no favours.' There it was, blurted out, the anger stored in her heart for so long. What else could she say, even though she was their guest?

'I know,' said Angus. 'He was a brave man in the end.'

There was something in the way he was looking at her that puzzled her. 'I don't understand . . .'

'My mother and I did correspond for a while. I just wanted to clear the air between us all. You still don't recognise me, do you?'

Now he was confusing her. She looked at his wife, who shook her head and left the table. 'Excuse me, I must get on with our dinner . . . I think what's said now is better said between you both alone,' she whispered as she put her hand on his shoulder.

What on earth was going on?

'Selma, you still think I'm Angus.' He spoke softly while lifting his forelock of straw hair to reveal his brow. 'So where's the injuries, the stitches that came when I dived and hit the rock?' His brow was smooth and pale under the flaxen hair.

Her heart missed a beat and she looked at him again. 'Guy?' she spluttered, her face flushing. 'What are you doing here? You should be dead and buried!' She stood up to leave but he grabbed her wrist. 'What game are you playing with me?'

'I am dead and buried. My brother made sure of that

437

when he stole my uniform and took my place all those years ago.'

'Let me go. I don't believe you. It can't be you . . . you let my brother die for the want of a good word from you. You couldn't be bothered to turn up. You brought me here on false pretences to make excuses. How dare you insult me! I'm leaving right now!'

'Don't go, Selma! I promise as God is my witness and I shall have to answer to Him on the Day of Judgment, it wasn't me. Hear me out, I beg of you. It has lain so heavy on my conscience. I beg you hear me out before you leave.'

Selma sat down, shaking at the sight of him.

'My mother played her part only too well,' he continued. 'It suited her purposes to let Angus pose as me but it all went too far. I was trapped in the house, sick, and I didn't know what had happened until it was far too late. Then I fled from what was done, as far away as I could. There was nothing I could do after that. How could I expose my brother or betray my family's honour?'

'Your silence betrayed *mine*. Even one word from you and he would have lived,' she cried. 'You left him to die alone.'

'How could I have known what was happening at the time until it was too late to change anything? It was a bad year for executions. The generals were wanting to quell any thoughts of mutiny in the ranks. They were heavy-handed and overruled so many pleas for leniency, but when I found out I wrote to Angus and left him in no doubt of what he had done. Mother did the same. Angus was many things: stupid, ignorant, full of gung-ho. He made a terrible mistake and it haunted him. I think he was too ashamed to survive after that . . . If you don't duck when mortars explode

438

around you, the end will come soon enough. If you volunteer for suicide missions . . . We can't turn back what happened then. I only wish I could.'

'So, you hid yourself out here in comfort. I don't understand. I'm not staying here to listen to more of your excuses. You let me think you were dead, not even a hint to me. You crept away. If I'd known I'd have helped you to escape. I was your friend.'

'I thought it was better to leave. You'd been sent away and I was confused and angry with everyone. Don't blame just Angus, blame the cruelty of war that takes a man to the brink of his sanity and beyond until his spirit is broken. What was done to Frank and many others was by the rulebook, by the letter of military law.

'Surely you realise now that whoever spoke harsh words to you at the forge wasn't me. It was my mother's infernal interference yet again. She wanted you out of my life once she knew . . .' He paused. 'I did what I thought was best. I wandered the earth in a drunken stupor for years before I found this haven. When I came to Springville, I became who you see before you: a farmer and man of the Mennonite faith. It has been a good life. I thought I could put it all behind me and then my son chooses to enlist against my wishes and history repeats itself. Don't you think it's strange? Now Charlie has paid a price for that enthusiasm as I once did. He needs my help, not my disapproval now.'

Selma could see the tears glistening in those blue eyes. How could she have ever mistaken him for Angus? She felt so confused, not knowing whether to stay or leave.

'Don't you think it's strange that these two young ones've found each other across the continent, and in England of all places? There's a sort of justice for us in that, I'm thinking.

What was denied us? The freedom to love where you find it, despite class, religion and nation. Theirs is this new world. Surely their love and happiness are all that matter now?' he pleaded.

Selma tried to concentrate on his words but she was shattered by this discovery. He must have known for months who Sharland was, and all this time they had said nothing. She shook her head, unconvinced.

'Don't you think they should be told this story and know what bigotry and misunderstanding and the cruelty of war did to us and our families?' Guy continued. 'Charlie will have found out all too soon, as I did in the trenches. We have to give them our support no matter what the consequences are for ourselves. If you withdraw because of me, then they'll have to take sides. It's so hard when you have to split your loyalties, believe me. I know the price I have paid for doing that. If families can't agree, what hope is there of everlasting peace between nations?'

Selma shook her head, still not convinced and unable to speak for shock.

Guy reached out for her hand. 'Please forgive me this deception. If I'd told you, would you have come? I wanted to unburden all this to you in private. How would you have felt if we'd met for the first time in public?'

She looked at him. 'I don't think I'd have recognised you if you hadn't said my full name like that. Why did you have to enlighten me?'

'Have I changed so much? You haven't,' he said.

She ignored his compliment. 'You seem to have found some measure of peace here. I'm not sure I ever will. I'm too angry at what happened to Frank.'

'Then put that anger to good use like Hester did. She

battled on about that monument. There still isn't one in Sharland or ever will be until this matter is resolved.'

'Don't preach to me, Guy. It doesn't suit you,' she snapped. How dare he tell her what to do!

'I'm not preaching – don't be so sensitive – I'm just making a suggestion. Come and let's join Rose on the porch. She's trying to be discreet. I do so want you to like her. Without her I'd have been dead long ago. We may come from different sides of the country but you and I love our kids, wayward or not. Better for us to pull together than apart. You and I were always good friends.' He smiled and she saw that grinning face of long ago. It was hard to stay sulking.

They sat in silence, each trying to think of something to lighten the heaviness of what had been said. Selma kept trying to go over Guy's story and make sense of it all: all their family secrets out in the open. She felt so exhausted by the journey and now by this amazing revelation.

It would be so easy to pack her bag and stomp off to LA in high dudgeon, never speaking to the West family again. She could slant everything so as to make Shari take sides against them, put her side of the story in such a way that Charlie's parents would be elbowed out of the room into the shadows, but was that fair? How did that help Frank's lost cause?

It was Rose who broke the deafening silence. 'How do you intend to celebrate the newlyweds' return when it happens? We will find it difficult under the circumstances . . . Mixed marriages are not condoned by our Church but they do happen,' she said, looking up at her husband with a smile.

Guy was quick to butt in, smiling, 'But there are ways,

Rose. Other members have found ways. Love finds a way . . .'

He really was quite the preacher man, Selma mused, not like the old Guy at all.

'I was thinking, how do we all intend to celebrate, together? That's why I came. I don't know how you folks do things round here,' Selma said.

'Like everyone else: a bit of a hoedown, a feast of shared offerings and a singsong in the barn,' Rose replied. 'Would that suit?'

'That would suit fine as long as there was a bit of liquor on tap for some of my friends,' Selma added.

'We can put it in the yard for those who choose to imbibe,' Guy was quick to answer.

'But judging from Shari's letters, maybe they'll want time alone to themselves before Charlie's ready for public scrutiny. Injuries can be exhausting.'

Rose smiled. 'Dorothy's already started asking if he'll have a hook on his hand.'

'It'll be a nine-day wonder and then they'll forget. I'll give her a talking-to,' said Guy.

'No, you won't. She's just being curious,' Rose snapped at him.

Selma watched their light-hearted banter with a smile and a sigh. This was how it should be in real family life, talking things over in the cool of the day after a mighty fine supper.

Here was Guy, the once love of her life sitting contented on a porch with a perky little wife in drab clothes. And here was she, feeling none of the old passion and envy or bitterness. How strange that her anger was evaporating like snow in sunshine. The two of them had been forced apart by life's experiences into different worlds. His had narrowed and hers had widened. Their shared memories were frozen in the distant past. Neither of them could thaw them now, nor wanted to. The only thing she did envy was that he had found a safe haven in his stormy life. When was she ever going to find one for herself?

26

September 1945

Charlie wasn't looking forward to the visit home. He'd had a polite note saying that they would be waiting for him on 20 September, and trusting he would bring his wife to meet the family. They hoped his wound was healing well and that he wasn't too exhausted by the journey back across the Atlantic. He'd tried to prepare Shari for any awkwardness, explaining that he'd not be welcome within the Church community and that they must expect a very quiet homecoming with no special ceremony.

Shari had smiled and said that nothing mattered except they were together. She had resigned her post and came back as soon as she could, making plans for when he went into rehabilitation later in California at the end of the leave.

Now that victory was secured against Japan they could celebrate the end of the war properly with flags and bunting and victory parades in New York.

How would Charlie make out? His attempts to build up his left hand were making slow progress, but he was assured that, given special training, he'd be as good as new.

Charlie knew he'd never be as good as new. The shine

was off his apple. He'd seen too much slaughter and madness. He'd seen the best and worst in human beings, lost too many buddies, but now it was time for a fresh start – once he got over facing his parents' disapproval. He wouldn't be shunned by them, but treated with polite distance, and he loved Shari too much to want to make her feel uncomfortable. It would be a short visit.

As they were driving back across the state along the turn-pike, he suddenly called out, 'Pull over! I'm not sure I want to put you through this. It won't be easy, so let's make an excuse and give it a miss.'

Shari drew up by the kerb to give him one of her piercing black-eyed stares. 'I never took you for a coward. They will want to see you, and your sisters will be upset. I'm dying to see where you live. I don't care if they make me wait in this car all afternoon, we're going there. You've done nothing to be ashamed of. You chose your opinion over theirs. Where I come from that's called free will. They are entitled to believe what is true for them, and we are free to do the same. Nobody in this world has all of The Truth. My pa was Roman Catholic, my mother was strict chapel, the Grunwalds were Jews, your parents are Mennonites. This is America – we have to live alongside each other and see the good in each other, not insist you must believe what I believe. The spirit of Love is in all faiths and none, I think.' She hesitated, flushing up, seeing the look on his face. 'Does that make any sense?'

'You do say the most beautiful things, Sharland West. You make it all sound so simple. I wish it were, but I'm scared. I love them and I hate having let them down.'

'Don't you think they might be feeling just the same?

Trust me, love will find a way through this, I promise.' She started up the car again. 'Do I have to leave the Ford at the end of the drive? Will they allow an engine on their land?'

'We do have a tractor,' Charlie laughed when they reached Springville. He noticed the yellow ribbons tied around the tree trunks: someone else was coming home, a regular soldier from a regular home where they celebrated his return in the regular Texan way.

As they drove ever closer to his house the ribbons were still there and as they turned into the drive there were flags flying. What on earth was going on?

'Look up there,' shouted Shari. 'Someone's put out a "Welcome Home" banner.'

'This isn't their way,' he gulped, confused now.

'But it's ours!' said Shari, laughing.

'You knew about this?'

'Just a little. My mom and my auntie had a hand in this, I'm thinking. Lisa loves a party.'

'Your mom's here?' This was getting stranger and stranger.

'Of course. You don't think she'd miss out on a party too?'

'She's visited here already?'

'Oh, yes. There's quite a story there.'

Charlie was shaking. This couldn't be happening. The Wests didn't mix with many English or make a fuss of soldiers. Then he saw his parents waiting on the porch, dressed formally but not in Sunday black, and his sisters were waving. There was patchwork bunting all round the porch. There were old schoolfriends and neighbours, and two women smiling, who must be part of Shari's family.

'Good to see you, son,' said his mother with her arms open to him, and his father was smiling. 'It's been a long time coming . . . but you've been spared.'

446

Shari's mother looked up and then looked at his pa. 'I don't believe it, Guy. It's like seeing a chip off the old block and no mistake. He looks just like you did!'

Guy? Who was the guy?'

Shari was tugging his stump end. 'All in good time. You'll never believe it when they tell you their story. Hollywood couldn't make this up!'

'Come in, Sharland,' said Rose. 'You're just how I imagined you to be only prettier . . . Welcome to our family.'

'They've got quite a party lined up for you both,' Selma whispered in his ear. 'The Wests and the Barrs; quite a combination, don't you think, young man? Forty years in the making,' Selma was laughing. 'From the Old World to the New and back . . . a special relationship through two world wars and a depression . . . but nothing gets in the way of true love,' she added. 'Welcome back.'

Remembrance Day 2000

What a formidable force a strong family can forge when it has a mind. What a heap of compromise it took to swallow pride and bitterness and strong opinions, to give these young people a day to remember for the rest of their lives; what a feast of pies, hams and cornbreads, sauces, shoofly pie and pumpkin and squash cakes, zucchini cake and cordials; what songs and dancing and laughter breaking down so much of my hurt and heartache that evening way back in 1945.

The barn was laid out with straw bales, the fiddler played and called out the dances, the lanterns twinkled under the starlit sky. I even sang my blacksmith's daughter song to cheers and clapping, made a right fool of myself, but it did the trick, I'm thinking.

To see young love in its first flush of passion softens the hardest of hearts. When your child is happy, how can your own feelings not burst with pride and joy? That's all that mattered then and matters now as I look down over the line of children we produced from this unexpected merger.

In that opening up of hearts, something shifted for me too.

When Charlie and Shari settled near my dream home in Prescott, Arizona, I found myself helping them set up the vacation trekking trail for horses and riders in Skull Valley, not far from the Santa Fe railroad, a little ranch down an avenue of cottonwood trees. It wasn't a happy time in Hollywood in the early fifties, with the McCarthy witch-hunts in the studios. We decided to pool resources and find something permanent, take a risk and make a dream come true.

It was in Prescott I met Andy McKade. He'd retired from the army, a widower, who liked horses and country life, just like me. We made good companions for many years and I took him back to Yorkshire, where he renewed his lifelong passion for English ale.

Rose and Guy came to stay awhile after his first major operation. They came to enjoy the warm winter sunshine. I can't say Rose and I were ever close, but her calm nursing was what was needed to see Guy through all the chemical treatments, all to no avail. He died a year later and with him a piece of my own history: the last connection with my West Sharland life until now.

Except that Shari, Charlie and Grace, their daughter, made contact with small groups in England, who worked behind the scenes to get those executed men pardoned. It was hard work to get even a hearing until the 1980s.

Those of us with relatives wrote endless letters to MPs and lobbied for our loved ones to be recognised as honest soldiers, many of whom were sold short measure of compassionate justice. It was a long slow process of gaining support in high places after that. A TV documentary helped, and books were written.

No one wants to be reminded of such uncomfortable

449

facts. Gradually more information was released and the names of the executed became public knowledge. More books were written on the subject and interviews given. I shared some of our precious letters to prove a point. The battle isn't over yet, but we are hopeful of some official pardon in the future.

Then West Sharland got fed up with having no proper memorial, and as part of their Millennium celebrations decided to raise one in Elm Tree Square.

Hester had left a sum of money for such purpose in her will, on condition, of course, that Frank's name was alongside his brother's. I made contact with them and told them everything I knew about his case.

There were letters of protest in the Gazette and others of commendation about this whole sorry subject. We became experts in sifting through public opinion to plead our cause, hence all the media interest in this occasion.

An invitation was issued to all surviving relatives of the deceased and now this simple lump of rock, in which is embedded a bronzed rifle and helmet, stands by the entrance to St Wilfred's.

Shari is standing by my side, but not Charlie. He passed away suddenly five years ago. Grace and her husband, Elliot, are here and my great-grandson, Curtis, who looks so much like Guy. He's on his first visit to England.

Later we're going to be entertained in Waterloo House, which is now, I'm told, a girls' boarding house for Sharland School.

No one in the family ever claimed Guy's inheritance. In proving his claim, the Cantrell history would have been made public. As he used to say on many occasions, 'It's only money.'

Shari replied it would have come in useful to help fund the

'Shot at Dawn' campaign. But it's somewhere gathering interest, never to be claimed unless my confession stirs things up . . .

We told all the kids about Frank, and my connection with Charles West, but I never told them his true identity. His children assumed he was Angus and we never enlightened them. What good would it do? It was his story and his choice to keep the illusion intact, but I think it has gone on long enough . . .

It's all here in my account, but some may discount this version as the ramblings of an old woman with an axe to grind against the Cantrells. I made my peace with them years ago. Providence has given us fair measure of recompense when I see these children, flesh of our flesh, making their way in this world.

Now it's two minutes to midnight in my long life. I'll not see another Remembrance Day. I've got all this stuff off my chest at last, but my bones are chilled with waiting to lay my wreath and take my leave of my brothers.

I hope Frank won't feel the need to keep roaming up and down the old high road, scaring the hell out of motorists now he's carved into stone with gold lettering alongside his brother at last.

Just the initials of first names are given with the full surname. That was another of Lady Hester's instructions. She had the last say, and quite right too, so no one was missed out, especially G. A. C. Cantrell. Guy or Angus? Take your pick.

Who is there left to tell their story but me? I'm the last piece of living history, and quite a burden it's been to bear at times. The truth and the rules that we lived by all those years ago are not what people can understand now. That's why men like Frank were shot by their own side. It was a

451

different world and can't be judged by today's understanding of things.

Time and silence quieten all the gathered assembly now the sacred moment of remembrance is here at last. What is there to pray but rest in peace . . . As long as this stone stands, none of you will ever be forgotten.

Read on for an exclusive extract of Leah's new book, *Winter's Children*, coming in Autumn 2010.

She glides through Wintergill House, drifting between the walls and closed up passageways. No floorboards creak, no plasterwork flakes as she brushes past, only a tinge of lavender betrays her presence. The once mistress of the hearth lists where she wills: ancient of ancients, she knows every nook and cranny, every dust bowl and rat run, loose boards and lost tokens, cat's bones crumbling in the roof spaces.

Hepzibah Snowden patrols her kingdom as she did in her own time, keys clanking on her leather girdle, a tallow candle in the pewter hold, still checking that the servants are in bed and Master Nathaniel, lord of her nights, is snoring by the fire. The once mistress of this household knows her duties.

She knows her dust is blown into every crevice of the old house, set high upon the hill like a cherry on a blancmange, circled by the four winds of heaven. The autumn mists froth from the valley cauldron but Hepzibah has no eyes for the outdoors. Her spirit imbues its benign presence only within the confines of these stone walls.

Soon it will be time to greet the old ones who gather in the recesses of Wintergill: the gone before, pilgrim spirits who return each year at All Saints to spread blessings on the house where once they too lived out their mortal sojourn.

November is the month of the dead. The barometer falls, daylight shortens its path across the sky. Shadows from stonewalls deepen across the moorland fields. She knows the year is beginning its slow dance of death when the leaves curl and rust and sap sinks to the roots. Time to dry the logs and burn the autum fires of Samhain. The air is stale, silence reigns. The house is empty of joy. She senses bitterness and tension left within these walls. These tenants, an old woman and her son ignore the patches of damp, the peeling plasterwork, the loose slates on the dairy roof. It is a cold, empty and barren hearth. What heat rises to the oak beams comes from the iron contraption that blocks the old kitchen grate. No servants warm their master's bed pans with hot ashes. No wife warms the master's buttocks. No horse's muck steams in the cobbled yard. She hears no shepherd's cough or stable boy's whistle. They have made another dwelling of the byre.

It saddens her heart to see all Nathaniel's toiling falling into disrepair, crumbling and soaking up the downpour of misery and pestilence in these parts. The Lord in his wisdom hath rained down such a plague upon these pastures of late. Now, not a living beast bellows from the byre; not a sheep bleats across the meadows. The Lord hath shown no mercy to Godless Yorkshire. All was lost to the summer slaughter in the killing fields below. Now is only silence and tears.

Hepzibah peers out from the mullion windowpane into the dusk. There is another out there that she fears, watching, waiting who saw it all. Her erstwhile dear cousin patrols around the walls, ever searching; the poor restless spirit who hovers between two worlds: the poor tortured soul who roams the fells with shadow fire burning in her eye sockets, flittering like a glow worm, bright in the hedge. Poor Blanche is out there in the gathering darkness, waiting to sneak through any open door, seeking what can never be found here in this earth.

Hepzibah shakes her head safe in the knowledge that this fortress is ringed against this troubled spirit by circles of rowan and elder, by lanterns of light no human eye can see, by sturdy prayer and her own constant vigilance. For Hepzibah is appointed guardian of this hearth. It is both her pride and penance to stay on within this place.

Each year the two of them must play out this ancient drama with dimmer lights and ever fainter resolve; an endless game of cat and mouse for nearly four hundred years. When, Oh Lord, will Blanche Norton's spirit be at peace? Who will help me guide her home?

Soon the Yule fires will burn and the seasons will turn towards the light. Hepzibah senses her own powers must fade in a Christmas house without the brightness of a child. Wintergill House needs new life or it will crumble. It is time now to open her heart for guidance, swallow her natural dissent towards such Popish festivities and cast her prayer net far and wide. Be this season pagan Samhain or Yule, Advent, Lent or Christ's mass, Wintergill waits for the coming of another winter's child.

Yet with such a coming there is always danger, Hepzibah sighs. For if her prayers are granted, she must summon her most cunning strategies to protect such an innocent from the all devouring hunger of cousin Blanche's passion. Lord hear my prayer, have mercy on Wintergill!

The recent campaign for the group pardoning of the soldiers executed in the First World War is well documented. The families in my story are entirely fictitious and the villages and towns apart from Skipton and Settle will not be found on any map of the North Craven Dales.

I am indebted to the following books:

Shot At Dawn: Julian Putkowski and Julian Sykes. Pen and Sword Books Ltd. 1998.

Blindfold and Alone: John Hughes Wilson and Cathryn Corns. Cassell Military Press Paperbacks. 2005.

Forgotten Voices of the Great War: Max Arthur. Ebury Press. 2002.

The Soldier's War: Richard van Emden. Bloomsbury. 2008.

All Quiet on the Home Front: Richard van Emden and Steve Humphries. Headline. 2003.

I would like to thank Roger and Gillian Walton for the tour of their lovely garden that sparked off so many 'what ifs' . . . Thank you, Jenny Hall and Kate Croll, for your continuing support and Lorraine and John Chilton for such wonderful Pennsylvanian hospitality and researches on my behalf. It was a privilege to meet Mr Sanford A. Alderfer who gave valuable insights into growing up on a Mennonite farm in the 1920s. A visit to the Mennonite Heritage Center in Harleysville. PA. enriched my knowledge of their faith and tradition.

Once more I'd like to thank all the team at Avon for suggesting the title, my eagle-eyed agent Judith Murdoch for her valuable input and my family for putting up with my 'absence' while I lost myself in the writing of this story.

Leah Fleming, 2009.